Praise for *USA TODAY* bestselling author Michele Hauf

"With action-packed excitement from start to finish, Hauf offers an original story line full of quirky, fun characters and wonderful descriptions. And the sexual tension between CJ and Vika sparkles. Readers won't want to put this one down."
—*RT Book Reviews* on *This Wicked Magic*; Top Pick!

"This quirky story has a fair amount of humor and a lot of heart as well."
—*Harlequin Junkie* on *The Vampire Hunter*

"*Kiss Me Deadly* is an addictive read, one that won't be put down until the final page is completed."
—*Examiner.com*

Praise for Deborah LeBlanc

"*The Wolven* seamlessly weaves a remarkably well-detailed mythology into the recent history of New Orleans. LeBlanc's dialogue sparkles and the sexual chemistry between Shauna and Danyon is delicious."
—*RT Book Reviews*

"An interesting new mythology and non-stop action make LeBlanc's story a fun read. Her descriptions are vivid and the chemistry between Viv and Nikoli is hot."
—*RT Book Reviews* on *Witch's Hunger*

Michele Hauf is a *USA TODAY* bestselling author who has been writing romance, action-adventure and fantasy stories for more than twenty years. France, musketeers, vampires and faeries usually populate her stories. And if Michele followed the adage "write what you know," all her stories would have snow in them. Fortunately, she steps beyond her comfort zone and writes about countries and creatures she has never seen. Find her on Facebook, Twitter and at michelehauf.com.

Books by Michele Hauf

Harlequin Nocturne

Her Werewolf Hero
A Venetian Vampire
Taming the Hunter
The Witch's Quest
The Witch and the Werewolf

The Saint-Pierre Series

The Dark's Mistress
Ghost Wolf
Moonlight and Diamonds
The Vampire's Fall
Enchanted by the Wolf

In the Company of Vampires

Beautiful Danger
The Vampire Hunter
Beyond the Moon

Visit the Author Profile page
at Harlequin.com for more titles.

THE WITCH AND THE WEREWOLF & THE WITCH'S THIRST

USA TODAY BESTSELLING AUTHOR
MICHELE HAUF
AND
DEBORAH LEBLANC

HARLEQUIN® NOCTURNE™

Recycling programs
for this product may
not exist in your area.

ISBN-13: 978-0-373-20868-5

The Witch and the Werewolf & The Witch's Thirst

Copyright © 2018 by Harlequin Books S.A.

The publisher acknowledges the copyright holders
of the individual works as follows:

The Witch and the Werewolf
Copyright © 2017 by Michele Hauf

The Witch's Thirst
Copyright © 2017 by Deborah LeBlanc

HARLEQUIN®
www.Harlequin.com

Printed in U.S.A.

CONTENTS

THE WITCH AND THE WEREWOLF

Michele Hauf

For Jeff. Our souls agreed to this.

Chapter 1

Feet floating up so her toes peeked out of the frothy bubble bath, Mireio Malory wiggled the little pink beads as she sang to the music filling her bathroom. She sang along with the Meghan Trainor tune about loving herself and not having time for a man because she was all about having fun. A fitting theme song for Mireio at the moment.

Guys were great, but she didn't have the time to focus on a relationship if her plans to achieve immortality came to fruition. A simple spell could prolong her life a hundred years, guaranteed. But to actually perform that spell—which involved drinking the blood from a live vampire's beating heart? She'd been avoiding the spell for years, but she couldn't do that anymore. It was time to honor her departed mother, and to take back her power.

Baths were a common ritual for her in the evenings, after a long day of work at the brewery, or after she'd flexed into a few yoga moves and watched an episode of

Bones on Netflix. Born a witch, yet pretty darn disappointed she'd not been born a mermaid, Mireio honored her water magic by feeding her body's innate craving for water. Surely she owned the biggest bathroom in the city. It was hexagonal, tiled like a Moroccan temple and the big round marble bathtub sat at the center of it all. It was the size of a hot tub, but there were no bubble jets in this tub beyond the sensory explosions from her homemade bath bombs.

Singing loudly, she blew a handful of bubbles skyward and laughed when some landed in her pinned-up red hair. The water was starting to cool, and she'd been in for forty-five minutes. Her fingers and toes were pruned, providing her traction—if she were an amphibian. Or a mermaid.

With a reluctant sigh, she rose from her watery haven and reached for a toasty towel hung over the towel warmer. It wasn't the wet porcelain tile floor that almost caused her to slip upon exiting the bath—it was the scream.

And a very familiar scream at that.

"Really?" Mireio wrapped the towel around her ample curves and padded wet tracks to the back window to peer out, though she knew she couldn't see into her neighbor Mrs. Henderson's yard from here. The windows were also fogged.

She often mentally compared her neighbor to Mrs. Kravitz, the nosy neighbor on the 1960s TV show *Bewitched*. They didn't look at all similar, but they possessed the same snoopy, and unwelcome, curiosity and annoying voices.

Yet another scream, this one curling the hairs on the back of Mireio's neck, prompted her to use the side door in the bathroom that walked out onto the patio.

Pushing open the screen door, she leaned out into the cool spring air and scanned her backyard. It was close to midnight, yet her yard was always illuminated from the house light above the door where she stood, and the dozen solar lights pushed into the lawn at five-foot intervals that framed the backyard.

Suddenly something ran into view. A deer? Wildlife always dashed through the neighborhood yards. Raccoons, beavers, deer, once even a black bear.

Mireio stepped out onto the bamboo patio rug, holding the screen door open with two fingers. She peered into the night, thinking her species, witches, had gotten ripped off because they didn't have cool night vision like vampires and werewolves. Suddenly an animal stopped, twenty feet away, in the middle of her yard.

She recognized the creature with an ease that made her heart sink.

"A werewolf," she gasped.

Removing her hand from the screen door to put her fingers to her mouth, she suddenly felt a cool breeze skim her bare skin. More skin than should have been exposed. The towel had gotten caught in the door and fallen away, leaving her standing naked beneath the house light, unable to form words as she met the werewolf's golden gaze.

The creature, who in fully shifted form was half wolf, half man, thrust back his shoulders and lifted his chest, looking ready to howl. But when his gold eyes dragged away from hers and down her body...

Mireio tried to cover herself as she actually said, "Eek!"

The wolf snorted and a low growling noise rumbled in the night. It didn't sound threatening. In fact, to her it sounded...amorous.

Mrs. Henderson's scream sounded again. It was the catalyst to setting the werewolf off in a dash out of the yard.

Released from the spell of the creature's piercing gaze, Mireio grabbed the door pull and opened it, reaching for the towel and quickly wrapping it around her body.

Just in the nick of time because from around the corner of her backyard appeared a policeman, and in his wake, Mrs. Henderson.

"Did you see it?" Mrs. Henderson, wrapped in a thick white terry robe, scampered over to the patio, the ears on her bunny slippers bobbing.

Tugging the towel up higher and this time clasping it firmly, she stood before the elderly policeman, whom she knew lived on the other side of Mrs. Henderson. Mireio nodded. "Uh, yes?"

"I told you!" Mrs. Henderson slapped the policeman's back, who shrugged and winced. He was accustomed to answering Mrs. Henderson's cries of wolf at all hours of the day.

But had this been a true cry of wolf? Best not to let humans know that.

"It was a deer," Mireio hastily tossed out. "Or maybe a moose. Yes, I'm sure that's what it was."

"A moose?" Mrs. Henderson jammed her bony fists to her hips. "It was Bigfoot!"

"All right, all right," the policeman said, placating his neighbor with a pat to her back. "Miss Malory here says it was a moose. She's got very good eyesight, and her backyard is well lit. So if she says it was a moose, I believe her. Let's go home now, Mrs. Henderson. Leave Miss Malory to…her bath."

To his credit he didn't eye her blatantly, only tipped a nod to her and turned Mrs. Henderson around, walking her back to her yard. All the way they argued over why a moose would be wandering through the tulips when it had very obviously been Bigfoot.

Mireio stepped inside the bathroom and closed the door and locked it. She peered out the now-defogged window, attempting to sight the werewolf. Perhaps spy a wolfish shadow backlit by the moonlight.

Whispering a protection spell to encompass her yard, she sent it out with a blown kiss.

Why had a werewolf been wandering through the neighborhood? That wasn't common. Too risky. And it wasn't even the full moon. Werewolves were much smarter than that. They knew to stay away from humans when shifted.

"It was a good thing for him I scared him off."

Mireio winced. She had scared the wolf away with her naked body? Not one of her finest moments.

On the other hand, that look it had given her. Definitely animal, but also…maybe kind of…sexual.

She shook her head. "You're a silly witch. Just be thankful you didn't flash the whole neighborhood. Ha!"

The music now blared Taylor Swift. Dropping her towel, Mireio performed a hip shimmy as she reached to drain the tub and then blew out the candles one by one, blessing the water goddess Danu as she did so.

Three nights later, Mireio stayed late after her shift at The Decadent Dames. She and her three witch friends owned the microbrewery in Anoka. Mireio was the master brewer. They all brewed and worked shifts and took turns scheduling, but Mireio was the early riser, so she generally arrived around six in the morning to start the day's brew and finished about an hour before they opened in the afternoon. Today, she'd gotten a late start so had finished the brew hours after opening.

A local band that covered current pop hits was set up before the front windows and the house was packed. At the moment, the lead singer belted out a cover of Meghan Trainor's "NO," which was an anthem to a woman not needing a man.

Singing the chorus, "Untouchable, untouchable," Mireio danced by herself amid the crowd on the dance floor, arms thrust high and hips swaying her short red-and-blue-tartan skirt. Nothing felt better than a beer buzz and dancing. And she had new, red, five-inch heels to break in, so much dancing was required. Tossing her bright red corkscrew curls over a shoulder, she let out an exhilarated hoot.

Eryss, the brewery's principal owner, danced up to Mireio. She and her boyfriend, a former witch hunter who lived in Santa Cruz, California, split their time between cities during the year and soon she'd be headed for the sunny West Coast. Her friend's long skirts dusted the hardwood floor and she grasped Mireio's hands and the twosome danced for a few seconds.

"You look happy," Eryss said over the noise.

"I am! I'm always happy!"

"It's contagious!" Then Eryss leaned in to speak close at Mireio's ear. "Did you notice the hunk at the bar who has been eyeing you up fiercely for the last ten minutes?"

"What?" Mireio abruptly stopped dancing and glanced to the bar, which was fronted by rusted corrugated tin in keeping with their rustic theme. She scanned from the left end of the bar to the right, and there at the end a big, beefy man with a mustache and beard, and long brown hair tied behind his head, lifted his pint glass to tip toward her. Handsome. "Huh." But. "Didn't notice. I'm in my zone, don't you know?"

"Yeah, I got that. I wish I could find the zone so easily nowadays. Whew!" Eryss blew a strand of long hair from her face. She had a six-month-old at home who lately had been keeping her up nights because of teething. "But don't be too untouchable tonight, okay? That man is sexy times two."

"Don't tell me that, Eryss. I'm not in the market for a— Oh, my goddess, he's coming over here."

"Then I'm going to leave you to him."

"No! Eryss!"

The man pushed by two people and deftly avoided a bull terrier sitting beside his owner's table. (Yes, the brewery was dog friendly.) He was halfway across the room.

"Please don't be a creeper. Please don't be a creeper." Mireio performed a hip swinging turn and he stood right before her. "Oh!"

Big brown eyes looked into her soul almost as deeply as if he could do a soul gaze. Of which, only witches were capable. And no one in town knew the owners of The Decadent Dames were witches. Well, mostly no one.

"Oh, hey," she offered.

Eryss had been right in her assessment of the man. But more like sexy times infinity. His dark brown hair was tied behind his head and his beard was trimmed neatly to reveal a snow-white smile. Chocolate brown eyes? Dreamy. Dimples? Oh, mercy. And he smelled like a forest after the rain.

"My name's Lars." He leaned in to be heard over the music. "I don't normally walk up to pretty girls and introduce myself." He looked aside briefly, then cast his eyes toward hers for only a few seconds. Nervous? "But there's something about you. Do I know you?"

"I've never seen you before. Unless you come to the

brewery often. I work here," she said, unable to keep her hips from swaying to the beat. "You like to dance?"

The man shook his head. "I'm not a dancer. Was hoping you wouldn't mind a little conversation."

He seemed nice enough. And he hadn't tried any pickup lines on her yet, so that earned him points. But, as she'd told Eryss, she'd been in her zone. And some nights a girl just wanted to be with herself. Maybe she should reinforce her white light. She always warded with a white light against psychic invasion—or energy vampires—before going out. It tended to wear down as the night went on.

"Sorry." He shrugged and smirked, interrupting her thoughts. "I think I'm out of line here. You don't seem interested—"

"No, wait!"

Ah hell, she wasn't a mean girl, and the guy was cute. What could a little conversation hurt?

"That table is empty. I need a break anyway. New shoes, don't you know." She didn't need the break, but again, the man was a tall order of nummy, so she'd be a fool to send him off like a stuck-up witch.

He wandered over to the table and Mireio assessed him as he did. His jeans were snug and showed off incredibly muscled thighs and legs that stretched much longer than hers. Good thing she was wearing the heels. But she still came up a head or two shorter than him. He wore a soft blue-and-green flannel shirt opened to reveal a plain white T-shirt beneath. And that shirt stretched over abs and chest muscles that screamed *this man works out*. A lot. Add in the beard, mustache and well-groomed hair and he sported the whole lumbersexual vibe.

She could dig it.

She stepped onto the lower rung on the stool to boost

herself up to the high table. Hey, she was five-two on a good day. Here at the back of the taproom they were set off from the dancers but it was still loud.

"Lilacs," he said.

"What?"

"You smell like lilacs." His dimpled smile was accompanied by a shy dip of his head.

She didn't wear perfume, save for essential oils once in a while, so if he smelled lilacs, then… "Oh. I was in the garden this afternoon. That must be what you smell on me. The lilacs are blooming. I love spring. Everything is so lush."

He nodded. "A familiar scent. I like it."

"You're a big one," she said absently. Then she realized what an idiot she'd sounded like. "Uh, I mean… Oh, witch's warts. I need another beer."

"I'll get you one."

"No, I got it." With a wave, she caught Eryss's attention behind the bar and made the pouring signal for another beer. "I work here. Not right now. But I own the place along with my friends. They know the fill-me-up signal."

"You ladies make excellent beer."

"Thank you. I brewed that oatmeal stout you're drinking."

"It's nice and creamy."

"I'm the head brewer," she said over the rising noise as the band kicked into a rousing '80s tune that everyone started to pound their fists to and bounce up and down.

"You say it's newer? Yes, I like it." He tilted back the drink and offered her a cheers with his half-empty glass.

She was never going to have a conversation with him surrounded by this noise. And she did want to get to know him better. Because why not? He was sexy and nonthreatening. And she wasn't against having a conversation with a handsome man.

"So, Lars, eh?"

"Yes. Officially Larson Gunderson."

"That's a fine Scandinavian name, if I've ever heard one. I'm Mireio Malory."

"Muriel."

"No, Mir-ee-O."

"Oh. It's loud in here with the band singing. My hearing is usually…much better." He winced then, as if thinking of something he'd forgotten. He shook the sudden lost moment away and offered her a smile that flashed his pearly whites from beneath his trimmed mustache.

"Muriel will do." She thrust up her hand for him to shake.

His hand clasped hers gently, wrapping with ease about it and up to her wrist. And then he held her more firmly, and the heat of their connection gave her a shiver. One of those really good, how-could-a-girl-get-so-lucky kind of shivers that she felt from head to nipples to toes—and everywhere in between.

And yet… She sensed something in his handshake. Something not quite human. It was the same feeling she got whenever the Saint-Pierre brothers stopped into the brewery. Those four ranged from werewolves, to a vampire and also a faery.

With a gasp, Mireio pulled her hand from his. He didn't notice her surprise, thank goodness. She was a water witch and spent a lot of time in nature working with streams, ponds, lakes and otherwise. She also communicated with the animals, and could always sense when one was near.

And Larson Gunderson gave off a distinctive animal

vibe. Could he be? Oh, mercy, he wasn't. Please, do not let him be the one who…

Mireio swallowed. If the lilac scent was familiar to him—witch's warts. He was the one.

Eryss suddenly popped up beside the table and handed her another pint of blueberry cream ale. She winked and sailed off before Mireio could grab her as an anchor. Something to hold her down so she didn't float too near the curious man who— This couldn't be an accidental meeting. But did that mean he'd followed her here?

She tilted back a swallow, then set the pint down on a coaster that featured their logo, a sexy witch casting a spell over a foamy brew. "So, Lars, uh…what can you tell me about yourself? I mean, I don't want this to sound like fifty questions."

"Fifty? You have that many questions for me in such a short time? I'm impressed." He pushed his glass aside and leaned his elbows on the table. She wanted to touch him once more. Just to be sure that what she'd felt was real. "I live out past Oak Grove. I come to town once a week for groceries and a pint. Just remembered this place was here so thought I'd stop in. I'm definitely coming back."

"And what is it you do, exactly?" Because if he didn't have a real job, she'd get suspicious. And fast.

"I…well, you could sort of call it security. On a private compound."

"Ah-huh."

That was vague. And she was getting more nervous about the guy by the second. But really, if he was the one, would he know things about her? Things she didn't want him to know.

"I'm also remodeling the cabin I live in. I like making things with my hands." He splayed them both on the table to reveal long, calloused fingers.

Oh, those were some fine hands that could certainly cover a lot of area on her if she was in the market for such handling. Which she was not. Was she? Mercy. Maybe giving up on men to focus on a spell she was too freaked about to give more than a few moments consideration to daily was too extreme?

Could be. But even more so? Talking to a man who may have very likely seen her naked a few nights ago was even more extreme. She couldn't deal with this. Not right now.

"Do you want more stout?" she asked and nodded toward his nearly empty pint.

"Probably." He tilted back the rest of the drink.

"Head to the bar." She reached over and touched the back of his hand. There was that sensation again. Hiding a cringe, she nodded toward the bar. "Eryss will give you a refill. On the house."

"Thanks. I'll be right back."

"I'll be here!"

No, she would not be here.

Mireio grabbed her little black purse, shaped like a fish, swung it over a shoulder, and beelined it for the door behind the band, well out of view of the bar, and the mysteriously delicious Lars Gunderson's eyesight.

She'd had three drinks, so she wouldn't drive home. If she were lucky, she might catch a bus this late.

Chapter 2

When he returned to the now empty table, Lars saw the sassy little skirt slip out the door. The woman with the bright red curls and sexy, deep cleavage had dashed out of the brewery.

He gaped. Really? Had he made that terrible of a first impression? She'd kind of seemed into him. Had touched his hand. Had even fluttered her thick lashes at him as she'd smiled a sweet pixie smile. And he hadn't gotten to ask her the burning question. The one he'd been wondering about since the scent of lilacs had led him here.

Devastated that the woman had taken off, Lars sulked. He should chalk it up as another rejection. And yet a deep, visceral part of him would not allow him to mark this off as defeat. He had to know if she was the one.

So, leaving his beer on the table, he pushed through the dancing people and slunk around the electric guitarist and pushed open the door. He could hear her high heels clicking on the concrete, though he couldn't see her. But he smelled lilacs...that way.

Turning left, he passed three storefronts, then swung another left and there she stood, near the bus stop, stepping nervously from foot to foot. He heard her mutter softly, "Oh, shit."

That utterance stabbed Lars right in the heart. Never had a woman rejected him so soundly as to run off. So he stopped about twenty feet away from her and put up his hands placatingly.

Should he really do this? Was he that desperate for more cruel treatment? She seemed almost *afraid* of him. Threatened? He didn't want her to feel that way. That wasn't his style.

But the heady scent of lilacs wouldn't allow him to turn away.

So what to do?

The woman wore a short skirt that looked like one of those tartans the Highlanders wore, along with a blousy red top that emphasized her ample cleavage. Sky-high heels matched the blouse color. And white ankle socks with a delicate ruffle kept drawing his eye down there. She was short, a good head shorter than him, even in the heels, but the shoes did make her legs look long and slender.

"You keep staring at my legs like that, I'm going to have to slap you," she said.

"Sorry."

She offered him a smile and a shift of her hips. "I don't do things like slap men."

He took that as a sign it was okay to approach. But only a few steps. "Couldn't help but stare. You've amazing gams. I, uh...did you have a previous engagement you forgot to tell me about?"

She rubbed a palm up one of her arms. A black fish swung near her waist. What was that? A purse?

"Sorry. I suddenly got a weird vibe about you. No offense."

"Really? Because if you think I'm weird I do take offense from that."

"No, I don't think you're *weird* weird. Just—hey, weird is good, right?"

"Still offended here."

Her wince was accompanied by a shrug. "I'm usually much better at explaining myself. I think you're a…" She bit her lower lip. Her lips were so red and plump. Kissable. Yet juxtaposed with her appeal was also her strange fear of him. What had he said to her to make her flee?

"I'm a what?" Lars prompted.

"I'm not sure how to say it. You said the lilac scent was familiar to you."

It had been in his nose since three nights ago when he'd been out of his head and had woken in the morning knowing he'd shifted again without volition. It had been happening with a disturbing frequency lately. And each time he risked being seen by more than a few humans.

Yet, he also sensed this woman wasn't necessarily human.

"I did, and do, smell lilacs," he said. "There's only wildflowers growing out where I live. I keep bees. They make me happy." *Ramble much? Just out with it, you idiot!* "So anyway, the lilac scent stood out to me the moment I entered the brewery. Let me see if I can approach what I think we're both trying to avoid. Okay?" He took a step toward her.

She clung to the bus stop pole fiercely.

"Tell me," he asked, "if the rumors I've heard about the owners of the brewery are true?"

Thankfully, no one else was out on the sidewalk, and the streetlights illuminated their conversation. Around the corner, the band could be heard singing a Billy Idol tune. Lars would love to give a rebel yell right about now. Anything to release his anxiety over talking to this goddess of a woman.

"What?" She teased a bright curl about her forefinger and her stance relaxed. That wasn't a motion that Lars could look at for long without wanting to do it himself. Tangle his fingers in her hair, that is. "That we spike the beer with a little something extra?"

"Is that a rumor? Huh. No, I'm talking about the one where you bewitch the beers. Because you're witches."

"Oh, that one." Her shoulders dropped. The fish purse slid down her arm to dangle near an ankle. A heavy sigh preceded her nod. "Well, we try to keep things as normal as possible for the human patrons. But…" Her pretty blue eyes dallied with his. "You have a problem with me being a witch?"

"Nope. I was raised by a wolf who was married to a witch."

"Which means…" She teased her tongue along her upper lip as she eyed him carefully. "I'm guessing you're not human either, are you?"

Lars dared a few steps closer to her. He cast a glance around toward the parking lot across the street—no one in the vicinity—then said quietly, "I'm a wolf."

"Shit." An accusing finger pointed at him and Lars couldn't be sure if it might possess a magical zap. "It's you."

He actually flinched. "I…don't even know what to say to that."

"You were the wolf the other night, weren't you? The werewolf in my backyard."

"Uh…yes?"

Talk about being caught out. Guilty as charged.

"Oh, I can't do this." She started across the street but avoided the parking lot.

If she'd been waiting for the bus, did she not have a car? Was she veering off course to get away from him? He'd gone about this all wrong. He'd scared her when he had only wanted to meet her and get to know the compelling woman who had not left his thoughts for days.

"Muriel, wait!"

"It's Mireio! And don't follow me, please. I'm embarrassed enough as it is."

"You shouldn't be. I can't remember much."

"What?" She suddenly stopped in the middle of the street that stretched down a quiet area between the parking lot and a closed restaurant. "So you admit it was you the other night?"

"I think so?" He approached with his hands splayed up and out. "When I'm in werewolf shape I know things and see them as the wolf, but my wolf mind shares space with my man mind. Things get a little confusing."

"Not confusing enough for you to be unable to find me tonight."

"It was the lilacs. I smelled them that night. Haven't been able to stop thinking about them since. Or of the soft woman I saw standing in the doorway."

"Oh, my goddess. You do remember that! I was naked!"

He offered a weak shrug. "Yes?"

"You said things were confusing. Do you remember me naked or not?"

He wobbled his hand before him. "Kind of? I don't have a good image of you, just sort of a memory imprint of seeing something really nice."

"I don't even know what to say." Gripping the purse strap with both fists, the fish wobbled before her as she took an exaggerated step backward. "You are freaking me out."

"I don't want to. I'm not like that. I'm not a guy who can— Do you know how hard it is for me to walk up to a woman and talk to her?"

"Couldn't have been that hard. You followed me out here!"

"I wanted to start over and hoped that maybe you'd talk to me." He stopped moving closer, knowing he'd blown it. He should not torment this beautiful woman anymore. Where the hell were his manners? "Forgive me. I've no talent approaching women. I mean, I do it all the time. Not like a stalker or anything—ah hell. I just… I'm embarrassingly awkward when it comes to this kind of stuff. I wanted to see the pretty woman who smelled like flowers once more. Sorry to have bothered you."

He forced himself to turn and walk off. *Idiot, Lars!* Way to spoil the chick's night. And to spoil his chances of getting to know her better. Yes, he'd seen her naked. And he remembered that image much better than he would ever admit to her. Soft, generous curves, and so much golden light glinting on her skin, which still had beads of water on it. Hell. His werewolf had been attracted to her. *He* was attracted to her.

"Wait!"

Now across the street, he stopped and turned back to her. The tiny witch toed the opposite curb with one of those sexy shoes, and offered a shrugging smile. "It was a remarkable beginning, that was for sure. You didn't do anything wrong, Lars. I couldn't be sure if you were leering at me that night—"

"Oh, never, no. I mean, I don't know. Honestly? I

might have leered a bit. You're worthy of a long, lingering look."

She clutched the weird purse tightly, and he realized what he'd said.

"I'm not saying anything right tonight." He checked his watch. Almost midnight. Shit. He had to stop by the compound, and soon. "It was nice meeting you, Muriel."

"Mireio."

"Right. You make great beer. And you have the prettiest blue eyes I've ever had the chance to look into. But I promise I won't come back to the brewery. I wouldn't want to make you uncomfortable."

He turned away again, and this time when she spoke, his shoulders straightened.

"Can we start over?" she called.

He nodded, and turned to look over his shoulder. All his anxiety swept downward and flooded out across the sidewalk. Offering her a confident smile, he said, "I'd like that."

She approached him and, as she did, tugged something out of her purse. It was her cell phone, which she handed to him. "Put your number in there for me, and we'll try again."

He almost shouted *score!* but controlled his nervous energy. If she knew how much courage it had taken him to cross the taproom to talk to her, and then to follow her after she'd run out on him…

And now he was entering his number into her phone. Some kind of awesome, that.

"I'd like to get to know you better." He handed her back the slim pink phone. "What would you think about going out for something to eat tomorrow night?"

"I have to work tomorrow night."

"Oh."

"But lunch tomorrow could work. Why don't you stop by my place around noon? I think you know where I live, right?"

"I should be able to figure that out." He tapped the side of his nose. "Lilacs. Thanks for the second chance, Mireio."

"It's—oh. Right. Mireio."

He winked at her, because he'd known her name since she'd first told him, then turned and wandered off. Halfway across the parking lot he turned and waved at her. She remained in the middle of the street. Probably waiting for him to leave before she returned to the bus stop. He wouldn't be rude and force her to wait long. Picking up his pace he aimed for his truck around the corner.

He'd talked to the girl! And it had turned out almost okay. Which was about how he rated his life right now. Almost okay, with a side of what the devil. The almost okay waited for him right now, so he shoved the key in the ignition and fired up the truck.

As for the what the devil? He'd been having weird symptoms for over a year, more than just shifting without volition, so had finally gone to see a doctor a few days ago. The doctor told him he'd give him a call in a week when the test results were complete.

But he wasn't going to worry about that. He'd been invited to a pretty witch's house tomorrow for lunch.

So he did indulge in a shout out loud. "Score!"

Chapter 3

Lars strode up the sidewalk to the little red cottage placed at the end of a cul-de-sac. He didn't recognize the area by sight, but by scent? He'd been here before. Yet, besides the naked woman, it hadn't been a pleasant experience. He remembered someone screaming, and then the sight of a beautiful woman—naked. He wasn't going to tell Mireio that as werewolf he saw things as he did when in man shape. His instincts and thoughts were more animalistic, but he did recall sights and sounds and smells.

And she had the sweetest curves on that tiny package topped with red curls and a Kewpie doll smile.

Now as he took the steps up to the door, he inspected the flowers he'd picked up at a gas station on the way here. Blue daisies. He liked blue. Her eyes were blue. But the flowers didn't have a scent and now he studied them closer, they actually looked…dyed.

"I can't even do flowers right." Thinking to toss them

aside in the little flower garden that hugged the front of the redbrick house, he paused. "She'll see them there."

For once he would like to get it right with a woman. It would be a bright spot in his life. And he really needed one. But his nervousness around the female sex could never be allayed by his usual confident alpha surety. Women made him go all stiff and fumble for his words. And hiding the stiff part could sometimes prove a problem, as well.

Smirking at that thought, he grabbed the door knocker and muttered, "Please let her like me. Give me this one, okay?"

Who he was asking, he wasn't sure. He believed in the possibility of God, so if there existed a higher power, he hoped his words would, at the very least, be noted by some force.

Rapping the knocker a few times, he then waited. After ten seconds the door swung open to reveal the flour-dusted face of a witch who sported a surprised look on her face. Hell, he should have called first. But she had told him to stop by for lunch. He must have misunderstood. Par for the course with him.

"Uh…?" Thick black lashes blinking over her blue eyes, she glanced to the flowers in his hand. "Oh! Right! Lunch! I forgot."

"I should have called."

"No, that's fine."

"You weren't expecting me. I can leave and—"

"Don't be silly." She grabbed him by the wrist and coaxed him over the threshold. "Come in! I was baking some bread."

"It smells great." He followed the scent toward the kitchen more than he followed her. Yeast and warmth and crisp browned crust. Mmm… He scanned the many loaves on the kitchen counter. He counted eight but also noted the oven light was on and there was another loaf inside. "That's…a lot of bread."

"I know, it's crazy!" She flung up her hands in surrender, then noted the flour on her fingers and wiped them across her pink frilled apron, which was covered with a white dusting of flour. "Whenever I get the urge to bake homemade bread I always go overboard. I really like the kneading process." She punched the air with a tiny fist. "Gets out some of my frustrations."

Lars wasn't sure if he should sit on one of the stools before the kitchen counter—that might seem too presumptuous—so he stood there holding the bouquet with both hands. Feeling out of his element and, as usual, awkward. "You're frustrated?"

"It's because of a decision I've been mulling over recently. A witch thing. A spell, actually. So, you brought some pretty flowers for me? I love blue."

"I do too. I can't smell them, though. It's kind of strange."

He handed her the bouquet and she pressed the oddly colored blooms to her nose, then sneezed. "Whew! Nope, no smell, but I think I got a petal up my nose. Ha! Sit down. Oh, we were supposed to go out for lunch, right?" She glanced to the oven.

"We can do it some other time. I can see you're busy. It was nice to see you again today. I thought I freaked you out last night. I know I handled things wrong."

"Don't worry about it. Today's a new day. And I have an idea. Because I certainly need to do something with all this bread. How about sandwiches and lemonade out on my patio?"

Spend time with the sexiest woman he'd met in a long time? "I'm in."

* * *

The opportunity to have lunch with the sexy werewolf was just the thing to knock Mireio out of her incessant worrying over how to locate a vampire for the immortality spell. It would also complement the fruitful results of her bread-making endeavors. Sure, she would hand out loaves to her girlfriends, and freeze a couple, but seriously, what witch needed that much bread?

So she sliced up a loaf of oatmeal rye, making the slices extra thick. The steam rose with a seductive invitation as she spread on some cucumber yogurt sauce, covered that with spinach, pickled onions, peppers and some slivered carrots and radishes. Top that all with broccoli sprouts and finely shredded red cabbage, and voilà!

With a glance and a wink to the candle she kept above the stove, she felt as if her mother was watching over her. She lit the beeswax candle once a year on her mother's birthday. It was her way of keeping her memory close.

Ten minutes later, the werewolf didn't seem to mind that there was no meat in the sandwiches. He was on his third half when Mireio returned to the patio with a refill on the blueberry lemonade for both of them.

"This is really good," he said. He sat on the wide-backed white wicker chair before the tiny wrought iron table. His big form seemed to suck up the chair and his knees kept hitting his elbows. It was doll furniture for the man. "What's that sour tangy stuff in the middle?"

"Pickled red onions."

"Love them. Thanks," he said as she poured him more lemonade.

"I'll send you home with a loaf of bread too, if you don't mind. I obviously have some to spare."

"I'd like that." He met her gaze only briefly over the sandwich.

He was a shy one, which surprised Mireio after his bold approach last night. But she'd sensed his nervousness then, as well. And knowing what he'd known about her, it had to have been tough to get up the courage to approach her. Especially when she could have reacted badly—and did.

She noticed his distraction as he looked over the small backyard, framed in on one side by ten-foot-high lilac hedges and low boxwood on the other. As he narrowed his eyes she suspected he was remembering. Merciful moons, she might as well rip off the Band-Aid and get all the painful stuff over with.

"Yes," she offered, "I was standing right there—" she pointed over her shoulder "—by the door that enters into the bathroom."

"Sorry. I didn't want to ask. It's the lilacs. They are what brought me to your doorstep today, and to the brewery last night. The scent is heady."

"You wolves have good sniffers. Did you happen to remember an old lady screaming from that night?"

"I, uh…" He set the remaining quarter of sandwich on the plate. "Yes?"

Mireio chuckled at his obvious confusion. "It's okay. Mrs. Henderson is a drama queen. She stopped over the next morning. Wanted to talk about the monster."

"Monster?"

"Yes. And get this—she'd changed her mind from her original assessment that it was Bigfoot. Now she's sure it was a Sasquatch."

"A—really?" His mouth dropped at the corners and his big brown eyes saddened.

"You're not a monster." She felt the need to reach over and pat his knee in reassurance. "But it's a good thing she thinks that, isn't it? If she was telling everyone she'd seen a werewolf, that could cause trouble for you. How many people actually believe in Sasquatches?"

"About as many as believe in werewolves?" He rubbed his palms on his thighs.

"Right. But don't worry about it." She sipped the lemonade. "So you said something like it wasn't normal for you to tromp through yards in werewolf form. Why *were* you in my yard the other night? Were you lost? Had you come through the cornfield that backs up to the yard?"

He picked up the lemonade and drank half of it. The man seemed nervous again. Yet much as she shouldn't push, curiosity was a witch's best tool when it came to making good choices and weeding out the wrong.

"Well, I mean, aren't werewolves much more cautious about shifting near humans? And it wasn't even a full moon."

"I don't know why it happened," he blurted out. "It's something I'm looking into."

"Really? Like, something is wrong with you?"

He shrugged. "I went to a doctor a few days ago and he checked me out. Said it was probably nothing to worry about. Might have been sleep shifting."

"Sleep shifting? I can't imagine."

"Neither can I. The doc took a bunch of blood and did some other tests."

"And?"

"And? Uh, he hasn't called with the results yet. It's nothing. I don't think you have to worry about finding me in your backyard in werewolf shape anytime in the future."

"Well, I'd rather you in *my* backyard than Mrs. Henderson's. You have to be careful."

"I am," he said forcefully.

And Mireio took that as a warning to curb the conversation topic. She did love an alpha, but she wasn't stupid. When you poke a wolf with a stick, it'll bite.

She prodded the bread crust on her plate. "So you said you're some kind of security guy?"

"That was just my roundabout way of saying I'm scion of the Northern Pack without actually telling anyone I'm a werewolf."

"Right. Gotta be careful. But since I know... What does being a scion entail?"

"At the moment? Not much." He chuckled and his shoulders relaxed. The wicker chair creaked as he settled into it. And those sexy dimples returned. "The pack I grew up in has been shrinking every year. A few years ago, Ridge Addison handed over the principal reins to Dean Maverick, which bumped me up to scion, his second-in-command. But there are only two other pack members at present, and the only one who lives on the compound is Maverick and his woman, Sunday."

"I know Sunday. She's good friends with one of The Decadent Dames owners, Valor Hearst."

"I know Valor. I've sold her queen bees for her hives. I'm also a beekeeper. I think I mentioned that last night?"

"That's so cool. I love bees. They're so fluffy."

"And industrious. They fascinate me. And Sunday is awesome. Lately she's been helping me with...a project."

Mireio leaned across the table and caught her chin in hand. "What sort of project?"

"Just something—" he held his hands in the air to suggest something bread-basket sized "—small."

A small project that he obviously didn't want to talk about. The man was either shy or shifty. Mireio would stick with shy. And he was a cute shy, so that made his reluctance to expound easier to accept. On with the next topic. "You said you've been remodeling a house?"

"Yes, my cabin. I'm fixing it up. I intend to add on two rooms to the back before winter. I live about a run away from the pack compound."

"A run?"

"I can jog back and forth from the cabin to the compound in about five minutes, or take a leisurely stroll in fifteen minutes. I moved into the old, single-room cabin years ago. I've got the outhouse all finished, but now—"

"Wait." Mireio set down her lemonade and sat up straight. "You have an outhouse? Like…no indoor bathroom?"

He laughed, and the sound of it felt like rough water rushing over river stones to Mireio. And for a water witch that was a very sexy sound. "It's how the place was when I moved in," he said. "But thanks to my remodeling it's all modern and has running water with good quality plumbing in the outhouse. Not a hole in a board."

"Whew! For a second there you had me worried. I'll have you know the bathroom is the most important room in my house. There are not too many nights I miss my bath."

"You were taking a bath the night I saw you standing outside the door. Uh, sorry." He rubbed a palm over his face and swiped across his beard nervously. "I have to stop bringing that up. It's rude of me."

"Not rude, just…" Mireio sighed. "So you've seen me naked. Just gives you something to desire, doesn't it?" And she sat back, satisfied that she'd stepped beyond the weirdness of the event and made it something she could control. If not a little weirder. *Ha! Go, Mireio!* "Anyway, my bathtub is huge. It's because I'm a mermaid."

Lars's jaw dropped open. "You are? So you're like a mermaid witch?"

"I mean, figuratively I'm a mermaid. I love water. I

work water magic. I think I was probably a real mermaid in a past life. You know?"

"I can imagine you swishing around in the sea. But would your hair have been green?"

"Maybe." She twirled the ends of her hair around a fingertip and fluttered her lashes at him.

And Lars fell into that puppy-dog, lovestruck expression again. Oh, dear, but he had it bad for her. And she wasn't beyond encouraging him, because now that she was getting to know him, she really liked the strong silent alpha.

Had she intentions to avoid a relationship? Silly witch.

"Mireio!"

At the shrieking female yell, Lars sat up abruptly, kicking the table and upsetting the plates. Mireio made a grab to keep them from falling onto the stone patio. "It's just Mrs. Henderson," she said quickly, as if to calm a spooked dog.

The old woman popped around the back corner of the house with a notebook in hand. She wore an olive green pencil skirt that Mireio imagined she'd probably worn in her heyday back in, well…whenever the skirt had been in style. Her black-and-gray hair was piled into a messy bundle atop her narrow skull and on her feet were the ever-present and quite beaten pink bunny slippers.

"Oh." Mrs. Henderson eyed up Lars. "I didn't realize you had a guest, Mireio."

"Mrs. Henderson, this is Lars Gunderson. Lars, Mrs. Henderson, my next-door neighbor. We were just finishing lunch. And I have a loaf of oatmeal rye for you that I'll bring over once it's cooled, Mrs. Henderson."

"Oh, that's lovely. You're always so generous with the baked goods. And quite a talent too." She still couldn't drag her assessing gaze from Lars as she held out the notebook before her. "I don't mean to interrupt but I wanted to show you the sketch I made of the—" she dropped her voice to a whisper "—you-know-what we saw the other night."

Mireio glanced to Lars, who, no doubt, had figured what the woman was talking about, but he didn't show that he had.

"Lars, was it?" Mrs. Henderson asked him. She tilted her head, taking him in with a discerning gaze. "Have we met before? You seem very familiar."

"Never," Mireio blurt out. "I mean, we've only just met, so of course you've never seen him here or in my yard before. Let me see what you've drawn, Mrs. Henderson. It's okay. I mentioned the, uh, incident to Lars. So he's in on it."

"Oh?" The woman's eyes brightened, pleased to have another conspirator present. "She told you about the Sasquatch?"

"That she did." He leaned his elbows onto his knees, giving her his full attention. "You must have been frightened something fierce."

"Who me? Oh, gosh, no. I may have been initially surprised to see such a big, ugly, hulking beast tromping through my prized tulips, but that didn't stop me from getting a very good look at the monster."

Lars's jaw tensed. It was a good thing he wasn't holding the glass of lemonade because Mireio guessed his clenched fingers might have sent shards flying.

Mrs. Henderson laid the notebook down on the table and Mireio turned it so both she and Lars could look at the—quite talented—sketch of what looked similar to an ape-like man with long hairy fingers and a hunched back and shoulders. The head was all wrong, not matching the werewolf's actual wolf head and long toothy maw, but instead more resembling a man with large ears and a flat monkeylike snout.

"Remarkable," Mireio said with a secret glance and smile to Lars.

"Is it how you remembered the beast too?" Mrs. Henderson asked eagerly. "I intend to bring this sketch in to the police, but I'm still not so sure I got the nose right."

"Oh. Well…" Mireio shrugged. "I didn't get a very good look at it. I had initially thought it was a moose… but I'm sure what you've drawn here is very close."

"But you said it stopped and stared at you for a moment. Surely you must have seen details? Did you look into its big glowing yellow eyes?"

Mireio met Lars's lift of his brows. He was smirking now, thank the goddess. He obviously understood there was no fear of him being found out with such a drastically wrong drawing, no matter who the woman showed it to.

"Maybe a little longer," she said, tapping the nose. "And did you get the tail?"

"The tail?" Mrs. Henderson picked up the sketch and studied it. "I'm not sure I remember…oh. Sure. A tail. Of course, Sasquatches have tails."

"Do they?" Lars asked.

"Oh, yes," Mrs. Henderson replied with knowing authority. "I'll have to add that. Thank you, Mireio. Oh." She placed a hand on Lars's shoulder. "Will you be around more often? To, you know, keep an eye on our sweet Mireio?"

"Uh…"

"I think I hear the oven timer for the last loaf of bread," Mireio interrupted. "We'll talk later, Mrs. Henderson. Lars, would you help me bring in the dishes?"

"It was nice meeting you, Mrs. Henderson," he offered as he dutifully and quickly followed Mireio's escape route into the kitchen.

The two of them watched out the window until Mrs. Henderson had turned the corner at the back of the house, then they both started laughing.

"That was the most awful rendition of—" she made air quotes "—'the monster,' I've seen. You don't look anything like that."

"Yes, I'm relieved. Must be interesting having that woman living next door, eh?"

"Never a dull moment." She opened the oven door, which emitted a whoosh of delicious bread scent.

"Mmm, now that scent will lead me back to your door over and over."

"Good," she said decisively. "Because I like you, Lars. I'm glad you had the courage to approach me last night. Maybe we can do this again tomorrow night? More like an official date? Because right now I have to go change and head in to work."

"I'd like that. Ah, but tomorrow night won't work. I won't be able to find a…" He winced, pausing to think his words through. "I have a previous engagement. It's not with another woman. Just something I can't get out of. How about this Saturday?"

Two days away. "Saturday works for me. But you'll have to pick me up at the brewery because I have the early shift."

"It's a date."

"Great! Let me wrap up a loaf of bread for you to take along." She pulled out some brown paper she kept for wrapping baked goods, and with a few folds and tucks fitted it perfectly about a warm loaf and handed it to him.

He took the gift and then glanced to the front door. Back to her. He rubbed a hand along his thigh. "Yes, I suppose I should leave. Thank you for lunch. It was really good."

"It wasn't that great. But you're a guy. Usually guys like any food that's been made for them that isn't a TV dinner."

"So you've seen the inside of my freezer?"

He smiled, and she fell into that pretty white gleam of his. He had no idea the impact those pearly whites had on her. And was she blushing? Parts of her suddenly felt very hot.

"Uh. Right. Then I suppose I should go." He turned, but didn't walk to the front door.

So Mireio stepped up before him, sensing what he couldn't say or do. And finding it sweetly endearing. "Did you want to kiss me before you leave?"

He nodded. Eagerly, but with a sheepish shrug. "I wasn't sure it would be okay."

The guy had scored one simply by being a sweet, uncomfortable lunk of shy. Mireio crooked her finger, gesturing that he should bow down, and when he got close enough to kiss, she met his lips with hers.

His mouth was not tentative, finding its place against hers with a surety and the promise of more confidence than his speech gave. He didn't open her mouth, but he lingered, and the pressure of him against her worked a delicious tingle in her core. Mmm, now that was a very not-shy kiss.

When they parted, his eyes darted back and forth between hers. Then his dimples dented his cheeks and his smile caught up. "Saturday can't come fast enough." He kissed her quickly, and then turned to leave.

Standing on the threshold and watching his long strides out to his pickup truck, Mireio touched her lips and whispered a blessing for the fact she'd not been a stuck-up witch last night and had decided to talk to the man.

"Good call," she said to herself. "May the witch and the werewolf get along. At the very least, have some fun."

Well past the midnight hour, Mireio startled from her sleep and cried out. She sat up, seeking in the darkness for a creature—with fangs. Heartbeat thundering, she pressed a palm to her chest and, realizing she'd had another nightmare, breathed deeply in and out to calm her fears.

It was always the same. The vampire stood before her holding a bloody heart that dripped onto the toes of her white shoes, forever staining her memories of a younger, more innocent time.

She hadn't had a nightmare in over a year, but the fact it had returned now disturbed her. She had to perform the immortality spell. But if so focused on preparing for the spell, could she then also concentrate on dating the shy but sexy werewolf?

"Am I doing the right thing?" she whispered into the night.

No one answered. Which was a good thing. That meant she was alone. No creepy vampire anywhere near her. Yet the only way to ensure she was safe from vampires was to rip the heart out of one of them and consume its blood.

She dropped back into the pillows and closed her eyes tightly.

Chapter 4

Saturday evening Lars stopped into the brewery. Mireio was ready to go, waiting for him by the door. She bounced on her high heels and her short multiruffled purple skirt caught his eye. And dangling near that skirt was the black fish purse. The woman was a character. And she was going out with him tonight.

He was the luckiest guy in the world.

Mireio waved goodbye to a woman behind the bar with dark hair and a calm, knowing smile, whom Lars waved to, as well. He hadn't been introduced, but did know Valor Hearst, who also worked here. She and Sunday, his pack leader's wife, were friends, so Valor popped up at the compound once in a while. They always chatted bees for a while when she did so.

"Where are we going tonight?" Mireio asked as she joined him and slipped her hand into his.

Momentarily captivated by the warm slender hand in his, Lars took a few seconds to answer. It actually took a squeeze from her hand to lure him back to what she'd asked.

"Uh, where? There's a new place in Tangle Lake. Supposed to be fancy and the scenery is pretty cool. You like a steak house?"

"Sure. I like all food. Your hand is so big and—" she turned it over to inspect as they strolled toward the parking lot "—rough. You must do a lot of physical labor."

"I've cleared out some fallen oaks from the forest near my place, so I've been chopping and stacking wood for winter fires. As well as doing some repair work on the plank path that leads to the outhouse."

"I need to see that outhouse one of these days. I can't imagine having to walk outside to get to the bathroom."

"I'm sure your bathroom with the big tub puts my little outhouse to shame."

"Oh, I'm sure it does." She skipped a few steps up to the charcoal gray truck. "This is yours? You men and your big trucks. You're going to have to boost me up for this one."

He opened the passenger door for her and held her hand as she stepped onto the lower step. Even then she had to stretch up a leg, and…he put a hand to her hip to guide her. He wanted to give a shove to that sweet little derriere, but that might be too forward. He was the kind of guy who would never manhandle a woman. Unless she'd given him permission to do so. And then he would enjoy touching her with abandon.

"I'm in!" she announced with a clap. "Let's do this!"

Chuckling at her enthusiasm, Lars rounded the front of the truck and hopped inside and started the engine. "How's business tonight?"

"It's a Saturday," she said as he drove out of the lot. "Comedy night."

"Really? Like stand-up?"

"Yes, and tonight is locals only. It's a big hit. There are some ridiculously hilarious people living in Anoka."

"You like music?" he asked, turning on the radio low.

"I love the oldies stuff like the '80s tunes."

"I think I know the station for you." He turned the dial to an '80s hit station, one of his favorites too, despite having missed the era because he'd been born in the late '80s. Culture Club was playing and Mireio gave him a thumbs-up.

"Did you eat all the bread I sent home with you?" she asked.

"Most of it. Had sandwiches for lunch, with enough left for a French toast breakfast tomorrow. You make great bread."

"You'll have to stop by when I'm in a cupcake-baking mood."

"Don't tempt me."

"Temptation is my thing, don't you know?"

He waggled his brows at her.

She giggled. "You're starting to loosen up around me. You were pretty shy initially."

He shrugged as he turned onto the freeway that would take them to their destination. "You're just so pretty. I admit I'm intimidated by most women. You're all so…tiny."

"That is understandable, coming from a big beast of a man. How tall are you?"

"Six and a half feet? Something like that."

"Good thing I like wearing heels. Oh! I love this song!"

Adam Ant's "Desperate But Not Serious" started playing and Lars turned it up. He would never consider himself desperate for a woman. But would he like to get serious with one? Hell yes. And Mireio Malory seemed a very good option.

* * *

The view was gorgeous, as promised. They sat on a patio situated about thirty feet from the lakeshore. The sun settled above the jagged line of pines across the lake, casting pink and silver shimmers on the water and the night air was surprisingly warm for spring. A fountain nestled in the center of the small lake burbled and a pair of white swans floated close by. Fortunately it was too early in the season for mosquitoes.

The brown butter shrimp with Gouda grits was excellent. The red wine sweet and not too dry. And the man sharing shy glances with her was slowly moving up to broadcasting more confidence in his brown eyes.

Mireio had never dated a man who wasn't in her face and always dropping innuendos about them *doing it*. Sure, she had dated a few who were polite, but none so sweetly masculine and devastatingly charming as this guy. A werewolf? She'd dated witches, faeries and once even a demon. But a wolf was new to her, and she was excited about the possibilities of learning more about this sweetie.

"I lost the muskie after that struggle," Lars said, ending his tale about ice fishing without an ice house or a line in the middle of what had turned into an ice storm.

"Do wolves have a greater affinity for cold weather?" she wondered.

"Yes, we can handle the Minnesota winters well. But I do like to bundle up when I know a storm is headed our way. That one took me by surprise. Froze my beard something fierce."

"Ha! I hope you had someone to help you defrost it with snuggly kisses."

He shrugged, that bashful move that endeared her to

his big, awkward appeal. "I was out with the guys. We never mix fishing and women. You ladies just don't get it."

"Oh, I think Valor is into ice fishing. But there are times I wonder if she's more a guy than a girl. I don't think I'd like to lie on the ice and dip my hand in the cold waters in hopes a fish will find me of interest," she said. Which was exactly how Lars had explained they'd done it. "I admit the winter bothers me. I need a big thick sweater to keep from constantly shivering. I prefer spring and summer. And warmth."

"Your tail would freeze in the winter," he said with a wink.

"Which tail are you talking about?" she asked teasingly.

"Both?"

"Ha!" She tilted her wine goblet to his and he met it with a *tink*. "To breezy summers and warm winter nights. And while we're at it, let's toss in a long life of immortal dreams."

"Immortal dreams?"

She shrugged. "It's a witch thing. Just a spell I've had on my mind lately. Anyway, back to the fishing. I certainly hope to never get hooked by a fisherman anytime soon."

"Is that so?"

"He'd rip my tail. And besides, we mermaids would never be caught swimming in any of Minnesota's ten thousand icy lakes."

"What sort of bait do you think would attract a mermaid?"

She leaned across the table and the small heat from the candle warmed her cheek. "Kindness and a sexy shy smile."

And there it was again! Those dimples were mermaid

bait for sure. But to think about it, she'd hooked him. And this was one catch she wasn't eager to toss back.

The waitress stopped by with the bill and Lars dug out his wallet from a back pocket and handed her his credit card.

"So what do you like to do for fun?" he asked. "I've already marked ice fishing off the potential date list."

"I don't have to be entertained in any wild or elaborate fashion. A movie. A book club. Dancing, or even just sitting in a park. I'm a chick who can find fun in most anything."

"I get that. You're what they call one of those eclectic women," he said with a wink. "Your bright hair and frilly clothes tell me that."

"How else is a girl supposed to dress?"

"You won't hear me complaining. But what's with the purse?"

She lifted her purse. A cool find on Etsy, crafted from black suede in layers that emulated a fish with scales. "Mermaid, remember?"

"Right. Let me guess… You're the chick at the summer festivals with the flowers in your hair, dancing in the mud with bare feet and not a care?"

"You got it."

"I think I'm the guy always standing off to the side, wondering if that beautiful blossom of a chick will ever notice him."

She placed her hand over his. "I have noticed you, Lars. And I think you're pretty cool. I'll get you in daisies and bare feet before the summer is out. Promise."

"I'd actually wear daisies for you. So why don't we…" He paused, staring off over the lake with the swans floating by.

The pause was…quite long. "Lars?"

"Huh? Oh. Sorry, lost my train of thought. What were we talking about?"

Daisies and flirtation. "Nothing much." But it was time to move it up to the next level. "Now do you know what I want to do?"

"What?"

"You said you live close?"

"About ten miles north."

"Then I want to see this mysterious outhouse with the modern plumbing."

He smirked and collected his credit card as the waitress swung by with it. But instead of dimples, he rubbed his jaw, with a wince. "I'm not sure. I have to make a stop on the way home, actually..."

"Am I being too forward? I'm not suggesting anything. I mean, am I? Maybe? If you're not ready to take me home with you, just for chatting, I get that. You're a guy who works more slowly than most."

"Not at all. I can do fast. I'm very fast. I mean..." He swiped his fingers over his beard in what Mireio was learning was a nervous gesture. "I want to spend more time with you tonight, Mireio. I just, uh...well..." A heavy sigh surprised her. "You'll need to know sooner rather than later. Guess now's as good a time as any."

"That sounds absolutely mysterious. But I'm in. Let's go!"

Ten minutes later, they drove up the long driveway to the Northern Pack compound, which was where Lars had to make a stop. It wasn't like a big military compound, which Mireio had expected, but rather a white plantation-style home with a massive tin-sided building out back that housed all kinds of building materials and lots of junk.

"So none of the pack members live here except Dean and Sunday?"

"Nope. We all live in the area, though. Packs used to share close living conditions, but you know, it's the twenty-first century. We like our privacy as much as we like the family we get from being in the pack." He parked before the house and swung around to open the door.

Just when she thought to step down, he lifted her and swung her out, setting her down carefully until she could get a sure footing with her heels on the gravel drive. How many times had a man helped her in and out of a vehicle? Exactly twice. Both of those times had been tonight. She could get used to this kind of chivalry.

"Shall we?" He offered his hand and that pushed her over the edge and into a giddy swoon.

She clasped his hand and beamed as he led her toward the front door, which opened to reveal a waving Sunday. The chick sported long, white-blond hair and was built like Valor—straight—and she seemed accustomed to hanging out in jeans and greasy T-shirts as opposed to frills and lace. She was a cat-shifting familiar, married to Dean Maverick, a werewolf and the pack principal.

"Hey, Lars!" A shout from near the storage building drew their attention to Dean standing near a huge steel beam he held at a diagonal, one end of it digging into the ground. "Come give me a hand!"

"Be right back," Lars said. "Uh, you know Sunday?"

"We've met once," Sunday confirmed.

Lars winked at Mireio. "This won't take a minute!"

"Hey, Mireio." Sunday gestured she come inside and held the screen door open for her. "I didn't know you and Lars were a thing."

She entered the house, which was dimly lit. The sun had set, and the soft kitchen lights gleamed on the white marble kitchen counter and copper toaster.

"Lars and I just started seeing one another. First official date tonight. Oh!" She spied a munchkin sitting in a baby seat on the kitchen table and her maternal instincts rushed her to check it out. "Who is this little sweetie? Can I hold him?"

"Sure, I just fed him. We call him Peanut."

Mireio picked up the warm bundle of blue fleece and baby softness and he nuzzled against her chest. The scent of warm baby was better than baked bread or chocolate any day. She rubbed her palm lightly over the thick crop of black hair swished to a wave on top of his head. "So much hair! And it sticks straight up. Adorable. How old is he?"

"Uh, about four months?" Sunday leaned against the counter, her T-shirt falling from one bare shoulder and her hair a little tangled as if she'd been through a tough day. Or she simply wasn't a fashion queen and didn't often bother to comb her hair.

"Did you and Dean adopt?" Mireio knew, from Valor, that Sunday couldn't have kids. Well, she could, but a cat shifter simply could not make a baby with a werewolf. Just didn't work that way.

"No. He's uh…" Sunday straightened and scratched her head. "You don't know who Peanut is?"

"Should I?"

The front door opened and Lars and Dean wandered in, chuckling about almost dropping the steel beam, but finally getting it loaded into the back of Dean's truck. Lars took one look at Mireio holding the baby and activated the nervous beard swipe.

"Hey," she offered. "Isn't he the cutest little button ever? He's called Peanut."

"I know that." Lars exchanged glances with Sunday.

"I'll leave you two." The cat shifter left the kitchen swiftly, grabbing her husband's hand and heading toward the front door. Dean protested with a "What's up?" as his wife tugged him outside.

"What was that about?" Mireio bounced as she held the baby. It was a natural motion, instilled from years of babysitting. His plump little body felt so good snuggled against her breast and neck. Someday she would have a million kids. Or at the very least three or four. "She must be babysitting for someone, huh?"

"She is." Lars smoothed his hand over the baby's hair. "Peanut is mine, Mireio."

"What?"

"He's my son."

Chapter 5

Mireio blinked a few times, then realized Lars was talking about the baby she cuddled against her shoulder. He held out his arms for the boy, and she handed him over. The big hulking werewolf gently cradled the sleeping infant in his arms as if he were a wise old granny who had been doing so for generations. He stroked the baby's hair and kissed his forehead.

"He's a sweetie," she offered because she was taken aback. But then she realized she was only surprised because she'd never expected such from Lars. "You're not married, are you?" came out too quickly.

He snickered and began to rock the baby with a gentle bounce. "No."

"Good. I mean—well, I don't date married men."

"I would never be so cruel to another woman. He's my boy, Mireio. I wasn't going to tell you like this. And I thought I'd wait a bit longer. But when you suggested I show you my place I figured now was as good a time as any. If you're not into kids, that's cool. At least you found out early on and can walk away."

"No." She touched his arm, and tapped the baby's tiny fingers. "I adore babies. And I'm fine with this. I mean, we're not lovers or anything. We've only seen each other a few times."

"Sure." But his wince told her he had high hopes for what might happen between them.

And she did too. Did she still have such high hopes with the introduction of this little number? It shouldn't change things. This was all a bit sudden and new. But if the guy had a baby, then she could deal.

"Let's take things as they come, okay?" She waited for Lars to meet her eyes. And when he did, she winked at him. "You should probably get this little guy home and tucked in."

"Yes, and he needs to be changed too. I uh…" He grimaced again. "I took the car seat out for our date tonight because, well, like I've said, I wasn't sure when or how to spring this on you. Usually I walk through the forest to drop him off and pick him up. Would you mind driving the truck to my cabin? It's just a winding road from here."

"That big monster truck?" Mireio gulped.

"I'll help you move the seat forward so you can reach the pedals."

"Do you trust me?"

He pressed his head against the baby's head and kissed his nose. And Mireio suddenly realized that the man probably trusted her more with the vehicle than he did with his child.

"Hand me the keys. I can do this."

The path through the woods had been there for decades. Lars knew that the very first pack members had built the compound and the cabin where he lived. He liked having his own place and had lived there alone since he was fourteen. But also, when the pack had been larger, he'd liked being close to friends, whom he also considered family. Now, it was nice for the two-mile distance between the places because babysitting was just a wander through the woods.

Sunday had been the one to suggest he get away from the cabin and go out and have a little fun. Lars had been cooped up with Peanut for months and generally walked around with baby spit on his shoulders, and who knew when he'd last washed his hair?

Yet in the process of "getting out" he'd hooked up with a pretty woman.

"I sure hope she likes us both," he said as he strode the beaten path over fallen leaves, cracking branches and crops of mushrooms that edged the lane. "What do you think, Peanut?"

The boy was awake and alert, taking in the surroundings, even though it was dark. Lars pressed a kiss to his bushy crop of thick hair. He loved that stuff. It was soft and black and smelled like nothing he'd ever known but everything he wanted to have forever.

Had he done things wrong tonight? Should he have kept Peanut a secret until he felt sure that he and Mireio might have a real thing between them?

No, better to give her opportunity to run now before they did get to know one another. And better for him. He'd hate to fall in love with her and then lose her because he had a baby. Much as she had claimed to enjoy babies, being a parent was different. It required dedication and sacrifice. And love.

Lars had never been in love. Until now. He hugged Peanut and strode swiftly toward the truck lights that approached his cabin.

He arrived at the truck in time to help Mireio down and tell her how to turn the lights off. The truck really was a monster in her hands, but she'd gotten here safely.

"Whew!" she said when she stood on the ground beside him. "That thing is huge and the road is narrow and winding. I think I just passed some kind of endurance test! Hey! Don't laugh at me, you little giggle butt," she said to Peanut.

Lars high-fived her and nodded that she should follow him in. "The road is crazy twisty. I've considered getting a smaller truck, but I haul a lot of wood and well…" He opened the front door, which he never kept locked and gestured she enter before him. "I do like a big truck."

"Men and their toys." Her heels clicked across the clean wood floor. "Wow, this place is cute. It's all just the one room?"

She turned, taking in the living area with the blue-and-green-plaid couch and low table made from half an oak trunk. The kitchen offered a small fridge, a porcelain sink and an old gas stove. A round kitchen table sat at the end of the foyer, which was right before them. Immediately to their right stood the queen-size bed hemmed in by a clothes rack against a wall. Peanut's crib was wedged between the clothes and the end of the bed.

"This is it." Lars grabbed a diaper from a shelf above the clothes rack and laid Peanut on the bed. "I gotta change him. I hope you don't mind. There's beer and water in the fridge."

"Sure. Looks like he's wide-awake now," she said as she rummaged around in the fridge.

"Peanut loves walking through the woods. Don't you?" He toyed with the baby's bare toes as the infant stretched out his legs. He always did that once diaper-free. Like, oh, yes, Daddy, let me dry out and be a nudist for a while.

"Soon you'll be running through the woods and putting your daddy through the wringer of keeping up with you."

"What is his name?" Mireio asked as she sat before the kitchen table with a bottle of water.

"Peanut." He secured the diaper tapes and replaced his son's onesie snaps. He tossed the diaper into the bin, which he emptied every night, and then got a bottle of milk he'd poured this morning from the fridge. He set it in the pot on the stove half-filled with water and turned on the heat. It took only minutes to get a nice warmth to the milk.

"You named your son Peanut?" He could sense the dismay in her tone. "That's…unique."

Lars sat next to her before the table. "I don't know his real name. His mother didn't tell me it before she ran off. And the name on the birth certificate simply says 'baby boy.' I thought he sort of melded against me like a little peanut when I held him against my chest, so…it works for now."

"Peanut. Sure. But you are going to give him a name?"

Lars shrugged. "When the right one comes to me. I have up to a year to fill it in on the birth certificate."

"Sounds fair enough. Oh, don't get up. I'll check the milk." She tested the milk against her wrist, then sat down and handed it to him. "Cool, but just about right. So…do I get to ask you about Peanut's mom and where she is and why you're doing the single-daddy thing? Oh. Did she die?"

"No, she's not dead, and yes, ask me anything you like."

Because that meant she was open to the conversation, and maybe he might still have a chance with her.

"I want to know whatever you're comfortable telling me." She pointed to the baby sucking voraciously at the bottle. "Explain that little bundle of sweetness and wild rock-star hair."

She hadn't made an excuse to leave yet. And she wasn't standing by the door, eyeing the escape. So Lars marked himself as lucky. So far, so good.

"All right, here goes. I spent a few nights with Peanut's mom last year. It was a two-night stand kind of thing. We met in a nightclub in downtown Minneapolis. We weren't drunk, but you know how sometimes you just want to get close with another person?"

She nodded knowingly. "Oh, yeah."

"And the feeling was mutual," he continued. "So, you know, it happened. She stayed the day and a second night, then told me it had been fun, and she was moving on. She traveled a lot for her job as a photojournalist. Was hoping to get an assignment in Africa that would last for years. I marked it off as a fun couple of nights and life went on. Human women, you know…"

He shifted to tilt up Peanut a bit so the baby wouldn't get gassy from sucking in air from the bottle.

"What about human women?" Mireio asked.

"It's hard for we werewolves to have a relationship with someone who is going to freak out the minute she sees you shift. We can't trust that secret with just anyone."

"You can trust a witch."

"I know that." He winked at her and she smiled and wiggled on her chair. "Ten months after that hookup I get a knock on the door and the surprise of my life. She didn't want a baby. Didn't need one messing up her life. And she got the African assignment. So she said it was my choice. She could put the baby up for adoption, or I could take him."

Mireio's jaw dropped open. Then she closed it. "Wow. Tough choice for a young, single man."

"Not really. I took one look at this little peanut and knew I had to have him in my life."

"Really? Have you always liked kids? Babies? Usually men aren't so paternal."

"I have never been around kids much. Never even held a baby before this guy."

"How did you even trust that he was yours?"

"She does ask the questions, doesn't she?" Lars said to Peanut. "I just knew. But also, his mom said I should get a DNA test, and she even had the forms and details on how to do it, along with all the info she'd written down for Peanut's feeding schedule. She was an orderly woman. And she said she knew he was mine because she hadn't had sex with a guy after me for months."

"Did you do the test?"

"I did. Peanut is one hundred percent mine. But I knew that before I got the test results."

"How did you know?"

He beamed at her. "My heart told me he was mine. But also, could you imagine putting this little sweetie up for adoption?"

"He is a sweetie. But he might have made some other family happy too. Adoption isn't horrible."

"I know that."

"Oh, but wait. Is he werewolf?"

Lars shrugged. "Not sure. His mom is human, but human women can give birth to our babies, and they can be werewolf. But I won't know until Peanut hits puberty. Another good reason not to put him up for adoption. Could you imagine human parents discovering their adopted son, once he hits puberty, suddenly shifts to a wolf?"

"So his mom didn't know you were werewolf?"

"No need for me to tell her. You know it's not wise to share stuff like that with humans. How many people do you tell you're a witch?"

"Zero. Unless I get a feeling about them. Like you.

Aw, look, he's sleeping. Sweet little Peanut. You really should give him a name, though."

"I'm working on it. I have to go to the county office and do a name change. I'm already on the birth certificate as the father. Peanut's mom had the foresight to do that, so he's got my last name."

"That was smart. Oh. Can I hold him?"

"Uh…" Lars set the bottle on the table and studied her pleading yet smiling look. When he'd walked in at Dean's place to find her holding Peanut, he'd initially felt angry. What right had she to barge in and take hold of his child? But then he'd realized she hadn't even known who the baby was then.

Now? He was being foolish. Possessive. And with every right to be so.

"Oh, sorry." She sat back. "You're his daddy. I'm sure he needs you to tuck him in."

"He sleeps through most of the night after his final bottle. I'll put him down."

Once he'd tucked Peanut in, and left him uncovered because it was warm tonight, Lars then rinsed the bottle and dried it while Mireio got up to admire the lamp base on the table beside the couch.

"This is beautiful," she said of the carved pine column. "It's so intricate. I can see deer and squirrels and that looks like a swan. Did you do this?"

Lars shrugged and nodded. "There's a lot of wood out here. Sometimes I see something in the wood that needs to come out."

"Like Michelangelo and his marble sculptures. You're an artist."

"No, I'm just a regular guy who amuses himself with a hammer and chisel once in a while." He set the bottle on the rack above the sink and then approached her. He shoved his hands in his back pockets. "So, I know this is a lot of baggage I've unpacked here. And I'll understand if you don't want to see me anymore. I wasn't even in the market for dating, but then Sunday said I needed to get out, have some fun. And after that morning at your place, there were the lilacs. It was almost like I had to find you. Then I did. I think it's better you know right away."

"Lars, don't worry. There are a lot of single parents nowadays. And we're not serious. Just having fun, right?"

"Right."

"Oh, and if Sunday can't babysit, call me. I adore babies. Would love to have a couple, or twelve, of my own someday."

"I'll remember that." He sat on the couch and she sat next to him, which he took as a good sign that she didn't want to leave right away.

"That is, if you can trust me with Peanut. I have baby-sat a lot."

"Oh, I trust you."

"Yeah? But you didn't want me to hold him just now at the table."

"Sorry. He's my boy and…well, you're new."

"I get it." She clasped his hand. "You're a protective alpha wolf. Do not apologize for that. Ever. Now. I want to see this strange but interesting bathroom. Can we slip out with Peanut sleeping?"

"Yep. I've got a baby monitor in the bathroom so I can hear him if I'm taking a shower. But I promise you, it's nothing to get excited about."

"Any outhouse that isn't two holes in a slab of wood is exciting."

Through the crisp darkness, surrounded by cricket chatter, they followed a plank path back to the outhouse.

The bathroom was indeed a small room with a toilet, shower and tub, and vanity. Plain but serviceable. But Mireio decided it would be a bitch in the winter if a person woke in the middle of the night needing to answer the call of nature.

"No holes dug in the ground," Lars offered as they stepped out into the night air.

He pointed out the wildflower field that backed onto his property behind the outhouse and the beehives he kept. He had eight stacks right now and would divide them in the fall and probably gain three more in the process. He'd promised to take some of Valor's bees when she divided the hives that she tended from the rooftop of her apartment building in Tangle Lake.

"So you're a keeper," Mireio commented, loving herself for the pun.

"I am? Oh. Uh, yes. A beekeeper."

She felt sure he blushed in the darkness. The man certainly was a keeper.

After the grand tour, Mireio suggested they call it a night. She'd felt bad he'd had to take Peanut out of his crib, but the infant had slept through being buckled into his car seat and the twenty-minute drive back to Anoka, and even her accidental slamming of the truck door when she got out at the sidewalk before her house.

"Can I call you?" Lars asked as he stepped down from the sidewalk to stand on the tarmac, which put their heights a little closer.

"I certainly hope so. Hey, how about an afternoon with Peanut tomorrow? I have to go in to work for a few hours in the morning. Valor and I are kegging the stout. But I'm free after one. We could go to a park and have a picnic?"

"I'd like that. You sure you're okay with this, Mireio?"

She shrugged. "I am right now. If I think about it

awhile? Who knows? But I don't think I'll change my mind. I'm enjoying getting to know you. You are certainly an interesting man."

"Maybe a little too interesting, eh?"

"Better that than dull, right?" She laughed, but stopped abruptly. "So tomorrow it's a date."

"Should I pick you up at the brewery?"

"Yes." She tilted up on her tiptoes to meet the kiss that he did not pause to give her this time. His breath tasted like the wine they'd shared over supper, and his beard brushed her cheek softly. And when she started to pull away he dipped in for a firm press that won her completely. She sighed into the kiss and drew her fingers down the ends of his long hair. Mmm, he was some kind of all right. "I do enjoy these not-so-shy kisses."

"Me too. I would kiss you longer but…" He glanced over to the running truck.

"I'm glad you told me about Peanut. You two are adorable together. We're going to have fun, the three of us."

Lars turned and waved as he got in the truck. And Mireio hugged herself and recalled that the man had given her a choice to walk away now if she wanted to.

Did she want to walk away? Could she handle dating a man with a baby? Neither option felt easy. And she needed easy right now. Because that would counter the nightmares and her wariness over performing the immortality spell.

Chapter 6

Areas of the park were overgrown with wildflowers stretching as high as Lar's waist in some spots. They'd picnicked with egg salad sandwiches, fresh veggies and blueberry lemonade in mason jars. While Mireio packed up the basket, Lars wandered into the flowers with Peanut, pointing out the yellow sunflowers. He held out his hand and a bee buzzed closer, probably attracted to his movement. He never flinched. Bees would not sting a person unless they were given reason to do so. And he intended to teach Peanut to not fear the insect, and to also respect it.

"That's a dragonfly." He stood still as the insect hovered but four feet from him. Strapped to his chest in a baby sling, Peanut stretched out his arms and cooed. "Yes, you like bugs? Of course you do. But you mustn't squish them. Insects are good. Especially the bees. Like that one. See the fat sacks of pollen on her legs? She's going to make honey with that. And then we can eat it."

Though he'd read not to give an infant honey in his first year. Or had the pediatrician told him that? He needed to get a guide or book on all the things a parent should do and watch out for. This whole baby thing was new to him. He was walking a tightrope with Peanut, and didn't want to wobble off the line.

"We'll find a book or something," he said to Peanut.

"A book on what?" Having taken off her shoes, Mireio joined him. A camera dangled from around her neck. She took some shots of a bright purple coneflower. Bending, she plucked a few tiny white daisies.

"A baby book," he said. "I need something that'll tell me what I should and shouldn't do. I was telling Peanut about honey. I know that's a no-no for the first year."

"Right. There are great books out there for parents. Dr. Sears or the What to Expect books. They cover a baby's first year, telling you what changes they go through monthly and about their growth."

"Sounds like exactly what I need. Can we stop by a bookstore on the way back into town?"

"For sure! But only if you don't mind me checking out the books on beer. I'm looking for a new and interesting recipe."

"Deal." He turned and fist-bumped her. "You a photographer too?"

"Me? No. But I like to take pictures of flowers and bugs. I have a macro lenses that I usually use. Takes amazingly detailed shots, but I forgot it today. I do have one of my pictures hanging up behind my bed."

"I'll have to check it out sometime." Lars wandered forward then, with a wince, realized what he'd said. Check out the picture or her bed?

Well, he'd like to do both. In good time.

Spying a thick crop of wild grass, he sat on it and

laid back with Peanut snuggling up to his chest. "Ah, this is the life. The sun is high and warm and I don't have a care."

Mireio leaned over him and snapped a few pictures. "Do you mind? You two look adorable lying there. He really is a little peanut all curled up on his daddy's chest."

"Go for it."

"Oh, wait. I forgot the daisies." She pushed a couple daisies into his beard. "I did tell you I'd have you in daisies, didn't I?"

"That you did." He even managed to smile, eyes closed against the sun, as she snapped the camera above him and Peanut.

After a few shots, she sat in the grass next to them and set down the camera. Tilting her head back to allow the sun to beam across her face, her hair tickled Lars's cheek. It was the color of overripe tomatoes, with a hint of golden sunshine within the strands. If her hair had a flavor, he decided it would be tangy cherry with a burst of lemon.

How had he gotten so lucky as to find a pretty girl who liked to spend time with him and his baby boy? While Dean Maverick had teasingly suggested that babies were chick bait, Lars had known that it wouldn't be so simple as strolling in to catch a woman's eye for more than a few oohs and aahs. But for some reason Mireio had stuck around after the initial reveal. So far.

He wouldn't count his blessings too soon. This thing they were doing was new and, as she'd pointed out, they were just having fun. So he had best stop worrying and get to the enjoying part.

"How about ice cream?" he suddenly said. "I don't think I've had any since I was a kid."

"Seriously?" Her blue eyes beamed above him. "There's

a shop not far from here. And I'm pretty sure a bookstore sits a couple stores down from that. What do you think, Peanut?" She stroked his fuzzy crop of dark hair. "Aw, he's sleeping. All tuckered out from the sunshine. We'd better get him inside so he doesn't overheat."

"Overheat? Do babies do that?"

"Well, he's not going to blow his top, but yes, his tender newborn skin will burn much easier than ours does."

"Darn it, and here I thought the sunshine was good for him." Lars sat up and tugged the blanket over Peanut's head.

"Don't worry about it. He's not going to fry. Lars, you're a great dad. You've some amazing instincts about taking care of a baby. Don't question yourself so much."

"It's hard not to do so. I've never done this before. Sometimes I feel like I'm a little bug standing in the middle of this big field, trying to keep my baby bug alive."

"You're doing great." She kissed him then. A soft, slow kiss that tasted his mouth and dipped her tongue across his bottom lip. It was a sweet connection that promised more. When she pulled away, she plucked the flowers from his beard and tucked them into her hair over one ear. "Let's get ice cream."

When they stopped by the bookstore, Peanut was fussing, so Lars stayed in the truck to change him while Mireio dashed in for the baby book and then skipped a few stores down to grab ice cream to go. They headed to her house, and by the time they arrived, Peanut was giggling and blowing bubbles every time she shook her bright hair before him.

"You must have grown up with brothers and sisters," Lars commented as they strolled into her house.

"Nope. I was an only child. I started babysitting when

I was ten. Every penny I made went toward spell stuff and crystals. And a really cool mermaid tail that I still have tucked away somewhere."

"A mermaid tail?" He dropped Peanut's bag of accoutrements on the floor near the sofa.

"Yes, it was rubber or something. I could pull it up like pants and there was room in the fin for my feet. It sparkled," she said, adding jazz hands because that was what one did when one talked about all things glittery. "I'd swim out in the backyard pool for hours wearing it. But it only fit me for about a year. I was so bummed. I think I expected it to grow with me. So you are going to stay for supper, yes? I make a mean zucchini parmesan."

"I'm not even sure what that is, but I'm in."

"Great! Let me get it put together. It'll take about twenty minutes, and then I'll pop it in the oven."

"Me and Peanut will take a look through the book you got for us."

He headed into the living room. Mireio called out that he could take the yarn afghan off the back of the couch and lay it on the floor for Peanut to crawl around on. "Will do!"

Utterly pleased after an afternoon well spent, she floated about the kitchen, gathering and slicing zucchini and onions, grating parmesan, while on the stove top she stirred a tomato sauce with basil and shallots.

Around the corner in the living room she heard Lars reading the *What to Expect the First Year* book out loud. In a very dramatic tone. She peeked around the corner and spied the big werewolf lying on the violet-and-blue afghan on his back—he held the book overhead while he pointed out the pictures to Peanut. The baby, lying on his back beside his daddy, followed his gestures with burbling fascination.

"Did you know a four-month-old is supposed to get his first tooth?" Lars called as she slipped back into the kitchen. "Peanut has had a tooth for two months. Heh. You're ahead of your time, my boy. Also, he might start to roll over. Is that so? You want to give it a go, Peanut?"

Whispering thanks to Demeter, the goddess of harvest, and snapping her fingers over the sauce, Mireio imbued it with a touch of love and confidence. It was difficult not to create something to eat without adding a spell. She'd been doing it forever. Nothing intrusive. But Lars could probably use the boost to his confidence. Goddess knows he must have been going through heck these past few months. But to judge from the infant giggles in the next room he was managing remarkably well.

Peanut, eh? That was a horrible name for a child to grow up with. She'd have to work on Lars, help him come up with something before the kid got too attached to the name.

Assembling the dish with layers of zucchini, cheese and sauce, she then put the glass baking dish in the stove and set the timer. Pouring two goblets of honey IPA from the growler she always kept stocked in the fridge, she then strolled into the living room.

Lars lay on his side facing Peanut; the baby was sleeping. "Sometimes I can't get over how much I like staring at him." Wonder touched his tone as Lars said, "I made this little guy."

"That you did. Or at least, you helped. I'm pretty sure the woman had a lot to do with it too. Brewing the little tyke for nine months and all." She handed him a beer as he sat up and leaned against the couch. The open book lay near his leg. "Do you mind if I ask you a personal question?"

"I already told you how me and Peanut's mom got together."

"Right, but do you think she might come back for her boy? I mean, after a few years? What if she has a change of heart? Or if her biological clock starts ticking? Wouldn't that crush you?"

Lars ran his fingers back through his hair, pulling it into a ponytail behind him, then releasing it with a growl. "It would annihilate me."

The alpha wolf lived inside him. And she had felt his protective instincts in that growl.

"I'm already so attached to him I couldn't imagine not having him around," he said. "But Peanut's mom won't come back. She had stars in her eyes. No desire to spend her days in a tiny cabin in the woods. She was pretty adamant about starting a new life in Africa."

"Did you offer to marry her?"

"Didn't have a chance. To be honest? I'm not sure I would have. We only knew each other two days. And we didn't share a lot of conversation in that time, if you know what I mean. But had she decided to give motherhood a go, I would have never backed down on my obligation to raise my son. I'm relieved, actually, that she thought to give me a chance to raise him instead of going the adoption route."

Mireio stroked the hair that spilled down his shoulders, then realized what she was doing and tugged her hand to her lap. He turned to look over his shoulder at her. "Whatever you're making, it smells great."

"Half an hour and you can test it. I hope you like oregano and garlic. How's the IPA?"

"Awesome. I can taste the honey."

"Got it from Valor's hives. So you've worked with her and her bees?"

He waggled his hand before him in an indecisive gesture. "I sold her some queens and suggested some good places to order equipment. Her honey is distinctively different from field honey. She lives in a city and has hives on the top of her building. That forces the bees to forage for flowers far and wide and they visit a greater variety of flowers, which makes for a robust honey."

"Do your bees produce a lot of honey?"

"Oh, yeah. I have to give most of it away because I'd never be able to go through it all. You want some?"

"I can always use honey, especially for baking. How do you do all that processing of honey in your little place? I didn't see any equipment."

"I keep it in storage at the pack compound over the winter. I'm hoping to build a room for storing my apiary and honey equipment with the addition. And an extra room for Peanut's bedroom."

"Do you know how lucky Peanut is to have a dad like you?"

He toggled the toe end of Peanut's sleeper. "You didn't see me that first month I had him. I was pretty crazed. And a walking zombie from lack of sleep. Wasn't sure which end was up on the poor kid and was pretty damn surprised how much stuff tends to come out of both ends. For the first time I truly believed a dirty diaper could kill a man."

She laughed and tucked her legs up onto the couch. Lars turned and she patted the cushion beside her so he moved up to sit beside her, making sure not to step on the sleeping baby.

"But by the end of the second month I'd gotten into a routine. I actually have one of those planner apps on my phone. I don't know how all the moms do it without a calendar and a personal secretary. Just call me Mr. Mom now."

"Mr. Dad more like it. You rock the single dad role. It's good for a kid to have a dad or mom."

"Or? You don't believe they need both?"

Mireio shrugged. "Not necessarily. I never knew my dad. And my mom…" She sighed, memories unexpectedly rushing to the fore. Though she'd long ago shed all the tears. A glance to the mantel over the hearth landed on the photo of her and her mom. Jessica Malory had auburn hair that hung to her waist and a smile that could have stopped wars. "She died when I was eight. I was raised by my grandma."

"Really? That's tough. Or was it?"

"Sometimes. I mean, it's been twenty years. But at the time, I was old enough to miss my mom, and her death was very traumatic." And she'd avoid telling him about that for fear of being reduced to blubbering tears. "But grandma was awesome. And you know with witches, if we've performed an immortality spell, we can look young for a very long time. Grandma looks like a fashion model from the sixties with her long brown hair and she seriously still wears bell-bottoms."

"You mentioned something about focusing on a spell. Does that mean you've performed the immortality spell I've heard about? Or are planning to?"

"That means I'm at this very moment prepared to do it. I've been thinking about it a lot over the past few years, and I'm ready."

"I think I know that spell requires a vampire, right?"

"You got it. It's never pretty for the vampire. We witches call them a source."

Lars lifted a brow. "Yes, but the vamps call those vampires ash."

"There is that result. And before you think I intend to destroy another soul to extend my own life, I'll have you know that I've hired a witch to track down one of the meanest and vilest vampires. One who has killed and is a danger to society."

He shrugged. "Doesn't bother me. I mean, if you take out a bad one. Vamps who kill to get blood when they only need a little to survive? That's unconscionable. I had no idea there was an actual person, though, that tracks down vamps specifically for you witches and your spells."

"It's Raven Crosse. She used to be a vampire hunter until she married a vampire. Now she does the search on the side for a very select clientele. And she costs a fortune."

"How much?"

Mireio pressed the glass rim to her lips, then shook her head. "I'd rather not say. Suffice it to say, it's something I want. Desperately. So it was worth the price."

"The idea of one lifetime doesn't sit well with you?"

"Nope." And could they change the subject please? If she had to tell him how traumatized she'd actually been by her mother's death she'd burst out in tears, and that was so not sexy or romantic. "I should check on supper. Be right back."

Lars followed Mireio into the kitchen, where the scents of oregano and roasted tomatoes made him hunger for a home-cooked meal. She'd sprung up from the couch to retreat so abruptly, he suspected he'd said something wrong.

"I'm sorry," he said to her as she bent before the open oven and tested the dish with a fork. "I think I went too far in there."

"No, you didn't." She popped up and set the fork aside. "I don't want to get into all the details about my mom. It'll make me cry. Okay?"

"Deal." At least she was honest. He could respect that. "How much longer? I could eat that whole pan if you let me."

"Let me have a little corner and you can go right ahead and attack the rest. Ten minutes. You want more beer?"

"No, I'm good. Gotta drive Peanut home later."

"Don't tell me you're a lightweight?"

"With beer? No. Takes a lot to get us wolves drunk. But I'm trying to do the responsible thing now. You know?"

"I get that. But if you ever want to not be responsible for a little while?" She pointed at her chest where her low-cut blousy shirt revealed ample cleavage. "You know where to find me."

"We do have a few minutes. Why don't you come on over and show me a little irresponsibility?"

She spun around the end of the kitchen counter and leaned toward him where he sat on a barstool. With him sitting, they came face-to-face, and he was thankful for that when he saw the kiss coming. Pushing his fingers up through her soft, bright hair, Lars accepted her sweet offering and smiled against her mouth. "You taste like tomato sauce."

"That's a preview for supper. You like?"

"I do." He kissed her again and this time delved in deeper with his tongue, tasting her tomato sweetness and dashing the tip of his tongue along her teeth.

Mmm, she was hot and soft and when she put her hands on his knees to balance, he wished she'd landed that touch a little higher up. There, where his erection was teasing rigidity. It had been a while since he'd been with a woman. And truly, after the past few months of endless diapers and spit-up, he had forgotten how good it could be to kiss one. And touch her. And mmm, just to inhale her.

He coaxed her forward by sliding his hand over her hip, and she followed directions and leaned into him without breaking their connection. Yep, everything was hard now. Not going to be easy getting through this night.

Her fingers clutched his shirt and the connection zinged his every nerve ending, sending scintillating tingles all over his skin. It was as if together they created a sort of sensual electricity. And he couldn't get enough of her mouth, her tongue, her sighs.

Pressing a hand against her back, he coaxed her forward again and bowed to keep the kiss. Her moan said everything he was feeling: yes, yes and all the yeses in the world. This tiny witch felt so right in his arms; he had to thank the gods for putting him in her backyard even if it had been a strange night that had scared the hell out of him.

A buzzer dinged, startling them to part their lips, and Mireio laughed. "Supper's done!" She kissed him quick, then wiped her finger alongside his mouth. "Got a little lipstick on you there." She tilted her head at him. "Can I have a few more of those awesome kisses for dessert?"

"You can have as many as you like."

Another *ding* drew her away from him, and Lars adjusted his position and winced as he tried to adjust his hard-on in his tightened jeans.

"A water witch, eh?"

Mireio dished up another square of zucchini parmesan onto Lars's plate and then refilled his water goblet.

She'd been telling him how she hadn't chosen the art of water magic but that it had chosen her.

"My grandmother could never get me out of the tub or the swimming pool. I used to tease her that I could make the water do things, so when she challenged me, I gave it a try. I cast my first water globe when I was ten." She held her hands apart but curved toward one another as if to hold a ball. "Then I threw it at my granny, soaking her. I had to clean the bathroom for a month after that."

Lars's laughter filled the quiet kitchen. Beside him on the counter, Peanut, asleep in his baby carrier, stirred but didn't wake.

She put a finger to her lips to shush them both. "So anyway, I mastered water magic by the time I was twenty. And that led to brewing beer. I like to change and control water. Add a few grains and some hops? Voilà!"

"So it's an innate thing with you witches? You're born able to do magic?"

"Some of it. As a baby I could swim underwater just like a seal. And I had a habit of curdling the milk before my mother could get it in the bottle. Or so I was told. But some magics we have to study and learn, and maybe never master. I'm trying to learn the healing arts. It should be easy for me. The body is made up of so much water, but I have real trouble invoking a healing spell."

"You'll master it. I know you will. You're so talented. And beautiful."

"You compliment me too much."

"What's wrong with that?"

"Nothing. I've got the Scandinavian gene, you see. We don't know how to take compliments."

"Uff da, you don't say?" he said with his best Minnesotan accent.

Mireio laughed. "Ya sure, you betcha. You've got the accent too!"

"Born and raised in Minnesota and damn proud to eat the lutefisk and lefse." He finished the food and pushed his plate forward. "I am stuffed. And relaxed."

She nodded toward his crotch. "I noticed earlier when we were kissing you were anything but relaxed."

He blushed.

"Oh, you're too cute. I'm going to keep you for a while. The baby too."

"Thanks?"

She stood up on the stool's bars and leaned over to kiss him quickly.

Peanut stirred in his carrier. "I should probably head out," Lars said. "I don't have any milk with me. Unless you can use your magic to turn water into milk?"

"Not quite that talented. And I'd hate to give the baby a tummy ache if something went wrong."

Lars packed up the baby's things and retrieved the book from the living room. Mireio walked with the two of them out to the truck parked in her driveway. After Peanut was fastened in and secured, Lars jumped back out and stood before her.

She waved at the baby and blew him a kiss. "See you later, Charlie!"

"Charlie?" He leaned against the truck door and gave her the eye.

"Yeah, thought I'd try out the name on him. You don't like it?"

He shrugged. "It's fine. I'll have to give it some thought."

"I've got a few more ideas rolling around in my brain. But I'll save them for another time. Give you a little time to try that one on a bit. So do I get to see you tomorrow? Uh, I have an appointment in the evening, but then…"

"What kind of appointment?"

"The one with the witch who hunts up vampires."

"Ah. Do you want me to go along with you?"

"Would you? She lives in Minneapolis. I know her but not well. I feel sort of weird about the whole thing…"

"I'll go along. For uh…" His gaze wandered over her head and took in the front of her house. The pause grew beyond a few seconds.

Mireio blinked, waiting for him to finish his thought. Did he do that often? Forget what he was talking about? He'd done it once before when she'd first met him.

"Wait," he said, focusing back on her. "What were we talking about?"

Strange. But she didn't want to draw attention to it. "Tomorrow night. Raven Crosse's place?"

"Oh, right! I can get Sunday to babysit tomorrow night. We'll stop by the witch's place, then do something after?"

"There's a new action movie I'd really like to see."

"I haven't been inside a movie theater in years. And action? Sounds like a plan."

He bent to kiss her and she wrapped her arms about his neck and bounced as she tried to get closer to him. So Lars lifted her by the hips and she wrapped her legs around his waist. That fit them together perfectly and made for a nice hold.

After a couple kisses he said, "You're so tiny."

"And you're like a basketball player. But I like a big strong alpha man."

Inside the cab Peanut giggled. Both looked to the baby, then back to each other and laughed.

"I think that's a hint," he said. "Time to stop kissing the girl and get the tyke home for his bedtime bottle. What time do you want me to stop by tomorrow?"

"Six!"

He kissed her again, quickly, then set her down and climbed into the truck. With a wave and a wink, he backed out and drove away.

And Mireio sighed one of those satisfied sighs that a girl reserved only for those moments she wanted to cherish. If she wasn't careful, she could fall in love. And she'd never been the queen of careful. Spontaneous, wild and free were her best attributes.

But what was wrong with the guy forgetting things midsentence? Hmm… Probably she had better not worry about it. She had a tendency to worry beyond the problem. There was no problem. Nope, none at all.

She had found herself a handsome werewolf. And a baby. Who would have thought?

Chapter 7

Raven Crosse lived in a downtown Minneapolis loft along with her husband of many decades, Nikolaus Drake. As a phoenix vampire, Nikolaus had survived a witch's blood attack (when witch's blood was once poisonous to vampires; that had been decades ago) and lived to tell the tale. The fact that it had been Raven's blood that had nearly killed him? That was a long story.

The witch, who had formerly been a vampire hunter, invited Mireio across the threshold, and drew her gaze up the long tall drink of werewolf who walked in behind her.

Only a little taller than Mireio, Raven scratched the back of her neck below the tight black ponytail and then pointed to Lars. "Who's he? I thought it was just going to be you?"

"Lars Gunderson." He offered his hand to shake, but Raven sneered at it. "I'm here for moral support."

Raven glanced to Mireio. "You're kidding me. If you

need moral support, sweetheart, you're not ready for this."

"I'm ready. I would have come alone, but he offered, and…" Mireio shrugged. It was good to have him with her. She wasn't intimidated by a witch who drove a street chopper and could slay vampires with a single shot, but well, okay she was a little. "He's my partner. In this endeavor."

Again Raven drew a long discerning gaze down Lars. Not impressed at all. Then she shoved her hands in her front jeans pockets and nodded. "Fine. But this is between me and Malory, you got that, wolf? No talking."

Lars zipped his fingers across his lips and closed the door behind him. Raven led them to the long stretch of kitchen counter and gestured they sit on the stools.

"Nikolaus is out of town. I don't do this when he's around," she said as she pulled a black file folder out from a drawer and slapped it on the counter before Mireio. She placed her palm over the folder and leaned in. "You got the cash?"

"Oh, yes." Mireio opened her fish purse and pulled out the envelope that was an inch thick and filled with twenty-dollar bills. "All there. You can count it if you want."

Raven shoved the envelope in the drawer and closed it. She pushed the file toward Mireio, then stepped back with arms crossed over her chest, eyeing Lars cautiously.

Inside the file was a single sheet of paper with two color photos printed alongside the details. Neither photo showed a clear face shot of the man. "There's no name?" Mireio asked.

"Names are not important, and intrusively personal. You get a name and you'll never be able to go through with it. The pictures and the details of that vamp's MO should be more than enough to ensure you get the right guy. He's a monster. Feeds in a very contained area in north Minneapolis, so finding him shouldn't be a problem. There have been unexplained deaths in that neighborhood over the last two months. It's his doing, I know it."

"How can you know that?" Lars asked.

Raven tilted a sneer at the wolf, and both Lars and Mireio heard the unspoken, *I told you not to speak, wolf.*

Lars cleared his throat. "I'm sure you know, being a vampire hunter and all."

"Former," Raven corrected. "You ever play blood games with vamps, wolf?"

"No. That's barbaric."

Raven lifted her chin, still assessing Lars. "You're from the Northern Pack. Amandus Masterson used to lead the pack."

"He's long dead."

The witch sniffed. Masterson had engaged his pack in blood games that had tortured vampires mercilessly. It was likely a sticking point for a witch married to a vampire.

Trying to cut the tension, Mireio tapped the information sheet. "He's mostly out after midnight?"

"Yes, all the information you need is right there. Now, did you need anything else? You got the immortality spell?"

"Yes. My friend is still working on getting the dragon's exudation. Few sell it nowadays."

"Very necessary to make the blood go down smoothly," Raven said. "Trust me. I've done this six times. Did it one time without the exudation. Nearly fucking gagged myself to death."

Mireio swallowed. Drinking the blood from a vampire's heart was not tops on her list of things to do. But if those few moments of suffering would give her another century of life, then she could rally. As well, if it would give her the revenge she sought against her mother's murderer, then she was all in. But that detail was not something she intended to tell Lars.

"You going to be her wingman?" Raven asked Lars.

They hadn't discussed him helping her, but when Mireio started to answer, Lars draped an arm across her shoulders. "Yep."

"Good. Tiny witch like you will need someone strong to crack open the vampire's chest and pull out the heart."

Mireio gulped down a gag, but kept a stoic expression as she nodded in agreement.

"So we're good," Raven said. "Business is complete. You two will be on your merry way. I'd love to say it's been peachy, wolf, but I'm still not sure I like you. You trust him?" she asked Mireio as she collected the file folder and walked to the door.

"I do." But she was still thinking about watching a werewolf crack open a vampire's chest and then handing her a bloody heart. That was the stuff of nightmares. And man, did she have nightmares. "I think we should be going, then. Thanks!" And she shot out the door, not caring whether Lars followed.

Scrambling down two flights and out to the street, Mireio rushed along the side of the building and turned the corner. Catching a palm on the rough brick wall she bent forward and exhaled forcefully.

A gentle hand pulled away the hair from the side of her face. "You okay?"

She nodded. "It was really stuffy in there, don't you think?"

"Uh…yes, I think it was. Everything is going to be okay, Mireio. I'll be there to help you with this. I promise."

"I didn't even ask you. I'm sorry—she just assumed…"

"No need to ask. I'm volunteering. There's no way a tiny witch like you can accomplish…well, you know. Will you let me help you?"

Righting, she dropped her shoulders against the wall and looked up at him briefly, then away. She was still shaken from having reality so blatantly laid out for her like that. No wonder her mother had died. She must have faltered in that moment when she'd needed to be strong. She hadn't taken anyone along with her. Mireio knew because she had followed her and had witnessed the whole terrible thing.

"Do you think I can do this if I can't even listen to the details?" she asked. "I mean, what will I do when faced with having to consume the blood from a vampire's heart? I am so not that chick from *Game of Thrones*."

"Yeah? You don't have a hoard of dragons to protect either. But you do seem to have a fear that can only be abated by meeting this challenge. And while I'm still getting to know you, I feel confident that when the challenge presents itself, you'll do fine."

He held out his hand and she clasped it as if it were a life preserver tossed into the wild and wicked waves. "Thank you for having faith in me. I need that boost of confidence. And, obviously, a big strong wolf to do the dirty work. Oh." She bent again, clutching her palms on her knees.

"I was thinking we could drive through north Minneapolis, take a look around," Lars said. "But maybe we should call it a night?"

She shook her head. The last thing she wanted to do was go vampire hunting. But she didn't want this night to end so quickly either. Especially not when Lars had hired a babysitter. "No, I'm good. Just needed to breathe in the air."

"We passed a movie theater on the way here." He clasped her hand and bent to speak softly. "What say you and I go sit in the dark, drink lots of sugary pop and then make out during the boring parts."

She squeezed his hand. "Here's wishing for a lot of boring parts."

Mireio couldn't recall a time when she'd made out in a movie theater. They were the only two in the small theater. The red velvet seats creaked and smelled stale. The screen had a tear on the right side that tended to give actors scars in inappropriate places. And the action they'd come for had lasted all of thirty-seven seconds. Now the characters were trying to find themselves emotionally and heal past wounds through therapy. Ugh.

So the key to intense action in a movie theater was to create your own. She currently knelt on Lars's lap, kissing him. The man was always a little slow to warm to her, but now he let his hands roam over her hips and ass. His wide strong fingers curled, giving her a squeeze. And she let her hands roam up under his loose gray T-shirt to the hard landscape of muscle and hot skin and some surprisingly soft chest hair.

"Never done this before," he muttered between breaths as they tilted their heads to change up the kiss. "Like it." Her fingernail glanced across his nipple and the man hissed into their kiss. "Like that too."

"If I were more daring," she said, "I'd shove you down across the seats. But the arms don't move, and I'm not quite that adventurous."

"This works." He pulled her in closer so her knees

hit the back of the seat to either side of him. "A little tight, but—"

"It's awkward." She flipped her hair over a shoulder and tugged at his shirt in frustration. "Let's ditch this place, yes? What time do you have to pick up Peanut?"

His slow smile beamed even in the darkness. "Not till morning."

"Nice. Let's go to my place and make out on the couch."

Lars felt like a randy teenager driving fast to get to the secret hideout so he could pull over, drag the clothes off his girlfriend and make out with her. Except, he wasn't sure if Mireio considered herself his girlfriend. Not that it mattered. They were adults. If they wanted to get their horny on, nothing would stop them.

And he didn't want to consider how hooking up could complicate things. What if they had sex and that was it? She didn't want to see him anymore? Could he handle that? He liked the witch. A lot. He didn't want to spoil the slow, sure connection they'd developed.

And yet, with Mireio snuggled up against his side, dragging her fingers along his thigh, he could not stop thinking about how quickly he could get her clothes off once the door to her house closed behind them.

He was a virile man. It had been months since he'd had sex because Peanut had occupied all his free time. He needed this. And he'd take the frenzied connection and worry about where the chips fell afterward.

Parking before the house, he shoved open the door, jumped out and offered a hand to help her out. Before she could step down, he took her in his arms and elbowed the door shut. He carried her up the walk and she punched in the digital code for the front door lock even as he held her in his arms.

"Set me down before we go in!" she said before he could step any farther. "No carrying over the threshold this night."

Uh. Okay. If she was implying some weird correlation to the whole carrying a wife over the threshold then, yes, he'd go with it. He set her down and followed her inside. After pulling the door closed, she turned and pushed her hands up under his shirt. He groaned at the sweet yet demanding touch against his tight muscles.

She shoved him none too gently and his shoulders landed against the foyer wall behind him. In the darkness, Lars raised a brow in question.

"Are we going to do this?" she asked, hugging her breasts against him, which landed them about gut level because of her shortness. "I want to do this."

"We're doing this."

"Good."

"Couch?"

"No. The bedroom is up the stairs."

She jumped then and he caught her as she wrapped her legs about his waist. Bypassing the couch and going straight for the bed? Oh, yeah, this was happening.

Bowing to kiss her, he then turned to navigate the stairs, which were beyond the kitchen. She kissed his jaw and stroked his beard as he took the tight square turns upward. At the top, only two doors were open and when he spied the bed and the big picture of the yellow daisy on the wall behind it, he knew it was her bedroom.

Carrying her in, Lars set her on the edge of the high bed, but she didn't unwrap her legs from him. Seeking fingers pushed through his hair and tugged the wood stick out from the leather hair wrap he used to curtail his long hair. She pulled his hair forward, drawing it over her lips and cheeks. Then she nuzzled her nose and mouth into his beard. With a giggle, she fell backward and stretched out her arms across the frilly bed.

"Goddess, you're a sexy man. All dimples and beard. I have to admit, I'm a little nervous."

Crawling over her, but not resting his weight on her, he propped himself up on his elbows, meeting her eye to eye in the hazy light. "Why? Is something wrong? Shoot. This is too fast. I knew it."

"No, Lars. This is happening exactly as it should. That's how the universe works. Things happen when they are supposed to happen. I'm nervous because, like I said, you're sexy. You're handsome and kind. And you're so big and I feel like a little bird beside you. But that's a good thing. It's like you protect me. And—oh, my goddess, I'm chattering!"

He kissed her quickly, then nuzzled his nose against her cheek and sought the thick curly shelter of her bright hair. "You're the opposite of me. You like to talk. I'm a doer. A man of few words."

"You can do me, Lars. I want you to take off my clothes and kiss me everywhere."

Directions? The woman just made his life a whole lot easier.

Lars pushed up her shirt and she pulled it off and leaned back onto her elbows to reveal a lacy red bra that barely contained her lush, full breasts. He laid a hand over one and kissed the other through the sheer fabric, teasing at her hard nipple until her moans rose and her hips rocked against his torso.

Her fingers danced down his chest and abs and she couldn't quite reach his jeans. His erection pulsed within his jeans, which were normally comfy and loose. But not now.

Nuzzling his face between her breasts, he decided this

pillow could hold his attention for a long sweet time. He glided his fingers over the red fabric, feeling as her nipple tightened even more. The red lace tickled his palm. He tugged down the bra and kissed her above the nipple.

"Do you have a condom?" she asked as he lashed teasingly at her nipple.

Lars looked up at her. Red hair splayed like goddess tresses across the bed. Lashes dusted over her blue eyes. Her mouth was plump and parted. A condom? Shit. Of all things he should be most vigilant about that was the one.

"No. I, uh…" Hadn't done this for a while, and—hell, he'd not planned this night very well. He'd never expected to bypass the couch and go straight to the bed. "Do you?" he asked hopefully, assuming since she'd asked, she must not be on birth control.

"Shoot. No. And there's a spell I can do for birth control but I've been waiting for the right moon phase. It's required for efficacy. Oh, Lars, I'm sorry."

Like that, his heart dropped an inch and he rolled to his back to lie beside her, blowing out a frustrated breath. But when her hand glided over his erection he popped up his head to meet her winking gaze.

"There are other things we can do. Yes?"

All the side stuff but not the big event? He'd never done anything like that before. He was a man who always got to the point. And he never left a woman high and dry. Nor did he often walk away without the big bang.

Now she squeezed over his jeans, which made his cock grow harder, if that were possible. "Lars?"

Everything but actually putting himself inside her? That would prove a challenge, but he was always up for a test. And no way in hell did he want to walk away from lush red hair, plump lips and lickable nipples now.

She tugged at his zipper and he winced, anticipating some pain should she make a wrong move.

"Mmm, commando. I'll be careful," she said. And she was, sliding her hand inside his jeans and over his cock and curlies as she pulled down the zipper. "You got a name for this big guy?" she asked. "Or should I assume you've named it after a legume?" Her eyes twinkled from her position hovering over his newly sprung erection.

A legume? Oh, right. Peanut.

"Mireio," he chided and tangled his fingers in her hair. "You can call it anything you like. It'll come when you call."

She giggled at that. "All I have to do is call, eh?"

"Oh, yeah…"

Her fingers slipped around his hard length, squeezing and setting off erotic shock waves that jolted through his system and made him hiss. A wanting utterance. Small as she was, the woman did possess a good firm grip. And she glided up and down his erection slow and easy, which he appreciated, because he hadn't any lube and wasn't all juiced up yet.

And thinking about that must have given her the idea to dash her tongue down the length of him. Lars gripped his fingers, then realized he still had them in her hair and didn't want to pull too roughly, so he swept them down her skin and dropped his hand to the bed, where he grabbed the coverlet as her lips closed over his swollen head.

"Oh, witch…"

Her mouth was a nice replacement for what he'd thought the lacking condoms had denied him. So hot, wet and… squeezing. She licked and stroked her tongue up and down the length of him. His entire body tingled and he felt a mad soaring sensation. And when she gently cupped his balls the darkness behind his closed eyelids took on color.

An animal growl came out, which stirred her head up.

"Mmm, my wolf. You like this."

"Oh, Mireio."

"You want to feel how wet I am?" He watched her slip her hand beneath her skirt, then she drew out her fingers and touched them to his cock. Sticky and hot with her wet dew.

Lars bit his lip and growled again. His body tremored and with a few more lashes from her tongue, he gave up the gold and came powerfully, hips bucking and breaths hissing.

Mireio's cell phone rang. She didn't stop stroking him. But he'd already come. He needed a few minutes.

"Get it," he said on a relaxing exhale.

"No, it's probably…" It continued to ring. With a heavy sigh, she said, "Sorry. Right, you need a little rest time, eh?" With a wink, she pushed aside her hair and retrieved the phone. "Hey, Valor… What? Seriously? That's the second time a keg has exploded this month… No, I can come in and help. I'll have it cleaned up with my water magic in two snaps. See you in a bit."

"You can't leave now." He sat up on the bed and pushed the hair from his face. Perspiration around his hairline made him swipe a hand across his brow. "It's my turn to make you come."

She sat on his lap, grinding her mons against his cock and moving up higher. "You can't imagine how powerful a girl feels when she brings a man to the edge like that."

"I might have some idea. I've done it a time or two to women."

"Only a time or two?"

"Aw, you know. I'm not going to detail my past conquests." He kissed her breast and suckled the nipple. His entire body was lax, yet humming with energy. "Five more minutes?"

"Lars, I know this is mean but the brewery basement is flooded. We've an old plastic fermenter that finally cracked open and gushed out eighty gallons of beer. Valor can clean it up with a mop and bucket, but I'm the one with water magic who can reduce cleanup time by hours." She kissed him as she pulled her bra back up. "Next time we'll both be prepared. Deal?"

"I'll add *condoms* to the list right above *diapers*."

She fist-bumped him then and slid off the bed, tugging her hair up and grabbing something off the vanity to pin it up as she sailed out of the bedroom. "I'm making a quick escape, because if I don't, I'll never be able to leave you. Don't be mad!"

Sitting up on the bed, feeling disoriented, satisfied, but also completely devastated that he'd not been able to do for her what she had done for him, Lars exhaled through his nose. What had become of his life of late? He couldn't please a woman. He had to be home by a curfew to feed his baby. He was waking up in the field naked, shifted out of werewolf shape, with no understanding of how he'd gotten there.

And…he pressed his fingertips together, wincing at the tingly pain that had begun a few minutes ago. It wasn't aftereffects from the orgasm. Soon the tingling would spread up to his elbow and he wouldn't be able to feel anything. He'd better get home quick before he wasn't able to drive. Wiping his T-shirt across his stomach to clean off the cum, he then headed downstairs.

They both rushed toward the front door, Mireio's fish purse bonking Lars on the knee as she made the dash.

"I'm so sorry the night ended this way," she said as

they sailed down the front step and she angled toward the garage. "You must think me terribly insensitive to one minute have my hand on your cock and the next be thinking about work."

"No." Maybe a little. "I understand." If it had been a call about Peanut, he would have done the same thing and rushed off. "It sounds like an emergency. And you're right, we weren't prepared."

She spun and pulled him down for a quick kiss. "Call me tomorrow! And don't forget about your shopping list!"

The garage door opened and she disappeared into the dark garage. Lars waved and watched as the little red Volkswagen backed out and she cruised away. Off to help her sister witch clean up the disaster at the brewery.

He fired up the truck. They'd started the evening by securing information on a violent vampire that Mireio would ultimately destroy to gain immortality. Then the movie theater, which led to an awkward, but strangely satisfying roll on her bed. What a weird night.

He shook his hand, fighting the tingling that would not relent. His whole life felt unbalanced and not quite right. And it only promised to get weirder.

Chapter 8

The next day, Lars stopped into the brewery with Peanut in the baby carrier. Mireio stood over by the brew tanks. And when he noticed she wasn't stirring the contents of the first tank, but the big wooden stir paddle was moving around and around, he set the sleeping baby on the floor and approached cautiously.

"Hey!" She winked at him and then stepped down from the short step stool she'd been standing on. "I'm in the wort production part of the brewing process right now. Come over. Take a look."

Lars peered into the open stainless-steel tank. A big wood paddle stirred the grains in the water—on its own. A little magic? Cool. He inhaled the rich oat smell. "You really do make magic."

"Just call me the resident hopcromancer. I can do magical things with water and hops." She noticed his hand shaking at his side. "What's up?"

"Huh? Oh." He smoothed his fingers down a thigh;

unaware he'd been moving his hand. "Nothing. Just some tingling I get every so often. Probably nerve damage from all the wood chopping I've been doing lately."

To distract her, he gave her a kiss, which she extended by pulling him down and wrapping her arms about his shoulders.

"Everything go okay last night?" he asked.

"It took less than twenty minutes to rally the spilled beer back into some kegs, with magic, of course. Then we were able to dump it down the sink."

"Bummer."

"Yes, but beer from the floor would not have been a big seller. Losses are to be expected." She hugged up against him, pressing her stomach to his hips. "How are you today, big boy?"

If she pressed a little closer and longer, she'd know exactly how he was feeling. Hard and happy.

"Still riding the high of you," he said. "It smells great in here. And it's not just you and your lilacs." He peeked again into the stainless-steel brew tank and saw the grains spinning round as they were magically stirred. "You always do that?"

"Oh, yeah. Stirring grains takes a lot of muscle. Some days I like to take it easy. And it frees me up to watch the controls." She pointed to the control panel on the wall. "Lots involved in the brew process. The boil comes next." She tapped the second tank. "All that sugar from the grains is sluicing into this tank. Then I'll boil it and add the hops and the secret ingredients."

"And by secret does that mean magic?"

She crooked a sly smile at him. "You bet. So what are you two up to today?" She skirted around the end of the bar to check on Peanut. "Hey, Oliver, how are you? Sleeping like a baby, I see."

"Oliver?" Lars scratched his bearded jaw. "I don't know about that one."

"Too Dickensian?" She shrugged. "Had to give it a try. So what's up?"

"We're headed out to do some grocery shopping. I always drive up to the market in Maple Grove. And since that takes me right by The Decadent Dames…"

"And you'll have to return this way too. Hey, why don't you leave Peanut here with me? The boil is my time to generally futz around and do nothing. I'd love to do nothing with this little cutie-pie."

"He does need a bottle soon. Are you sure?"

"Sure? Are you kidding me? Some free time to hug and kiss and cuddle all this awesome baby?" She fluttered her lashes at him and her smile slipped into a seductive curl. "Don't you trust me yet, Lars?"

"I do. And if you keep looking at me like that I'll have to put you up on the bar and spread your legs."

"I'm game."

He glanced to the baby. "Not in front of the kid. Or…" He gestured toward the front windows of the brewery, not thirty feet away, where people walked by and peered in constantly.

"Sure, but can I take a rain check on that offer? Later? When you get back from shopping?"

"Hell yes. But as for leaving Peanut here, I don't want to impose. You are working."

"I'd never offer if I didn't want to and if I couldn't manage it. The boil begins soon. That'll give me some time to blow raspberries on Peanut's toes."

"I could make the grocery shopping quick."

"No. Take your time. I'll be here for hours yet. Go on."

"I might take a few minutes to run by the Jiffy Lube and have them top off the fluids in the truck."

"Yes, do that. Run all the errands you need to get done. We'll be good." She squatted near Peanut's carrier and ruffled the sleeping babe's hair.

Lars's cell phone buzzed. He tugged it out of his front pocket and checked the text. He frowned.

"Hot date cancel out on you?" she asked.

"What?" His face felt hot and his heart beat fast.

Mireio pointed to his phone.

"Oh, this? Uh, a text from my doctor."

"Really?"

He shrugged and shoved the phone back into his pocket.

"Is that normal? I mean, I've never heard of a doctor texting a patient."

"Oh, uh, I don't know. He's like a small-town doc. Not a lot of patients, and all of us are werewolves. He, uh… wants me to meet with him this afternoon for the test results. It's all good."

"How do you know? You could be dying."

Lars chuckled. "I'm going to live forever. And I don't have to eat a vampire heart to do so. We wolves tend to live three or four centuries."

"I know. Hardy genes." She bent and kissed Peanut's forehead. "So you go, and fit in your doc appointment while you're at it. We're good for an afternoon. And I promise I won't let the little guy drink too much beer."

"He's a teetotaler, that one. Thanks, Mireio."

As Lars started toward the door she called, "Don't forget the condoms!"

"Tops on my list!" With a wink and a wave, he wandered off.

Geneva Curtis, one of the four witches who owned the brewery, clicked over to the far end of the bar in the highest of red crocodile leather heels. Likely bought for her by a billionaire. In Dubai or some other fabulous vacation getaway that Mireio could only dream about. Geneva swept off her Chanel sunglasses, then startled at the sight of what sat on the floor near the bags of rye grains.

"What the hell is that?"

Mireio laughed and took her friend by the arm, hugging up alongside her. "Oh, Geneva. This. Is a baby."

"I know that, joker. I mean, what are you doing with one of those? Did you have a baby and not tell me about it?"

"Dear, sweet Geneva. You would know if I had a baby. Though you have been pretty scarce around here lately."

"Our shifts never overlap. You're the morning bird. I'm a midnight raven. So what? Did you think a baby would draw in customers during happy hour?"

"I'm watching him for Lars."

"The man you're dating?"

"Yep."

"Ugh. How can you? I mean, it's a baby. They're just so…"

"Adorable?"

"Sticky." Geneva cringed and took a step back from Peanut's setup on the blanket below the plastic play gym. Lars packed the baby bag like a pro. "What's its name?"

"It is a boy. And his name is Peanut."

The witch flashed Mireio a disdainful pout of her deep red vamp lips. "Seriously?"

"He doesn't have a name yet. Lars has been calling him Peanut. So what are you here for? You're not scheduled until tomorrow night. And I'm almost finished. Was waiting around for Lars to pick us up."

"Where is the guy? You just start dating and already he's using you as a babysitting service? Sounds sketchy."

"He's gone out for groceries and a doctor's appointment. And you know I'll babysit anytime, anywhere."

"What's wrong with him? I thought he was a were-wolf? Werewolves don't get sick."

True. Huh. Mireio should have asked him to explain.

"It's nothing. Lately he's been experiencing some weird tingling in his fingers and toes. He thinks it's from cutting wood."

"Sounds not at all sexy to me."

"The man has a beard and a baby, Geneva. My ovaries can't handle all that sexy."

"A beard?" Geneva mocked a shudder.

"Oh, sweetie, you've obviously never been on the receiving end of *the beard*. It has some amazing powers, let me tell you."

"Like catching food and being smelly?"

"Lars's beard smells like him. Sort of like a forest after the rain. Mmm…" Mireio wiggled her shoulders appreciatively.

"Ah-huh." Geneva slid onto a barstool and patted the stool next to her. "Well, leave Cashew to his baby stuff, and come sit with me. I need your advice about a man."

"Really? This is new. You know I can't begin to comprehend the level of financial status you require from all your men?"

"I'm not dating a rich guy at the moment. And it's driving me mad. Mad, I tell you. The man is positively…"

"Rustic?"

"Yes." Geneva followed with a drawn-out moan. "At least he doesn't have one of those." She thumbed a gesture toward Peanut, who giggled and kicked his feet as he eyed the spinning objects above him.

"As far as you know." Mireio climbed onto a barstool. "So what's up? Why did you even go after a man with no money?"

"I thought it would be a lark, you know? Sort of a

reassurance that I really do enjoy dating rich guys and being treated like a princess and getting jewels and cars and stuff all the time."

"If there's a *but* to follow that statement, I will stab you in the heart. Do you know how lucky you are, Geneva?"

"I thought I did. But." She caught her chin in hand and flashed her million-carat sapphire gaze at Mireio. "I think I like this man. But he's a grocer." She squeezed her eyelids shut and put up a palm before her. "I can't believe I told you that. Argh! He works at a grocery store putting food in bags, Mireio. That is so…"

"Beneath you?" Mireio tried, but hoped her friend wouldn't nod in agreement.

"No. It's…different. We don't do big fabulous things like yachting or shopping in Dubai or even renting the penthouse of a New York apartment for a week. We just… talk a lot. And last night was the first time in ages I actually sat in a dank old dark movie theater."

"Hey, me and Lars were in a theater last night too."

Geneva shuddered. "The horrid popcorn smell and those lumpy seats. But do you know I enjoyed myself?"

"Oh, sweetie, you're in love."

"I can't be." Geneva actually cast her arm across her forehead in the classic tortured-heroine move. "What am I going to do?"

"Just let it happen, I guess. Seems to be the thing lately with us Dames and our men. And with Scorpio rising…"

"Oh, goddess, that means our sexual energy is so high right now. And me and Mr. Rustic haven't slept together yet."

Mireio almost said, "I don't believe that," because she knew Geneva went at her men fast, furious and with a mission, but she stopped herself. It had to be tough dating a man so out of her planetary orbit.

Thinking of which, she'd taken a bold, brave step by dating a man with a baby. Wasn't so bold. Wasn't even brave. It actually felt right.

"It's a good thing," she said, about her and Lars, but then Geneva hugged her suddenly.

"Thanks for the chat, Mireio. It means a lot. I know I spend a lot of time away from The Decadent Dames because I travel so much. So I appreciate you dropping everything and giving me some time. I really like this man. He might be the one. Even if his checkbook is flatter than Valor's chest."

Valor was the resident tomboy who had a body like a boy, but she'd caught herself a sexy faery man—one of the Saint-Pierre brothers—who appreciated her exactly as she'd been designed.

Geneva pulled on her scarf and sunglasses. She stepped down from the stool and gave Mireio air kisses to both cheeks. "Thanks, sweetie. I'll be in tomorrow night," she called as she walked toward the door. "Bye, Hazelnut!"

Mireio sat on the blanket beside Peanut and tapped the mobile so it spun. "Don't listen to her, Peanut Butter. We'll get you a name soon. How about… Horatio?"

"Nope."

She hadn't heard Lars walk in. He must have entered as Geneva had walked out.

"Hey! Get all the necessaries?"

"You know it." He winked, indicating he knew exactly which necessity she was most concerned about.

"How did it go with the doctor?"

"Uh, fine. Just some routine stuff."

"Routine? Then why did he make you go in? I mean he sent you a text. That was so weirdly urgent."

"Huh? Oh. Uh…" He shrugged and shoved his hands in his front pockets. "He wanted to do one more test. I had to give some more blood. It's nothing. So I'm going to take Peanut home and try to get some work done this evening before the sun sets. And I need to check the hives. It's swarming season. I don't want to lose my queens."

"Okay." The man seemed...not right. Nervous? Definitely not telling her something. But he was also a shy guy so she'd give him that. For now. "I do have some inventory to do in the basement. I could continue to watch Peanut if you have things to do today?"

"No, we're good." He bent to disassemble the baby gym and shoved it in the diaper bag. Pulling out the soft flannel baby sling, he wrapped it around his neck, then picked up Peanut and tucked him against his chest. "He need to be changed?"

"Just did it. Are you sure, Lars? Because Horatio and I were starting to get into a groove."

"Not Horatio." He shoved the blanket into the bag and stood. "I'll talk to you later. Thanks!" And he strode out of the brewery.

And Mireio could but sit there on the floor, wondering what she'd said to make him act so curt and abrupt with her. He hadn't even kissed her before leaving.

No, it wasn't anything she'd said. Something had gone down between the time he'd left her with kisses and smiles earlier to visit the doctor and now.

"But werewolves don't get sick," she repeated Geneva's statement. "Do they? Hmm..."

Wood chips flew furiously about him as Lars slammed the ax down. Again, and again. He split the oak log, tossed the cut piece aside. Again. Split. Toss. Slam.

He'd been working for an hour and the sweat spilled down his face and bare chest. The overalls he'd shoved down to his hips were soaked about the waist with more sweat.

He glanced to the baby monitor but the red light that would indicate sound remained green. Peanut tended to nap in the early evening for almost two hours.

Swinging his arms up he brought down the ax with another forceful show of brute strength.

Yes, damn it, he was strong. He wasn't… Fuck!

He was not. He couldn't be.

He hadn't been able to get out of the damn doctor's office fast enough. What the doctor had told him had made no sense at all. And the man had been so sure, even though he'd suggested one more test. As a confirmation. But really? Werewolves didn't…

Lars let out a guttural shout as again he swung down the ax and the chips flew. At his feet a heavy pile of wood shavings had formed and he shook them off his work boots and grabbed another oak log. The air was thick with dry wood scent but he didn't enjoy that spring perfume this day.

He hadn't been able to walk away from Mireio fast enough when he'd picked up his boy. He hadn't wanted to stand in the brewery and try to act normal and happy to see her when…

"Fuck!"

The ax found its mark. He kicked the cut wood aside to the stack, which was turning into a haphazard pile. Picking up another piece, he slammed it on the wood stump before him.

The doctor was wrong. Had to be. Whatever the heck was going on with him right now? It would pass. Yet the doc had treated his dad in the months before he had passed so long ago. He'd kept those records and had nodded sadly as he told Lars he was confident he'd the same thing his dad had. But to alleviate any worries, he'd do one more test.

But seriously? Why take *more* blood from him after he'd announced such a dire diagnosis?

Swinging down the ax, he winced as his biceps stretched and a sudden piercing pain radiated from his left wrist toward his elbow. He flung the ax to the ground and gripped his wrist. To his side, the monitor flashed red. He heard the gurgling sounds of Peanut coming awake.

Bowing over the wood stump he caught his palms on it and shook his head. Never in his life had he cried. And he wouldn't let that happen now. He was strong. He was a man. He could handle this shit.

He glanced to the monitor. Heaven help him, what was he going to do with Peanut?

Chapter 9

The next day Mireio glanced at the clock above the stove. It was late afternoon. Lars had not called. She hadn't spoken to him since yesterday afternoon when he'd picked up Peanut from the brewery.

She licked the buttercream icing from a finger and pulled the bowl of fresh-washed blueberries and raspberries closer. She was making a lemon poppy seed cake and the topping would be an artfully arranged assortment of fresh fruit. Lars would love it.

Or would he? Why the silence?

She'd called him a few hours earlier. His phone had forwarded her to messages. She'd left a quick one: "Call me. Thinking of you." But she couldn't help feeling unsettled. Worried for him.

What had the doctor told him?

On the other hand, she did have a tendency to think too far ahead, as Eryss often said. She had to stop worrying about a future that generally never turned out as she thought it would. Lars was fine. He was probably busy doing whatever it was the guy did. Maybe he'd started a big project yesterday and hadn't time to chat?

She wondered about the baby. Did the poor thing sit in the baby seat all day while his dad worked away? No. Lars would probably stop what he was doing every so often to entertain the boy. She knew that he must. He and his boy were like two peas in a pod.

"Peanut." She sighed and toggled a blueberry under her finger. "Who would have thought I'd fall for a man with a baby. A baby who has the most handsome, irresistible dad, a dad who kisses like I'm the only woman in the world. And oh, that beard."

She shivered to recall it brushing her skin as he'd kissed her breasts. Indeed, it had some kind of sensual power.

She picked up the cell phone, smearing it with frosting. Tapping the voice messages app, there were no return calls from Lars. "I'll send him a text."

That way he wouldn't feel the need to call her, if that was the problem. Though why he wouldn't want to talk to her—the man had to have gotten over his shyness with her—argh! She was freaking out over nothing. Women had this terrible time schedule in their brains about how long people should go between conversations, yet she well knew men were not like that. They could go for days without talking, and then arrive at a girl's doorstep eager for fun, like no time had passed at all.

She typed in a message: You must be busy. I can make supper if you're interested. Thought maybe one day we could drive and look for vamp...

Yeah, give him a reason to want to see her. Like helping her out with looking for the big bad vampire. Unless he'd decided he didn't want to see her anymore and this was the dreaded "I'm ignoring you because I don't like you anymore" kiss-off?

"Oh!" She caught her forehead in her hands, smearing frosting across an eyelid in the process.

At that moment her phone buzzed. A message!

It was from Lars.

Sorry, she read. Been busy. Tonight's not good. Vamp hunt sounds necessary. Try me tomorrow?

She set the phone down and nodded reassuringly. "Okay. That's cool. He's busy. So chill, Mireio. Maybe tomorrow night. This cake will still be good by then. Of course it will be. I'll…put the berries on tomorrow so they don't get mushy. Right. I have to work on my water spells anyway."

The following afternoon, Mireio called Lars but again he did not answer, so she texted him. This time she didn't know what to say. Was he really that busy?

"Just checking in," she whispered as she typed. "Call me."

What was up with her chasing a man? She did not phone-stalk men. Until now. Mireio dropped her head and sighed again. "I guess that means more spell practice."

The afternoon crept toward evening while she managed to wrangle a water elemental to help her in the garden. The elemental would tend her flowers and alert her when they needed a squirt from the hose. The tiny liquid creature slid down Mireio's finger and landed on a wide peony leaf, hugging it gently. She liked to keep her elementals happy.

A text reply did not come until around six that evening when she was staring in the fridge at the frosted cake, wondering if it would look odd if she presented her lover with a cake missing a slice. The bowl of berries sitting beside it was getting mushy. They needed to be eaten today.

Mireio spun around and grabbed her phone. Lars had texted her. Sunday can watch Peanut after ten. Will swing by, pick you up. Vamp hunt!

Letting out her held breath, she nodded. Then performed a triumphant fist pump. Then, she caught a hand at her throat. Why did she feel as if tonight could be the last time she saw the man?

"I need some rhodonite and...rose quartz."

She wasn't going into the unknown without some sexy backup crystals. And with the new moon she could also finally work a birth control spell. Might be best, just in case the condoms were forgotten again.

"So much to do before he stops by." She closed the fridge door. The cake could wait.

As far as dates went, this one ranked as strange and unusual. But it afforded Lars time with Mireio, and he hadn't seen her for two days, so he was in for the ride. And what a weird ride.

Before leaving her place, the witch had insisted he eat cake. Lots of it. He'd finished half the cake and more than enough berries to make his skin turn blue (yes, he was a fan of *Charlie and the Chocolate Factory*), and then she'd grabbed him and made a dash for the truck.

Once in northern Minneapolis, they'd decided to park in a four-level open parking ramp. Upon exiting the truck Mireio pointed out a dark shadow pursuing a woman below in an alleyway. Lars could smell the blood and violence on the man. Definitely vampire. They could observe from the ramp, so he suggested they remain there, near the truck because he didn't want Mireio to get too close to a dangerous vamp.

And they were just scoping things out tonight. She had said there was a necessary spell ingredient she'd ordered. Dragon's blood or piss. Something disgusting like that. So tonight was simply to see if they could locate the vamp, get an ID on him, then return to his turf when Mireio was ready.

And besides, if they were both focused on the vampire, then they didn't have to make small talk. And he wasn't sure he was ready for that.

"My grandmother never let me go in this area of the city," Mireio said. "Too dangerous."

"Your grandma?"

"She raised me. My mom died when I was eight."

"Oh, right, sorry about that. That's rough. My dad died when I was young, as well. I was raised by the pack leader and his wife." He pressed a hand over his stomach.

"Still hungry?" she asked eagerly.

"Oh, no," he said too quickly. "I mean, it was great cake. But that was a lot of cake. Whew!" A movement drew his attention. "There's something down there."

Both of them leaned over the concrete balustrade and followed the action below that wound deeper into the dark suburban landscape. A man pursued a woman, whose frantic breathing Lars could hear. He could also sense her heartbeat thundering madly.

Suddenly Mireio clutched his hand and he sensed her intense fear. "He's moving in on her. He'll bite her."

"That is what vampires do," he said.

"Yes, but he's a known killer. What if he kills her? Oh, I can't watch this. Lars?"

The witch was squeamish, which he decided was a good thing. But not if she intended to ultimately eat a vampire heart. Blood drinking only seemed palatable if you were a vampire. Well, it was what vamps did. And if a guy was going to accept that the world was filled with all species that sometimes destroyed others to survive, then he had to allow each their own survival methods. But Lars knew vampires didn't have to kill to survive. They committed homicide because they wanted to. Raven Crosse had reported this vampire had killed many. And that made all the difference to Lars.

"Nobody is going to die tonight," he said, trying to hide the resignation in his voice. He'd hoped to remain a bystander. But there was obviously a price to pay for such voyeurism. "Stay here."

He climbed over the cement balustrade and stood at the lip of the fourth-floor level. Pushing off into a free fall, he landed on the tarmac crouched in a solid stance, his boots stirring up earthy dust. He turned up to Mireio and winked at her, then took off in the direction where the vampire stalked his victim. The fear scent was stronger down on the ground. As was the acrid tang of blood. Lars quickened his pace.

The woman struggled against her captor when Lars came upon them; the vampire had her pinned to the wall by both wrists. The blood scent teasing the air sickened him. He growled, alerting the vampire.

The longtooth turned to him, fangs dripping with blood. The vamp hissed, and took off.

Taking chase after the fleeing vamp, Lars followed him at a leisurely lope for three blocks. He wasn't about to go full-out assault werewolf. Not in the middle of a neighborhood populated by humans. And besides, Mireio needed this vampire to live for the night she would return.

When he decided he'd scared off the flesh pricker, he

quickly veered back toward the victim, who wasn't there when he returned.

He sniffed and cast a glance around the dark alley, peering into nearby shrubs and between trash cans and parked cars. The human scent trailed west.

To follow her or not?

He glanced upward, his gaze meeting Mireio's. Even at a distance he could see her give him the thumbs-up signal. The victim must have wandered off to safety.

He returned the thumbs-up, then wandered back to the parking garage. When he reached the truck, Mireio ran up to embrace him. Wrapping her legs about his hips, she held him in a long hug. That connection brought him down from the adrenaline high of the chase. It was a sweet landing in the arms of a soft and sexy witch.

"I saw her wobble off," she said. "A car pulled up and two women got out to help her into the back seat. I hope they're taking her to the emergency room." Her body shivered against his. "It's been so long since I've seen a vampire attack a person. It kind of freaked me out. I wish I could have gotten a better look at his face."

"I saw him. It was dark, but I'm sure he's the one Raven Crosse told us about. This must be his territory. We'll return when you're ready to do the spell. Okay?"

She nodded, and he helped her up inside the truck. As he drove to her place, Mireio remained quiet and Lars sensed she'd been more shaken by watching the attack than he'd first thought. How desperately did a person have to want immortality to commit such an act?

Immortality. If only werewolves were immortal. Hell. He'd better not go there. He'd never get through this night if he allowed the doctor's diagnosis to do battle with paying attention to the girl.

Arriving at her place, he walked her into the living

room and helped her to sit. "I'll make you some tea. It'll settle your nerves."

"Thanks," she whispered.

"She's going to be okay," he offered. "The victim."

Fortunately, he'd gotten to the vampire and his victim before the bastard could drink too much. The woman would survive. With luck the vamp had used persuasion to make her forget what had happened, but Lars guessed his showing up might have prevented that. That woman was going to have some hellacious nightmares.

In the kitchen, he found a cup and some tea, then filled it with water and set it in the microwave for a minute and a half. While he waited, he stared into the living room, spying Mireio, who had put her bare feet up on the end of the couch. Her reaction prodded at his own morals.

Raven Crosse had assured them this vamp was the baddest of the bad. That he had killed. Many times. He probably deserved a cruel and painful death. But how could Lars be the man to deliver that death? No matter how horrible the vampire was, he should not place judgment on him and decide it was okay to end his life.

Should he?

Mireio had asked for his help. He'd said he would. He was a man of his word. But now...

Shit. Things had changed. And it had been two days that he'd stayed away from Mireio, knowing when next he saw her he'd have to tell her all. He didn't want to. How could he? Could a guy get a rope to pull himself to shore?

Feeling a dizzy wave wash through his head, Lars slapped a palm to the counter. A weird feeling of dread crowded his thoughts. And then...his legs gave out and he went down.

Chapter 10

Hearing a clatter in the kitchen, Mireio sat up. Lars didn't answer when she called out, so she raced into the kitchen to find him lying on the tile floor between the counter and the fridge. Unconscious.

He still held a tea bag in hand. He couldn't have bumped his head. She didn't see any blood. Had he…fainted?

Giving his shoulder a shake, she jostled him awake. The big, muscular man sat upright with a sudden movement and a groan.

"What happened?" he asked.

"I think you fainted." Saying it out loud ratcheted up the anxiety she hadn't realized had tensed her fingers into claws. She shook out her hands. "Let me help you up so you can sit on the chair." She grabbed his arm but he roughly tugged away.

Turning onto his knees, he used the stove to heft himself up, and wobbled over to the barstool before the counter, where he collapsed in a huff. Hands shaking, Mireio filled a glass of water and brought it to him. When he refused it, she insisted. Finally he took a few sips, then he drank the whole thing and handed it back to her.

"Your tea water is ready," he said curtly.

"I don't need tea. I feel better now. But you are not fine. Lars, you fainted!"

"It was nothing."

She exhaled, hands to her hips. Grown men who were as strapping as Lars, and seemingly healthy, did not all of a sudden faint.

"It is something. Something you're not telling me. What is it? It's about the tests the doctor did, isn't it? You've had the blackouts and the shifting without volition. And you forget things in the middle of conversations. And you said something about your fingers getting numb."

"Mireio," he said warningly. He pressed a fist to his forehead and winced.

She wasn't going to be chided. The man was not okay. And she needed him to let her in, trust her and tell her what was up. She needed that for her own sense of well-being.

She placed both hands on his shoulders. "Lars, you can trust me. And I worry about you. Is it your health? What's going on?"

He exploded up from the stool, shoving her aside. Pacing between the counter and the front door, he paused in the center of the room. He eyed her sternly. His breaths were heavy. He glanced to the tea bag, still lying on the kitchen floor.

Then he turned and marched out the front door, leaving the screen door to slam in his wake.

Mireio gaped at his fuming exit. "Did I say something wrong?"

Just when she felt a tear wobble at the corner of her eye, the burly wolf marched back over the threshold and again paced a few times in the center of the room before her.

What was going on with the man? And why did men have such a hard time—

"You're right," he said. "It's—" he squeezed a fist before him "—something."

Of course it was. And it was a big something, to judge how upset he was. By the goddess, she didn't know how to keep doing this. The man had a way of dropping surprises on her left and right. What more had he to hide?

No. She would not accuse or berate him for keeping things to himself. Lars was a private man, never one to boast about himself. Or, obviously, bring up his problems. So she'd be open and prepare herself for whatever he had to say. "Tell me?"

"Mireio, I—" He swung a fist through the air in defeat, then stopped his pacing. "Fuck!"

"Lars, please, you're scaring me."

Turning to face her, his arm swaying out in helpless abandon, he looked at her as if for the first time. For a moment his mouth compressed and he blinked his eyes, as if tears might fall. But then he nodded and pressed his palms together before him as if in prayer. "Sorry. I thought taking a few days to think this over would make it easier to tell you. It's not. And it never will be. But you need to know." He scrubbed a hand over his hair, gripping it, then releasing it with another forceful swing of his arm. "I've got…this thing. A disease. The doc says it's rare and exclusive to werewolves."

She stood there, arms down and open to listen. Because any wrong move would surely send him fleeing. But already Mireio felt her stomach clench and tears began to well.

"I've been having symptoms. Involuntary shifting. Memory loss. Disorientation. And now this? Blasted fainting? I hate this! It makes me feel so weak. But I'm not, Mireio. I feel good still. I'm strong. I feel…" He sighed.

"What is it called, that the doctor says you have?"

"It's some fancy medical name. Lycanthorpus…" He searched for the words, then punched a fist into his palm. "I can't remember the full term, something crazy. All I know is it's degenerative." He glanced to her for reaction.

Mireio touched her breast over the thudding heartbeats as the definition of that word coalesced in her thoughts. "Doesn't that mean…?"

"It means I won't ever get better. I'll only get worse. And then?" He spread out his arms in what seemed surrender, and stated, "I'll die."

Her mouth dropped open at that statement. Issued forcefully and finally. She didn't know what to say. She'd never… Feeling light-headed herself, she steered around the counter and climbed onto the stool. "That's…" Heartbeats thundering and skin prickling, she looked to him.

The big, strong werewolf whom she had come to care for. Pine for. Think about constantly. He was her boyfriend. They hadn't come out and stated their relationship status, but he was. He was hers. And she was his. And… The world faded in and out on muffled vibrations that at once made her heart pound loudly, and then she could not hear a thing.

Degenerative? He was going to die?

She sought his gaze and he initially looked away, but then, he met her eyes straight on. Shoulders rounded and hands still spread loosely beside him, he said softly, "The doc gave me a few months."

Mireio stood. "A few? But that's... Seriously?"

"I've been having symptoms for over a year. I didn't want to go to the doctor." He sighed. "But after shifting without volition one too many times, I finally figured I'd better check it out."

Oh, damn. Her heart dropped to her toes. She couldn't move. Her hands shook.

And she noticed Lars subtly shook too from shoulders to hands. And that was all she needed to break out of her shock and plunge against him and wrap her arms about him. At first he stood there, caged within her arms. But she hugged him tighter until he put his arms across her back and then bowed his head over hers and pressed his forehead against the crown of it.

Blessed goddess, she never wanted to let go of him.

They stood there for long moments. She could feel his heartbeat against her throat, could almost hear it. His heavy breaths that rose and fell with a world-weary exhale... Death?

"You need to get a second opinion," she suddenly said.

"Yes?"

"There's only one werewolf doc in this part of the States, sweetie. He's been taking care of the Northern Pack for much longer than I've been around. I trust him. He did all sorts of tests. Brought out books and explained things to me. He believes it was inherited."

"Inherited? But your...family?"

"My dad died when I was little. Not sure where my mom is. She left me alone with the pack after dad's death. It was hard on her. Ridge Addison and his wife, Abigail— a witch—raised me."

"But if the doctor has been looking after your pack? Didn't he take care of your dad?"

"He did. My father had the same thing. And—" he swallowed and dropped his hand down her shoulder and back "—he said he went quickly."

Compelled to give comfort, she hugged him even tighter, wanting to draw out whatever it was inside him that was making him sick. To cleanse him of it. To renew him.

"Maybe there's a spell?" she suggested. "There must be."

He stroked her hair and tilted her chin up so she would look at him.

"You won't die. We won't let it happen. I'll search my spell books. We'll figure something out."

He hugged her against his chest, so broad and strong. The deception of his outer appearance had surely fooled her. Her mighty werewolf was dying. There were simply no words to put that into proper focus right now.

"I want to make sure Peanut is taken care of," he said. "Thought about that a lot the past few days. I just get that sweet little piece of heaven and now he's going to be taken away from me. Or rather, I'll be taken from his life. Just like with my dad. Something's wrong with that."

She clung to his shirt, squeezing too tightly, but to let go of him might see him fade away. And then she'd never get him back. Because he was skittish in a way that always surprised her. Except earlier...

"Oh, my goddess." She pushed from him, turning away because she didn't want him to see her. "You went with me this evening. And the whole time you knew you were going to..." That he would die. And so quickly. Two months? "I can't believe I could have been so cruel."

"You're the least cruel person on this planet. What are you talking about?"

"Me!" She stabbed her chest with her fingers. "I've been seeking immortality, and I drag you along to make it happen. There you are standing with a death sentence on your head. How dare I?"

"Mireio, you didn't know. And this has nothing to do with the spell you want to cast. You need that immortality. You said you've been thinking about this for years. And I will help you get it."

She shook her head and spun her shoulders to face him. That he could suggest such a thing now revealed the capacity of his wide and giving heart. She truly was a monster to even think to ask him for such help.

"Can we sit and hold hands?" he asked softly. "I need that right now, Mireio. I... Please?"

His hand slipped into hers and she led him into the living room, where they sat on the couch. Tilting her head against his shoulder, they cuddled in the darkness, quiet, yet their minds racing. Two hearts who had found one another under the strangest circumstances.

Perhaps a half an hour had passed when Lars glided his hand along her arm and tilted up her chin to kiss her. Slow and easy, he tasted her mouth, taking his time and lingering on the sensitive inner dip behind her lower lip. It was such an erotic touch. She sighed into him as his hand cupped the back of her head and his thumb stroked her cheek.

He bowed his forehead to hers and asked quietly, "Make love with me?"

"Yes" fell out in a gasp. "Take me upstairs."

Standing, he took her hand and she followed the stoic werewolf up the creaky stairs and into her clove-perfumed bedroom. The pale mint walls glinted with sparkle dust she'd blown on while the paint had still been wet. Moonlight shimmered everywhere, as if in an enchanted haven.

A pop art portrait of Marie Antoinette stuffing cake into her mouth hung beside the window. A sunflower burst above the high bed. It was covered with a patchwork quilt comprised of shades of green, mint and violet. Her grandmother had sown it for her. The stitches wove wards and protective sigils and blessings for love into the fabric. Draped over the canopy, a sheer blue scarf with violet and yellow flowers dangled its long betasseled hem over all four sides. It was her mermaid's escape from the world.

Lars sat on the bed and pulled her to stand before him. The side of his face was illuminated by moonlight and his big brown eyes took her in as if she were magic.

Now was no time for thinking dire thoughts or discussing a dreaded future. Now…this man needed her.

He pulled her hand to his mouth and kissed the palm, burying his face there as if to imprint the lines that told her life story, past, present and future, upon his soul. Keeping her hand in his he glided her palm over his cheek and she tickled her fingers down and into his soft beard. He wore his wild on his face, but his tender, gentle soul revealed itself in the curve of his smile and the perk of his dimples as he cradled Peanut in the crook of an arm.

"Touch me everywhere," he whispered. "Make me yours."

For a moment she thought of his confession down in the kitchen. Her heart dropped. But mining bravery, she pushed that feeling aside. Didn't want to think about it. Not now. Now was for the two of them, getting to know one another on a deeper level. And she needed that desperately from this lovely yet broken werewolf.

Stepping up to stand closer to him with one of his legs between hers, she leaned forward and slid her hands down the back of his head, finding the wood stick and pulling it from the leather hair clasp. Tossing that over a shoulder onto the floor, she ran her palms over his thick, wavy hair and drew it up to press against her cheek, lips and nose. He smelled like wood and wild and salty, musky masculinity. His beard was thick and soft and so…fun to run her fingers through. He purred as she stroked it. Mmm…

And when he looked up into her eyes, she got lost. Her hands slipped away from him. Such deep memories of earth and ancient things in his irises. His soul was old, steeped with ages, perhaps millennia, of experience. He may not realize it. And Mireio was not a soul reader, but she sensed that they may have walked into one another's lives once or twice previously. It was possible. All things were possible.

She traced both his eyebrows with her forefingers, drawing that touch out and along his cheeks to stop at his dimples. His smile warmed her belly and spun that rush of heat to her toes and back up to her ears. So she touched his mouth, framed by a thick mustache and beard that was so dark it was almost black. He parted his lips, and she tickled across his lower lip. His tongue tasted the whorls on her fingertips and curled an erotic vibe all the way to her belly, where it coiled in anticipation.

Wetting her finger by allowing him to dash his tongue about the tip of it, Mireio then touched her own lips and tasted him. His eyes followed her motions intently. Outside this enchanted sanctuary's windows, a crow cawed and the maple trees that spread their leaf-frothed limbs over her entire backyard rustled. Inside, her heartbeats were calm and steady, but desire warmly flooded her skin and opened her pores to every sensation.

She leaned in and barely touched her mouth to his.

Gliding her wet lips across his she didn't so much tease as leave a promise to return. And then she kissed down his bearded chin and neck to the top of his shirt where so much more dark hair tufted out.

"Take this off," she said quietly, and he obeyed, pulling off the T-shirt and tossing it to the floor.

His chest was a mastery of muscle and steel shaded with a manly brush of dark hair that grew sparser as it neared his belly. Mireio pushed her fingers through the silky hairs and shoved him backward to lie on the bed. She crawled up onto the bed, lying on a hip beside him and leaned over to brush her cheek over his chest hair. Following the hard line of a pectoral that pulsed under her touch, she made a slow journey to the tiny hard nipple that looked from her side vantage point a boulder standing in a clearing in the forest.

He hissed as she toggled her fingernail over it and then teased around the areola that tightened and textured under her touch. Leaning over him, she cast a glance toward his face. His eyes were closed, one hand rested over his forehead. Under her palm, his chest rose and fell in anticipation. And as she touched her tongue to his nipple, he groaned. Like a quiet animal. Like a man in need of touch.

The tiny bead she toggled in her mouth, dashing it, licking it, sucking it and then giving it a pinch between her fingers. Slickened with her saliva, it reacted to every lash, taste and hush of hot breath.

Not to give the other short shrift, she glided over and did the same, while dancing her fingers through the wild dark hairs, down around his belly button, and lower to slip under the waistband of his jeans.

"Mireio," he whispered as if he were invoking a blessing. Or a goddess.

"I need to touch you with all of me," she announced and tugged off her shirt.

Lars's eyes opened and he watched as she unsnapped her bra in the back and tugged it away. When he reached to touch one of her breasts, she caught his hand with hers, fully intent on touching him everywhere, as he had requested. "Close your eyes again. I like knowing you can only feel, hear and taste me, but not see me."

"But you're so beautiful." His words came out as another worshipful prayer.

"You can look and touch all you like soon enough." She bowed to kiss his eyelid, then the other, and he kept them closed as she lowered her breasts against his chest and delighted in the tickle of his chest hair against her tightening nipples.

The glide of her thick nipples across his tiny ones made him rock his hips. "Mine are bigger than yours," she said.

"Yeah, and they feel great."

She reveled in the tease of his hard maleness against her heavy breasts as she moved lower. The musky salty scent of his arousal lured her to unbutton his jeans. Oh, mercy, the man was commando again. The head of his erection loomed right there, begging for attention, so she took care in unzipping him, gliding in her other hand to protect his skin. He was so hot and hard she wanted to get him in hand, but she cautioned her eagerness. For a little while anyway.

Tugging at his jeans, she bent and placed kisses at the ridges of muscles that arrowed down toward his groin. And while his penis bobbed against her chest and chin she paid discerning attention to those cut muscles because that was where the man's magic lay. Those muscles, on any man, were capable of drawing women's eyes. Of stopping them dead and making their jaws drop. Of inciting fantasies. Of making ovaries sing. Of inviting and luring to the real treasure.

He swore on another hiss and his fingers twisted into her hair, not pulling but instead holding on. Anchoring himself. He lifted his hips and she was able to shove down the jeans and forget about them as the heavy material slid over the edge of the bed and below his knees. Brushing her breasts over his cock stirred his hips to rock subtly, so she pressed the ample girls together and around his hardness. A boob hug.

"Mireio…" Another roughly whispered prayer.

Nestling beside him on an elbow and leaning in closer for better study, she drew her fingers lightly up his bobbing cock, mapping out the thickness, the pulsing veins that bulged and made him even harder. She'd not taken such time to linger on the night when it had seemed a second best option in the absence of condoms.

Up she moved, along the heat that must surely drive him to some kind of edge, and tucked her fingernail under the ridge of the plum-firm crown. Circumcised. And the head of him fit against her palm as if she were cupping a juicy fruit that filled her grasp. Down the backside, she lightly journeyed into the nest of his curls where she wandered lower to trace the tender yet tightly tucked testicles.

Every bit of him was a masterpiece. Designed for pleasure. For study. For creating and sensual adventure. And much as she wanted to straddle him right now, knowing he would fill her completely, she knew putting off that pleasure would prove a sweeter reward.

So she slid off the bed and tugged down his jeans. He'd left his shoes at the front door, so the pants dropped to the floor. His socks she discarded, left and right with a flip. His legs were taut with muscle and thick with dark hairs.

A wolf under her command. She imagined what it must be like to stand before him in fully shifted werewolf shape. And then she remembered that she had. And she had been fascinated. What an awesome creature, both man and wolf. Wild and tame. Aggressive when need be, yet so gentle he could quiet a baby's tears with but a touch of his lips to the child's forehead.

Mireio bowed before him, palms to his knees, gauging the race of her heartbeats and knowing beyond doubt that she had fallen. Plummeted into his arms and so happy to be there. No matter the darkness. Because he, the big strong werewolf, faced so many struggles. She wanted to be a soft place for him. A comfort when he needed it. And a lover when he required the world to slip away.

Licking up his length roused a deep and throaty moan from him. His penis bobbed in approval so she gripped it firmly to keep it at her mouth. The taste of him made her sigh, and with a secret inner giggle she thought that if she had the inclination to use a wand for magic, she'd very much like it to resemble this exquisite rod.

She looked up and found he'd propped himself up onto his elbows and was looking at her. Waiting? No, just… being. There. Sharing. Knowing.

Hastily, she slipped off her skirt and panties. She crawled up over him and pressed her breasts against his hard chest, her stomach to his rigid abs, and her mons placed firmly against his erection.

"Kiss me," she pleaded. "Take what you want from me, wolf. I'm yours."

He bracketed her face and before he kissed her asked, "What is it you witches say about things coming around threefold?"

"For everything we put out into the universe it comes back threefold."

"Then everything I take from you, I will also give to you threefold."

He rolled her onto her back and hovered over her. The man's hair slipped from behind his shoulder and spilled across her breasts. Mireio took the ends of it and tickled it over her nipple. And he bowed to brush his beard gently over the other.

With a glance up to her, he winked, then kissed the top of her breast. "I've never had sex with a mermaid before."

"It could get slippery," she warned on a tease.

The man's hot kisses explored her breasts with licks and gentle nibbles and when he took a nipple in a suckling squeeze, she moaned and dug the fingers of one hand into the bedspread while tangling the other in his hair. His fingers clasped her other breast, containing her abundance with his sure touch.

"So much," he breathed against her skin. "Your tits are big and round. Makes me mad for you, Mireio."

He sucked in her nipple and at her other breast pinched gently, then none-too-gently, causing her to arch her back as she sought the intensity of him. The tickle of his beard heightened every touch, coursing exquisite shivers through her system. Mmm, beard. Behold the power.

Shoulders pressing into the bed, she sucked in her lower lip. Nuzzling her mons up against his stomach she rubbed her clitoris against his hard abdomen, heightening the coiling tightness that promised a luscious release in her belly and loins.

"You're so hard." She clutched his head, keeping him there at her breast, silently telling him that what he was doing was perfect. It teased her closer, made her pant, stirred in the clove scenting the room with his wanton musk and salt, and it dizzied her.

"Come for me, Mireio," he whispered. "I can feel you so close."

She was. Just. There. Waiting to spill over. The texture of his hot tongue easing and prodding and suckling drove her giddy mad. His lips closing over her nipples. The erection thrusting against her thigh...

Breaths gasped and caught in her throat. She moaned, twisting her fingers in his long hair. Drawing up a leg, she squeezed her inner muscles, tempting her to jump, to make the leap.

And when he slid a hand down her stomach, over her panting belly, and glided through the dark strands that didn't match those on her head, his finger slicked across her swollen clit and that set off a chain of explosions inside her.

Mireio shouted and jerked upright as the orgasm overwhelmed and commanded her limbs, shaking her, extending her moan into a luscious pleading. And when she felt the lash of Lars's tongue move across her clit she bellowed with joy and spread her arms out wide as her shoulders and head landed on the bed.

The wolf had truly given back threefold.

Chapter 11

Mireio's body quaked beneath his hands. At once Lars wanted to contain her, to hug her close and tend to her shivers. And then, he wanted to open her wide and allow her to soar. So he hovered over her, kneeling on the bed, knees to either side of her thighs, head above her breasts, and watched her expression. It moved from gasping glee to a wincing but satisfied ache and then to panting relaxation as he felt her limbs settle beneath him and the flush that colored her cheeks and neck softened.

"Oh, my goddess," she said on gasps, "you…you really know how to do me right…whew!"

He chuckled and kissed her breasts. Her nipples were so sensitive and he could suckle at them all night. Lose himself in her lush, bountiful breasts. He nuzzled his cheek between them, rubbing his beard softly against the underside. It wasn't so much a sexual move as one of possession. The wolf in him was marking his scent on her, but she didn't need to know that.

He pressed his hard cock against her thigh, working it to a rigidity that tempted him to get to the really good part where he lost himself inside her, but he knew all parts of this were good. And taking his time, as she had when she'd stroked him, was important to him.

The curls inviting him lower were darker, almost black. Not that he'd considered her bright red hair color natural, but one never knew with witches. He nuzzled his nose and beard into them, meshing their tresses and seeking her alluring perfume. It was a lush aroma that enticed him to drag his tongue over her heated skin.

"Oh, Lars, you made me come, it's…"

He reached up to tweak her nipple and that quieted her protest. "Let me do this my way, witch. I have to taste you. And if that makes you come again, then so be it."

"You are a wicked wolf." Her toes curled at his hip. "Oh, sweet mercy, when your beard brushes my skin…"

Smiling, he swished his beard softly over her. Heh. Instant pantie dropper, his beard. But he wasn't cocky about it. He only wanted one particular witch's panties to drop. And…they had.

He slid an arm under her leg and, gripping forward over her hip, pulled her closer as he nuzzled the lush folds of her and parted them with his tongue. She tasted like earth and woman and wild and salt. And magic.

He wondered briefly if she'd bewitched him, and then he knew that she had. But it hadn't required a spell or a snap of her fingers. He'd been bewitched since the night his werewolf had stood staring at her bathed by the porch light, naked and unashamed.

Skating his tongue upward, he circled it about her swollen clit. This was where all the magic happened, and perhaps it was the source of her true magic. A woman's strength lay in her core and in the womb. He sucked the tender bud and the moan that spilled from her pleased him immensely. Her hips rocked and her fingers clawed at the bedcover. He liked that he could make her squirm.

Tasting her deeply with his tongue, he pushed in a finger to curl up and forward. There, she felt rigid and slick and his gentle strokes increased her moans to fervent yeses and panting pleas.

He reached down and cupped his balls, which were so tight against the base of his cock he knew he could explode any moment. And then he remembered…

"I have a condom out in the truck."

"No! You stay right here. After our last attempt, I worked a birth control spell. We're good, lover. Promise. Oh, do that more. Like that, please, Lars."

She rocked her hips and squiggled down on the bed to embed his finger deeper within her, so he took that as a good sign, and pushed another finger into her squeezing sweetness.

She swore, and such a word had never sounded more like a prayer, yet also demanding. He pumped his fingers as if they were his cock and licked her clit, teasing her to a shiver. Her thighs squeezed beside his cheeks and her heels slid and slipped over his tense delt muscles as she sought to steady herself. He wouldn't allow her to fall into anything but his arms.

Pulling out his fingers, he gripped his cock, wetting it with her lush heat and marking himself with her scent. Mercy, he wanted all of her.

"Come inside me," she begged. "Put that big, thick cock inside me, Lars. You want to. I'm right there, and so are you. Oh, come on!"

Edged as it was with a touch of annoyance, he would

not ignore that insistent command. Pushing up her legs so her knees bent, he lowered himself onto her. He groaned deep in his throat, bowing his head to hers at the heady meeting of skin and skin. Heat melded the soft and hard of their anatomies.

She groped for a hold of his cock, but his torso was long and her arms wouldn't quite give her the reach she required. It was a tease he'd prolong.

Gripping his shaft, he nudged the head against her, slicking it upward over her clit. Now she panted, gasping out oaths that he hoped weren't actual witchy curses. Maybe he should get to it or risk getting hexed?

Gliding into her was like entering a new world. Jaws tight and eyelids shut, Lars moaned forcefully as she enveloped him in a tight hug. He rocked slowly at first, testing and feeling every inch of her on every hard inch of his cock.

"So thick," she murmured. "Goddess, give me more."

Words a man loved to hear. He hilted himself, which shoved her up against the pillows, hands reaching behind and above her to clutch one of the frilly concoctions. He thrust deeply, slowly, gliding in and out of her. Learning her. Memorizing her. He could do this forever…

How much longer do you have?

He chased away that nasty, intrusive thought with a growl and a fist to the bed beside her shoulder. Pumping faster, he fed the beast that demanded satisfaction. He answered her cries to go faster and harder. To give her everything. She could have all of him. He needed to expose himself, open himself up and let it flow out.

And with a flick of his finger over her clitoris, he set her off, her hips ramming upward against his, and that squeezed her tightly about him and stole his last moment of control. The surrender rocketed through him, shaking him above her and dancing in his veins.

This night the witch had given him magic.

Lars woke to sunlight prodding at his eyelids. He winced at the brightness, then felt his body waver and lean to the right. He slapped out a hand to the right and caught it against a pinewood nightstand. Then he glanced down at his position on the bed. He was stretched lengthwise from pillow to the end, but only had about eight inches of mattress for his big wide body.

And the reason for his lacking space was the diminutive red-haired witch who lay on her back, arms outstretched and legs spread, to take up the entire bed.

He chuckled softly, then let his body answer gravity and slid off the bed without disturbing the queen of the mattress. Wandering out of the room, he glanced down the hallway to the only other door on the upper floor. No, he remembered she'd said the bathroom was on the main level. He took the stairs carefully because he'd heard them creak when coming up before and managed a nearly silent descent until the last step groaned loudly.

Flashing a look upward he listened but didn't hear her stir. Once in the bathroom he intended to veer toward the toilet but he had to stop and take it in. Had he stepped into a Moroccan palace? A princess's hideaway? Tiles painted in jewel tones danced under his bare feet and traveled halfway up the walls. The upper half of the walls was painted a deep maroon and stenciled with elaborate gold arabesques. Fixtures gleamed gold, and the morning sunlight danced in the cut-glass panes that hugged the back of the room and curved in a half hexagon. The room was nearly the size of the living room and a huge round marble tub mastered the center of it all.

"Like something a mermaid would bathe in." He smiled at that thought, then wandered over and found the toilet behind a half wall.

While he did his business, he scanned the room. A shower was tucked into a cove behind him, and that was big too. Definitely made for two people. The entire bathroom ceiling was domed and a couple panels were stained glass. It was like a mini cathedral or something. So cool. He could imagine soaking in the tub under that ceiling. Everything was brightly colored and there were fresh flowers everywhere. Totally Mireio. His bubbly, hippie witch.

His witch?

Sure felt like it. He wanted her to be his. But he didn't expect that one night of sex—amazing, mind-blowing sex—would make her his. Sure, they'd gotten to know one another well these past weeks.

She'd even accepted Peanut.

He flushed the toilet and then washed his hands, noting the tips of his fingers tingled. Stupid numbness. What was that about?

The news about his health was something he wasn't sure how Mireio would deal with. Hell, he wasn't dealing with it. He was avoiding it. But he was glad he'd told her about it. Gotten it out there. Now he could push it aside and think about other things. Better things. Because what man who's been given a death sentence wants to think about his life ending?

He pressed a palm to the doorframe and blew out a heavy breath. He was that man. How could he *not* think about such a thing? The sentence had been shackled to him with a heavy yoke and he could no more shuck it off than he could have put Peanut up for adoption. This disease lived inside him. And it was doing things to him. Things he couldn't control.

And it would only get worse.

He shouldn't do this to Mireio. This was his trail to walk. It would be cruel to spread the misery. But, besides Peanut, she was the best thing that had happened to him. Could he simply enjoy what time he had with her? Would that be fair to her?

It wouldn't be, but he couldn't walk away from her. Not now. The witch had gotten inside him. He couldn't imagine a day without her in his life.

Pushing his fingers back through his hair, he strolled out to the kitchen and poured and drank a glass of water. Then he refilled it and carried it upstairs, where he found a landlocked mermaid witch lying on the bed all smiles and yawns.

"I'm not sure how someone so tiny as you managed to commandeer the bed." He handed her the glass and she sat up against the pillows and drank. "I almost landed on the floor had I not caught myself."

"I like to use the whole area." She swished her legs back and forth over the wrinkled sheet. "What's the purpose of having a bed if you don't use it all?"

"I can get behind that." He sat beside her and flipped a curl of her hair between his fingers and held it to his nose as a mustache. "But didn't your grandma teach you how to share?"

She laughed. "Sorry. I don't often have a big strapping man wolf sleeping beside me."

"I'll count that as a good thing. No other werewolves before me?"

"Nope. Not that I'm a slouch in the dating department,

but you don't need those details. Nor will I ask for yours. Though I'm guessing you've had some gorgeous lovers."

"What does their appearance have to do with anything?"

"Really? But you're so handsome."

He shrugged. "I like women in all shapes, personalities and, apparently, sizes. Tiny is my new favorite flavor."

"Good. Because I have mastered tiny with a side of curves."

"I want to devour your curves." He kissed her breast and sucked in the nipple.

"What time do you have to pick up Peanut?"

"I told Sunday I'd be there before noon. It's ten now."

"Then we have plenty of time for a shower and breakfast." She crawled to the edge of the bed, but he caught her around the waist and pulled her onto his lap. His cock was already hard and her thigh crushed it against his gut.

Pulling the hair from her face and tucking it over her ear, he kissed her. She tasted like him and her fierce magic. "Last night was the closest I've ever felt to a woman."

"Really? Not even with…"

"I told you that was just a couple nights."

"Yes, but this, between you and me, has only been one night. What made this different from…you know?" Lush lashes dusted over her bright blue eyes.

"Everything. And things I can't put into words. Do I have to put them into words?"

She shook her head.

"Wait. I can," he offered. "She was a good time. A good time that gave me my amazing little baby boy. But I didn't have the time to learn about her and care about her. Nor did I want to. But I believe that baby was meant to be, and I was meant to raise him without his mom. We came together for reasons neither of us may ever realize. A grand-scale kind of thing."

"The universe was at work, making sure Peanut arrived in this lifetime to be with you."

"Yeah, I like the way you put it." He kissed her cheek. "But me and you? I care about you, Mireio. You mean something to me. You are a part of something I can't really explain either, but I know we came together because we were meant to do something great."

"Like have fabulous sex?"

"Oh, yeah. So let's go with it and see where it takes us, yes?"

"I'm all in. It was amazing. And let's not let it stop. You and me. Shower. Race you!"

And with that, the naked witch took off and ran out of the room. Lars followed close behind, only stopping when he turned to close the glass shower door behind them.

After a long hot shower and two orgasms—or had it been three?—Lars and Mireio finally dried off and got dressed. Standing before the bed, he kissed her and pulled on his shirt. "I have to rush off. Gotta stop by the compound to pick up Peanut. I don't like to leave him too long with Sunday. Don't want to take advantage of her kindness."

"That's cool. I'm brewing apple ale this afternoon, so I'm headed in to work. Can I bring you supper later?"

"I'd like that."

He kissed her again and winced as the muscles wrapping his torso tugged.

"How you feeling?" she asked.

"Never better. And I don't want to talk about it. Okay?"

She nodded and Lars made a quick exit. He didn't groan from the pain that had suddenly wrapped about his hips and torso until he was inside his truck.

Chapter 12

Lars stood before the door to Dean and Sunday's home, his palm pressed to the white wood siding. Yet he couldn't feel the warmth of the wall against his skin. His fingers felt dead, lifeless, and his wrist tingled. He shook out his hand fiercely, trying to force the feeling back into it, but he knew it wouldn't work. He could but ride it out.

Gripping his stomach with the hand he could feel, he winced at the creaking ache in his lower abdomen. When he'd found him on the property, Lars had barely had enough time to tell Dean he had to run up to the house before he'd dashed away to avoid his principal seeing him in pain.

He swore under his breath as he pressed a shoulder to the door and rode out the pain that shivered all over beneath his skin. Felt like a bad sunburn, on the inside.

"Damn it, this better not get worse," he muttered.

"What's getting worse?"

He twisted and there stood Sunday, Peanut propped on her hip and smiling at him. The sneaky cat shifter must have seen him groaning in pain as well as heard what he'd said.

"Nothing. Hey, Peanut."

"There's something wrong with you." Sunday stepped up closer and her blue eyes took him in as her nostrils flared. It was a cat thing. He'd gotten accustomed to her scent so no longer read it as offensive—cats and wolves, you know—but she always did the scenting thing around him. "Oh, great goddess Bastet. I can smell the disease in you. Lars?"

"It's nothing, Sunday. I don't know what you think you scent—"

"I have a thing for picking up disease and cancers in people, Lars. Oh, shit, do you have cancer? I didn't think werewolves—"

"Sunday, please. It's not cancer. Just..." He blew out a breath and shook his numb hand, thankful that some of the feeling was returning. "I told Dean I'd help him move some hay bales, and he's waiting for me. But let's go inside. I'll tell you what's up."

Mireio was finding it difficult to concentrate on the laundry spell. She'd put too much lavender in the potion and it overwhelmed the hyssop. It was a quick and easy spell to cast a white light over her whenever she wore the clothing. But at this rate, she'd have to start over.

Blowing out a breath, she dumped the mixture outside onto the lawn—right on the brown spot where she suspected the neighborhood rabbits liked to mark their territory—then wandered back inside to the kitchen and the assortment of spell items strewn about the counter.

Measuring out the black sea salt into a clear glass mixing bowl, she paused and leaned forward to catch her elbows on the counter and her chin in her hand.

She'd had amazing sex last night. More orgasms than she could count? Check. World? Rocked.

And her lover was dying.

What the hell?

How was a witch supposed to deal with that? Magic did not enable a witch to bring back the dead. Not unless the witch practiced dark magic and wanted to deal with zombies as a result. But could she heal the dying? Her healing skills were miserable. If she suggested to Lars she wanted to give it a go, would that push him away from her? He did not want to talk about his condition. And she got that.

Yet, they'd grown closer last night. The man was amazing. Like no man she'd ever shared her body with before. He looked at her like she was magic. And he treated her like a princess. And he was kind and so gentle with Peanut. What more could a girl want in a man? She had to keep him.

But if she managed to do so, for how long would that last?

Lars set aside his work gloves and sat on the bale of hay. The pack rented some acreage to a nearby farmer who used the land to grow wheat and barley, and in turn, all they asked was a few dozen bales of hay. A stack stood four bales high out behind the compound. Dean used it around the compound, and Sunday spread it over her garden in the fall to protect the plants from the harsh winter chill.

Dean had gone inside the house to grab them some water and he returned carrying a thermos. Yet the wolf walked purposely toward Lars, as if something urgent were up. Suddenly feeling as if he were a teen who had pissed off the principal and was waiting for a talking to, Lars stood, hands flexing nervously near his thighs. And Dean grabbed him and pulled him in for a crushing man hug.

Ah hell.

"Sunday told me," Dean said. He slapped Lars's back a couple times. Stepping away, he studied Lars's face. "You're dying?"

"Don't make a big thing about this, man. It's—the doc says it's probably the same thing my father had. You weren't here when he died. It took him…quickly."

"Oh, man, that's rough. I'm so sorry. Whatever you need, you know you just have to ask. Sunday and I are here for you."

"Thanks, but uh, I'm good." And it felt too awkward between them right now. He wasn't a feeble thing. He was still strong and could toss around hay bales as if they were Lego blocks. "Don't tell the other pack members."

"I won't. I'll be cool. Just want you to know I got your back, man."

"I'll let you know if I need anything. I should get Peanut home. I have a lot to do this afternoon. You good here?"

"Of course! Next time tell me if you're not feeling well. I never should have asked—"

Lars gripped Dean by the shoulder, tightly. "I'm capable. I am not an invalid. So don't treat me like one. Okay?"

"Got it." Dean slapped his bicep. "Thanks for the help."

Lars wandered up to the house and made quick work of packing up Peanut. He sensed Sunday hung back, probably feeling as though she'd done something wrong by telling Dean. Good. He didn't want to talk to her. To have to fit himself into the mold of "dying."

He didn't plan to die. He planned to live every day until his last breath.

He wasn't as mad at the wood he was chopping today. Mostly. Still tracing a bit of anger over Sunday having told Dean he was dying, Lars brought down the ax on the head of a pine log and crisply split the column in two. He gripped one half and split it again.

Out of the corner of his vision he saw a flash of pink, and for a second Lars thought his vision was starting to blur. A problem that was showing up more often lately. Was blindness in his future? Had his father suffered such? He couldn't recall. He'd been young and had spent his days playing with the other pack wolves with no concern for how his father had actually felt.

He brought the ax down with a forceful grunt. The pink lingered in his peripheral vision. What next? Had Sunday returned to check on him? He should have been more clear with her regarding not treating him like an invalid, as he had been with Dean.

"Hey!"

At the shout, he startled and whipped around to find it was not failing vision but rather a particularly tasty witch dressed in a short pink skirt, white lacy ankle socks and black high heels, and a tight T-shirt that said Mermaids Like to Get Wet stretched across her ample bosom.

"Whew! You surprised me."

"I guessed that from the way you swung around with an ax aimed at me."

He looked at the weapon, still hoisted high in readiness for defense, then set it down by the tree stump.

"Sorry," she said. "I should have expected that. You

were in the zone. The cutting zone, or whatever you call it. So what's that you're sporting today? A man bun?"

"A what?" Oh. He shrugged and bobbed his head to test that the hair was still secure and tight at the back of his head. "Keeps it out on my way when I'm working. Man bun?"

"You haven't heard that term before? You're working it, let me tell you. Add in the beard and the overalls and ax? Most definitely a lumbersexual."

"A…? I don't even want to know."

"It's a good thing!"

"Sounds…skanky."

Her giggle lured him over to kiss her, but she squirmed and swiped a hand down her cheek, which left a dirty streak in its wake. "You're all sweaty."

"You don't like me sweaty?" He rubbed at the dirt smudge he'd left on her cheek but he only managed to make it worse.

"I like you sweaty in my bed, but this is, hmm… You have wood dust all over you and dirt streaking down your chest."

"Yeah, I got some dirt on your cheek. Why don't you run in and wipe it off." He stepped back and picked up the ax, but the handle slipped through his grasp and the heavy metal blade landed right before Mireio's feet. The witch let out a peep. "Shit. Sorry. I didn't mean to…"

He grabbed the wood handle and again couldn't get a good grip around it. He flexed his fingers, working them in and out, but it was no use.

"Loss of feeling again?" she wondered. "Oh, Lars. What can I do? You should maybe quit for the day and get some—"

"No!" he shouted a little too loudly.

Mireio stepped back from him, clutching the fish

purse to her gut. It wasn't quite fear in her eyes, but concern for sure.

"Don't do that," he said with a forceful sweep of his hand between them.

"Do what? I was worried—"

"That," he said. "I don't want that from you. None of that—" he waved his hand wildly before him "—feeling sorry crap. I'm fine. It comes and it goes. I need to walk it off. Kick some logs or something."

At that moment the baby monitor blinked and the rustle of a little body kicking in his crib could be heard.

"I'll get it!" Mireio rushed out. "You're right. I'll leave you to finish up your man stuff here. I brought stew and some bread that needs to go in the oven. I set it on the step before looking for you out back. Come inside in about half an hour?"

He nodded and turned to face the woodpile while she wandered into the house. When he heard her coo over Peanut and pick him up, Lars held back an oath. He'd been mean to her just now. What was wrong with her being concerned for him?

"Everything," he muttered.

He did not want to be treated like an invalid. By anyone. Such treatment would only make his diagnosis all the more real.

He punched a weak fist into his opposite palm, hoping to feel the pain, but all he got was a brush of his knuckles against skin. He couldn't even feel the tingle in his fingers now. They felt...dead.

Setting aside Lars's anger as just that—a well-deserved reaction to the sudden awful circumstances he'd been forced to face—Mireio put the stewpot on the stove top to warm and slid a pan of dinner rolls in the oven. Soon the cabin smelled like bread, potatoes, rosemary and caramelized carrots.

"Mmm, wait until you can eat real food, Peanut." She bent before the infant she'd placed in the baby seat at the table and dangled her hair before him. He swiped at it and managed to grasp a hunk but his little fingers slipped easily because they were sticky with his saliva. The kid did like to suck on his thumb. "I wonder if you're teething? You think so? Is that right? I remember your daddy reading to you about getting your teeth right about now. You need something to chew on."

She sorted through the neat collection of toys kept in a box on the shelf next to the other baby supplies. A puppy rattle, a squeaky bunny… "Yes! A teething ring." She washed off the nubby blue silicon circle and helped the baby get a good grip on it. It went right to his mouth and he kicked his legs and cooed as a means of thanking her. "Do I know how to make my menfolk happy, or what?"

"That you do." Lars strolled in and tossed aside his work gloves. He'd kicked off his boots on the step. His chest was soaked and his face streaked with dirt. "Sorry about that out there."

"No problem. You got the feeling back in your fingers?"

"Yes. Just now. Sometimes it lingers all day. Other times it's a short while. Damn, that smells great. Do I have time for a shower?"

"You do. Me and Thor will get the table set and have everything ready for you when you get back in."

Towel in hand, he paused at the door and cast a look over his shoulder. "Thor?"

Mireio nodded encouragingly.

"Nope." He strode out, leaving the screen door swinging gently back to close.

"Yeah, I didn't think so. But it is a good Scandinavian name, don't you think?"

With great dramatics, and a devilish grin, Peanut emitted a disgusting sound that she knew signaled time for a diaper change. The kid had definitely spoken against that name.

When Lars returned, she had stew in bowls and the table was set with dinner rolls glossed with melting butter. Peanut sat with his bottle, eyelids drooping heavily and a drool of milk trickling out the corner of his mouth.

Lars kissed his son on the crop of bushy black hair, wiped the milk away and then swiped his fingers across the towel he wore wrapped about his hips.

"Do I need to get dressed for supper?" he asked as she poured them water into two mason jars.

"Well, it will be a distraction. And I haven't eaten all day."

"Just checking. Wouldn't want to distract you from nourishment. I'll pull on a shirt." He winked at her.

His mood had bounced from angry to cheery. It was because of Peanut, she knew. The man adored his son.

After putting back his second serving of stew, Lars reached for what was probably his sixth roll and spread butter across the still steaming insides. "You, witch, know how to cook."

"Why, thank you. I like conjuring up spectacular things in the kitchen and in the brewery."

"Is there anything you can't make?"

She shrugged and considered that a moment. "Tofu?"

"I'm glad about that. You know how to keep your men happy, that's for sure. Look."

Peanut was asleep in his chair, the bottle lolling out of his mouth yet still his tiny bite held the end of it.

"Aw, Connor was tired."

"Connor?"

She waited for his reaction but got merely a shrug. "Really?"

"I don't know. Sort of wussy sounding."

"Lars. You do realize if you let the poor boy keep *Peanut* that when he grows up the kids in school will call him Pee for short. And I'm not talking about the vegetable either. Do you want that?"

"Not exactly."

"And if not Pee, then he'll be Nuts. How does Nuts Gunderson sound to you?"

"I'll come up with a name. I appreciate you giving me suggestions. Keep them coming. Something will stick, sooner or later. His mom left that up to me."

"What if you ever marry?"

He paused with a chunk of dinner lodged in his cheek.

"I mean, will the mother's name always be on the birth certificate?"

"I'm pretty sure that's a given. But if I should marry someday my wife could adopt."

"That makes sense. Only you don't want her to have to adopt a Peanut."

"I'll take care of it. Just keep the suggestions coming. It's a quick change I can do with a visit to the county records office. Sunday told me that."

"So Sunday is like your secretary as well as baby-sitter?"

He stopped chewing again and narrowed his gaze at her. "Don't be jealous of her, Mireio. She's married to Dean."

"I know. I just…" She set the spoon down in her stew and pushed aside the hair from her face. "Maybe I am a little jealous. I mean…well, I'll just ask. What are we, Lars?"

"We? Uh…you mean like…"

She nodded eagerly.

His shy smile surfaced and those dimples were anything but coy. "Well, you're my girl. Right?"

"Yes," she said immediately. "I'm your girlfriend. And you're my boyfriend?"

He took another bite of the dinner roll and smiled around the chew. "I'm all in."

She couldn't prevent a gleeful clap and a wiggle on the chair. Sometimes it was hard to define whatever she had going on with a man. And men were often reluctant to commit to labels such as *boyfriend* and *girlfriend*. He really liked her. Yes! Lars Gunderson was her boyfriend.

"I never thought you'd be happy about that," Lars admitted.

"About being your girlfriend? Are you kidding me?"

He shrugged. "With all that's happened lately."

"You mean with you telling me…? Oh, Lars. Don't even go there. I'm glad we said it. I like to know what's up between us. You're mine. I'm yours. Like it or not. Do you like it?"

"More than anything."

"Good. Then no doubts. Promise?"

He nodded. "So that reminds me… Did you sleep okay last night?"

"Sure. Why?"

"I was lying awake for a bit, watching you." He dipped his head and smirked. "You're so pretty when you sleep. And your breasts were highlighted by the moon. But at one point you called out like you were having a nightmare."

"Oh." She shrugged. "Ah…it happens. I'm a witch. I've seen things that are bound to come back to haunt me. I don't remember having a nightmare last night."

"I was worried about you."

"Don't be."

Kissing him on the forehead, she took his empty bowl and cleared the rest of the dishes to the sink, where she'd already filled one side with warm soapy water. She'd had a nightmare again? Why hadn't she remembered that? Usually the nightmare woke her in a sweat and sometimes she even screamed. Always the same thing. A vampire holding a heart and grinning at her.

Shoot. She didn't want Lars to know what was up with that. The man lay awake watching her sleep? While it should seem creepy, she couldn't go there with her new adorable boyfriend. Time to look up a spell to silence the dark and disturbing dreams.

Across the room, Lars cleaned up Peanut's face and then lifted him to pat him on the back. The baby burped loudly, gave a little giggle, then promptly fell asleep.

The twosome chuckled at that, and Lars, bouncing as he walked with Peanut, kissed Mireio on the cheek. "He's my boy."

"I can't say I've seen that obnoxious side of you yet, but I am duly warned."

He strolled over to the crib, big hand smoothing across Peanut's back and stood there a while, bouncing gently. The setting sun illuminated his silhouette. Eyes closed, he looked a man at peace. Content in this world.

Sometimes he hid his emotions well, Mireio realized. And she brushed a wet hand across her eye to wipe away a nonexistent piece of fluff. Wasn't as if a tear had dropped down her cheek. Nonsense.

Rinsing the dishes while Lars tucked in Peanut, she stacked them in the rack and wiped down the counter. Lars snuck up behind her, his hands slipping up under her skirt and surprising her into a peep.

"Watching your ass wiggle while you work gets me horny." He squeezed the aforementioned body part and she pressed against his hands and wiggled slowly. "Did you have plans to eat and run or...you want to stick around and see what comes up?" He leaned into her and his erection nudged against her derriere.

"I think something is already up." She made to turn around but he caught her wrist and turned her back, placing his hand over hers on the counter. "Oh, yeah? Bring it, big boy."

He dropped the towel and flipped up the back of her skirt. His hair, still wet from the shower, fell across her back and shoulder as he fit himself between her legs and she squeezed tightly to hold him there. She wasn't quite wet, but it wasn't going to take too long...

His hand glided around to cup her breast and pinch the nipple through her shirt and bra as he dragged his erection between her clasped thighs. His wanting growl tightened her nipples and...that was all she needed. She was ready for him.

Drawing a heel along the side of his calf, she thrust up her ass, begging for his entry. His big wide hand slapped to her stomach, covering it completely, then moved down under her skirt, where he simultaneously guided himself inside her and toggled her clit at the same time.

He was so thick, a man of girth and talent with that remarkable magic wand of his. He pumped slow, allowing her to feel every inch of his entry and pull-out. Add to that the wet slickery dance of his finger over her clitoris.

Mireio grasped the faucet over the sink with one hand and pushed against the marble counter with the other, wanting to hilt him inside her. In this position she could feel him so deep. A few times he lifted her shoes from the floor as his thrusts moved her entire body, pairing them together in a bond of skin and lust and wanton need.

He bit the back of her top and tugged as he growled. "Not going to be able to hold off much longer."

"Go for it, lover. Take me hard and fast. Oh, yes!"

His hand slapped onto the counter beside hers. He held her pinned there on his cock as his body tremored and he pumped inside her. And then a gasp of relief and joy. He slipped both hands around and over her breasts and pulled her body back against his. "Inside you is where I always want to be."

Chapter 13

A few days later Lars brought in Mireio's mail when he stopped by her place. She opened a package to find the dragon exudation had arrived. Okay, so it was dragon sweat. But she couldn't imagine what it required to get such an item from the source. Did dragons sweat much? And who stood nearby to catch it? Didn't sound like a job that would offer a lengthy employment. But perhaps the death benefits for next of kin were included. Eek.

It was exciting to finally have all the ingredients that would allow her to perform the immortality spell. She tossed the bubble packing material in the garbage and before she could tuck away the vials in a drawer, Lars pointed to her closed fist that hid the ingredient.

"Is that what I think it is?" he asked.

"What do you think it is?"

"Dragon piss?"

"Eww. No, it's dragon sweat!"

"And that doesn't rate an eww? Huh. I'll never understand witches." He winked at her and the dimples joined in. "So now that you've got the secret ingredient, are you ready to go vamp hunting?"

Not as much now that she knew he was dying. "I need to study the spell a bit more and do an inventory of all the ingredients."

"Well, what if we stalk the longtooth again? I want to get out. It's a beautiful evening. Sunday's got Peanut. And afterward we can get ice cream."

"I'm in!"

As they walked the alleyway following what Lars had called "his sniffer," Mireio could only think about what neither of them dared bring up. She wanted to live forever. Lars had been given two months to live. And that count was ticking down daily. That was completely and utterly insane.

She could not do this! Especially not with him—a dying man—helping her. No question about it, she had to call it off. Now. Before it got out of hand and they actually found the vampire. She picked up her pace and just as she opened her mouth to call to Lars, his body suddenly contorted.

That did not look comfortable. Or warranted.

"Shit." Mireio rushed up and grabbed him by the arm but he twisted it out of her grip. "What is it?" He bent and slapped a hand to the brick wall of a residential garage. "Lars?"

"Shifting," he ground through his teeth. "Need to… get out of here. Can't stop…it."

"Witch's tits, this is not cool. Can you relax and let the urge pass?"

He growled at her through gritted teeth. And his hand

began to shift. The knuckles bulged and his fingers contorted.

"Right. Not in your control."

He shoved a hand in his front pocket and pulled out the keys, thrusting them at her. "Get the truck. Go home," he said. "I'll…"

"You can't run around in the city. I'll get the truck and come for you." She took off and, remembering where the truck was, veered left. "Don't howl!"

As she scampered down the alley, she heard him swear again. Turning, she saw him pull off his shirt and unzip his jeans even as his feet tore through his boots. The shift happened so quickly. He hadn't even time to undress? Pulling off one pant leg, he hissed when the other leg split down the seam. His chest expanded and his head changed. Drastically. Fur grew over his body as claws curled out from his fingers. No, not fingers…

"Paws," Mireio whispered in awe. She couldn't be afraid of him. She wasn't. He was beautiful.

But not in public. This was so bad.

Finally the fully shifted werewolf stood, slapped a paw against the wall, and sent crumbled bricks flying. Then it turned, scented her with a flare of its nostrils and took off the opposite direction.

"Oh, crap. He's on the run."

Scrambling over to gather up his clothes, Mireio then clicked down the alleyway, cursing her need to always wear high heels. Short girl problem number fifty-five. But she made it to the truck without stumbling. She climbed up into the cab and started the engine. She had no magic to stop him from shifting. Or to make him invisible to others.

Rolling down the window she heard the wolf's howl.

"No, no no. Don't do that, Lars. Someone will see you."

On second thought, the howl would help her to track him. Sliding forward and stretching on the seat so her foot could reach the gas pedal, she shifted into gear and rolled around the corner in the direction he had run. Passing half a dozen teenagers walking and biking she winced. They couldn't see him. She had to find him first.

Turning abruptly left, the tires squealed as she headed toward a dangerous shadow moving swiftly before a high hedgerow, plunked right before a row of two-story houses with their porch lights on.

"That's him!" She sped up and slammed on the brakes beside the wolf. Leaning over she opened the door. "Get in!" Please goddess, let him understand her.

The werewolf crept forward. Somewhere down the street she heard, "Hey! Look!"

And in the next instant, Lars jumped into the front seat, and she took off without worrying that the door swung wide and probably her boyfriend in shifted form had no clue or idea how to pull it closed. Turning left again, she made it a sharp fast turn, and the door slammed shut.

The wolf yipped. Its big furry head bowed forward to fit his bulk inside the cab. Its toothy maw opened, drool dripping, and it barked at her.

"Dude, do not give me the sassy bark. I'm your girlfriend! Mireio. Friend." She reached for him but when he snapped at her she retracted. "Okay, stay in the truck and I'll get you home as quickly as possible."

Ahead, a well-lit intersection advertised flashing red and blue lights and another set of bright headlights aimed skyward. A car accident? The last thing she needed was to pass the police with a werewolf sitting in the passenger seat.

"Duck," she said, but he obviously didn't understand her speech.

The wolf suddenly shoved the steering wheel with a paw and Mireio focused back on the road. She'd narrowly avoided colliding with a parked car. Had Lars not done what he had, they would have crashed.

"Shit. Stop panicking, Mireio. This is just another night out on the town with your big handsome wolf. Relax. Smile at the cops as you drive by."

She gave a little wave as an officer ducked his head and appeared to look through and to the opposite side where she sat. Passing slowly, when she cleared the scene she stopped at a light and turned to Lars.

A naked human man sat on the seat, his head bowed and caught against a palm. Werewolves shifted so quickly, but she wasn't startled.

"Lars?"

"Drive!"

"Yes. Drive. I am driving." The light turned green and she slid forward again to reach the accelerator and headed back to his place.

Reaching over and under the front of her seat, Lars adjusted the seat forward so she could reach the pedals without having to skooch up to get close enough.

He picked up the clothes she'd tossed on the floor and pressed them onto his lap but didn't move or speak to her again. When she pulled up to his cabin, he hopped out of the truck and slammed the door behind him. The naked man stalked up to the front door and disappeared inside.

Mireio turned off the ignition and the lights. Her car was parked beside a weeping willow tree. She could drive home and leave him to sulk. Was he embarrassed? Probably at a loss as to why he was shifting without volition. The man was in pain, and he needed someone to hold him.

Would he let her in?

Hopping out of the truck, she swung her purse over a shoulder and stepped up to the threshold before the cabin. No lights on inside. She lifted her hand to knock, but couldn't do it.

Moonlight glinted on her silver rings. She touched the larimar crystal entwined within a platinum wire-wrap, wishing she had a water spell to make him feel better. A bath always made her feel better after a rough day.

She wouldn't be so stupid as to suggest a bath to soak away his insurmountable worries. And Lars's days would only get worse. He had to be careful if the shift were to again attack without his volition. Perhaps stop going near humans.

Sighing, she turned away from the door. And then heard him call from inside, "Come in. Please."

She entered the cabin quietly, seeming to walk on the balls of her feet so her heels wouldn't click too loudly. She stood there, acclimating to the darkness.

Lars lay on the bed, curled in on himself. The shift had come on him so suddenly that he couldn't stop it. He'd felt so helpless. Yet, thankfully, even in werewolf shape he'd recognized the truck and known she'd wanted him to get in. He'd felt small and defeated as she'd driven him home. Shifting back to were shape beside her, he had felt more naked than when he stood before her when making love to her. Exposed and wretched.

He still didn't want to talk. But he did need to feel her against him. Mireio was his safe place.

He stretched out an arm and she walked over to take his hand. "Stay?" he asked.

She kicked off her shoes and climbed onto the bed and cuddled up against him. Kissing his forehead, she then pulled his hand up to her mouth and held it there, her lips sealing warmth onto his skin.

"Sleep," she said. "I'm here."

Chapter 14

Mireio stayed at the cabin to make breakfast for Lars while he went for a morning run to pick up Peanut from the compound and bring him home for Mireio to feed a bottle.

He immediately headed out again, feeling he'd not spent enough time outside and mostly because he still didn't know what to say to her about what had happened last night. He felt like a failure. A werewolf who couldn't control his own shifts? There were no curse words strong enough for that one.

Tracking through the woods on the path he'd beaten down over years of running—both in his were, or man, shape and wolf shape—he suddenly realized the moon had been very round last night. It must be close to the full moon. Well, he knew it was. He'd been horny as hell lately. Of course, he had good reason with such a gorgeous witch as his girlfriend.

He smiled at that. He had a girlfriend. And life was good when he was with her. But if the moon reached fullness tonight or tomorrow, that meant he'd have to let out his werewolf, no matter what. Had it been full last night? Was that why he'd shifted? No, it hadn't felt like the moon pull shift. That moment in the alleyway he'd been completely out of control of his body. A passenger who hadn't signed up for the wild ride.

Stopping and bending forward to catch his hands on his knees, he panted. A lot. Normally his casual jog didn't wind him so much. He wasn't going to consider that he was growing weaker. It wasn't right.

"Screw this." He turned and raced down the path toward the cabin, pushing full speed and pumping his arms.

Five minutes later he wandered to the back of the cabin, wheezing and coughing. He sat on the log splitting stump and hung his head. If he was going to die, he wished for it to happen quickly. No long endless days of suffering. Or to be bedridden?

"No, please…no."

He'd never imagined that death could be humiliating, but if he were reduced to a feeble invalid, that would be the worst possible condition. He wasn't sure he could face that.

But he would. He had to. For Peanut. And his girlfriend.

Suddenly a bee landed on the ground right beside his bare foot. Its wings buzzed but its furred body was slick with wet.

"Poor guy." He bent to gently stroke the tips of the bee's wings. "All tuckered out after a morning dew bath? I know the feeling."

He turned his hand palm up and nudged it beside the bee. The insect climbed onto his hand and sat there, content to soak up Lars's innate warmth.

He lifted his hand and studied the bee. Its big black eyes took him in, antennae flickering. "You live such a short lifetime, and yet you accomplish so much. You, my sweet little worker bee, are remarkable." He closed his eyes and shook his head. "What have I accomplished?"

Nothing of significance came to mind.

Standing, he padded over to the hive, his passenger still in for the ride. He set his hand at the entrance and waited until the bee climbed off and into the hive. There she would be warmed by hundreds of her fellow worker bees and then could return to collecting pollen. Accomplishing so much.

Did he have to leave a mark on the world before he left? He wanted... He wanted so much for his son that he might never be able to give him. Mercy. What would become of Peanut when he was gone?

"Lars?"

Mireio walked around the side of the cabin. He sucked in his winded breaths and gave her a nod.

She carried a wide-eyed Peanut, who chewed on the teething ring. "I'm sorry, but I forgot to mention last night that I need to go in early this morning. I'm brewing some IPA. I left breakfast for you on the table. Peanut has had a bottle and he's burped. Loudly." She handed the baby to him and he reached for him, but knew he wouldn't be able to hold him securely. His fingers tingled, as did his feet.

"Could you bring him in and lay him in the crib for a nap?" he asked.

She assessed him momentarily, then nodded. "Of course. You going to be able to eat?" she called back as she made haste toward the cabin door.

"I sure hope so," he muttered, forcing himself to walk. The going was slow. With every step the sensation in his feet decreased. But he made it to the front door, where Mireio kissed him quickly. She was acting brisk and he sensed she was in a hurry.

"Your fingers again?" she asked.

"And my feet." He nodded. "I'll be fine."

"I know you will. Call me if you need anything. Can I come over after work?"

"I'd like that. Uh, but, Mireio, what day is it? I mean, do you know when the moon is full?"

"Tomorrow!" she offered gleefully. "I know you wolves shift on the night of the full moon."

"Sometimes the day before and after too. I'm going to shift tonight. Or I'd like to."

"Does that mean I get to watch Peanut? Because I'd love to."

"I'd appreciate that." He kissed her, but didn't lift his now completely numb hand to touch her.

"See you later. Remember to call if you need anything!" She wandered over to her car and turned it around and drove down the winding drive.

And Lars fell to sit on the threshold because he could no longer stand on feet he could not feel.

Around four in the afternoon Mireio popped her head up from cleaning the stainless-steel brew tank and waved as Valor strolled in. The brewery didn't open until five, and Valor had the night shift.

"Here to help," Valor called as she tossed her backpack behind the bar and leaned over the sink, plunging her hands into the soapy water.

"I appreciate it when you come in early to help clean. You know Geneva would never think of doing such a thing."

"Well, hey, my hands are covered in motor grease so I figured all this sanitizing solution will cut that and get me clean in the process."

"Just don't get it on the parts," Mireio warned as she decided the tank was clean, and she could now move on to disconnecting the remaining hoses that led from tank to tank and run those through the wash. She really should concoct a spell to automate the process, but she felt the equipment got cleaner when it was hand washed, not…spell washed.

Valor's long chestnut hair, streaked with blue of late, was queued back in a loose ponytail. She wore combat boots, short jeans cutoffs, a Decadent Dames T-shirt and strands of talismans hung from leather cords about her neck. She was the tomboy of the group and generally did the heavy lifting and liked to close.

Mireio joined her at the sinks and started rinsing the items Valor had washed. They were stainless-steel clamps and rings and assorted parts she broke down and cleaned after every brew. The cleaning part was the most tedious, but with a helping hand things went quick enough.

"So I hear you've got a new man," Valor said. "A wolf?"

"Yes, Lars Gunderson."

"Yeah, Sunday told me about you two. I've spoken to him a time or two when I needed help with my bees. Very quiet. But man, is he a big one, and sexy."

"He's almost twice the size of me, and I adore every inch of him."

"Cool. So you two getting serious? Because I know that Sunday babysits for him. A single father? That's gotta make for some interesting dates."

"The two of us serious? I hope so. I really like him,

Valor. And the baby thing doesn't bother me at all. You know how much I love kids."

"You do, but that doesn't mean you have to become the kid's mom."

"I didn't say I was going to do that. But a man with a baby is not a deal breaker. You would be amazed at what a kind and gentle dad Lars is. So attentive to Peanut."

Valor chuckled. "I can't get over that name. Every time Sunday mentions him I laugh."

"The mother didn't give the baby a name."

"Crazy. You know how all this affects Sunday, don't you?"

Mireio held a dripping clamp over the water. Other than knowing the facts about cats and wolves mating, she hadn't thought beyond that. "Why? Did she and Lars have a thing? I thought she and Dean had been married awhile?"

"It's the baby thing. Cat shifters can't have werewolf babies. Just isn't possible."

"I know that."

"So Sunday will never be able to have Dean's children. And even though she acts like it's no big thing, she wants a baby. So while she loves babysitting, it also tears her apart having to hand that kid back over to Lars. And now you."

"Oh, no. Did she say something about me? Is she… jealous of me? I'm not trying to be the baby's mom. But, well, Sunday shouldn't be either."

"Yeah, I know. It's her little weirdness she needs to work out. So don't take it wrong if she acts strange around you, okay?"

"I won't. I'll try not to. But could they adopt?"

"They had considered asking Lars about adopting the boy. But Sunday quickly realized that would have been awkward to the nines. Both men in the same pack and someone else raising his kid?"

"Lars would have never let that happen. He's in love with Peanut. He'll raise him alone no matter what—oh, my goddess."

"What?"

"I hadn't given the baby's future a thought. Oh. What's he going to do now about Peanut?"

"Mireio, you're freaking me out. And you're shaking." She took a heavy steel ring from her and set it aside. "What's up?"

"Oh, Valor." Mireio turned and leaned her hips against the sink, pushing the hair from her face. "Lars has this thing. A werewolf disease. It's rare. Hereditary. His dad died from it. The doctor gave him only a few months to live."

"Whoa. And you're getting involved in all this? I know you like to take care of people and are compassionate, but are you sure about this, sweetie?"

"I am." And she was. "But what will happen to Peanut if Lars were to die?"

"Then Sunday and Dean could adopt him."

"Oh, my goddess, what am I saying? I don't want him to die." She turned and gripped the edge of the sink.

"Oh…uh…hmm…" Valor spread an arm across Mireio's back. Of the witchy quartet, she was the least comfortable with hugging and had always claimed she didn't have much empathy.

"He's so young, you know? This isn't fair. And he's just gotten this beautiful little baby that makes him happy. I know it's what puts the smile on his face every day. Here I've been sad because he has to go through something like this. But I didn't consider the struggle he must be facing knowing he may not be around to watch his son grow up. He can't die, Valor. He can't!"

She turned and hugged her friend. Even as she sensed Valor's initial reluctance, Vaolr soon returned the hug and smoothed a wet hand across Mireio's back.

"What did the doctor say?" Valor asked. "Can he take something for it? Is it like cancer? Can he do chemo or radiation?"

"No, it's degenerative. No pills or chemicals can stop it. He's got neuropathy and he loses feeling in his hands and feet. And last night he shifted without volition. He can't control his werewolf. It scares him. It scares me. I want to be there for him. But I feel so helpless. This morning I wanted to wrap him in my arms and tell him it was going to be all right, but I could sense he didn't want that from me, so I tried to do the nonchalant thing. He puts on this stoic werewolf act. I'm tough. Don't treat me like an invalid. How can I help him?"

"Have you tried healing him?"

Mireio pulled away from Valor. "You know I'm not a healer. I wouldn't have the skill or the power."

"Well, neither am I. But I have been known to bring a drowned faery back to life with my pitiful healing skills. And what if we combined our powers? Geneva is a master healer. I know we witches can't give back life or raise the dead, but…he's not dead yet. Maybe we could infuse Lars with some life-sustaining magic?"

"Oh, my goddess, I think it would be worth a try. But Eryss is in California now."

"As long as we have a triad, we're good."

"Right! Oh, I wonder if Lars would let us try?"

"Ask him. I mean, sure he's putting up a front, trying to act all tough and cool. But you gotta think the man would be desperate to try anything to stay alive."

"I'll ask him. Oh, he has to agree to it. I'm not sure if it'll work, but we can't not try, right?"

"I'm in," Valor confirmed with a fist bump to Mireio's wet fist. "And I'll make sure Geneva won't say no. Just let us know when you need us."

Mireio hugged her again. "I love you. Thank you!"

"Sure, but chill on the hugs, will you? I think I got enough hugging to last me a year now."

Mireio hadn't had much time for baking lately, so after picking up some things for supper to make at Lars's place, she stopped into a local sweet shop near the brewery and, after much debating over the triple chocolate bomb and the cherry pistachio cream delight, she went with the chocolate. It was a small cake, but it would serve the two of them. Or rather, it would serve a big hungry wolf, and offer enough for a taste for his girlfriend.

When she arrived at Lars's cabin, he met her at the door and grabbed the bags she was carrying, only kissing her quickly. He set the bags on the counter and started unpacking them. "I didn't expect you this early."

It was after six. She couldn't determine if he was angry or busy. "I usually finish up at the brewery around three or four. Valor stopped in to help me clean today. Where's...oh, there you are, Peanut."

The baby lay on a blanket before the couch beneath the bright plastic toddler gym. He kicked his legs eagerly when she sat next to him and tugged one of his toes. "You look so happy! Were you and Daddy playing before I got here?"

"He just got up from a nap," Lars offered over his shoulder. He had unpacked all the groceries and now seemed a little too concerned over the food, remaining by the counter with his back to her.

Mireio kissed the baby's exposed belly. "You're a little tub, you know that? A little tub! What do you say to that, Loki?"

She waited for Lars to react, but he was studying the red pepper she'd brought for the enchiladas.

"So that's a good one?" she asked, again waiting for a reply. "Lars?"

"What's that?"

She got up and walked over to the counter and he grabbed the onion and opened the fridge door. "Do you like the name Loki? Lars? What's up with you? Is everything all right?"

"It's fine." He finally turned and, even with the hair falling over the side of his face, she noticed the red streak by his eye. "I'll maybe take Peanut out for a walk while you make supper."

"Wait." She stepped in front of him, forcing him to look at her. The red mark was actually a cut and it looked new. "When did you cut yourself? Right before I got here?" Because she knew werewolves healed quickly, sometimes almost instantaneously.

"Mireio, I said it was nothing."

She grabbed his hands and did not back down. Without saying a word, she peered behind the shadows in his gaze and coaxed up the truth.

"Fine. I…might have fainted right before you got here. I came to right away. So like I said. Nothing." He tugged out of her grip and stomped over to collect Peanut.

"Nothing? Lars, you fainted? What if you had been holding Peanut?"

"I wasn't." He turned with an air of anger darkening his expression. "It's happened twice now, and I know that right before it happens I get a weird feeling of dread. So if it ever happens when I'm holding Peanut, I'll set him in the crib."

She put a hand to her hip. That was an utterly ridiculous defense and he knew it. But if she pressed him, she would only push him away. So she forced herself to nod. "I get it. No big deal. You've got everything under control. Why don't you give me half an hour to get supper ready? Are the two of you going far?" She realized what he'd think of that question only after it had come out.

"Just out back." He grabbed the baby sling, fitted Peanut against his chest, and headed outside.

And Mireio finally let the teardrop fall that had been threatening since she'd realized Lars had fallen and hurt himself. Had he been holding Peanut at the time, the baby could have gotten hurt too. Was the man degenerating so quickly? Did he need someone around to watch him? A caregiver?

Heartbeats thumping, she pressed a fist over her chest and shook her head. She would be that caregiver if he asked. But she knew he would never ask. And she didn't want to make the man feel more helpless than he likely already did.

Navigating Lars's right to privacy and need to ignore his disease was a tough situation. And it would only grow more difficult.

Could she do this?

After supper Lars helped Mireio wash the dishes then, after she'd folded the drying towels over the sink, he took her in his arms and hugged her. "Sorry," he said. "It's how I'm dealing with this…stuff. For now."

"I get it. But allow me to stumble as I'm dealing with it too?"

"Of course. I'll try not to be such an asshole from now on."

"No, you've every right. I mean, not to be an asshole, but to be as unsure about how to deal with your feelings as any man would be. I can take it. I'm a big girl."

He squeezed her hand, then smiled. Just a little. "A big girl?" His eyes focused on her chest. "That you are."

"Oh! I have a surprise for you. For us, actually. We'll need two forks." She grabbed the bag she'd left by the door because it hadn't needed to go in the fridge and pulled out the white bakery box. "I didn't make this, but I know it'll be good. It's called triple chocolate decadence."

He held up two forks. "Deal me in."

Mireio sat on the couch, before which Peanut lay on the floor on his stomach. She opened the box and the sides folded down to make a plate. Lars sat next to her and kept both forks.

"This looks like mine," he said taking the makeshift plate from her. "Where's yours?"

"I only want a few bites. I think there's enough sugar in there to keep me awake for two days."

He forked the first bite and then turned to feed the next bite to her. The soft chocolate frosting melted on her tongue and she groaned.

"That good?" he asked.

She nodded. "But not better than sex."

He tried a few more bites and nodded in agreement. "But very good."

On the floor, Peanut suddenly rolled to his back and kicked his legs and arms.

"Hey! He's getting good at that," Lars said. "He'll be crawling soon. Probably before the book says he will. My kid is smart."

Mireio dashed her finger through the frosting and leaned over the baby. "Let's see if he likes chocolate."

"Wait!" He grabbed her wrist. "I don't know. He's not on solid food yet."

"I'm just going to put a little on his tongue. Let him taste. Okay?"

He considered it and she almost sat up and licked it off herself, but then he said, "Sure. A taste can't hurt."

"You're very protective of him." She touched her finger to Peanut's mouth and the baby tongued at it. "I like that about you. So fierce in everything you do, be it chopping wood, helping me to track a vampire or taking care of your boy."

He tilted his head against her shoulder and gazed up at her. "You forgot sex."

"No, that was next on my list. You are a fierce lover." She bent to kiss him and he dashed out his tongue to touch hers, giving her the sweet lush chocolate heat. "Mmm… More of that, please."

He peeled off some frosting with his fork and when she thought he would feed it to her, he dashed it across her lips, smearing them with chocolate. And he quickly followed with a kiss that devoured her more thoroughly than cake.

But the baby cooing at their feet lured them both forward to find Peanut bright-eyed and giggling.

"I think he wants more," she said.

"You've created a monster."

"So he really does take after his dad?" She nudged him with a teasing elbow. "I mean that in the nicest way."

"I'd better get him a bottle. He might go down early tonight. We did a lot of work out back today."

"Is that so?" Mireio picked up the baby, bummed that

Lars had taken the cake with him to the fridge. She wiped a smear of chocolate from Peanut's mouth. "What did you and Daddy do today? Did you build something?"

"I finally got a building permit for the plans I handed in to the city. Soon as I get materials, I can start on the addition to the back of the cabin." Lars forked in another bite of cake while he set the bottle in the pot on the stove. Then he picked up the last piece with his fingers and ate it all. "You're right. That cake will have me flying high. Good thing I plan to stay up tonight."

"So tell me what happens when you wolf out under the full moon? I know you wolves have to do it. It's innate. But what do you do? Where do you go? Is there a werewolf party I'm unaware of?"

He laughed and joined her on the couch. When he held out his arms for Peanut she handed him over, knowing she'd have another chance later before bed to sit and feed him. The baby fit against Lars as if there were no other place he belonged. Truly Daddy's boy.

Once Peanut started to drink, Lars flipped his long hair over his shoulder and sat back. Noticing his eye where the cut had been, she touched it. "It's almost gone. Just a faint line now."

"Normally that would have healed within minutes. I'm hoping getting my wolf on tonight will restore my fading strength. Maybe that's all I need? To wolf out and race toward the moon?"

"Or toward a party?"

"There's no party. We werewolves need to answer the call to the moon once a month or we get really fucked up inside. Our bodies need the shift. So we run and race and sometimes even catch small animals."

"Seriously? Oh, I don't want to know."

"Then I won't give you details. Once in a while Dean

and I run into one another and we have a good tussle and then race along the hill. We can run for miles and miles without worry of getting close to humans. It's why the compound is way out here."

"You tussle? So you have a werewolf fight?"

"Yep. Sometimes I win, sometimes he does. It doesn't get too nasty. And we always see each other the next day and bump fists. It's our nature. We need that. Like what about you witches? You must have something that you absolutely need to do in order to live and exist?"

"Practicing our magic. Not letting it go stale. And…" She sighed.

"What? Tell me?"

"It's just… I can't."

"You want to live forever. Who doesn't?"

"I do, but some people aren't given that chance. I'm so selfish."

"Hey." He kissed her but with Peanut in his arms it was only a brush of his mouth over hers. Always delicious, though. "It's what you want. It's what you need. Don't apologize for that." In his arms the baby burped, and that ended the serious portion of their conversation.

And Mireio was thankful for that. "When are you going out?"

"In a couple hours. I like the sky to get really dark."

"Despite the moonlight?"

"Exactly." He stood and bounced as he patted Peanut's back, mining for another release of gas. "I'd ask if you want to watch some TV before I go out, but I don't have one. So that leaves sex."

"Hmm…" She tapped her lips, making a show of giving it some good thought. "I suppose I could manage that."

"You suppose?" He spun on her with a smiling gape

on his face. "Well, if you're going to be that way." He turned and bounced Peanut over to the crib.

Mireio stood and pulled her shirt off as she walked over to the bed. She slipped off her skirt and climbed onto the bed before Lars had turned around. And when he did, she pushed up the girls in her bra and winked at him.

Chapter 15

Making love with a baby lying not six feet away from their embrace didn't bother Mireio. Why should it? Peanut was asleep. Parents across the world had been doing it forever. Not that she considered herself a parent, but it was hard not to feel parenty when around Peanut.

But right now, she felt like a lush, desirable woman as Lars, hands to the bed beside her shoulders and beard brushing her bare breasts, thrust inside her slowly. His eyes were closed in bliss. They'd both come once together. Now the slow and steady, stay together as long as possible, was happening.

His tense abs gleamed with the moonlight beaming through the window and onto the side of the bed, and she wondered if they might have had too much sex. Because on the night before and after the full moon, some werewolves chose not to shift. One day during the month was enough. But in order to keep back that urge to shift they had to have sex until they were sated. Lars seemed insatiable.

"What are you thinking about?" he asked. "You've got this curly smile on your face like you know more than everyone else."

She pulled his hips toward her, urging his motions to speed up. "I was thinking how much you love sex. And how much I love having sex with you. But is this too much? Will you be able to shift later?"

"I'm already feeling the pull to shift. Don't worry, it'll happen. Just a little longer, please?" He bowed his head and nuzzled his beard across her nipple. "I like being inside you."

"I like your big, thick cock making itself right at home. Stay there always?"

"As long as I can, lover. But I'm almost there…"

She put her hands to his forearms, which tensed and the veins bulged as he neared orgasm. Fashioned of steel and suede, this man. So sexy. And he smelled like chocolate and sex. Yet when he slammed his hips to hers and she awaited his climax, he suddenly pulled out.

He kissed her mouth and then rolled off the bed. "I gotta go. I'm feeling it."

"But you didn't come."

"Can't. Or rather, won't. Gotta save my energy for the shift."

"Do you want me to wait up?"

"No, I should be out all night. Make sure Peanut gets another nip in an hour?"

"I will." She watched him stroll to the door, naked. Of course, he didn't need clothes. "You don't even bring along a towel or something?"

"Why?" He spread his arms, giving her a good long view of his physique. The muscles were steel, and his hard cock jutted upright. "I usually keep extra towels out in the bathroom. I can get dirty loping through the woods. Promise to shower before I come back in. See you in the morning." He blew her a kiss, then left the cabin.

Mireio sat up on the bed and realized Peanut was lying awake in the crib. "He's pretty awesome, your daddy. You're one lucky baby."

Peanut giggled and kicked his legs in response.

Lars leaned against the huge oak trunk where he had established a sort of base for his moonlight outings. He'd been standing here for—hell, he didn't know how much time had passed, but it felt like an hour. A raccoon family had wandered past him, casting him shifty looks with their night-mirrored eyes. He growled at them, and they scrambled off.

He panted and shook his fingers and stomped his feet. The neuropathy wasn't rearing up, but he couldn't shift. What the hell? Normally the process was a seamless, minimally painful flow from human shape into werewolf shape. He'd done it hundreds of times since that first shift when he'd been a thirteen-year-old boy living with his adopted parents, Ridge and Abigail, at the compound. Shifting wasn't even a second-nature thing. It *was* his nature.

So why couldn't he do it now?

Had Mireio been right? Had he had too much sex?

That had to be it.

"Shoot." He kicked the grassy forest floor with his bare foot.

He still had the night of the full moon. So tomorrow night he'd try again. And he'd have to keep his hands off Mireio to ensure nothing went wrong next time.

"That'll be a challenge," he said as he turned to march back to the cabin.

Ten minutes later, Mireio muttered a sleepy "Really?" She lay in bed, naked, the sheets not covering her beautiful breasts. Lars had checked on Peanut. Sleeping soundly in the crib. "You couldn't…?"

"You were right," he said as he slipped between the sheets beside her. But he didn't snuggle up close. "I had too much sex. I'm going cold turkey until after the shift tomorrow night. You okay with that?"

"Sure."

He kissed her forehead quickly, cautious not to touch her tempting breasts, then turned his back to her. When her fingers teased at his hip, he wiggled and scooted closer to the edge of the bed.

"Right," she said on a yawn. "Touch not the wolf. See you—" Yawn… "—in the morning."

The next night Mireio handed off Peanut to Lars, who wanted to tuck his son in before he went out to howl at the moon. There was something about the sight of a big, burly man rocking a little nugget of baby hugged against his chest and clutching his beard with chubby little fingers that made her ovaries quiver. Oh, mercy, she had it bad for the man and the baby. And the beard.

After Peanut was down, Lars kissed her. "We going to make another date to do some vamp hunting soon?"

"Uh, sure. But I'm still working on memorizing the spell. No rush."

"I made a promise to you, Mireio. I will help you with the vampire. Just tell me when we're good to go."

She gave him a thumbs-up, and kissed him at the door. He'd not taken off his clothes in preparation to go out and shift. Because he didn't want getting naked to make him even hornier than he was.

"See you in the morning," he said and slipped out the door.

Tilting a hip against the doorframe, she watched him stride away and around the back of the cabin.

"The vampire," she muttered. "I don't think I can do it anymore. How can I? I can't be so selfish. To ask a dying man to help me gain immortality?" She shook her head and sniffed back a tear. "I can't do it. But I still want that vampire dead. By the goddess, what am I going to do?"

Around eleven, Mireio checked on Peanut. He'd been fussy after Lars had laid him down, but after carefully sliding her finger inside his mouth she'd felt the edge of a tooth he'd been working on for days. So the fuss had been well-earned. She hadn't minded rocking and walking with him a little longer. Now she fluttered her fingers over his wild crop of black hair. So soft. She wondered if that's how wolf cubs' fur felt when they were little? Natural wolves, that is.

Werewolves gave birth to a human and the child was never actually a cub. They didn't have their first shift until puberty. What if Lars's son only ever remained human? With a human mother it was possible. Would it be a disappointment to the man? She couldn't imagine anything about Peanut upsetting Lars. The two had already bonded. No matter what the future brought...

She winced, realizing how far she'd let her thoughts wander. Lars would never live to see his son experience his first shift. Maybe?

Could the doctor be wrong? So what if Lars did have some crazy mean disease. Maybe the degeneration part wouldn't happen so fast as the doc expected? A few months? She'd known him almost a month. Time was moving too quickly. He had to have longer than that. And by all appearances he looked healthy. A strapping, fine man. What man could ever know when another would breathe his last breath? People, no matter if they were human or paranormal, had no such powers. And to believe such a proclamation to death would only make it real.

"Bastard," she muttered about the doctor. "He shouldn't have given him an expiration date." She could only imagine it must occupy his thoughts constantly. And it clawed at her insides that her proud man had been given a dark ending to a story she had only begun to create with him.

Tiptoeing over to the sink so as not to wake the sleeping baby, she quietly rinsed out the bottle and set it on the drying rack. Lars lived such a stark, simple life. No modern conveniences like a television or microwave or even a computer. He did have a cell phone, but she wondered about the Wi-Fi reception up here.

Not feeling tired, she decided to sit out on the front stoop for a while and listen to the crickets chirp. A blessing for the insects, and Lars's bees, would cap off the night perfectly. But when she opened the screen door she found Lars sitting there, a towel wrapped about his hips, head bowed and hair concealing the side of his face.

She sat next to him and hugged up to his shoulder. "Did you have a good run? I thought you were going to be out all night?"

When he didn't answer, her mind jumped to what could be the only reason he was not racing through the woods free and wild right now. "Oh, goddess. Again? You couldn't…?"

She tilted her head against his shoulder and rubbed his

forearm. And he reacted by wrapping an arm around her and pulling her in tightly against his bare torso.

"It's crazy," he said on a whisper. "I've never felt so… incapable. So small. This is not me, Mireio. How do I stop this? I don't want to…"

She tightened her lips as they wobbled. Tears heated the corners of her eyes. This big strong man was being reduced to something lesser, and he was struggling. He was trying to fight back, but how to defeat the inevitable?

"How's Peanut?"

"Sleeping like an angel," she said bravely.

"You don't have to stay if you don't want to."

Hurt that he'd suggest such a thing, she had to mark it off as his feeling badly for not having shifted. Again.

"I want to stay with you, lover. Always. I want to climb in bed beside you and feel your skin against mine." She leaned forward and caught his gaze. Moonlight gleamed in his pupils. Only there did the moon possess him.

"When you look at me like that," he said, "you make me feel like a man. Like you've never seen me with baby spittle on my shirt. Or raging because I'm frustrated. Or even down because of…this. You make me feel sexy, Mireio. And whole. You make me want to live."

She touched his mouth then, feeling the quiver of his struggle. Moving around in front of him on the step, she slid between his legs and gave him the gaze that made him feel like the world.

"You are a man," she said. "You are my man. You are strong and proud. You are so patient and flexible. Kind and wise. You make me feel protected."

"Will you…" He glanced aside, and she stroked his hair over an ear. But he couldn't look back up at her. "Will you stay with me…for all of this?"

Tears spilled down her cheek and she nodded, knowing exactly what he was asking of her. She would never abandon him. The idea was inconceivable to her. He needed her. He needed a hand to hold his. Someone by his side, for good and for ill.

"You don't have to ask," she said. "I'm here, Lars." She took his hand and placed it over her heart. "And you are here."

He bowed against her, cheek brushing hers and head landing on her shoulder. And she held him while the crickets chirped cautiously and the moon continued to taunt at its trick against the werewolf.

Chapter 16

The morning was no better to him than the night had been. Lars woke hugging his allotted eight inches of bed and rolled off, glancing over to spy on Mireio, who had claimed her usual queen's portion of the bed. He had to smile at that. But when he straightened to stand, his back tweaked. He winced. Wandering over to the stove to put on a pot of coffee, he even felt the arches of his feet ache. It was as if he'd climbed a mountain wearing poor equipment.

He stretched up his arms and did a few twists. Man, he felt exhausted.

Coffee. He needed plenty. He flicked on the burner and put on a kettle of water, then noticed that Peanut stirred in the crib. He walked over, feeling as if he were an old man struggling against aging muscles, and looked over his smiling son. The kid never woke grumpy. Always that bright smile. So happy to be found, even though

Lars suspected his diaper was mush. Which, when he thought about it, was the likely reason for his glee at finally being noticed.

Grabbing a clean diaper, and lifting Peanut, he wandered over to the blanket still spread on the floor before the couch. When he bent, his back again tweaked and he stumbled forward. One hand slapped the couch and he just managed to tug up Peanut to his chest like a football and roll to his side before he hit the floor. The baby giggled, but Lars squeezed his eyelids tight. That could have been a nasty spill.

He glanced over to the bed. Still sleeping. She hadn't seen his mishap.

"Your old man is feeling his thirty years today, Peanut," he whispered as he changed the infant's diaper. "I sure hope whatever it is I have, I didn't pass it along to you. Whatever you do? Live life. Don't waste a moment, okay? Make memories and…"

He glanced over to the bed again. "And…yes. Make memories all the time. Don't let death beat you to the end. Race that fucker."

With a determined nod, he knelt, fighting the pull of his sore muscles as he arranged Peanut under the baby gym. "I'm going to tilt back some coffee, then we're going to make some memories today. What do you think of that?"

Peanut kicked his legs vigorously and his fist pumped.

"That's what I thought. Good idea, right? How are you taking your milk this morning? Fresh from the fridge or with a splash of warm water in it? You know that cold stuff puts the hair on your chest? It does."

He wandered to the stove to check the kettle, which was already at a low boil. All he had left was some instant coffee, but that would serve. Stirring up the brew, he sipped. Heat trickled down his throat and warmed his gut.

What to do today that he'd always wanted to do? He had never been a man of great and wild dreams. He lived a simple life; he took the days as they came to him.

But life as he knew it had changed. And he wasn't going to sit around and let his body fall apart and then suddenly drop dead. He needed to grab life and enjoy it.

"Kayaking," he decided. Dean had a couple yaks stored in the compound shed and he'd wanted Lars to try them out. "I'll give Sunday a call and ask her to watch the babe."

The lake was smooth as glass, for the wind had taken the day off. Mireio skimmed her fingers in the water, drawing up the energy and feeling it invigorate her entire system. As a water witch she drew her power from the wild vibrations humming in the lake. Felt like a jolt of vitamin B straight to the cortex.

She'd worn her swimsuit beneath a life vest and almost felt compelled to jump off the kayak and into the dark depths, but Lars was paddling quickly and it was all she could do to keep up with him.

"Slow down!" she shouted to the wolf, who stabbed an oar into the water to spin himself to face her. "I need to enjoy this," she said. "Or are we still participating in the race portion of the event?"

He chuckled and paddled up to her, gripping the edge of her kayak to hold them together. "Sorry. Got carried away. You going in for a swim, Miss Mermaid?"

"When we get closer to shore. I brought my phone along, so I don't want to lose it if I dive in." She clicked a few shots of him with the camera. The man's smile was easy. And those dimples were worth a thousand flashes.

"This lake is beautiful. I've never been here before. And we have it all to ourselves!"

Lars laid the oar across his kayak and leaned in. She met him with a kiss. "Wow, that one zinged me."

"Yeah? I'm in my element here on the lake."

"So what would sex with you be like in the water?"

"I do have a very large tub at home that will fit two people."

"Challenge accepted," he said.

And then she remembered that maybe she could beat him at a race.

"Race you to the shore?" She pointed to the distant shore that must be a good three or four hundred yards away.

"So now you want to race?" He eyed her curiously. "No magic involved?"

She pouted.

"All right. Let's see what the witch can do. But I get a head start."

"Go for it."

As he turned around and began to paddle off, Mireio pressed her palms to the water's surface on each side of the kayak. Calling on the water elementals and summoning a swift wind from the depths of the forest edging the lake, the kayak soared forward. Quickly. It took only a few seconds to catch up to Lars, and pass him by.

She waved and blew him a kiss. Arms spread out she tilted back her head as the rush of air breezed over her face and blew back her hair. Headed straight for shore, behind her she heard Lars cheer for her.

The kayak docked softly in the sand and she pushed it up and set her phone on her bag, which contained a towel and dry clothes. Instead of getting dressed, she waded into the water and dove, swimming out to meet

Lars, still fifty feet off. She surfaced near his kayak and treaded water.

"Sing to me, mermaid," he said, setting his oar aside.

"You know if I sing to you, you'll become enchanted and fall in. Then I'll kiss you and drag you to the depths."

"Sounds like a sweet way to go." He bent to kiss her.

But Mireio suddenly realized what she'd just implied. That she could drown him. Why had she said such a cruel thing? The last thing they should talk about was death.

Lars opened his eyes, still waiting for her kiss.

She tapped his lips with a wet fingertip, then pushed away from the kayak, swimming on her back. "Race you to shore!"

He beat her this time, though only by a hair. But he was cheating, not even paddling very much. She met him in the sand as he dragged up the kayak and only then did she feel okay to kiss him. Away from the depths.

He lifted her and she wrapped her legs about his hips, keeping the kiss. Their connection always started easy, then picked up to a deep and delving intimacy that soared through her every nerve ending, brightening her soul as if with a million volts. Nowhere else did she feel as if she'd found her place but in Lars's kiss. His mouth. His soft, sexy beard. The skim of his mustache beside her cheek as he moved to whisper at her ear.

"Today has been a good day."

"Best day ever," she agreed. "Thank you for giving the mermaid a chance to swim."

"I haven't forgotten the bathtub challenge."

"I should hope not."

"You want to get something to eat?" he asked as he loaded the kayaks into the pickup bed. "Someplace fancy?"

"Fancy?" Mireio looked over their attire. Lars wore

long swim trunks and a wrinkled T-shirt. And she wore a sheer swim cover-up and sand-covered flats. And she was pretty sure her hair would dry a disaster. "I'm dressed for McDonalds, though I crave steak and potatoes."

"We'll swing by your place and let you change. You think I'll pass muster?"

"Sweetheart, you've but to smile at the hostess with your pearly whites. Flash those dimples, and give a suave rub of your beard, and you're in. Anywhere."

"What if it's a host?"

"Same result. Trust me."

At her place, she slipped into a flowered sundress that fell below her knees but fit her body like a hug. Flats felt appropriate with the dress, even though it would make her look as though she was a child standing next to Lars. She didn't care.

Skipping outside to where he waited by the truck, she saw Mrs. Henderson had discovered the hunk and was chatting him up.

When Mireio approached Lars, he said, "Your neighbor has been doing some research online about the Sasquatch. She thinks it only comes out on the night of the full moon."

"Oh. Did you see it again last night, Mrs. Henderson?"

"I did not see it. Exactly. But I did hear some mysterious rustling in the cornfield behind our houses. It was a very *particular* rustling."

Mireio and Lars exchanged winks.

"Particular rustling. Hmm," Mireio said. "You should be careful, Mrs. Henderson. I certainly hope you don't go outside after dark."

"I would never! But I do have my camera set up on a tripod now so I can take pictures from the window. Your

Lars was telling me he didn't think Sasquatches were a danger to humans."

"Is that so?" She clasped hands with him and he squeezed her fingers quickly and added another wink. He was feeling fine today, and she loved that he'd been able to enjoy the day and not fall into a funk. So this teasing she encouraged. "I imagine they are more afraid of us than we them."

"Oh. Do you think so?" Mrs. Henderson's eyes widened as she peered beyond the houses toward the backyard. "I wonder what they like to eat? I might leave out some lettuce."

"Oh, Mrs. Henderson," Lars said. "You stay safe inside. Don't try to approach the beast if you see it again. In fact, give Mireio a call and I'll come over."

"You will?"

Again, he winked. "Promise."

"You don't know what a relief it is to hear that I've such a big strong man willing to protect me."

"Sure thing, Mrs. Henderson. We're on our way out for supper. See you later."

The neighbor stood curbside, watching them drive off, and only when they'd turned the corner did Mireio laugh. "She's got a crush on you."

"You think? But what would she do if she learned I was her Sasquatch?"

"That's not going to happen, is it?"

"Fingers crossed." He crossed his fingers and drove toward uptown Minneapolis for seafood on the rooftop at Stella's Fish Cafe.

After eating, they strolled, hand in hand, back to the truck in the parking ramp near the Lagoon movie theater. Mireio decided that since Lars was in such a good mood now might be the time to toss out what she'd wanted to suggest to him since seeing him so down about being unable to shift.

She turned and walked ahead of him, backward, and he slowed and grasped both her hands. "I'm going to say something to you," she said, "and I don't want you to react. Just think about it a little before you rush out with a quick no. Promise?"

"I'm not sure I should make a promise when a witch says something like that to me."

"Please?"

"What is it?"

They stopped before the parking ramp building. The moon was high, and neither had mentioned anything about the fact it was the day after the full moon and that Lars should want sex right now in order to stave off the irresistible urge to shift.

"What would you say about letting me and Valor and Geneva work a healing spell on you? Now listen. Valor and I are not expert healers. But Geneva has some amazing talents. And we witches simply cannot bring back the dead. But maybe our healing skills could help you. In some way? Would you be willing to give it a go?"

He tilted his head, fixing his gaze on hers. When his jaw tensed, she expected a definite no. So when he nodded and said, "Okay," she plunged into his arms for a hug.

"Thank you. I want to take care of you," she said.

"I know that. If a bunch of witches want to work their witchy magic on me, what's there to lose?"

"Maybe your pants."

"What?"

She led him into the building's shadows and walls of concrete cinder blocks. "The healing works best in water. We'll plop you in my tub and see what we can do."

"I thought *we* had a date to get it on in the tub?"

"It'll happen. But first let me try this? I'll give them a call and we can do it tonight."

"Tonight?"

"Well, Sunday's got Peanut until morning. I figure we should take advantage of the free time while we can."

Lars sighed and nodded again. "I'm in."

Chapter 17

Valor and Mireio were busy blessing the bathroom with sage and witchy chants, while Lars stood by the big round marble tub. He felt out of his element, and was a little freaked by the suggestive looks the third witch, Geneva, was giving him. Sleek black hair hung straight to chin level and she wore some kind of fitted yellow silk dress that gave her a cosmopolitan flair, yet Mireio had told him she was as Scandinavian as the rest of them. With a finger to her red-lacquered lips, her bright sapphire eyes took him in.

The tub had been filled with warm water and sprinkled with Epsom salts. Now Valor began to tap some sparkly dust into the water, which she explained to him was actual faery dust courtesy of her boyfriend, Kelyn Saint-Pierre. The Saint-Pierres were a family of wolves, a vamp and a couple faeries. Lars had never met them, but he was aware the eldest brother, Trouble, lived up to his name.

"You can get in now," Mireio said to him. She clasped his hand and hugged up against his side. Her blue eyes beamed up at him with such wonder and respect Lars always experienced a second of disbelief that he'd actually found a woman like her.

"Uh." He eyed Geneva and she winked at him. Whispering to Mireio, he said, "You know I go commando, sweetie. I'm not sure about this."

"You don't want to get in with your clothes on. And garments will only impede the magical energies. Go ahead. They won't watch you undress."

"Oh, I'm watching," Geneva said as she circled around to the vanity where the witches had set candles and incense and crystals and all sorts of mysterious magical accoutrements. "Strip, big boy."

"Geneva," Valor admonished. She finished the circle then walked to the doorway. "We'll stand out in the hallway, Lars. You two let us know when you're ready. Come on, Geneva!"

The witch pouted and slowly glided toward the door, yet when out in the hallway, she kept the door open and, even though Valor turned her to face away, she cast a thick-lashed wink over her shoulder.

"Ignore her," Mireio said. "She's not interested unless your bank account has a minimum of ten figures. Besides, she'd have to go through me to get to you, and she knows that's not worth the fight." She helped him tug up his shirt and then unbuttoned his jeans.

Lars caught her hand over his waistband. "I can do this."

"I know. But I'm always so eager to get your pants off, lover."

"Not around those two," he whispered.

"Are you going all Mr. Shy on me again? They've seen naked men before. And you have so much to flaunt."

"You're not making this any easier," he said as he shoved down his jeans and stepped out of them, now completely naked. A glance spied Geneva and she was looking right at him. Her brow arched and she dragged her tongue along her lips. Lars clasped his hands before his cock, which, despite his embarrassment, was quickly growing erect. "I knew there was something about witches that should creep me out."

"Not me?" Mireio pouted at him.

"Never you." He kissed the crown of her head, then stepped into the tub. It was warm and inviting. Sinking down, he noticed Geneva was the first in.

"Now that's something to be proud of," Geneva said as she clapped softly. "Bravo!"

Thoroughly embarrassed but not about to let her see that, Lars lifted his chin and winked at her. Hey, he could play this game too. Even if it did make him uncomfortable.

"All right, witches, so the man has an impressive dick," Valor said as she strolled by the tub and toward the altar. She glanced back at Lars and said, "Well, you do."

He could but lift his shoulders a little higher. Yeah, so he did have his talents.

"But let's focus, shall we?" Valor insisted. "The preshow is over. Geneva has briefed us on the spell. It's time for the magic. Mireio, it's your game now."

"Let's perform the blessing," Mireio announced.

The three witches clasped hands over by the spell stuff and bowed their heads. Mireio recited a blessing that asked for their safety and his, and then she slipped into Latin, which Lars had no clue how to interpret. The tones of her voice were harmonized by her fellow witches with hums.

Lars swept his hair over a shoulder and, spying a pink hair clip by the tub used it to hold back his hair in a messy tangle. Not a man bun. He didn't do man buns. Nor did he soak in a tub like some kind of spoiled...

Eh. Well. So this day was turning out to be challenging in ways he'd never expected to face. But still. The soak was kind of relaxing. The water was not clear, thanks to the salts and some black specks floating on the surface— he suspected it was ash and hoped it wasn't something like crushed frog brains. He tilted his head back against the curved headrest and stretched out his arms along the marble edges.

He quickly sat up as the women convened from their prayer and circled the tub.

"Everyone ready?" Mireio asked. "How about you, Lars?"

He shrugged. "What do you need me to do?"

"Just sit there. Maybe close your eyes. Take in everything that comes your way. We will touch you at certain points in the spell..."

He cast a look at Geneva, who winked at him.

"...but those touches will be to ground you and allow our magics to flow into you. So be open."

"Open. Got it."

"All right, witches." Geneva spread her arms wide and opened her palms faceup. "Let's do this!"

What followed was more chanting and humming, and it, at once, gave Lars the chills and then made him feel kind of dreamy. Almost as if he were falling into a hypnotic state. Realizing that, he shook himself back to alertness. Valor had leaned forward to touch his right shoulder. Eyes closed, the witch murmured something in a low, haunting voice. Geneva followed by touching his left shoulder. Her chant seemed to trickle up his spine and radiate out through his veins. She was the witch with the healing powers, so he certainly hoped she knew what she was doing.

And from behind him, Mireio placed both her hands to his head, spreading her fingers along the sides and whispering what sounded to him like nonsense syllables, but he felt her energy. He felt the energies from all of them. Vibrations hummed through his body, singing an ancient tune. So he closed his eyes and accepted it all, taking it in and daring to hope.

Five minutes might have passed. Or maybe a half an hour. But eventually the touches left his body and he felt the pulling away like a snapped connection. But he didn't startle. As the women filed out of the room, Lars floated there, peaceful and content. Someone blew out the final candle, leaving the room dark, but he felt the moon beam through the stained glass behind him dance across his exposed skin and glimmer on the water's surface. And if he went there, to that place where hope lived and witch magic really worked, he felt…lighter. Actually happy.

And he knew that Mireio had returned to the bathroom and stood in the doorway, quietly observing him. He didn't call out to her. He was content to share this moment and know that something had happened tonight. Whether or not their magic had cured him or simply delayed the process of his death didn't matter.

What mattered was that he was pretty sure he loved the woman who stood watching him. And that no matter what, he'd fight for her. Always.

Chapter 18

A day passed, and Mireio only received a text from Lars. But she wasn't down because his text consisted of hearts, flowers and a thumbs-up emoji. He wrote that he was working on the framework for the back of the house and was making headway.

As well, he was probably rising into the healing they'd performed on him, allowing it to enter him completely.

Everything was good. And after a day at work brewing cherry cream ale—one of her favorites—she had stopped by Target on the way home. Now she spilled the bag onto the kitchen counter and sorted through her booty. Because there were bootees. Little blue-and-purple socks with cats paws on the bottoms (she intended to tell Lars they were wolf socks), a baby T that said I'm Wild and some teething chews and another soft blanket because Peanut only had two and there were days when he spit up on both and Lars had to do laundry before bedtime.

And who could resist the beanie with the floppy gray bunny ears on it?

Mireio now understood why babies always had so much stuff. Buying the things had given her such a cute high it was even better than a slow sip of wine after a long day at work.

A knock on her front door surprised her. Suspecting Mrs. Henderson might have another Sasquatch sketch to show her, she pulled a white light of protection over herself as a means to not take on the craziness on the other side of the door.

Before she even touched the doorknob, the door opened and in burst Lars with Peanut clutched to his chest. He strode in and set the diaper bag down, along with the baby carrier, then turned and pulled her in for a kiss sandwich. Peanut cooed between the two of them as Lars made it very difficult to be in cute baby mode when all systems in Mireio were heading toward *please take me now* and *don't even bother to get undressed.*

"Wow. What was that for?"

"You don't like my kisses?" His dimples were irrepressible as he brushed a palm over the baby's bushy coif. "Peanut approved."

"I love your kisses. Anytime, any way. But why so happy today? Did you get a lot done at the cabin?"

"I finished framing in the back of the house. But—" he put up a finger to pause her from cheering for him "—I have even more exciting news." Smoothing a hand down Peanut's back the man burst out with "I shifted to wolf this afternoon! And it was because I wanted to, and not without volition. And I shifted back with the same ease. I feel renewed, Mireio. And I have you and your witchy friends to thank for that."

He bracketed her head and kissed her forehead, then

spun and picked up the diaper bag. "Gotta change Peanut. He had a blowout on the way here."

"I noticed that," she said, waving her hand beneath her nose to disperse the rank air. "I'm so happy for you, Lars. Who was watching Peanut when you went out?"

"Sunday. Both Dean and I went for a run. Man, that felt so good." He laid the blanket out on the floor and starting changing the baby. "And I have so much energy today. But I think it's my normal energy. I didn't realize how run-down I've been lately. You got any coffee?"

"Uh, no coffee for you. I think you're flying high enough. Oh, please put that one outside in the garbage can. I'm thankful tomorrow is pickup day. Whew!"

"I gave him carrots this morning. We're starting to try some food."

"Awesome. You know, I could plant a garden for you on your land and make homemade, all-natural baby food for Peanut. It shouldn't be too late to plant."

"Would you really do that?" With Peanut all fresh and beaming, Lars walked over and handed the baby to her. "I'll be right back." He headed outside with the stink bomb.

"I would do anything for you, sweetie." She kissed Peanut's head, loving his soft sweet scent so much, and she nuzzled her cheek and nose into his silky hair.

When Lars returned he stopped halfway to the kitchen and stared at her.

Mireio felt as if she might have forgotten to comb her hair. Or maybe she had baby spit on her she hadn't noticed. "What?"

"You're so beautiful standing there in a beam of sunlight. Your hair is like fire and your eyes like ice. And I can feel you right here." He slapped a hand over his heart.

"You and Peanut are my two favorite people. How'd I get so lucky?"

"We're not always beautiful. One of us has mastered the stink bombs. And the other can work the cranky vibe once a month. So watch out."

"I'll take the stink and the crank. I'm so blessed."

"The one that's truly blessed is this little guy. Erik."

"Hmm, not so sure about that one."

"Oh, come on, it's very Scandinavian."

"It is. I'll put it on my possibilities list."

"Do you have such a list?"

"Maybe." He tugged the baby book out of the diaper bag and sat on the couch but didn't open it. "I should have picked up something for us to eat. I wasn't thinking clearly after the stink bomb hit in the truck."

Mireio laughed. "Want me to order pizza? I could actually go for a big cheesy slice with lots of pepperoni and sausage and…"

"Mushrooms and onions?"

"Oh, yeah, your kisses are going to be very savory later."

"As will yours." He winked. "Order an extra-large. I'm starving."

After they'd made the pizza disappear, Lars fed Peanut a few spoonfuls of mashed peas, which the baby promptly spit up. The kid was developing a bubbly giggle, and even with peas splattered all over his face and beard, Lars could but laugh along with him.

"I'm going to run a tub," Mireio said as she breezed by them toward the bathroom.

"For you?"

"Aha-ha-ha!" She paused and gestured toward his beard in a circling manner. "You're starting to look like the swamp thing with all those peas in your beard."

"'Bout time we do the tub challenge!" he called after her.

After burping his son and changing his diaper, he laid Peanut down on the floor to read to him while Mireio was in the bathroom. It was after nine and while he wasn't at all tired, he didn't expect to sleep too much later. Not with a sexy woman in the house.

He really felt great. And while he wasn't so hopeful as to think the witches may have actually cured him, he was going to ride this good feeling for as long as he had it.

Finishing the chapter on what to expect during the fifth month, he closed the book and turned to find Peanut sleeping. The infant sucked in his sleep sometimes, his little lips pushing out repeatedly. Such dreams he must be having.

A crop of bright red hair popped around the corner. Then Mireio stuck out a bare foot, and followed by stepping into view. Lars propped himself up onto his elbows and whistled in appreciation for the woman wearing only a towel.

"You going to strip for me?"

"No, I'm going to take a bath." She disappeared behind the wall again, and then the towel landed on the floor.

Lars dug in the diaper bag for the baby monitor he never left home without and turned it on. Then he rolled a blanket and placed it on one side of Peanut, and took the roll cushion from the couch and placed it on the other side. Standing over the boy he decided there was no way, if he woke without a sound, he could roll himself into trouble. Check.

Tugging off his shirt, he headed down the hallway and into the bathroom. He set the monitor on the vanity by the sink.

A witch lounged in the vast marble tub, sipping a goblet of wine. She fluttered her lashes and blew a handful of iridescent bubbles into the air. "Ready to screw a mermaid?"

"Yep." He couldn't get his jeans off fast enough. But before Lars could dip a toe in the tub, he paused, looking over the vast, sparkling bubbles. It was very different from herbs and healing salts. "Uh…"

"What? Do you want to bring Peanut in here?"

"No, he's good. Got the monitor set. It's just…there's so many bubbles. And it smells like fruit and flowers. It's all so…"

"Delicious?"

"Girlie," he decided.

"Oh, lover, I'll still want to have sex with you if you smell like a girl. Promise. And pomegranate is an aphrodisiac. The scent should drive you wild."

"I don't need anything to make me wild for you."

"Just give it a try." She slid her hand down a breast, wiping away the bubbles and her nipple peaked above the water's surface.

Lars stepped into the warm water and lowered himself cautiously. It was just bubbles. Nothing to freak about. And his woman looked so lickable, all wet and with bubbles in her hair. When her hand stroked up his thigh and found his cock, he forgot about the smell and the silliness of a grown man sitting in a bubble bath and glided up to kiss the nipples that teased at him.

Mireio cooed in response and hooked her legs over his hips. He caught his hands on the curve of marble behind her shoulders and suckled her breast until she squirmed so much the waves threatened to slosh over the edges.

"Steady on deck," he said while dancing his fingers down her body till they were between her legs. "Mmm, this mermaid doesn't have a tail. And I've found something interesting. I think it's treasure." He slid fingers inside her and circled her clit with his thumb.

"You'd make a terrible pirate," she said, gripping the sides of the tub to stay above water. "But I'd walk the plank for you any day. Oh, Lars, yes, just like that. Slow and firm." She bit her lower lip and groaned deeply in her throat.

He loved the sound of her unabashed pleasure. And he was the man who was so polite and respectful with a woman—until she begged him for more.

Pulling her toward him and kneeling on the bottom of the tub, he used the wave of water to glide her body against his torso and then fitted her neatly onto his jutting erection. Mercy. Nothing felt better. Not. A. Thing.

She began to rock upon him, sending water over the sides of the tub. He encouraged her motions, tensing his jaws as the exquisite tremor of orgasm rushed to his core and coalesced in one perfect blast of oblivion.

Lars howled and clutched the witch against his chest as he released inside her and sighed out a satisfied breath.

The bubbles had dissipated and the wine was gone. Mireio's body hugged his as if she were an exhausted mermaid clinging to her earthbound lover. The world was right. No matter the darkness that germinated within his body. As long as he had his two favorite people, Lars could face anything. And he would do anything for Mireio. Thinking of which...

"Did you want to go out again one of these days on a vampire hunt?"

"No. I uh..." She pulled from him and floated to the back of the tub, sliding her arms along the edges to anchor herself. "I think I'm going to put that search off for now. I don't need to rush into things."

"But you paid Raven Crosse a lot of money to locate a vamp for you."

"I know. But I feel differently about it now."

And he suspected the reason behind that change of heart. "Mireio, you have to do this for yourself."

"I will. Someday."

"It's because of me, isn't it?"

"What do you mean?"

Sitting up in the water, he bent his knees and propped his elbows on them. "I know what you're thinking. How can you seek immortality when I might drop dead any day?"

"Don't say that. You're feeling so good today."

"I am. And I intend to take it one day at a time. But it would make me feel better to know your future is secured."

"To be honest? I've decided not to do it. And that's that. So don't argue with me, okay?"

The staticky baby monitor alerted them both.

"Peanut's up," she said. "You go get him and I'll drain the tub. We can have midnight margaritas out on the patio if you want."

"Midnight margaritas?"

"It's a *Practical Magic* thing. I love the Owens witches, even if they are fictional." She sat up and flipped her wet hair over a shoulder. "Go get your son."

Lars reluctantly got out, wrapped towels around his hair and hips, then wandered off to claim the stirring baby.

Mireio propped her chin on the edge of the tub and tapped the wine bottle with a fingernail. "I'll figure some other way to get revenge on the vampire. When Lars isn't looking."

Chapter 19

The next day, Lars stopped into the brewery. Mireio had told him she'd be finished brewing around three, so he made a point of getting there at two. Just in case she'd let him help a bit, maybe even learn a few things. With Peanut in the baby carrier, he strolled inside the empty brewery to find no one behind the bar or back near the brew tanks.

"Mireio?"

Someone walked up behind him and hugged him fiercely. He set Peanut on the floor, letting the carrier rock, then turned and pulled his tiny witch into his arms. She wrapped her legs about his hips and dove in for a kiss.

Lush red hair spilled across his face and hands as he tasted beer and salt on her tongue. He leaned back and studied her. "You been drinking?"

"Ha! No. Maybe. Okay, yes. I had to test the stout. And all I've had all day to eat is a bag of stale pretzels. Did you bring me food?"

Estimating that she was a bit tipsy from her "beer testing," he offered to pick her up a sandwich from the deli down the street.

"Yes!" She pumped the air with a fist and did a little shimmy before Peanut. It ended in a wobble and a spat of giggles.

"How much beer did you test, sweetie?"

"Half a pint? Of the stout. And then maybe a few tasters of the honey IPA and the pale ale. The Scottish ale has gotten rangy. That stuff never lasts for long with the happy spell on it."

"A happy spell." That explained a little. The woman was certainly in her happy place.

He hugged her to him and she made to jump for another kiss but landed awkwardly on her high heels and he had to catch her before she toppled backward.

"I'd better get you some food, stat." He glanced to Peanut, who gave him a wondering look. He'd be fine with the drunk witch for the ten minutes it would take him to find food to sober her up. "Be right back. Don't dance too suggestively for Peanut. The boy's an innocent!"

He left to a spill of giggles and quickened his steps down the street. The shop wasn't busy, and besides an all-veggie sandwich for Mireio, he grabbed a foot long with all the fixings for himself, as well. When he got back to the brewery, Mireio lay on the floor next to the baby seat, toggling the puppies hanging from the mobile. He'd wanted wolves but the closest thing had been blue plastic puppies.

"You finished brewing for the day?" he asked as he set out the food on the bar. "Everything all washed up? I could help."

"I didn't get to brew at all. Ended up kegging the stout

with Valor earlier. Since then I've been doing some dusting, inventory and…"

"Beer testing?"

"You know it!" She slid onto a barstool and dove into the sandwich.

Surprised that a woman who actually brewed beer for a living could get so tipsy from her own brews, Lars took it all in stride. But something about Mireio's actions bothered him. She was smart and had a good head on her shoulders. She knew better than to get drunk at work. Something must be bothering her. Had to be.

She finished the sandwich and twirled around behind the bar. She turned up the radio and grabbed an empty pint glass.

"Uh—" he gestured toward the fridge "—maybe you should have water?"

"What's up with you today?" She set the glass down with a clink. "You're harshin' my vibe."

"Harshin' your— Mireio, what's wrong? Is there something you want to talk about? You're not yourself today."

"Can't a girl indulge in a little beer therapy once in a while?"

He shrugged. "Sure, but during work hours? Is it about the immortality spell? I know you said you were going to set that aside, but, sweetie, if that's what you want…"

"It's not that." She waved him off, then turned to grab a bottle of water from the fridge. "Did Peanut eat yet?"

"Gave him a bottle and some peaches before coming here. I think he likes peaches."

"I volunteer to *not* change that diaper." With a giggle she glided around the bar and plucked a few chips from the bag he'd opened. "What are we going to do tonight? Have any plans?"

"What do you want to do?"

"I thought you were all about doing things that made you happy? Going for the adventure."

"How adventurous can we be with Peanut tagging along? Sunday can't sit for him tonight."

"You should find a backup babysitter."

"It's an idea. I haven't needed a babysitter so much until I met you."

She blanched.

"That's a good thing," he said to alleviate her pout. "I could spend every hour of every day with you and still want more time together. Even when you're drunk."

"I'm not that drunk. And I'm starting to sober up. The food is helping. Thanks. You're right. Something was probably bugging me earlier and…" She blew out a breath and dove to the floor to kneel before Peanut and toggle his toys.

So she didn't want to talk about it? He could respect that. She'd tell him when she felt like it. Or not. But if it was something about him, he'd like to know.

"I think he looks like a Vladimir today," she declared.

Lars turned to see if she was being serious or if that was still the beer talking. The witch leaned over Peanut's carrier, toggling his toes. She then lay on her stomach, knees bent and feet tapping in the air. She looked like the kid's mother, playing with him. And that thought put a catch in his throat.

Would he ever find a mother for Peanut? Before he died? And what about Dean's request the other day that he change his will? It felt right. Like the responsible thing to do. But something held him back from committing to such a drastic move. Because nowhere in that legacy would there be room for Mireio.

"I love this song!" She stood and traipsed to the other

side of the brewery, where the speakers sounded best. Freddie Mercury crooned softly. The woman wrapped her arms across her chest, eyes closed, and swayed as she sang.

Lars wiped his mouth with a napkin and wandered over to her. Compelled by the magic of her being, he held out his hand for her to take, and she stared at it.

"But you don't dance," she said, brushing the hair from her face. "You made that clear the first night we met."

"I can dance to this slow stuff. It's just swaying back and forth, isn't it?"

She put her hand in his and hugged up to him, and Lars bowed his head over his tiny witch. Her melting up against him was the best feeling in the world. Holding her close. Feeling her heat mingle with his. The brush of her hair against his bicep tickled in the best way. The world was right.

Until he caught a few of the song's lyrics. It was about living forever. Or maybe not? Mercury asked him if he wanted to live forever.

Hell. This was her favorite song?

Sighing, Lars tuned out the words but the one stuck in his brain. *Forever.* So he put a positive spin on it.

"I want to hold you like this forever," he whispered.

Suddenly she pushed away from him, swiping at a surprising tear that rolled down her cheek. "Don't say that!"

"What? Mireio, what is wrong?"

"Don't you get it? I'd like to hold you forever too. But that can never happen because you're going to die! Oh, my goddess, this stupid song! I don't want you to die, Lars. I…don't…"

She dropped to her knees on the hardwood floor and bowed her head, the tears coming full force as the song ended and segued into something more upbeat.

Lars knelt before her and, unsure what exactly to do, he first bracketed her head with his hands, but didn't try to lift her face. She sobbed. And he felt her pain pulse in his heart. It was a wicked, relentless pain that promised to bring him down if he didn't defeat it. But there didn't seem any way to do that.

Suddenly she looked up, clutched his shirt and said, "I love you, Lars. I don't want to lose you. And I know there's no way to change that. That's the toughest part."

"You might have changed it. I still feel great from the spell you witches worked on me."

She smirked but her tears continued to spill. "M-maybe."

He pulled her in close and stretched his legs out before him so she could sit on his lap. Holding her there, he nuzzled his face against her hair. Nothing sweeter than his tiny witch. Yet the thought that he might lose her, and Peanut, cut through his heart like a blade.

"Why did you happen to me now?" he whispered, "When I've just learned that life isn't going to go the way I expected."

She brushed her hair away. "No one should ever expect life to go a certain way. We signed up for this. You and me? Our souls agreed to this before we were even born. But that still doesn't mean it won't hurt. A lot."

He kissed the back of her hand. "You said you love me."

"Because I do. How can I not? You're the most amazing man I've ever known. And how lucky is Peanut to have you as his daddy? I don't mean to be so forward, but if I'm going to let everything out, I have to be truthful. What are we going to do when you're gone?"

That blade that had cut into his heart? It now sawed it in half. And Lars knew that kind of wound could never heal so swiftly as he wished.

"Life always goes on," was all he could say.

"I love Peanut so much," she said. "I hate to think of this—of you dying—but should it happen, I want to adopt him."

Lars bowed his head to hers. He hadn't told her about the will change yet. And now, more than ever, he knew his decision to think about it had been a good one. But how could he deny a couple who could never have children of their own simply because another woman who had known Peanut a short time had fallen in love with him? Mireio could have kids someday.

How he wished he could have a family with her.

"What do you think about that?" she asked.

"It's a generous offer. But I also have a lot of thinking to do about a lot of tough things. And I'd kind of like to linger a bit on that part about you loving me."

She turned on his lap and met his gaze. "I do. I really do."

"I feel like if I say the same to you—and damn it, but I do believe I do—that I might only break your heart all the more. I don't want to do that to you, Mireio. I…" He choked down the rising pain. "I don't want to die…"

She wrapped her arms about him. The two sat there on the floor as the music continued, oblivious to their pain. Peanut had fallen asleep. And Lars's heart had broken open.

It felt good to have told Lars what had been hanging over her head lately. And the tears had helped, as well. Part of her witchy water magic.

And hearing him confess that he didn't want to die had reassured Mireio in ways she hadn't realized she'd needed. What man *did* want to die?

So she'd take it one day at a time. With the man she loved.

A man who was afraid to tell her he loved her because he didn't want to break her heart? She understood where he was coming from and was glad he'd put that into words for her. They were on the same page. Only, some days it seemed like he was slowly sliding away from her. She intended to grasp his hand and hold on tight.

They got up from the brewery floor and Lars checked on Peanut. Though the infant was sleeping soundly, he was smiling, which indicated a diaper change was necessary.

"Hate to wake him," Lars commented.

She waved her hand before her nose. "Oh, please, you have to or I will perish from the stink bomb."

He laughed and carried the baby into the bathroom, where the brewery provided a pull-down baby-changing table, which was installed on the wall.

"You still haven't suggested what you want to do tonight!" she called.

No answer from behind the closed door. She gathered the food wrappers and tossed them in the trash. It was close to suppertime, but she was full. And no longer tipsy. Okay, bad judgment letting her angst rule and her better senses take a vacation earlier. She should never have had that last half-pint of bad ale. Lesson learned.

On the other hand, her relaxed inhibitions had allowed her to make her confession to Lars. So she'd take the good with the bad. Even though some days it felt all bad. But she wasn't going to get down on herself anymore. She wasn't the one with the death sentence. She had to stay strong for Lars.

As for immortality? Nope. Not going to do it. Even if the one vampire she most wanted dead was out there stalking the streets.

"I know what I want to do tonight." Lars strolled out of the bathroom with a smiling Peanut and a small plastic bag that he held away from him as if it were labeled Hazardous Materials. "It could be a family date."

His choice of words warmed her very soul. "What?"

"Not sure how you'll feel about this, but uh… Would you like to go bowling?"

Mireio clapped her hands once and bounced. "Yes!"

He gave her a surprised dodge of his head.

"Sorry, was that too enthusiastic? You don't know how much I've always wanted to go bowling. The glossy lanes and the sparkly balls! And the shoes! Everyone gets their own special shoes!"

"Uh, okay? I've never seen a woman so excited about the prospect of wearing shoes someone else just got done sweating in, but let's do it!"

Chapter 20

Bowling was…complicated. And while Mireio had yet to knock down a single pin after six attempts at tossing that ugly pink sparkly ball down the lane, she didn't feel at all upset. How could she when watching Lars was like staring at a kid in the candy store? The man loved bowling.

He was talented with the bowling ball. And he had a style. The tall, hulking wolf approached the sacred line beyond which you shouldn't step—which she'd slid across four times already—and with a bend and a glide of his right leg behind his other, he released the ball in such a smooth, speedy throw she could but marvel. Even the lanes paralleling them stopped and watched as the ball crashed into the pins and, most of the time, knocked them all down. This time all went down.

Lars pumped an arm and did his little "strike dance" as she'd come to call it. Hips wiggling, he twisted on the toes of his shoes.

She glanced to Peanut, who seemed to watch eagerly, though it could also be the squishy teething ring that made him look so enthralled. "Your daddy is a rock star, Peanut Butter."

"What was that?" Lars cupped a hand to his ear as he glided back over to the chairs behind the ball holder. "Did someone call me a rock star? Oh, yeah!" Another fist pump was well-earned. "You going to let me help you on the next one, sweetie? I think all you need to do is bring your swing back a bit more. Put a little more oomph in your delivery."

"I know what I'd like delivered with some oomph." She winked at him and stood to collect her ball. The thrill over sparkly balls and shoes had dissipated. Seriously? Who put on shoes that someone had just got done sweating in? Well, she did. Because it made her man happy. And that was all that mattered. Of course, she did have one trick up her sleeve. She glanced to him as she held up her ball. "I got this one."

He bowed grandly, gesturing she go for it, then bent to kiss Peanut on the head.

Cautiously she approached the do-not-cross line, eyed up the neighboring aisles—everyone was chattering or focused on their games—and with a whisper of Latin, Mireio then sent the ball flying. It traveled slowly, but this time it was almost straight.

With her back still to Lars, she lifted her hand near her stomach and directed the ball with a finger and another whisper. "To the right." The ball corrected and rolled right up to the pins and…knocked one down. "Yes!"

Lars ran for her, lifting her in his arms and spinning her around. "You did it!"

"I'm so close to being a rock star, I can feel it." She

kissed him. "Maybe the rock star's groupie. It's fun watching him do his victory dance."

"I have a victory dance?"

"Seriously? You do that hip shake and toe twist thing every time you knock them all down."

"Huh."

He didn't realize he did that? That made it all the more sweet.

After four more attempts at hitting the pins, and with the use of magic, Mireio was able to add two and a half more pins to her tally. The half one wobbled, looked like it would almost fall, then decided not to. But she was going to count it anyway. Stupid, magic-resistant pin.

Wandering back to the chairs, she sat beside Lars. Peanut was fussing, kicking his feet like a sumo wrestler and twisting uncomfortably in his carrier. "You want me to pick him up?" she asked, surprised that Lars hadn't already done so.

"Would you?"

"Sure. You go knock 'em all down again. I got this."

"I think I'm going to sit the rest of them out. We've had a good game. But this rock star has taken his final bow for the night."

Mireio picked up Peanut and as she did she noticed Lars sat with his hands between his legs, and his fingers dangling, and, while it wasn't an odd pose, she immediately knew what was up.

"Fingers numb?" she asked as nonchalantly as possible. Making a big deal out of it would only make him feel weaker.

He nodded. "Feet too."

"Okay. I'm going to head into the bathroom to change Michael. I'll be right back. You good?"

"Yep. And… Michael isn't bad, but I once knew a bully by the same name."

"Ugh, Michael? What an awful name." She kissed Peanut's head and strolled off. "How about Mason?" she tried. "Or Morty, Maxwell or Mouse?"

The poor kid needed a name soon. He couldn't be named after a legume for the rest of his life. She then thought maybe she shouldn't have left Lars sitting alone, but with a glance over her shoulder she saw him conversing with a man on the seat behind him. He'd be good for a few minutes.

Thankfully, the bathroom had a changing station and she made swift work and then kissed Peanut's head. The woman at the sink eyed him and cooed. "Your son is adorable. Look at all that hair! Oh, I saw you and your husband out there. He's a big tall drink, isn't he?"

"He certainly is." No need to correct her mistake. Mireio left the bathroom, but her thoughts scurried toward a surprising future.

What if they got married? She could adopt Peanut, and if anything did happen to Lars—because who knew how long the healing spell would be effective—the baby would be taken care of. It wasn't a ridiculous notion to entertain. Sure, she'd only known him a short while, but what she knew of Lars was that he was honest, kind, hardworking and so true. And a good lover. What more did a girl need?

Not that she'd expected to get married so early in life. What she'd expected was to perform the immortality spell and gain a good hundred years. And then a hundred more. And a hundred more. And so on. Marriage? That could wait, because she'd have centuries to find the perfect man.

Who would have thought that without even searching she would have netted such a perfect catch?

When she returned to the chairs, the diaper bag sat on Lars's lap.

"You got the feeling back?"

"A little. I think we should head out, if that's okay with you. Everything aches. I want to get home so I don't have to face this in public."

"Deal." Hooking Peanut on her hip, she then dug into Lars's front jeans pocket and grabbed the truck keys. "I'll drive."

"I think you just shifted gears." He pressed up against the back of her to show her that some part on him wasn't giving him problems. "Think you can manage the diaper bag too? I might have to use the ball shelves to lean on to get out of here."

"Not a problem. Hook it over my shoulder. You want me to help you?"

"Nope. Just give me some time."

"Fine. I'll walk ahead and get Peanut in the car seat. We'll drive back to pick you up." She turned to kiss him and he caught her head with both his hands and delivered her a long, deep, promising kiss. One she hadn't been expecting. It reminded her exactly what a hold he had on her heart.

"You're too good to me."

"You make it easy to want to be so good. Let's go."

She walked ahead, trying to act casual as she kept slipping looks over her shoulder. Lars walked a little hunched over, pressing his fist to the shelves for support, but he made it up the two steps to the carpeted landing and gave her a nod of reassurance. So she dashed outside and put Peanut in the car seat. She'd gotten good at climbing up into the monster truck and adjusting the seat. She made it to the front door as her lover wobbled out. At the door, he stepped up but his foot slipped. She saw his hands cling to the door and seat as he attempted another go at it. Jaws tight, he was in pain. She wanted to lean over and pull him up, but she didn't. She would allow him his pride.

Finally, he made it up and with a "Whew!" he gave her a wink and said, "Home, Jeeves."

Once at her place, Mireio suggested Lars go upstairs and lie down for a while. He didn't say a word, only crept slowly up the stairs as if an old man struggling in his twilight years. She hugged Peanut to her, wishing she could help the man, but she was at a loss as to how. The healing spell was apparently starting to fade.

There had to be something she could do.

Spinning Peanut about, she realized he would be staying the night if Lars wasn't feeling better, so she would give him a bottle now. He'd have to sleep in the baby carrier. It was better than laying him on the hard floor, even on a blanket. Although, she could make a little nest for him…

"Nah, the carrier should work for a night. It'll get you toughened up for those nights when you're in college and you have to couch surf, or when your girlfriend kicks you out of bed. You little rascal, you."

After giving Peanut a bottle, Mireio ran upstairs to check on Lars. He lay facedown on the bed, as if he'd fallen there, arms outstretched. Snoring filled the room.

"Oh, sweetie."

Carefully, she removed his boots and set them on the floor by the bed, then she kissed his cheek and went back down to find Peanut snoring, as well.

"I've got to do something for him." She glanced about the room, feeling helpless, and yet, when her gaze landed on the red witch ball she kept over the kitchen sink—not a charm against witches but to keep out demons—the most obvious answer struck her.

Chapter 21

Eggs and bacon bubbled in the frying pan, but the scent had yet to wake Lars from the coma sleep he'd fallen into last night. Mireio didn't mind.

Blowing raspberries on the bottoms of Peanut's feet was interrupted by a knock at the front door. She promised the baby more fun amid his delirious giggles and hastened to answer. It was Valor, on her way to work. Mireio had called her earlier, asking if she could drop off some grimoires.

Valor handed over a tote bag. "It's all I have and that I'm willing to loan you. And Geneva sent one along too. You think you can find a spell to reverse imminent death?"

"Not sure. Maybe delay the actual dying process? I mean, I know we witches can't bring back the dead. And I'm pretty sure we can't stop an inevitable death, but…" She sighed and clutched the tote bag to her chest. "I have to try, Valor. The healing we performed has weakened. Lars was feeling pretty awful last night."

"That's tough. Big guy like that must feel so…"

"Small, is how he puts it. Oh, it kills me, Valor." She hugged the tote bag to her stomach. "But thank you for this. It means a lot."

"Let me know if you need my help. I'm always willing to do what I can. But no dark stuff, got it?"

Mireio nodded, but couldn't quite get behind an enthusiastic agreement. She'd do what was necessary to help Lars. And if that required dark magic? She'd face that hurdle if it approached. "You waxing the floors at the brewery today?"

"Yes. I'm excited to use the buffer. Rented it from Home Depot. It's going to be a blast."

"Only you could get excited about stripping hardwood floors and waxing them. Thanks, Valor. I'll get these back to you as soon as I can."

After Valor shut the front door, Mireio laid out the books on the coffee table before the couch and browsed through them, keeping Peanut in peripheral view. She loved grimoires. Bound in leather, velvets and other fabrics, some were so old, having been preserved through centuries of family, or sometimes even belonging to the same witch for those many centuries. The pages always smelled of herbs and age, and some even came alive with the proper incantation or a knowing eye.

The stairs creaked, signaling the wolf had woken. Lars wandered into the kitchen, rubbing his beard. He wore only jeans and Mireio's eyes veered to his tight abs. Mercy.

He sat before the counter and the plate of breakfast she set out for him, but before lifting the fork, he apologized with a yawn for falling asleep last night.

"It's not your fault, lover. Besides, Peanut and I partied it up while you were sleeping."

"Oh, yeah?" He ruffled the infant's wild hair. "Did she get drunk again?"

The baby kicked his legs and cooed. It seemed like a very definite yes.

"Telling stories!" Mireio protested. "He's a sneaky one."

"So what's all that stuff on the coffee table?" He shoveled in eggs and growled a satisfied noise.

Mireio pulled out the ingredients for the cupcakes she intended to make after the breakfast dishes were cleared. But now that he'd asked, she had to tell him. "It occurred to me last night that I'm a witch."

He cocked a brow above a dimpled smirk.

"And that witches cast spells. All kinds of spells."

"Thus, the healing spell," he said.

"Right. But we can conjure so many other kinds of spells. Some, which are dark, ancient and very powerful, can even possibly save lives."

"Is that so? I thought there was something about witches not being able to bring back the dead?"

"Exactly! But you're not dead, are you? So there's hope. I called Valor and Geneva and asked them to gather all their grimoires and spell books. Valor dropped them off. There will be something in one of them. I know it."

"A spell to save my life? Didn't you just basically try that?"

"It was more a general healing spell. And after last night, I feel as though it wasn't as effective as I'd hoped. So what do you think? Can I give it another go?"

She squeezed his hands and bounced on her heels, hoping he'd get behind the idea, but preparing herself for an argument.

So when he nodded and kissed her mouth and said,

"Go for it. I approve," she squealed and wrapped her arms about him.

"I love you," she said. "Thank you."

"I'm all for trying everything in our power. But that's a big stack of books."

"It is. But can you feel it?"

He shrugged.

"The magic emanating from all those sacred texts. It's in there, Lars. I know it!" Skipping around to collect his plate, she set it in the dishwasher. "Now, I'm going to make cupcakes because some guy gave me a lot of honey and I need to do something with it."

He smiled at her.

"You take Peanut in the other room and read to him, why don't you?"

"Are you suggesting I look through the witch books?"

"If you want to."

Glancing over the assortment of grimoires, he scratched his beard. "What am I looking for?"

"You'll know it when you read it." She tapped a finger to her lips. "Probably don't read anything too dark aloud. But me and my friends don't practice dark magic, so you should be safe. On the other hand…some of our relatives may have dabbled in the dark arts. Hmm…"

Lars glanced to Peanut. "She's a little nutty. But I like her. Come on, Charlie, let's do this."

"Charlie?" She beamed at him. "That was the first name I ever suggested."

"I know." He winked at her. "I like it. But I'm not committing to it yet. We'll see if it fits him, okay?"

She nodded eagerly.

Lars lay on the blanket on the floor next to Peanut-Maybe-Charlie. He'd paged through one of the grimoires that smelled musty and of lavender, but the writing was in some kind of hieroglyphs. Must be witch writing. He didn't know if that was a thing, but he knew he didn't need glasses.

Another book, from which he read a few pages out loud to Peanut, seemed to feature only love spells and those for womanly concerns. Women had a lot of issues. Who would have thought softening freckles would require a spell?

Now he picked up a dusty book bound in scratched blue leather. The spine was laced with wide red silk stitches. He smoothed a hand over it and thought it felt warm, as if alive.

"What do you think of this one?" he asked his son. "Let's take a look inside."

As he opened to the first page, Peanut cooed as if in marvel. And there was quite a reason for such a reaction. The first page featured a kind of family crest or logo that seemed to leap off the page at him. Like a 3-D design or hologram. The stags clashing horns at the top of the crest turned to look at him and their blue eyes glowed.

"Now that's freaky. But cool, eh?"

Peanut blew spit bubbles, a sure sign that he was enjoying the book.

"So the first spell is…" Lars loved reading to his son and no matter what it was, from the morning paper to ads to nonfiction or fiction, he always tried to add some dramatic inflection. "Casting out transgressions of the heart. Ooo… Now isn't that interesting? And see here? The insects drawn along this page…" He moved the page slightly and the bugs seemed to turn fluorescent and glow. "Do you think they could fly off the page?"

Out in the kitchen Mireio called, "How you two doing? We'll have frosted cupcakes in about ten minutes."

"Great! We're reading about bugs in magic books."

"Sounds awesome. You want chocolate or vanilla buttercream frosting?"

Lars thought about it only a second. "Both!"

"Both it is."

He turned to meet Peanut's pale blue eyes. "She spoils us." The baby cooed.

"Okay, next page…"

He read through spells for opening the third eye, a charm for attracting health—hmm… No, he'd read the squiggly text wrong. It was for attracting *wealth*. But on the next page he was pretty sure it did say health. The words were written in blue and emerald ink, and the dark brown ink that depicted a raven in the corner he suspected could be dried blood. Scents of earth, ash and flowers emanated from the page. And something darker.

When he turned to the next page, which was blank save for some decorative scrollwork, all the pages fluttered and the corner of the upper page suddenly blackened, as if burned. He smelled sulfur and could taste blood at the back of his tongue. He traced a finger along the ink scrollwork that edged the left side against the spine and he pulled back with a flinch. A blood drop formed on the cut he'd gotten on his thumb. And before he could wipe it off it dripped onto the old stained paper.

"Oops." He glanced into the kitchen. Mireio was too busy to notice him damaging her book.

He tried to wipe off the blood but the droplet seeped into the toothy paper and crept outward, forming words in bright red. It was fascinating, but also a little scary. Lars looked to Peanut, who sucked his thumb with great intent.

Turning over to lie on his stomach, he set the book on the floor and watched as it filled with text. And within the text were tiny drawings of skeletons, hands pointing in various mudras and at the bottom crawled a snake. He flinched when he saw that. The snake lashed out its tongue at him, then rolled into a circle, biting its own tail.

And the final text formed a title across the top of the page. He read in a whisper, "To Dissuade Death."

Dissuade meant to deter something or to stop it. Had he found a spell that could save his life? This was remarkable. It was almost too good to be true. But maybe it only meant putting if off for a little while? Eventually death would come.

"Even a little while is better than what I have now," he muttered. "What do you think, Peanut?"

The baby rolled to his side and his chubby hand slid across the page. And behind the brush of his skin over the scrollwork, another tiny pinpoint of blood showed.

"Ah hell." Lars grabbed the boy's hand and saw he'd been cut. But he must not have felt it. The infant held his head up with some effort, grunting. Lars pressed his lips to the cut, then licked it. Then he rolled Peanut to his back and gave him the teething ring. "Such magic is not for you, Charlie."

Hmm, maybe that name would work. He did like it.

Turning back to the book, he watched his son's blood crawl over the page in a perfect bubble, not leaving a trail but seeking… The bubble stopped over a word. "Immortality," he read. Then the blood dispersed into the paper and left a faint pink stain.

Immortality?

Lars saw that the word was part of an ingredients list. Dragon's blood. A baby's cry. Pixie dust. Ashes of vampire. And… "A witch's immortality. She must ransom her borrowed years for thee one on whom thy spell is focused." Lars caught his forehead in hand. "Shit. That means…"

The witch performing the spell had to have already performed an immortality spell for herself. And what witch would give up such a precious thing?

Didn't matter because Mireio had told him she no longer wanted immortality. Which he didn't believe for a second. She would go after it. Someday. When she didn't have to stand alongside one who was dying. She shouldn't feel bad for having such a desire. She wouldn't have sought it if she hadn't genuinely desired it.

If Mireio read this spell she'd probably perform the immortality spell just to help him. He knew that she would.

Such a sacrifice was too much to ask of her. And he could never live knowing what she had given up to save him.

"Everything all right in here?"

He jerked around, slamming the book shut.

"It was so quiet I figured I'd better check to see if one or both of you were taking a nap."

Lars looked to Peanut, who was napping, arms splayed and teething ring lying on his chest. He twisted forward, effectively hiding the book behind him with a sweep of his hair.

"One of us is still awake. Cupcakes ready?"

"Yes! And they've cooled enough to frost. So, uh, did you find anything?"

"Nope." He sat up, wrapping his hands about his knees, and shrugged. "Nothing but some ways to cure monthly cramps or get a man to fall in love with you."

She narrowed her brows. Could she see the damn book behind him?

"Let me bolster Peanut in and I'll be right in to sample the goods," he said, shooing her off with a gesture.

"Okay." She spilled her gaze over the floor one last time. "You want some coffee too?"

"Yes!" he called.

Turning, he grabbed the blue leather-bound book. What to do with it? If he didn't draw attention to it, and slipped it back in the pile… No, she was going to look through them all, surely. Panicking, he shoved it under the couch. Then he stood, made sure he couldn't see any part of the book from where he stood. Grabbing the bolster pillows from the couch, he set them on either side of Peanut. Good for a few minutes.

And he swung around the corner, following the delicious aroma of chocolate and sugar.

After Lars's fifth cupcake, Mireio refilled his coffee. If he wanted to eat a dozen she wouldn't be happier. She would like nothing more than to cook and bake for this man every day.

"What's that?" he asked.

Standing across the counter from him, she straightened and looked about. "What's what?"

"That look on your face. Like strange stories of romance and adventure are taking place behind your eyes. I'd love to know your thoughts."

"Honestly? I was thinking how happy it makes me to watch you eat the stuff I bake. I've always considered food a form of love. You eat my food, that shows me how much you love me."

"Then I'm not leaving until all these cupcakes are gone." He winked at her. "Though I probably should slow down a bit, eh? Whew! These are sweet."

"I promised Valor a couple. Going to drop them off tonight as thanks for her hard work at the brewery today.

It's supposed to rain tonight and tomorrow. Are you going to take Peanut home?"

"Yeah, we should hit the road. I used the last diaper in the bag."

"You can keep some diapers here if you like. And I wouldn't mind if you kept a bassinet or something for him to sleep in here, as well."

"That might be a good idea." He leaned over the counter and met her lips with a kiss that tasted like chocolate frosting. "Sorry I didn't find anything for you in the spell books. We paged through most of them. You'll have to bring them back to your friends. Or I could drop them off on the way home."

"No, I can keep them awhile. I want to look through the one Geneva brought. It's one of the oldest and is filled with ancient magic."

"Which one was that?"

"It's got a red cover and gold foiling. Very elaborate. Did you look in any of the living grimoires?"

"Are those the ones that have pictures that move and put out scents? Yes. A little creepy, but kind of cool too. I couldn't activate any of those spells by reading them to Peanut, could I?"

"Definitely not. I hope we find something."

"Mireio." He clasped her hand and pulled her around the counter to stand between his legs. Bowing his forehead to the crown of her head, he swallowed, then bracketed her jaws with his hands and tilted her gaze to meet his. "I'm dying, sweetie. You and I both have to accept that. It could be in a few months like the doctor predicted. It could be years. No man ever really knows when he'll take his last breath. Let's live in the now, okay?"

Chin wobbling, she staunchly defeated the need to

break out into a wail. "But you said I could try another spell. Have you changed your mind?"

"No. But I don't want you getting upset if you can't find anything in those dusty old books."

She stepped back and said defiantly, "And what would Peanut say if he could speak?"

"What do you mean?"

"He'd say he wants his daddy around for a long time and that no matter what he should never stop trying."

Lars swiped his hands over his face. The nervous beard swipe ended in a squeeze of his fist. "You can't change what nature intended."

"I will!"

"I'm not going to let you sacrifice—" Lars grabbed the diaper bag sitting on the floor behind him. "I should get going. When Peanut wakes, he'll need a diaper change."

"Sacrifice what?" she asked as he tromped into the living room to gather up the baby things, along with the baby.

"It's nothing. You do too much for me, is all. You make sacrifices."

"Nothing I don't want to do. You know I would do anything for you, Lars."

Baby and supplies in hand, he hustled toward the front door.

"Why are you in such a hurry to leave? Are you mad at me?"

He stopped on the threshold and turned with Peanut clutched to his chest and the diaper bag over a shoulder. The baby's face skewed into a pre-cry twist.

The man's jaw tensed but he shook his head. "Sorry. I'm…having a weird moment, I guess. I'm not mad at you. But I don't like to talk about…this. You know?"

She nodded, understanding. The man was dying. He

knew that. No need to constantly remind him. "Can I still come over tomorrow? For the rain?"

"Just for the rain?" He managed a wobbly smile.

"And you, of course. But mostly the rain. I need to recharge."

"I can't wait to find out what that means. Come here." He nodded because his arms were full. "I'll see you soon. And bring me the rest of the cupcakes, yes?"

"Of course." She tilted herself up on her tiptoes and barely managed to brush his lips with a kiss because he didn't want to bend too far and crush Peanut. She kissed the infant's head, which stopped what could have become a loud wail. "See you later, Charlie."

"The name is growing on me," he said.

"Me too. See you later, lover!"

As soon as Lars was out of the driveway, Mireio dodged into the living room and scanned the stack of books. He'd been trying to hide one with a blue leather cover. And he'd done it so obviously, as if he were up to something. What was in that book he hadn't wanted her to see?

Chapter 22

Mireio laid her hands on the various grimoires stacked on the floor, trying to sense a lingering remnant of Lars's touch. On one, she immediately felt his gentle warmth, and she opened it and paged through. It was the grimoire dedicated specifically to women. This one he must have explored with more than a little discomfort.

Setting that volume aside, she sat on the floor, legs stretched before her, and caught her weight on her palms behind her. "What is he trying to hide from me?"

She lay back and decided it had been months since she'd dusted the ceiling lamp that dangled with purple crystals. Sighing, she turned her head to the side. A book under the couch? And so far under.

"Well, well, well, what's that?" Something like that couldn't have possibly been an accident. It had to have been pushed under there.

Reaching under, she slid out the thin volume bound in blue. "Valor's great-grandma Hector's grimoire."

She knew it from the family crest on the inside front page. That witch was still alive. Mireio had no idea what she was up to lately, but she and Valor had been close because she'd raised her granddaughter. So many witches had been raised by their grandmothers. It almost seemed the norm as opposed to an exception. Hector Hearst had also practiced dark magic on occasion, so what was compressed between the covers of this grimoire gave Mireio a warning tingle.

Had that same warning frightened Lars, someone unfamiliar with the intricacies and dangers of magic? That would have been enough to make him skittish and try to shove the book as far away as possible.

Hmm, that didn't convince her that he hadn't read something inside, which could have also freaked him.

Paging through, she marveled at the ornamental designs and elaborate writings. Some pages were blank. She knew those spells could only be activated with blood magic. That was definitely dark magic.

"Oh." She turned a page and her finger came away sticky. It was… "Blood? But how…?"

How had he known to activate a page with his blood? Impossible. He must have cut himself on the paper. But the spell title took her breath away: "To Dissuade Death."

"Oh, my goddess, this could be it. The spell that could save his life."

She quickly read the incantation and the ingredients. All of it was easily obtainable, and it promised to dissuade death. And to her, dissuade meant to stop it.

"Did he read this spell? Is this really his blood? Why wouldn't he say something to me?"

And then she tapped one of the words on the ingredient list that was stained pink: *immortality.* The witch performing the spell was required to sacrifice her immortality as the final ingredient.

If she went through with the spell she'd been angsting about lately, she'd have to give up that newly won immortality to save her lover. And she knew damn well the last thing Lars would ever ask of her was such a sacrifice.

She closed the book. What to do? The answer was simple.

"It's not a sacrifice for someone you love."

With Peanut-Maybe-Charlie down for an afternoon nap, Lars set the baby monitor on top of the outdoor closet that contained his beekeeping equipment and then approached the hives. He wasn't going to check them today. He'd done that three days ago. Disturbing the bees overmuch wasn't good for their productivity.

Since ancient times people had been telling the bees their good news, their bad news, about their celebrations and also about their family deaths. It was a tradition that Lars had started a few years ago when he'd needed someone to talk to. He always landed in a different place by putting his thoughts, fears, dreams and emotions out there by telling the bees.

And he needed to do that now.

Wildflowers and grass freshened the air. The sun hung high. And a gentle breeze listed through his hair. Spreading out his arms, he tilted back his head and took in the gentle hum from the hives. Their busy noise seemed to vibrate in his veins. The sensation felt like a symphony, and he was humbled by it. A few bees buzzed about his head. Bees wouldn't sting unless threatened. His bees had yet to sting him.

"Bless you for your hard, endless work and for the gifts you've given to me" was always how he began.

Standing straight and putting his hands down, palms facing the hives, he mentally reached in and put his heart out before him. "My life has been filled with some ups and downs lately. Some really awesome ups." Thinking about the past weeks with Mireio put a huge smile on his face. "You may have noticed the witch who comes here all the time. I love her."

It was the first time he'd said that out loud other than suggesting he couldn't say it, even though he wanted to, to Mireio. Because to give it to her in words? He didn't want to break that vow when he died.

"And she loves me, which is some kind of awesome. She also loves Peanut. I'm thinking his name should be Charlie. It's a good name. I have to remember to run down to city hall next week to fill out a change for the birth record. So there's the up. Love is indescribable. It's like I can't breathe without thinking about her. She keeps me alive."

He caught a palm over his chest. If only it were so easy to stay alive.

"And then there's the down." He rubbed his jaw, stroking his beard tentatively. "I've been struggling with this stupid death sentence. Damn! Why did this have to happen now when I've found the one I want to spend every day with for the rest of my life? A life that is supposed to end soon, rather than later. I can feel it in my bones. I haven't told Mireio. I ache all the time. My fingers and toes always tingle. But I can function and hide it most of the time. It's as if I'm being eaten up from the inside out. And I don't want to get to a point where I'm frail and incapable. I…couldn't bear that. Me. The big guy who's always been strong enough to push a tree over with but a shove."

He knelt then because it felt right to honor the bees

that way, and telling all this was difficult and his voice subtly shook. "And my wolf. I feel as if I've lost that part of me. Yet when it comes on me without my volition it feels like a punishment for not being able to control myself. I wish… I wish I could understand this. I wish my father was here so I could talk to him. Ask him questions. Learn from him. Why do we die like this?"

He'd not known at the time what had taken his father from him. Only that it had hurt his child's heart like no physical injury ever had. And when he'd most needed his mother to wrap him in her arms and tell him the world would not end and life would go on, she had fled the pack, never to be seen again. It had taken years for Lars to forgive her. He knew she hadn't known any other way to handle her grief. Or at least, he hoped that was what had allowed her to abandon her son without a look back over her shoulder.

"What should I do? I need guidance. I want… I think I want to leap. To take life and rip it to shreds and live every moment. But then I've a little boy to take care of. I want the best for him. And Mireio. Do I dare? Can I? What should I do?"

Catching his palms in the grass before the hives, he listened as the bees flew out en masse and formed a swirling cloud above his head.

Straightening, Lars lifted his arms and closed his eyes, taking in the flutter of thousands of wings against his hair and skin. They had never responded this way before. And he sensed what they wanted him to know.

He needed to leap. Be damned, the fall.

Chapter 23

Mireio set the plate of cupcakes on the table, which caught Lars's eye. He had been making the bed when she wandered into the cabin with a cheery "Hello!" She had no intention of discussing the spell she'd discovered in Hector Hearst's grimoire. It could wait. Until she had a solid plan.

It had started raining as she'd driven the winding tree-lined road up to the cabin, and her skin absolutely tingled in anticipation of her plans.

"A dozen left for you," she said, licking a smear of chocolate buttercream from her thumb. "Where's Peanut?"

"Sunday has him. I wanted it to be just us tonight." He winked, then shoved a pillow into the case. "So what's up with your plans for the rain?"

"I've come to renew. I am a water witch," she said as she unbuttoned her red short-sleeved blouse. Drawing her fingers down to her cleavage, she eyed him through her lashes. Darting her tongue along her upper lip seemed an appropriate tease. "I have needs."

"Needs?" He tossed the pillow behind him without a care. The man could work the overalls and wrinkled T-shirt. And talk about dimple overload. Goddess, he looked sexy tonight. His gaze aimed for her bust, barely contained by the red lace bra. "Any sort of needs I might be able to assist you with?"

"Not really." She draped the blouse over the back of a chair before the kitchen table, then shimmied down her skirt to land about her four-inch plaid heels.

"Then you've really got me confused." He pulled her closer by her hips and bent to dust the ends of his hair over the tops of her breasts.

She cooed with desire and stroked his beard. "Mmm, hold that thought for a bit, will you? I intend to go out in the rain and draw in its power. Revive and reinvigorate my water magic. I can't do it so often at my place because, while my backyard is private, you know Mrs. Henderson and her sketch pad."

"That I do. You think she's ever sketched a naked witch?"

"I hope not!" She giggled as he moved up and licked under her chin. His hair was what tickled, and yet it also set her skin on fire with desire. "Give me an hour to take it all in."

"An hour out in the rain? And…in your underthings?"

"Not exactly."

She reached behind her back and unhooked her bra, then let it slide off. When she stuck her fingers under the waistband of her panties, Lars put his hands over hers and helped her slide them down, slowly, his face moving over her stomach, his breaths drawing up the goose bumps on her skin. He knelt before her, breathing heavily at her mons.

"I said you have to wait. Can you manage that, wolf? I don't want to miss the rain. It's only supposed to fall for a couple hours."

He pouted up at her.

She stepped out of her shoes and bent to kiss the top of his head. He cupped her breasts as she did so. A squeeze of both her nipples did not make her want to step outside into the rain, especially since the night was beginning to cool off.

"You're cheating," she said with an admonishing wave of her finger. She snapped upright and marched to the door. "Maybe all I need is half an hour. Eat some cupcakes, why don't you?"

"Can I watch?" he called as she stepped outside.

"I can't stop you, but it'll be weird if you do. You'll know when it's cool to come outside and find me."

Still kneeling on the floor, he saluted her, then reached for a cupcake.

Arms spread, head tilted back and eyes closed, Mireio called on the rain to embrace, baptize and renew her. She whispered an ancient chant that her grandmother had taught her. One that spoke to the water elementals that clung to the raindrops and that flittered among the soaked grasses. The water skittered over her skin, gliding and teasing and infusing its wild and vibrant energies into her.

Her body hummed with power. And she felt her smile grow as she flicked her fingers and snapped away the rain droplets. And with each bend and flick of her fingers she controlled the drops, sending them spraying out in a fan, and then an arc that coiled above her head and performed a rain dance for her, the master.

She liked to think of rain as a direct infusion of star stuff. Because that's what everything was anyway. Ancient and ever alive, the soul never faded as it journeyed through the ages. And perhaps this rain was the same that had fallen on her bare skin centuries earlier as she'd performed much the same spell. It was a nice thought, and she truly believed it.

Her ritual ended by crafting a water cage sphere around her. It was her way of sealing her commitment to water magic. Out of the corner of her eye, she noticed Lars standing close.

"Sorry," he offered. "I couldn't resist watching. You're more beautiful than anything I can put to words. And your magic is incredible."

She swept her hand through a swath of the water cage before her, which opened a door. Then she crooked her finger at him, welcoming him inside her haven.

"Really?" he asked.

She nodded. "But you gotta get naked first."

"I can do that."

She was pretty sure no man had ever shucked off his clothing so quickly. Never would she tire of admiring his muscles and long sculpted body. The rain misted his skin, tightening her nipples as she thought about how fun it was going to be to lick the moisture from his hard lines. Padding through the squishy wet grass, he looked over the rain cage first before carefully stepping inside.

"Don't worry—it's strong. Only I can break it," she said.

"You're more than a witch." He pulled her slick body against his. "You're a goddess."

"Flattery will get you anything you desire, lover.

Mmm… I think we need a bed to lie on." She swept her hand and produced a knee-high flat surface fashioned from water.

Testing it with a palm, Lars flashed her a look of awe. "Can we really sit on this?"

"Lie down and try it out."

He did, and his body almost stretched to both sides of the cage, so, in complete control of her magic, Mireio teased the sphere a bit wider with a push of her hands outward.

She climbed onto the bed. Straddling Lars, she lifted her wet hair and splayed it out, commanding it to dry, so by the time it fell the red coiled curls brushed her cheeks softly. Inside the sphere they would be protected from the rain, which had picked up again. Not that she minded a lot of wet.

Reaching down, she gripped Lars's penis and slicked her hand up and down, drawing up a hiss of pleasure from him. He propped himself up on his elbows. "I'm still worried we're going to drop through this funky bench."

"Trust me." She leaned down, almost touching his erection with her lips. "You do trust me, don't you?"

"Yes?"

Smirking, she licked the head of him, then took him in deeply and sucked him until he orgasmed.

Sitting naked on the edge of the framed wall behind the cabin, Mireio fluffed her bright hair, which did not seem to get any more than a few droplets on it, even though it was still misting.

Lars was soaked. And he hadn't felt this good in days. His muscles were stretched and lax and his heartbeats still thundered from his orgasm. The moment felt enormously promising. The air was fresh and, even though there was no moon in sight, the night was bright.

"So you want to go in and snuggle under a blanket?" she asked coyly and added a flutter of her lashes.

The woman owned him with that sexy lash-fluttering smile. Every part of him belonged to her. Wanted to be inside and out with her. Forever and always.

"I have to say something to you first," he said. "And I need to apologize because I said before I wouldn't say it, but now I don't care. Or rather, I do care. A lot. I have to put it out there. For you to know."

"Sounds ominous."

"It could be. Mireio…" He knelt on the ground before her and threaded his fingers with hers. Eyes meeting hers he felt her power in the blue irises, and her compassion and kindness. "I love you. And…uh… I was wondering if you'd marry me."

Her mouth dropped open as she pressed a hand over it. "Really? You're not on a sex high right now and will regret this later?"

"No, lover, I thought about this after I got home yesterday and talked to the bees. I don't want to spend a day without you. And nothing would make me happier than if you'd become my wife. Oh, and…that includes accepting Peanut into your life, as well. I know it's a lot to ask—"

"Yes!" She plunged into his arms. Not expecting that reaction, Lars toppled backward. They landed on the slick ground with kisses and squeals from Mireio. "Oh, yes, yes, yes! I've been thinking the same thing lately. I love you so much, Lars. And I want to be with you always. No matter what the future brings."

"And Peanut?"

"I adore Peanut, you know that. I would be honored to be his stepmother."

"I think he'd like having you as his mom. You have a way with him. Just like you have a way with me. You've bewitched us both. And I'm happy for it. Can we get married soon? Like this weekend? I know you women like a big fancy to-do, but—"

Her kiss stopped his protest. "I don't need a to-do. I just need you. But can we have my girlfriends there? And you might have some friends you'll want there?"

"Dean and Sunday for sure. And Peanut can be my best man."

"Yay! Let's do it this Saturday. That'll give me a few days to find a dress. I do need to find the perfect dress, even if we go to the courthouse. I guess I need a little to-do after all."

"Pretty yourself up. Do what you want to. Do I need to get a suit?"

"You can wear whatever you like. Oh, Lars, we're getting married?"

"We are."

Chapter 24

Mireio turned before the mirror in the tiny department store dressing room. Geneva sat on the bench observing with the practiced eye of a seasoned fashion designer. Mireio had found a sequined pale pink dress that stopped at her thighs and whose back plunged to above her waistline. In front it draped to reveal her cleavage. Add to that the five-inch silver Pradas and she was in love with her bad self right now.

"I'm not sure." Geneva tilted her head against the wall where half a dozen rejected dresses hung.

"Oh, come on, Geneva, this one is perfect. And I am so not going to wear white. I'll spill beer or drop a cupcake on it. I think Lars will love this one."

"The dress is gorgeous. Your bright hair falling over the pink sequins makes it all rock. But I'd wear red shoes with it."

"Good call. Back to the shoe department! But uh, what are you not sure about?"

Geneva stood and unzipped Mireio down the side. "You're getting married in two days. You've dated the guy for what?"

"Long enough. I love him, Geneva. And he loves me."

She crossed her arms, unconvinced. The perfect cat's-eyes black liner she always wore gave her a majestic demeanor, even though she was shooting daggers at Mireio right now. "You sure this isn't some freaky rushed thing so when he dies his kid will have a mom?"

She gaped at Geneva, but the woman merely shrugged and waited for a reply.

"No. It's not like that." Mireio slipped the dress from her shoulders and spied her lying eyes in the mirror. "Okay, so part of it might be me wanting to have as much time with him as I can. And I love Peanut. I would much rather he comes to me than become a ward of the state, or whatever happens if Lars should die." She slipped down the dress to puddle around the high heels. "Which he's not going to do."

"I thought the doc gave him a couple months? Seems like his expiration date should be coming up pretty fast."

"You're rude, Geneva."

"I'm playing devil's advocate here."

Yes, and she couldn't blame her for that. But Mireio had thought about all this. She couldn't change any of it. Well, not without one last attempt.

"What's so wrong about me wanting to grab a little happiness? For wanting to make Lars happy?"

"Nothing. But you're trying to convince yourself he's not going to die. What do you know that the universe doesn't?"

"Let me tell you."

Two days later, Lars drove to Anoka with his bride at his side. They decided to hold the wedding ceremony down by the Rum River, behind The Decadent Dames so that afterward the party could move to the brewery. Lars had picked up Mireio, who had bounded out of her house in sweats and a T-shirt. Strange attire for her. Was this her idea of a casual affair? He was feeling itchy in the dress slacks and white shirt. He'd even rented a tie, which clipped on, thank the gods. He'd mess with that later.

He cast Mireio another glance. She twisted to make faces at Peanut, who sat strapped in on the back seat. Before he'd left this afternoon, Sunday had stopped by to give Peanut a present. It was a onesie that looked like a tuxedo with a little black tie at the neck. That was one smart-looking boy.

"What?" Mireio asked as he cast her yet another glance.

"Just never seen you so dressed down before."

She patted the plastic dress bag. "I'm not going to let you see me in all my stunning beauty before the ceremony. I'm changing at the brewery."

"You're going to make my heart stop. But then, you do that every time I see you." He winked at her and turned from the highway and into town. "You know, I realize that by marrying you I'm agreeing to wake every morning clinging desperately to my eight inches of the bed?"

She waggled her shoulders. "Got a problem with that?"

"Nope. I'd fall on the floor every morning just to be near you, and I have a few times already."

"We could get a king-size bed. It would fit at my place. Where are we going to live? Your place is awesome with all the woods and quiet. And there's the bees. You couldn't leave them or move them. But...it's one room."

"I'm working on that."

"Right. Doubling the size would be nice. And then Peanut could have his own room. Could we keep my place until that happens? I'm not attached to living in my neighborhood but there is my bathroom."

"The mermaid's throne. I wouldn't dream of asking you to give that up. We'll figure something out. But I don't ever want to spend a night without you."

She clasped his hand. "It'll never happen. Promise."

"So uh, I need to tell you something."

"That sounds ominous. You mean you still have more secrets? I can't imagine what they could be."

"Not a secret, just…facts you need to have before signing on the dotted line. About me. When I'm werewolf."

She tapped a finger on her lower lip. "Like what?"

"When we werewolves take a mate, it's for life."

"I know that. I wouldn't agree to marry you if I wasn't in it for forever."

"As short as that might be," he said, then shook his head. "Sorry. I have to stop thinking like that. Take one day at a time."

"That's the way I intend to do it. So it's me and you. For life."

"Right, but we wolves? We like to also take our mates when in werewolf form."

"Oh? Hmm, I think I knew about that. So you, all shifted to werewolf shape and, uh…little ole me?"

He nodded. If he thought she looked like a teenager standing next to him now, she'd be positively dwarfed by his werewolf. "I would never harm you, Mireio. You know that. But my werewolf will want in on the action."

"I love all of you, Lars. And I would never deny you a thing. But can we take it slow? Work up to that experience?"

"Of course. Just the fact you're open to it is all I need to hear. We can go really slow. Like months. Years." He cleared his throat and swallowed. He didn't have that long, but he wasn't going to be a downer. Not today. Not on the best day of his life.

"Since we're doing the confession thing here…" She twisted on the seat to face him. "There's something I have to tell you. You need to know this before you marry me."

"Is it worse than anything the two of us have already been through together?"

"I don't know. Depends on your perspective."

"Tell me, Mireio."

"I've had a change of heart about the immortality spell."

Lars's jaws tensed. "You want to do it now?"

"Yes."

"I see."

"You're not cool with that? I thought you were."

He was. Until he'd found that spell. And really? He shrugged. "I might have had second thoughts about taking the life of an innocent vampire."

"He's not innocent, and you know it."

"I only know what Raven Crosse has said about him."

"Lars, I had Raven search for a very specific vampire. Which is the part I need to confess to you."

"And this specific vampire? Why would he make you change your mind about performing the spell?"

"He was the vampire my mother went after when she had plans to invoke the immortality spell. Except before she could rip out his heart, he ripped out hers."

Lars slammed the truck to a stop at a stop sign at a four-way in a quiet neighborhood. Both of them shot a look into the back seat. Peanut slept.

"Sweetie. Really?"

She nodded. "Mother left me alone that night. I knew she was going out to invoke the spell to live forever. So I followed her. I was eight. And…" She sniffed. "I instead watched the vampire murder my mother. Thank the goddess, my grandmother had followed us, as well, and was able to get me away before the vamp came for me. You'd think that would have scared me away from casting the spell. But all my life I've wanted immortality so that I'd be protected against a vampire attack."

He nodded, understanding.

"But, as well, I've wanted revenge against the bastard who took my mother's life. Those nightmares I told you I didn't remember? I do. They are about my mom dying. I always see that bastard vampire standing there, holding her bloody heart."

"I had no idea." He clasped her hand and met her teary gaze. "Then I'm in. All the way. You want revenge?"

"I—I want immortality."

"Truth, Mireio."

She nodded decisively. "I want revenge too. To stop the nightmares."

"Don't say another word. It's done. Just let me know when we need to go out on the hunt."

"Thank you. For understanding."

"I'd do anything for you, my love. Anything."

He wished she'd told him sooner. He would have never said anything against going after the vamp. So long as she didn't find the spell, he could be okay with helping her to track down a vampire and kill it. A vampire who had haunted her since she was eight. A bastard longtooth who had murdered her mother while Mireio had watched. Hell, what a thing to have experienced.

He'd take away her nightmares. If it was the last thing he did.

A goddess in pink spangles walked down the sidewalk toward him. The small gathering of friends stood on a shaded path alongside the river. The day was bright and warm and ducks swam in the river. Maple, elm and oak leaves performed a cancan in the breeze. To his right stood Dean Maverick. And Sunday held Peanut. Charlie. The best man.

Lars watched with awe and a reverence that pushed up tears at the corners of his eyes as Mireio approached, led by Geneva, who was dressed to the nines in a long black sheath dress and who held white roses.

Mireio's bright hair spilled in luscious coils over her shoulders and down her back, and…did her shoes match her hair? What a fiery bundle of witch and mermaid-wannabe he'd gotten for himself.

Lars adjusted his stance and swallowed a lump in his throat. Yeah, so he was getting emotional. That this woman wanted to marry him did not cease to amaze him. Did they deserve one another? Maybe. Would she be better off finding a man who would live long enough to take care of her and have a family with her? Yes.

But he wasn't going to question his luck. She had said yes because she loved him. And her love was what kept him going.

One of her hands slipped out from under the bouquet of red roses. Fingers beringed in silver and crystals, she took his hand and beamed a smile up at him. "You ready for this?"

"Let's get hitched, sweetie."

The ceremony took ten minutes. It was a long ten minutes. Lars didn't hear much of it because his focus was on the part where he finally got to kiss his bride. And when prompted, he tilted his new wife back and bent over her for a long, binding kiss. Their friends cheered. Peanut giggled as a flutter of rose petals was tossed in the air. Then they all convened at the brewery where the DJ had already set up, and word had spread. Dozens of friends were already partying it up inside.

"You know we have to do the first dance," Mireio said as she kissed him. "I'll request something slow."

"I'm good with that. Where's Charlie?"

"I love that you're keeping that name! He's…" Both of them scanned the taproom. They spotted the baby in the midst of a half dozen women cooing over him and arguing who would get to give him his bottle. "I think he'll be fine for a while. You want to check on him?"

"No, let him party it up. See? He's already a ladies' man. He's got more chicks surrounding him than I've dated in my lifetime."

"Ha! And now you're mine so you are off the table. Come on, husband, let's dance."

Two hours later, Mireio sensed Lars was tired. He didn't say anything, and he was very good at hiding it, but she saw him flicking his fingers behind his back as if trying to work the circulation back into them. And he took mincing steps. His joints must be bothering him. When he found a moment to himself, his smile dropped and his jaw tightened. Then a friend would congratulate him and he'd force on a cheery demeanor.

It was time to call it a night. But first, she'd collect Charlie. Who was currently sleeping in his carrier on the bar with Sunday dutifully watching over him.

"Has he been sleeping awhile?" Mireio asked as she gathered his blanket and looked around for the diaper bag.

"Ten minutes. Oh, Mireio, don't worry. Dean and I will take Peanut home tonight. You and Lars go on— have your wedding night."

"Really?" Though she expected her new husband

would probably crash as soon as he saw the bed. And he deserved it.

"Yes. I've got this," Sunday said. "I stocked up on diapers and even bought a crib for the house, so we're all good to go."

"That's quite a commitment. We won't be needing a babysitter so much now. Well, I'd still like to go out with my new hubby once in a while."

"Mireio." Sunday placed a hand over her wrist. "You are aware that Dean and I will get legal custody of Peanut should Lars die?"

"What?"

Chapter 25

In the morning, Mireio brushed the hair from her face and rolled over to find her new husband clinging to the edge of the bed. One leg hung over the side of the bed, and so did one arm. But somehow he managed to snore through it all. The guy *had* stated that he'd known exactly what he was getting into by marrying her.

But had she known everything? What Sunday had said to her last night still bothered her. She'd wanted to ask her to explain, but Lars had come up to her and put his arms around her waist from behind, nuzzling his face into her hair. It had been a silent signal that he wanted to leave, so she'd left the baby with Sunday and driven him to her place. Lars had almost fallen asleep on the ten-minute ride, but he had made it upstairs and to the bed. By the time she'd showered and anticipated a little wedding-night snuggling? Snores.

Good thing he wasn't a loud snorer. More of a gentle

whispering type. And to be fair, there were times she'd woken herself with her own snoring. Not proud of it either. Maybe a little proud.

She stroked his hair along his arm, and that touch startled him awake. He lifted his head, snorted, then wobbled and fell off the bed.

Mireio leaned over the side of the bed. "Good morning, husband!"

After a groan, he gave her a thumbs-up from the floor.

"It's actually closer to noon," she said. "So what will we do with ourselves on our first official day as husband and wife?"

He exhaled and rubbed a hand over his abs, blinking as he came fully awake. "Sorry about denying you wedding night sex last night. I was beat."

"I understand. We can still have 'morning after the wedding' sex."

"That we can."

And with an energy that surprised her, he lunged up onto the bed and crawled on top of her. She, of course, had slept naked, but he still had on his dress trousers. So she unzipped him and he swiftly kicked the pants to the floor.

"How's it feel to be married?" he asked, then lashed his tongue over her nipple and sucked it deeply.

"Oh...goddess, yes."

"That good, eh?"

She raked her fingers into his hair and held him there at her breast. Her body reacted to his intense motions by arching and squirming and...every nerve ending sang.

When his fingers slicked between her legs and pressed firmly against the edges of her opening she gasped. The man knew she liked pressure there, that sometimes he didn't even have to enter her to coax her song to a wild, rocking anthem.

"I think I found the right spot," he murmured against her ear, then tugged the lobe with his teeth. "Like this?" He glided his fingers firmly along the opening, contacting her clitoris, and occasionally slipped his thumb over her swollen pearl. "Oh, yeah, my witch is so happy she can't even speak."

Clinging to the sheets, she threw her head backward and it slid off the edge of the bed. He kissed her throat, laving her skin with his hot tongue. And his fingers increased pressure as he slowly stroked her to a long and moaning climax.

"I love to listen to you come," he said. A shift of his thigh pressed his erection against her leg. "So loud and proud."

Panting and laughing at his admiration for her, she gripped his hair and tugged him down to kiss her. Hard and messy and delving for the deepness of him. Heartbeats still thudding and the high fluttering away, she pushed up from him and gripped his cock. "My turn."

"I've got a better idea." He stood and pulled her into his arms, standing and swinging her over his shoulder in a smooth move. "Let's take a shower."

Half an hour later, wrapped in a towel and with wet hair tickling her shoulders, Mireio felt ever so satisfied. She brewed tea and fried up some vanilla cream French toast. She stirred honey into some mascarpone cheese to make a topping, sprinkled it with cinnamon and set the plate before Lars, who also wore but a towel.

"You spoil me," he said, as he dug in with fork and knife. "Mercy, this is amazing. I don't think I've ever eaten so good as when I'm being fed by you."

"Food is love," she said. "And I love you lots. More toast?"

He put up three fingers and she happily dipped more bread into the mix and fried the slices up for him while she ate one herself, standing before the stove.

Domesticity came easily to her. And now knowing she'd wake every morning next to the man she loved, well, life couldn't be better. Add to that a sweet baby boy?

"So, uh… Sunday said something to me last night that confused me."

"What's that? I suppose I should head over and pick up Charlie. Hate to leave him there too long."

"I'm so glad you're going with Charlie. It fits him. But Sunday said that she and Dean would get custody of Charlie if anything should happen to you. Why would she think that?"

Lars set down his fork and looked aside. After a long draft of water he stood to walk around and lean against the counter opposite from the stove where she stood. "That's not completely true."

"But partially true?" Her heart thudded loudly.

"The pack has been pressuring me to change my will. They want to make sure they get Charlie when I die."

"But why would you do that? Lars, I'm your wife. When I agreed to marry you I knew what I was doing. I knew that I was becoming Charlie's stepmom. I adore him. I can take care of him if…well… Don't you trust me?"

"You're the best mom Charlie could ever have. I've had the will sitting out. But I've delayed calling a lawyer to make changes because of exactly this. Us. I know you would make an excellent mother to my boy. But…"

"But? But you're still going to change the will?"

"I don't know." He raked his fingers through his wet hair. "Have you ever raised a werewolf?"

"No, but I'm sure I can learn."

"Mireio, my boy could be an entirely different species from you. Don't you think it best he be raised by a pack? His own kind?"

She eyed the browning toast in the frying pan, knowing it needed to be flipped. Sweet vanilla could not coax her from the sudden anxiety she felt tightening her jaws. "Is that what you want?"

"I honestly don't know. It's why I still haven't made changes to the will. I need to think about it. Is that okay with you? I want to do what's best for my Peanut."

Affronted that he didn't immediately fall in favor of her, Mireio cautioned her anger. He only wanted the best for his son. And a werewolf would thrive if brought up in a pack, living and learning among others of his kind. What could she, a witch, offer him?

On the other hand, no one knew if Charlie was actually werewolf. He could be human. And she could handle that fine.

But he was right. She needed to give him some space on this. Some time.

Lars reached around and grabbed the spatula and flipped the toast. The top side was burned. He bowed and kissed her softly, slowly. His mouth melted against hers, giving her the sweetness the vanilla promised. Had she been angry about something? And then he met her gaze, seeking, searching, asking without words.

She nodded. And he kissed her forehead and scooped the toast out to toss in the garbage. "Let me make the last few. You sit down and eat."

So she did, because she was unsettled at learning she wasn't her husband's first choice to raise his son.

* * *

That night they sat out on the back porch. Fireflies fluttered in the garden above the jasmine and primrose. Cicadas droned in a nearby oak tree. And relaxing on the hammock with Charlie tucked between his arm and chest, Lars read the only thing he could find that wasn't a spell book or a cookbook.

"Sign up now to receive your free toaster when you open an account," he narrated to his son.

"I promise tomorrow I am getting some kid books," Mireio said as she returned to the porch from the kitchen with apple ale for both of them. She set Lars's on the wood floor beside the hammock, then curled into the big wicker chair that swallowed her with its wide white wings. "You just like to read, don't you? Anything and everything."

"I do. Finally found someone who will listen to me, so I'm going to take advantage of that." He sat up and, gripping Charlie's torso, dangled him over the summer grass so the infant could test his legs. He was in a bouncing phase. "I'm sorry about our talk earlier. I didn't give you a chance. And I've been thinking about it. I'm swaying toward you for adopting Charlie. In fact, I called the county records department today, and there's a form that needs to be signed for you to become his official parent."

"Really?"

"Yeah, one issue, though. It needs the real mother's signature."

"Oh." He read her pout and suspected she thought all hope was lost.

"I know she'll do it. It's just tracking her down and getting the paperwork to her and back to me that could be the challenge. I only know that she headed off to Africa."

"What about her family?"

"We didn't talk family trees or contact information during those two days we had our fling. And while she left me with a stack of legal documents, there wasn't an address to contact her because, well, at the time, she was on the move."

"Right."

"But the birth certificate lists an address in Minneapolis."

"Maybe you could start there to find a family member?"

"It's an idea. But how do I do that? Show up at her mother's door. Hey, I'm the guy who fathered your daughter's son, whom you probably don't even know about, and I want her to give me complete custody."

"I'm sure her mother must know about it. Kinda hard to hide a pregnancy from your mom."

"If she has a mom."

"True. Do you have any computer hacker friends? They might be able to track her down somehow."

"Computer hacker friends." He chuckled. "Do I look like a guy who has friends like that?"

"No. Maybe Valor could give it a go. She's always the one who fixes our computers when something goes wrong. She's handy with a wrench and hammer, as well."

"I could hire a skip tracer."

"What's that?"

"A person who tracks down people who don't want to be found. It's not as if she doesn't want to be found. But it's the same kind of situation."

"You look into that. And I'll ask Valor. Hey, Charlie, can you walk over to me?"

Lars led the boy who tested his feet forward, Charlie eagerly trying to get to Mireio's outstretched hands. He wanted her to be his son's mother. Forever. But he had to think of the pack too. And make sure his son got the best guidance through life. This was a tough decision.

And the fact that he even had to consider such a decision? Hell.

Mireio grabbed Charlie and swung him through the air. The boy giggled effusively. He had developed a full-throated belly laugh that always made them both laugh in kind.

"Oh!" She grimaced. "I know why you handed him over to me."

"The one holding him gets to change him," Lars teased. "I am busy reading." He picked up another piece of junk mail and fanned it before his face.

"Fine. But that means I get to feed him his last bottle and tuck him in. So there." She stuck out her tongue at him and wandered into the house.

Lars tossed the mail to the patio floor and sipped his ale. Life had never been better.

Chapter 26

Mireio woke to a strange sound. She couldn't have been sleeping very long after that third orgasm had lulled her into a blissful, sighing slumber. But now she searched the dark room seeking what had sounded like a growl.

Standing near the bed was a shadowed, hulking figure that stomped the floor...with a paw.

"Oh, my goddess."

Lars had shifted to werewolf.

And the baby, likely having been woken by the noise, was crying in his carrier on the floor.

"Lars!"

The werewolf glanced to her and growled. And then he howled a long and rangy sound that Mireio felt sure the whole neighborhood could hear. He stalked toward Charlie, bent to sniff at the infant, then swept a paw through the carrier handle and lifted the infant.

"Oh, no, Lars!" She stumbled off the bed, tangled in the sheets. "You can't. He's not strapped in!"

The werewolf snorted at her and took off down the stairs.

"Oh, shit!" She grabbed her night robe and tugged it on.

By the time she graced the top stair she heard the screen patio door open and swing shut. A glance outside saw Mrs. Henderson's lights go on. Charlie wailed.

"Stop!" Mireio cried as she broached the patio and hit the grass at a run.

The werewolf had fled through the pasture that backed onto their neighborhood yards. The corn grew higher than her shoulders, but a werewolf should have no problem navigating it. But a baby, not strapped in…

"Oh, mercy!"

"Mireio!"

"Not now, Mrs. Henderson! He's got the baby!"

"Who? The Sasquatch?"

"No! Uh…" She ran toward the corn. What to say? The last thing Mrs. Henderson needed to know was that Mireio had married a werewolf. Or even a Sasquatch, for that matter. "A stranger! I've got to get the baby."

"I'm calling the police!"

Ah shit, that was not what she needed. Police and a werewolf? That could mean the end of Lars. The end of werewolves. The end of a reality where humans believed werewolves only existed in movies and books. She couldn't let the police see Lars.

But more, she had to get to him before the baby was hurt. She knew Lars would never intentionally harm his son. But how much of his man's mind could control his wolf brain when in werewolf shape?

She followed the path of trampled stalks through the cornfield, tracking the werewolf's grunt up ahead. He was far off, his powerful legs moving him more swiftly than she could run. The long cutting corn leaves slashed across her face and bare legs. She tugged the night-robe over her naked body and tied it as she ran. Should have put on some shoes; the broken cornstalks proved rough to run over.

Charlie's wails spurred her on and his cries grew louder and closer. She burst out into a clearing where the farmer must turn his tractor, for the cornstalks that lay broken down were in an almost perfect circle. The werewolf stood before the baby carrier, which sat on the ground. Not toppled. And now Charlie had strangely settled, his wide eyes taking in the creature who loomed above him.

"I know you couldn't help it," Mireio said as she approached cautiously. She just wanted to get to the baby. Behind her, she heard police sirens in the distance. "You've got to shift back, Lars. Or get the hell out of here. Go!" She clapped her hands toward the werewolf and it cringed from her.

But then it growled and snapped. Actually snapped its teeth at her.

"I'm not afraid of you. I'm your wife, for goddess's sake. Listen to me. If you want to protect yourself and your son, run!"

And of a sudden the werewolf's head jerked to the side and then forward. His shoulder bent painfully backward as his legs bent and he fell to his knees—human-shaped knees. Lars shifted back to his were shape within three seconds. He crouched there on the crushed cornstalks, panting, naked.

Mireio rushed to Charlie and grabbed the carrier. "You have to go, Lars. Mrs. Henderson called the police and I can hear the sirens. Run…somewhere. I'll leave clothes out in the backyard for you. Go! I'll say whoever took the baby got away, but that doesn't guarantee they won't keep looking for the culprit. Please, Lars, go!"

He nodded and scampered off into the cornstalks.

She checked Charlie. He looked fine, though it was dark and there was no moonlight. Lars hadn't shifted because of the full moon. He'd shifted because his body was mutinying and forcing him to surrender to his shift at the most inopportune times.

"Poor man." She glanced down the path he'd taken, thinking he left a lighter trail now that he was no longer in werewolf shape. She hoped it would be an impossible trail to follow.

Wandering back the way she'd come, she met two police officers with guns pulled when she was about twenty feet from her backyard.

"Hands up!" one called.

"It's me," she answered, but she set down the baby carrier and put up her hands. The flashlight beams forced her to squint. "Don't shoot! I've got the baby with me. I'm the stepmother. I woke up and heard someone leaving the house with the baby. I chased after the man and found the baby alone in the middle of the cornfield."

"Keep your hands up, ma'am."

The officers approached her. She'd never been more frightened. Not even a vicious werewolf could make her feel so vulnerable as standing before two men holding guns aimed at her.

"Which way did the intruder go, ma'am?"

She pointed down the path. "That way. But I think he's long gone."

"Let's take a look," one of the officers said to the other.

"You can take the baby inside, ma'am. We'll be back to talk to you after we check this out."

She nodded and picked up the carrier. Mrs. Henderson

waited on the porch, wringing her hands. Her hair up in curlers, the elderly woman shrieked when she saw Mireio approach with the baby carrier. And that set Charlie into a new stream of wails.

"Oh, the poor boy," the neighbor said. "The kidnapper got away? Why would someone do that? Was it someone you know? Where is Lars?"

"Lars is…at his cabin tonight. He worked on it all day and stayed over. Just me and Charlie here. And I have no idea why someone would do this. Must have been a burglary. I don't own any valuables, so the intruder must have decided to take the baby instead. I need to go inside and see if I can get Charlie to calm down."

"Do you need me to come in with you, dear?"

"No, Mrs. Henderson. Thank you for calling the police." Not really. But, she had to play nice. "Go back to bed. The baby is safe—that's all that matters."

"All right, but I'll come over in the morning to check on you two. You call your husband and have him come home right now."

"I'll do that. Thanks."

Inside the house Mireio poured herself some water and then picked up Charlie and paced the floor with him. He was wide-awake but no longer crying or frantic. That was a good sign. Could he have known that was his daddy who'd taken him on the crazy run through the cornfield?

"I hope he's okay." She glanced out the back screen door, spying the bobbling orbs from the police officer's lights. With hope, they'd give up the search and mark it off as a failed kidnapping or maybe even drug-induced idiocy. "Please be safe, Lars."

The next morning Mireio awoke to a constant knock at the patio door. She climbed out of bed, checked that

Charlie was still sleeping, safe and sound in his baby carrier, then pulled on her robe and wandered down the stairs. She spied the dirt tracked through the kitchen and couldn't recall if the police officers had done that.

Last night two officers had returned from a search of the cornfield and had knocked at the patio door. They'd informed her whoever it had been was nowhere to be found, and then had taken half an hour going through her home and the bedroom. She'd had the forethought to toss Lars's clothes, which he'd pulled off before they'd made love, into the hamper so they wouldn't question where the man of the house was.

And now she followed the dirt tracks down the hallway, even as the knocks sounded gently at the back door—Mrs. Henderson could wait—and into the living room, where she found Lars sleeping on the couch, one arm thrust over his head and hair splayed across his face. His jeans were unzipped and he wore no shoes. He'd found the clothes she'd laid out for him after the policemen had left and must have quietly slipped in sometime during the early-morning hours.

Tiptoeing to the back door, she opened the creaky screen door and stepped out onto the patio so Mrs. Henderson could not come inside.

"Everything is okay," she offered immediately. "I called Lars last night and he came home right away. He's inside sleeping now. And so is Charlie. We're all good."

Mrs. Henderson clutched her arm with a squeezing reassurance. "You know what I was thinking last night as I watched the police search the cornfield?"

"What's that?"

"What if it was the Sasquatch?"

"Oh, Mrs. Henderson, I don't think Sasquatches exist. And if they did, I'm pretty sure they wouldn't have the stealth to sneak into a house and steal a baby. I followed a man through the cornfield. It was probably a burglar who decided to give kidnapping a try. The police said they'd return today when the sun was up to look for evidence."

Of which, she hoped, none would be found. Lars had been naked. He couldn't have left anything behind. Except DNA. No. All they'd find might be a stray wolf hair.

"I brought you some orange cranberry muffins." Mrs. Henderson pointed to the plate she'd set on the patio table. "Are you sure you're okay, Mireio?"

"Positive. Now that my husband is here, we're good."

"You make sure he stays with you tonight. Just in case."

"I will. Thanks for the muffins. Lars will appreciate them."

Her neighbor reluctantly left, waving as she crossed into her yard through the narrow space in the lilacs. Mireio was beginning to wonder if she should plant roses, with thorns, in that space. The woman was a busybody. If she had never called the police everything would be fine.

As it was, she wouldn't stop worrying until the police returned and marked the case off as cold.

She returned to the kitchen and grabbed her phone just as it buzzed with a text. She didn't want it to wake Lars. Eryss texted that she was headed back to town and had left the baby with Dane in California. She wanted to get together to party.

"Will do," Mireio whispered as she texted back.

Then she opened her photograph app to look for a party pic to send, but smiled when the first ones to come up were from the day she and Lars had been kayaking. And the one before that when she'd captured him lying in the tall grasses with the baby snuggled up on his chest. White daisies dotted Lars's beard and he'd beamed as if a ray of sunshine. The man was so happy when he had Charlie in his arms.

Sighing, Mireio tiptoed into the living room, where Lars snored. The poor man. He was degenerating faster. And now, more than ever, she was determined to go ahead with her plan. She had to.

To save her husband's life.

Even though the lasagna didn't have any meat in it, it was hearty and filling. Lars finished his fourth square and eyed the casserole dish. One slice left. His pretty new wife winked at him and nudged the dish toward him.

"Thanks. This stuff is awesome."

"I promise to feed you until you're stuffed every night. That wasn't in the marriage vows, but I will make good on it."

"I know you will. And I promise to help you plant a new lilac shrub where that space is in the hedges."

"Leave it for now. If I end up moving, we'll leave the new owners to figure out Mrs. Henderson. I will really miss that bathroom, though."

"Then I'll make another promise to create a bathroom even more grand than the one you now have. Anything for my wife."

She kissed him, and didn't notice his wince after he'd said that. Would he have the time to do that? Today he felt all achy and his joints were stiff. He felt half in and half out of a shift, actually. Though he wasn't. He was completely in were shape. Yet the shift from last night lingered. Painfully.

By the gods, he'd endangered his son by stealing him away while in werewolf shape. He hated himself for that. Might he have to sleep elsewhere so he wouldn't risk harm to his family? Chain himself up at night? The idea of such a thing sickened him. But even more, if he had harmed Charlie, he would have never forgiven himself.

"Let's go vampire hunting tonight," Mireio said with a hopeful lilt.

He'd been surprised when she'd told him she wanted to perform the immortality spell. But her reason for doing so, because the vampire who killed her mother was the one she'd targeted, was solid. And if his wife wanted revenge? Then he would be the man to stand beside her and support her.

"Sounds like a plan. Do you mind if Sunday babysits?"

"She doesn't threaten me, Lars. In fact, I appreciate all she has done for you and Charlie. She would make a good mother."

"They'll have kids someday."

"I know they will. Sunday will make it happen, one way or another. As for us? I love my little glop of Peanut Butter. Are we going to call him Peanut when we're old and he's grown and married?"

"I certainly hope so." Because that meant Lars would be alive to see such a day.

Chapter 27

It was after midnight and the sky was dark. Clouds blocked the moon. Mireio had brought along all the supplies for invoking the immortality spell. Candles, black salt, lighter, the dragon's exudation, faery dust, a baby's cry and various herbs and crystals. She'd practiced the incantation this afternoon. And had invoked a confidence spell to bolster her efforts tonight.

She was ready to hunt a vampire. And to cast the spell upon herself.

Silently they walked the alleyways they'd followed previously. It felt covert to Mireio, as if they were on a mission and both knew their roles and would only speak if necessary. She wished this night could be as easy as they made it look in the movies.

Lars immediately picked up a scent. Following his silent gesture, she caught up to him.

"You're sure about this?" she asked him.

"The longtooth killed your mother," he said with a strange detachment. "You need this revenge."

"You were reluctant to kill a vampire, no matter what. What's changed your mind?"

"Because I want to remove the threat to you. And if that means you get the bonus of another century of life, then so be it. Let me give you this, Mireio." He stopped to look at her. "Life."

She swallowed back tears. He wanted to give her something he couldn't grab for himself.

He touched the corner of her eye, releasing a teardrop. "No tears for me. Shed them for your mother. You honor her tonight. Yes?"

She nodded and summoned the bravery she would surely need to make it through the next few hours.

"You ready?" he asked. "It's gone that way. Up on the rooftop."

The vampire saw the two of them approach and stood up from his victim. Closely cropped dark hair shaved with zigzags gave him a ridiculous look. And the gold gauges in his earlobes hung heavily near his jaw. His face was so gaunt Lars at first thought he was starving, but the blood dripping down his chin indicated he'd fed. And well. Lars sensed the human at the vampire's feet still had a pulse and Lars saw his legs twitch. But if he didn't act swiftly, the victim could lose too much blood and die.

"What's this?" the vamp said. He made a show of sniffing the air, then sneering. Gold rings on his fingers clicked as he clasped his hands together. "A wolf? And a pretty little bite?"

At Lars's side Mireio bristled, but he tapped her arm. He wouldn't hold her hand. He didn't want to show the vampire any weakness. Though, he was feeling suddenly dizzy. The world wobbled, and his eyes felt loose in their sockets. Damn it, this disease was challenging him in ways he wished would not show up at the most inopportune moments. But he wouldn't get any better thinking about it.

They had to do this now.

Lars stepped forward and delivered a punch up under the vamp's jaw. His victim was wily, though, and he shook it off, spitting blood to the side. He skipped over the victim's inert body. Lars lunged and slammed him against the wall, fisting him in the kidney once, then again. The bastard didn't deserve to walk this earth. He'd taken a woman's life and had left Mireio alone and haunted.

Gritting his jaws, he narrowed his gaze to see through the dizziness as he delivered another punch that he felt go up under the longtooth's ribs. He would pay for the atrocities he'd served others—

Mireio yelled, "Wait! Don't kill him."

Why was his sweet witch here? She should not be… Oh. Yes.

Lars came down from the sudden murderous rage and glanced to his wife. He'd brought her along with him. For good reason.

The vampire in his grip squirmed and spat blood, which landed on Lars's cheek.

The witch planted her feet squarely and lifted her chin. Thrusting out a hand, she spoke firmly, "Let me have his heart."

Lars nodded. He'd almost forgotten. "Right. Speak the spell, witch." He gripped the vamp by his shirt. "Here is your source."

"Oh, shit! Not this!" The vampire kicked, landing a toe at Lars's thigh, which didn't hurt.

As Mireio began to recite a preliminary spell that she'd explained would put the vampire under a temporary thrall, Lars struggled with the thing as if he were a slimy octopus. The creature was not going down without a fight, that was for sure. And Lars's strength had waned quite a bit over the past weeks. Normally he could have controlled the bastard with ease. But he wasn't seeing clearly right now, and if he wasn't careful, the vampire would slip from his grip...

No, he wouldn't let that happen. He slammed the vamp against the brick wall.

A spark flashed in the vampire's eyes and he suddenly went limp in Lars's grasp.

"It took! We've got only a few minutes," Mireio said. She stepped up and blew green dust into the vampire's face. Then pressed her hand over his mouth and nose, forcing him to inhale. "That'll hit his blood stream and render him incapacitated."

At their feet, the human victim scrambled up and clapped a hand over his neck. "What the hell?"

"Did you work a thrall on him?" Lars shook the vampire. "Tell me!"

"Yes," the vamp muttered drunkenly.

"Go!" Lars yelled at the victim. And when he stood there, stupefied and confused, Lars growled at him, which sent him running.

Enthralled, the human would not remember how he'd gotten the bite on his neck. Nor would he transform to vampire. And with hope, he'd not remember Lars and Mireio either.

Shoving the vampire to the rooftop, Lars stepped over him, straddling his hips with his boots. The dizziness had him wavering over the vampire, but he gripped his shirt tightly to anchor himself. He glanced aside to Mireio, who stood up from setting out candles at four points. Her nervous energy hummed in the air and he wanted to ask her one more time if this was what she really wanted. But there was no going back now. He wanted her to have this revenge. And she would.

"Ready?" he asked.

She nodded. Bending, she sprinkled ashes from a glass vial around her and then placed four black crystals at the compass points between each of the candles. A snap of her fingers ignited the candle wicks. "This is for my mother, Jessica Malory. Thy will be done."

She stood inside a protective circle, but also one that would enhance her magic and make her receptive to the spell. As she began to chant words that Lars suspected were Latin, he bent over the vamp. He knew his role. He tore open the bastard's shirt and tapped his chest right over the heart… This was not going to be pretty. Then he dug in his fingers and pulled up skin, muscles and ribs. The vampire moaned, but not loudly. He was under Mireio's spell and still alive, which was the necessary key to this spell. Gripping the slippery, beating heart, Lars gritted his jaws against the smell and this vile act.

It's not vile. It's punishing a murderer and giving a good woman life.

Life. How crazy was it that he couldn't control his own life, yet could hand over so many more years to someone else?

He gasped, wobbling, but managed to slap a hand to the brick wall nearby to steady himself.

"Lars?"

Mireio's voice startled him out of the swirling dizziness. Shaking his head, he cleared his thoughts. Gripping firmly and tugging, he pulled up the organ from the vampire's chest. Arteries and veins burst and severed. The heart continued to beat as he turned swiftly and thrust it toward his wife.

Mireio took it with both hands and, closing her eyes, pressed it to her mouth.

Lifting his chin and setting back his shoulders, Lars watched. Because he was as much a part of this as she was. Together, this act bonded them in a strange and mysterious way. For life. No matter how long or short that may be for him. She sucked at the blood. And as she did, Lars felt his veins tighten. His muscles cramped.

No, no shifting now. He squeezed his fists tightly, mentally begging for a brief escape from the disease, if only to help his wife.

Beneath him the vampire's body suddenly lurched and then relaxed. Dead. The body began to disintegrate and ashed.

And the heart in Mireio's hands ashed, spilling over her bloody fingers and sifting away on the wind. The candles around her flickered and snuffed out, imbuing the blood-tainted air with sulfur.

"Did it work?" he asked.

"I hope so." She dropped to her knees, bowing her head. And Lars knelt beside her, hugging her against him. She trembled. But he only wanted to hold her and make the world right for her.

"No regrets?"

She shook her head. "I did the right thing."

Once at Lars's place, Mireio jumped out of the truck and ran around the side of the cabin. Lars called after her but she begged him to stay away. She needed time to herself.

What she really needed was to make it to the field of

wildflowers so she could… She dropped before the flowers and expelled the contents of her stomach. The horrible act she had committed tonight would not allow her to callously accept the immortality. Had so many witches over the ages done the same without regret? How could they not feel remorse for such a foul act? No matter that the vampire that she'd reduced to ash had been a homicidal madman.

As bees buzzed nearby, hovering over the blood she'd expelled, she spat onto the ground and gasped as tears fell and splatted the backs of her hands. "I'm so sorry," she whispered to anyone who would listen. What had happened to "and ye harm none"? Why was such a spell not considered dark and forbidden? "Oh, goddess. What have I done?"

And then, she shook her head. No. She could not be sorry for taking the life of the vampire who had killed her mother. It was a wish she had held for years. And she felt her mother's soul could feel the revenge and would condone it. Nor could she be sorry for obtaining the one ingredient she needed to give her husband a fighting chance at life.

What was done had been done. She must remain strong.

Standing, she wobbled, then straightened her skirt and stepped away from the spattered wildflowers, which now hummed with hundreds of bees. In the darkness, she wandered around the side of the cabin and into the house. Her shoulder bumped the wall. She redirected but then turned and pressed her forehead to the wall. Lars slipped up behind her and wrapped his hands over her shoulders.

"Don't ask," she said softly.

"I won't. Something happened tonight. Something good and not so good."

"It's a lot to take in."

"You going to be okay, lover?"

"I need to sleep."

"Why don't you let me run you a nice hot tub first? You've some blood on you, sweetie."

"Yes, a bath would be nice." And she needed to brush her teeth. Like fifty times. "Thank you, Lars."

"Sit down." He helped her to sit on the couch. "I'll be back in a few."

He let the screen door bang shut as he raced out and around to the bathroom. Ten minutes later, Mireio was submerged in the hot water, which smelled like Lars's mint shampoo. Very few bubbles, but the man had tried, bless him.

"I'll sit here quietly," he said, settling onto the closed toilet seat.

"No, please. Give me some time alone, will you?"

He nodded, and only when Mireio heard the screen door on the cabin creak once again did she allow herself to cry.

Chapter 28

The next morning Lars drove his family to Mireio's place. She didn't have a change of clothing at the cabin—her shirt had vampire blood on it—and she was kind of cranky, so he decided to do what he could to make her happy. She'd gone upstairs to change an hour ago, so he snuck up to check on her and found her in bed. Sleeping? No, he didn't hear the soft, rhythmic snores. Probably sulking.

After making toast and coffee for breakfast, he took Charlie out to the patio to feed him his bottle. The day was bright and he actually felt pretty good, save for the twitch at the base of his spine. He prayed that did not indicate another unintentional shift. He generally didn't feel it coming on until he was in the midst of it. Which gave him two or three seconds to get away from his son.

Charlie giggled at a passing monarch butterfly that fluttered close to Lars's hair. "Butterfly," he said. "Can you say that?"

Charlie burbled nonsense. And Lars hoped he'd get to hear his son say "Daddy" before life decided to up and leave him.

A rustle in the lilac bushes verified what he'd just sensed. Mrs. Henderson stepped through the leaves and when she spied him gave a little wave. She carried a plate of some kind of baked good that Lars had no intention of turning down.

"How are the Gunderson boys today?" she asked, handing Lars the plate.

"We're both chipper and eager to chase butterflies."

Charlie grasped out for Mrs. Henderson and she gave Lars a hopeful look. "Can I hold him?"

"Sure." He handed the boy over and the woman seemed to handle him well enough. Charlie was a little chunk and growing heavier by the day, but she propped him at her hip and pulled a face to make the boy laugh.

So Lars peeled back the plastic wrap and dug in to the sliced banana bread.

"It's my grandmother's recipe," she said. "Uses cinnamon and walnuts. You don't have a nut allergy, do you?"

"I don't think so. This is great. I might even save a piece for Mireio to try."

"Where is she today? Inside cooking?"

"No, she's…" He wasn't going to tell the woman his wife was depressed because she'd consumed the blood from a vicious vampire. "Taking it easy today. I'll tell her you stopped by."

"Oh, sure. This tyke is sure an adorable guy. Where's his real mother?"

Lars stopped midbite and swallowed awkwardly. So the woman just came out with the tough questions, eh? She wasn't as unassuming and bat-brained as she made others believe.

"Not in the country," he offered, holding out his hands to take Charlie back. "I should go inside and see if Mireio needs help with the laundry."

"But I thought she was taking it easy?"

Oops. "Thanks, Mrs. Henderson."

She stepped back slowly but didn't make her way toward the hedges. "I could watch the boy while you run in to help your wife."

"No, we're good. Aren't we, Charlie?"

The baby in his arms suddenly tilted back his head and let out a howl that would make any wolf pup sit up and howl back.

"Well." Mrs. Henderson pressed a hand to her chest. "That's unusual."

"Heh. He's making baby noises." But Lars was so excited about the howl, he nearly knocked the table over when he stood. "See you later, Mrs. Henderson!"

He rushed inside the house. Lars held up Charlie and the boy howled again. "That's my boy! Mireio!"

He ran up the stairs. His wife lay in bed, awake, but he suspected she wasn't in any mood to actually rise and face the day.

His excitement could not be contained. "Guess what Charlie did?"

She shrugged and sighed.

"He howled at Mrs. H! Howled! Just like a little wolf. He's werewolf, Mireio. I know he is."

"That's sweet."

"Aw, honey." He sat on the edge of the bed and Charlie reached, trying to grab at her tangled hair. "You feel like lying around today?"

She nodded.

"Can I bring up something to eat? Some tea? Mrs. H brought over banana bread."

"Maybe later."

"Okay. You take all the time you need. I'm going to head to the lumber store today. Need to pick up drill bits. You want me to get you anything when I'm out?"

She shook her head and turned her back to him.

At the sight of the blinking baby monitor, Lars set his hammer down. He'd considered asking Mireio to watch Charlie today while he worked on finishing the framing, but he hadn't wanted to leave the baby with her since she was still in a funk. She had gotten out of bed this morning and made him breakfast, but she had still been in a robe and her hair had been uncombed when he'd decided to leave around eleven to work on the cabin.

Had the immortality spell not worked? Had something gone wrong?

Or was it as he suspected? She was feeling guilty over taking the vampire's life to prolong her own.

She should not feel that way. A vicious predator had been taken out of circulation. Yet, he couldn't convince himself he'd had such a right to be judge, jury and executioner. That night, in the moment, he had wanted to kill the vampire out of a rage even before Mireio had reminded him she needed to take the heart. They were both responsible for that death.

So why was he here now? He should be standing by his wife, giving her the hugs and compassion she needed. And in turn, he could get the same from her.

Wow. He'd handled this one wrong. But he intended to fix it.

Packing up his tools, he then found Charlie inside in his crib, bubbly and ready for a bottle. Instead of tucking him into the car seat right away, he let the boy roll around on the floor a bit while he reread the will he'd not taken a moment to look at it. Could he do it? Should he do it?

"What do you think, Peanut?"

The boy rolled over and burbled out bubbles, which was his latest trick. He took joy in the sounds the sputtering saliva made, and obviously the drooling mess.

Lars swiped a cloth across Charlie's chin and neck. He dropped the cloth as the numbness struck him suddenly. His feet and legs began to tingle, as well. The tingling traveled swiftly from his extremities and focused in his spine. So fast! He dropped to his back next to his son and closed his eyes. The numbness was coming on more often and swiftly now, and it seemed to travel toward his center, coalescing at his spine. He had learned that if he lay down and rode it out, it seemed to pass more quickly.

He felt so helpless like this. If a man was going to die, he decided it would be better to be quick. Not debilitating or degenerative. This shit was nuts. He wasn't a weak man. He was a vampire killer, damn it!

Yeah, so maybe he'd had to prove something to himself by killing the vampire. Idiot. And look how the universe rewarded him?

Stretching out an arm, he was able to nudge Charlie onto his back and the infant kicked and squealed, unaware his dad couldn't pick him up if the world were ending.

And with that thought, a tear spilled from Lars's eye.

It had been three days since they'd killed the vampire. And Mireio had, supposedly, gained immortality. Physically, she didn't feel any different. Except tired. But the fact she'd been moping about for days was probably the reason for that. So this morning after Lars had taken off for the cabin with Charlie in tow, she'd gotten up, taken a long bath with Epsom salts and rose quartz crystals, and then wandered out to the garden to pick some lavender. Then she cast a spell to lift her spirits and help her to see the goodness around her.

Sometimes a person could get so mired in one detail that the wide, bright world surrounding them faded into the background. No longer. What had been done was done. She said a blessing to her mother's soul and asked her for a blessing in return. And when the beeswax candle above the stove suddenly flickered to flame, Mireio got her answer.

Her mother approved.

And that was all she needed to lift her head and move forward.

Thinking she might make something sweet for Lars as an apology for her funky mood, she paged through the recipe book she and her grandmother had cobbled together over the years, but nothing leaped out at her.

So when the door opened and Lars and baby entered carrying a little brown bag from Nothing Bundt Cakes, she was thankful the man was on the same page as her.

"You're up," he noted as he situated Charlie in the highchair he'd bought the other day to keep here at the house. He then swung into the kitchen, swept the hair from her cheek and kissed her.

His masculine, fresh-rain-in-the-forest smell drew her to tilt her head for another kiss. And another. And when he landed on her mouth, she turned against him and pulled him down to make it a long and luxurious kiss.

"Wow," he said when he pulled away. "I think you're feeling better."

"Much. Sorry, but I think the enormity of what we did sort of whacked me off balance for a few days."

"I understand that." He took her hands in his. "It affected me too."

"Oh, I know. I've been terrible to ignore you. What can I do for you?"

"What's done is done," he said. "We both need to accept that. And if that's too hard, I picked up something that might help." He grabbed the paper bag and shook it. "Red velvet and chocolate chip."

"Oh, mercy. I'll get the forks!"

Half an hour later, they lay on the couch, naked, with bits of buttercream frosting on Mireio's breast and in the crook of Lars's elbow. Eating cake had started out innocently enough. Until Mireio had dropped some frosting down her shirt, and then… Well.

On the floor, wide-awake in the baby carrier, Charlie gazed at the two of them with a wonder that widened his eyes.

"We'll have to stop having sex in front of the legume," Mireio said.

"Agreed. But we can always eat cake in front of him." They clinked forks together. "Deal."

A shower to remove frosting and cake crumbs was necessary. Afterward, Mireio dried off with the towel and tossed it over Lars's head. He wiggled his butt and then tugged it off and winked at her.

"I hope you don't mind, but I'm going to meet the girls tonight for a gab session."

"Sounds like what you need."

"Why are you so good to me?"

"Because I love you. Because it's easy to want to please you. Because you're the cutest, tiniest witch I know. Because Charlie loves you. Because—"

She pressed her fingers to his lips. "Okay, I get it. You

love me. I love you. We're one big happy family. Do you want me to make you something to warm up for supper before I leave?"

"No, I'm good. I can manage a few things by myself. I've survived this long."

"Indeed, you have."

"You could bring home a growler of the oatmeal stout, if you like. I love that stuff."

"That's the only brew I never put a spell on."

He winked at her. "You've already bewitched me. Spells aren't necessary."

"No, I suppose not," she said, but her mind rushed to the plans she had. A spell would be very necessary.

Chapter 29

Eryss had returned from California but had left her six-month-old with Dane. He was flying into Minneapolis in a week. So the party was held in her conservatory. It was two stories high, designed all of glass panes and resembled a Victorian garden house. It had been damaged last year when a fire had started in her kitchen and Dane had broken through the glass to run in and rescue her. But the repairs made it look as if nothing had happened, and the lush plants and real grass carpeting the floor flourished. There were even dragonflies flitting about among the flowers and crystal grids.

Geneva snapped her fingers, invoking her fire magic, which set the candles sitting on the coffee table to flame, yet the flames hung suspended above the wicks. She winked at Mireio. That's how she liked to do it.

Valor's air magic floated those candles above their heads as if in a candelabra. And Eryss's earth magic had sprouted mushrooms about the emerald velvet sofa where they sat. Mireio's water magic spilled a fine mist over the flowers behind them, which released lush, heady scents.

Eryss tilted back the pink and purple drink Valor had mixed for all of them. "Mercy! What is in this stuff?"

Valor winked. "Faery dust. They're called Dust Bombs. I got the recipe from a witch in Paris."

"Seriously?" Mireio dabbed the sparkling surface of her drink with a fingertip. "What do you have to do to get the ingredients? Give your man a squeeze to get it out?" she asked. "Wait. No. I don't think I want to know the answer to that one."

Geneva hooted. "Faeries expel dust when they come. So we all know how she got this stuff!"

Mireio considered her drink for a moment. Kelyn had…? No, better not to think about the collection method. She tilted back another swallow and smiled so widely her cheeks were beginning to hurt. "To faeries!" She lifted her glass, and the other women joined in the toast. "Long may they sparkle!"

"And to wild and wolfy men," Geneva said with a wink. Then she sighed dramatically. She'd broken up with her rustic fellow a few weeks earlier. Truly, his checkbook hadn't had a chance with her expectations.

Valor plopped her head onto Geneva's shoulder. "We need to hook you up, girlfriend."

Eryss, lying on the couch nursing her drink much more slowly than the others said, "Yeah, but none of us knows any millionaires."

"I prefer billionaires," Geneva replied haughtily. Mireio downed the last of her drink. "We need music!"

"I got it!" Eryss snapped her fingers. "Music!"

Panic! At the Disco filled the room with an erratic yet

bouncy beat. Geneva bobbed her head and performed a hand jive.

"So Geneva needs a billionaire," Valor said. "And I've got myself a delicious faery man."

"Is it true what they say about faeries and their wings during sex?" Mireio asked.

"Oh, hell yeah. When I touch his wings..." Valor mocked a shiver and exaggerated it into a lolling collapse back into the couch.

"Tell us about werewolves," Geneva coaxed. "Have you ever fucked your husband in werewolf form?"

"Not yet. But maybe someday. I will never rule it out."

"That sounds creepy." Geneva tilted back the rest of her drink.

"I think it sounds like an adventure." Eryss winked at Mireio.

"You need more faery dust." Geneva stood up to gather more drinks, but she wobbled and landed back on the couch among giggles.

"So tomorrow night, ladies?" Mireio asked. "That'll give us time to sleep off the hangovers we all know we'll have in the morning. I hope you have room on your bed, Eryss, because I'm not going anywhere tonight."

"Last time I remember sharing a bed with you, you kicked me onto the floor in the middle of the night."

"Then lay down some pillows on the floor. Lars loves me for my bed-hoarding proclivities."

"That's a big word for such a very drunk and tiny witch," Geneva said.

And all four of them burst out in laughter.

Lars drove up to the cabin. He'd dropped Charlie off with Sunday, who had asked him again about the will. He'd said he was still thinking it over and she'd frowned.

He was beginning to get annoyed that the woman was trying to take away his son. And while he knew Sunday was kind and only had the best intentions, she was making it easier for him to sway toward making sure Mireio got full parental custody of his child.

But first he had to get Charlie's mom to sign the paperwork. Sunday had actually found a friend living near the address listed on the birth certificate, and he'd given Sunday the email address where they could reach Charlie's mom. She agreed to sign the adoption papers without question and would sign and scan the documents he sent her way, then send them back to him.

A black Firebird and a Prius were parked before the cabin. He wasn't sure who those vehicles belonged to, but he would guess Mireio's witchy friends. Mireio hadn't come home until nine in the morning. She'd texted him last night that she was too drunk to drive. Had they carried the party over here?

Hopping out of the truck and hitching up his jeans, he realized they were looser than usual. He was always rucking them up of late. Was he losing weight? Mireio had been feeding him well, and he always ate like a horse. Was his body somehow protesting? Hell, he didn't want to think about it. So long as he could walk and use his hands and not wince at the ever-present pain that seemed to clench his spine, he would call that a good day.

Wandering up to the front door, he paused when he heard the female laughter around back. Were they out by the hives? Hmm… Better go say hello to the wife and check out what the witches were getting into. Because with a crew of witches gathered together? Something had to be up.

They stood near the entrance to the woods, not far from the hives. Lars wandered over cautiously, not wanting them to see him until he was sure he wasn't sneaking up on anything. Witches were supposed to gather and get skyclad and cast spells. And he did owe the flirty one for seeing him naked. Hmm...

Mireio placed something on the ground. Valor sprinkled sparkly stuff into the air. The one with the dark hair that he remembered seeing that first night he'd met Mireio in the taproom must be Eryss. She was lighting candles. And the fourth, the witch with the wandering eye for his privates, spun in a circle with a crystal wand held high.

Enchanting the forest creatures this day? Must be some kind of wacky spell. Wonder when they'd all get skyclad? This might require he watch a bit longer.

Leaning against the back wall of the bathroom, Lars crossed his arms and watched, for only a few seconds, before Geneva let out a chirp and clapped her hands, alerting her friends to his presence.

"Lars!" Mireio called, and gestured he approach. But when she looked about to take a step forward, she suddenly paused and stood. She wore a short red dress. Her feet were bare and her hands were bejeweled with crystals and rings. "Come give me a hug!"

He wandered over and nodded to the witches, noting they had set up some kind of ritual. As he got close to Mireio he saw the circle that glinted on the grass—in which his wife stood. He stopped at the outside edge.

"Come here," she encouraged.

A sudden twinge of unease shivered down his spine. He wasn't going to step inside a witchy circle. No way. Not after watching her invoke the immortality spell. He needed a break from witchcraft after witnessing that horror show.

"Come give me a kiss," he tried. If she had no desire to leave the circle, he would grow suspicious pretty darn quick.

"I can't. You have to come to me."

"Why?" He cast his gaze about the circle, meeting each of the other three's gazes for a few seconds. None betrayed their intentions. "What wicked witchery are you ladies cooking up?"

"It's nothing," Mireio said. A flutter of lashes wasn't going to win her any seduction points this time.

Lars noted the three witches who had gathered beside him gave him sidelong glances. His hackles prickled. And considering how screwed up his instincts and body had been lately, that warned him. Deeply.

"Just a renewal spell," Mireio added. "It's something we do with each of the four seasons. Step inside and you'll feel it, as well."

"I, uh..."

"Don't you want to be renewed?" Eryss asked from beside him. "It won't hurt. Mireio has been in the circle for ten minutes. Look how beautiful she is."

Indeed, his wife had never looked more lovely. Her hair spilled like goddess coils about her face, her cheeks were rosy and her lashes were so thick and tantalizing. The hand she held out to entreat him closer seemed to glow with warmth and positive vibes. A renewal spell?

What could it hurt? It might even settle the ache in his spine. And if he got a few days of relief out of it, as he had with the bathtub spell, then he couldn't argue against it. But why did he suddenly feel like a guinea pig?

"Lover," Mireio cooed. Her voice wrapped about his heart.

Ah hell. He'd do anything for his tiny witch.

Lars stepped over the line and into the circle. And as he did so he felt as if he'd permeated a skein and it wobbled to a bubbly close behind him. The air inside the circle felt electric and cool. The hairs on his arms and chest prickled.

Around him, the witches immediately started jabbering something, speaking in tongues. He saw the candles surrounding the circle all take to flame and they lifted from the ground to float. The crystals on the ground glinted as if they were glowing LEDs. And as he started to back up, Mireio lunged and grabbed his hand, tugging him forward. She pulled him down for a kiss and it was so wanting and deep, he lifted her up until she wrapped her legs about his hips and held her in an intimate connection. He didn't care if they had witnesses. He would kiss his wife and make her know how much he loved her.

And yet…

He didn't feel right. Since stepping inside the circle his muscles had tightened. His fingers began to tingle. And his spine pinched. Would he have another attack in front of so many?

She bracketed his face with her palms. "I love you, Lars. And I'm going to save you now."

"What?" Every hair on his body stood alert. His instincts screamed mutiny.

"I found the spell in the grimoire you tried to hide. Did you think I wouldn't want to sacrifice immortality if I had it?"

Shit. So that's what this was about. "Mireio, you can't. You went through so much to have immortality. What about the revenge you got in your mother's name?"

"The only reason I took that vampire's heart was for you, lover. Only for you. Now. Like it or not, we're doing this."

She wiggled out of his grasp, and in the next instant he felt a burn down his forearm. He was bleeding? She'd cut him. And she proceeded to cut herself with a small blade that glinted with black crystals on the hilt. Then she slapped her arm over his, grasping him at the elbow, and forcing him to do the same to her. The cuts aligned and he felt the electrical energy fuse them together. Bright white light burst out from their clasp. The witches' chants rose in intensity.

Mireio chanted, her eyes closed and her grip tight.

Lars wanted to shake her away. She couldn't do this. She'd only just gotten immortality. He'd killed a vampire for her...

Yet in the next instant his entire body jolted. His free arm swung out, extending with the shock. He gritted his jaws at the intensity of the volatile sensations that skittered over his skin. Was she feeling the same? This was insane. It didn't hurt, but it racked every bone in his body.

Lars fell to his knees. Mireio went with him to maintain the hold on his forearm.

"Listen to the words," she said close to his ear. "Know that my love can heal you. Say goodbye to death. Say it!"

"Goodbye," he managed, feeling his throat close up and wanting it to be real. To not be some silly healing ritual performed in a bathtub. To be something that would really work this time and give him forever with his family. "Goodbye, Death!" he shouted again. "Get the hell out of me!"

"Yes!" Mireio shouted. "We honor the deity Hel, who wishes to take Lars Gunderson's life, but now we request his course be changed and the disease rampaging his body be vanquished. Clear his soul of the darkness. Fill him with light!"

His body hummed with what he could only imagine was light. Vaguely aware that around him flames had ignited the glittering circle and a swirl of wind whipped them around into a wall of gold, Lars spread out his arms.

His wife placed her hand over his heart. In that moment he could feel all of her. Her heartbeats. Her joy. Her determination. Her love for him.

Bless her for what she'd done. He prayed that this would work. For he had nothing left to try. And so he exhaled, and let go, surrendering.

And all of a sudden the fiery wall dropped. Tiny spatters of flame scattered across the grass and extinguished with a glint. The three witches, placed at intervals around the circle remained silent, their heads bowed.

Mireio pushed her hands through his hair and kissed his eyelids, then his forehead. "Blessings, husband. The spell is complete."

He opened his eyes to look into pure blue love. Mireio's smile grew slowly. He touched her mouth, then smoothed his finger along her cheek. She felt so soft. So real. So powerful. He still felt the magic vibrating through his system. It was strong. Did her body shudder?

"You two need to stay in the circle awhile, let the magic settle in," Eryss said from outside the circle. "We've done what we came for. We'll leave you two to bind the magic as tightly as you can. Blessed be."

Geneva and Valor both said, "Blessed be."

"Call us later!" Valor called as the threesome made their exit.

"We need to bind the magic now." Mireio stood and pulled off the dress over her head and tossed it outside the circle. "You ready for this?"

Thoroughly taken aback by all that had happened, Lars could but nod and grin. Anything involving his wife's being naked was all right by him.

Slowly she rocked upon her husband's prone body, feeling the glide of him deep inside her being. Becoming a part of her. Owning her. The magic still hummed within him and her. It heightened every sigh, every touch, every slick of skin against skin to an intense sensation. He cupped her breasts as she rode him, and moaned as she used her inner muscles to squeeze him.

They needn't speak. The moon was nearing fullness. Probably tomorrow, Mireio realized. Tonight should be a night Lars had sex until he was sated because his were-wolf would want to be set free. But he hadn't had control over his wolf for months. When he'd wanted to shift he could not. And when he least wanted to shift, his body decided otherwise.

But that would all change now. It must. The spell had been invoked. And they bound it tightly with sex, the joining of their souls and bodies.

Lars slicked his fingers over her clit, drawing up a moan from deep within her. Her body began to shudder, matching his tremors. And together the two of them came in an exquisite blending of magic and wild.

A fierce magic, that.

Later they sat in the center of the circle on the soft grass that still glinted with the faery dust they'd used in the spell. Mireio sat on his lap, her head tilted against his neck. She wanted to set his wild free. To give him the freedom that his very species demanded for survival.

Had the spell worked? Only time would tell. She didn't feel any different. As if she'd lost the immortality she'd only had for a few short days. She didn't miss it. She hadn't had time to embrace it, so how could she miss it? She'd never have the opportunity to work the spell again. It was a once in a hundred years kind of thing. If she lived naturally for another hundred years, she could attempt the spell, but it was unlikely that would occur.

Another seventy or so years was enough if she could spend every day with Lars.

"What are you thinking about?" he asked, softly stroking her thigh.

"How I'm looking forward to spending seventy years with you. Every day."

"Seventy? Where'd you get that number?"

"I don't know. I'm almost thirty. I figure I'll shoot for one hundred."

"Sounds like a good goal to have. Do you think the spell worked?"

"You tell me how you feel."

"Besides the fact that my body was just put through a wringer and then injected with awesome and now I feel like I'm sparkling like a faery? Who can know?"

"We'll take one day at a time. The moon is watching us."

"I can feel her in my veins. She is calling me to shift."

She gave him an incredulous look.

"I know," he said with the same doubt. "I haven't felt such a calling for a long time. I think I could shift if I wanted to."

"Then do it. Let me meet your werewolf on much better terms than we have the past few times he's come out."

"I don't know. If I can't control the werewolf, he might, you know…"

"Try to have his way with me?"

"Possibly."

"You said that's how we bond."

"But you're not ready for that."

"No, I'm not. But I think you can control that part of you. You would never do anything to harm me."

"Never." He kissed her cheek. "You really want me to try? I could go for a run. It would feel great. I have all this energy coursing through me. I feel like it's ready to burst."

"Then do it." She stood and pulled him up. "We can leave the circle now. Our sex bound the magic. The spell has settled into you. I think shifting might even help it sink in further."

"You don't need to tell me twice. Maybe you should go inside."

"No. I'm staying right here. I want to watch you howl at the moon."

"All right, then." He kissed her, lingered on her soft, swollen mouth that felt as fiery as his heart. "I love you, witch."

"I love you too. Now shift!"

"Here goes. I think I'm going to stay in the circle when I shift. Can I do that?"

"Sure. It still has some minute energies flowing within it." She stepped outside the circle, picking up a red candle and her dress. With a whisper, the candle ignited. Bowing, she touched the flame to the faery dust circle Valor had laid down. It glowed white, a match to the moon. With another whisper, she sent her intentions from her heart about the glow, imbuing it with love, peace and her wish for Lars's healing. "Go for it, lover."

With a growl and a controlled jerking of limbs, Lars shifted from his beautiful, muscled man shape into the befurred and clawed werewolf with a wolf's head and maw that revealed pristine white canines and a soft black leathery nose. His ears were tufted with black fur among the brown, and from his paws sprouted razor sharp ebony claws.

The werewolf turned to her, flared its nostrils and then stepped closer. Mireio held up her palm, and the wolf pressed its paw to it. It was twice as large as her hand

and the claws curled over the tops of her fingers, but it was so warm, and the toe pads were as soft as Lars's skin.

"Husband," she said.

The werewolf bowed his head and sniffed at her hair and face. It stood tall, its golden eyes glowing and claws flexing. And then he tilted back his mighty head and howled toward the moon, his chest expanding and back arching.

"Magnificent," she whispered.

And she fell in love with her husband's werewolf that night.

Chapter 30

A week later...

Mireio stood before the beehives after the sun had set. Hundreds of insects buzzed in the air, returning to home base with their pollen loads for the evening. Lars was in the cabin reading to Charlie about how to unclog a drain. She'd suggested he look it up online before going after the kitchen sink that had been causing them issues for days. And her wolfie man was always eager to read and learn.

He'd been exuberant to a fault since the night she and her witch friends had performed the death-dissuading spell. It had worked. It had to have worked. And while she'd suggested Lars go to the doctor to have those tests done all over again, he would have nothing to do with such nonsense. He said he felt great. Leave it at that.

Which, she could do. Mostly. Yet she pined for some sort of reassurance. Some promise that the future she had with her husband would be long and not cut short by a disease that may or may not have been defeated by witchcraft.

"No one ever knows when they'll die," she whispered to the bees. "I had immortality for a few days. Now it's gone."

And for a good reason. She'd given her husband life. And that was all that mattered. She would never again have a chance to cast the immortality spell. Worth the sacrifice. No question.

"He is such a kind man. I love him beyond words. Take care of him," she said to the bees. "Please. And watch over our whole new family. I promise I will never stop loving him."

The bees continued to buzz, their wings busy and their furry bodies industrious. Mireio said blessings to them and then cast a spell across the meadow, stirring the flowers to tilt up their petals and reach for the setting sun.

Lars gripped the edge of the bed to prevent himself from falling onto the floor and instead rolled to his side, snuggling up close to his wife's warm, naked body. Her hair tickled over his face and he nuzzled into it, seeking the faint cinnamon scent that still lingered on her. She'd made cinnamon rolls last night and put them in the fridge so when he rose in the morning he could pop them in the oven. She intended to get up when the oven timer went off and deliver to him the warm rolls while he worked.

The witch had a curious method to doing things that all seemed to revolve around food and creating delicious memories. He liked that about her. He kissed her head and she moved slightly but still slept. Gliding his hand down her arm, he closed his eyes and drew in the softness of her skin. The warmth that emanated from her. The utter grace and beauty that had agreed to be his wife. Charlie's mother. The witch to his werewolf.

Life was good.

And it was really good lately because he'd not experienced a single symptom nor shifted without volition. The spell had worked. He'd beat the disease.

Maybe.

But he wasn't willing to risk going to a doctor to find out otherwise. Life was to be lived without caution. And he intended to do so.

In fact, he had finally gotten the courage to tell Dean and Sunday that he was changing his will, but only to reflect that Mireio was his wife and, should he die, all his possessions would go to her. And Charlie's mom had signed the papers and emailed them back. Now Mireio was officially Charlie's legal mother. And should Lars ever die, Charlie would remain with her.

All was well with him.

Rising, he pulled on his jeans and a T-shirt, then tiptoed over to the crib. Charlie lay on his back, arms spread and legs splayed wide. He slept like the witch, using up all the mattress. Lars smirked at that. He'd sacrifice all his space for his two favorite people.

He padded over to the fridge, pulled out the cinnamon rolls and removed the beeswax-coated cloth, then he turned on the oven, set the timer and placed them inside. Grabbing his boots by the door, he walked outside and around the back to the framework. The south wall was almost complete. He planned to order windows today and they'd be in by next week.

He walked between the back of the new work and the bathroom. Only about ten feet. He could either craft a narrow hallway that led to the bathroom, expand the expansion even further or move the bathroom up to nestle against the main house. Which would involve a whole lot of plumbing work.

"A hallway to start," he decided. "At least for the winter. Can't have my bride walking out in the dead of winter after she's soaked in her bath."

The Sheetrock needed to be put up today. It was a tedious job, but he had all the right tools, which made it easier. Lars walked over to the stack of Sheetrock. He'd left his tool belt in the bee shed yesterday because, before coming in for the evening, it had started to rain.

Striding over to the shed, he smiled because he realized he had everything he'd ever wanted in life. And more. How had a wolf like him gotten so lucky? And to have dodged death?

Must have been due to the magic that had entered his life. Mireio had called it fierce magic. Indeed, it was.

To his right, the sun flashed on the horizon, pinking the sky and promising a warm August day. Already the bees were headed out on their pollen routes, which would take them across the field of wildflowers, and miles away in some cases, in search of nectar.

He walked past the spot where Mireio had fallen to her knees the night that she'd drunk the vampire's blood. He knew she'd gotten sick and the next morning when he'd come out to toss some dirt over it, he'd seen that it was gone. The bees had landed on the blood-covered flowers and drunk it. Weird. But that was bees for you. He'd once read about bees producing blue honey because they'd gotten into some melted sugar candies tossed into an open factory Dumpster.

And now that he thought of it, he wondered about experimenting with planting some new flowers next summer. Pollinators thrived on a variety of flowers. He'd have to talk with Mireio about it. She knew about things like flowers.

Stopping before the bee shed, he reached to open it, when a sudden twinge in his chest stopped him. He clasped a hand over his heart. Something stabbed at him. And burned. It clenched his spine from neck to hips.

He cried out, but that sound was abruptly cut off as he blacked out and his body dropped, there on the dew-frosted grass before the hives.

Mireio had listened to Lars carefully place the rolls in the oven and then sneak out. He was so thoughtful trying not to wake her. She loved the big ole wolf. But Charlie had stirred as soon as the screen door had closed. So she dragged herself out of bed, pulled on one of Lars's worn gray T-shirts that fell to her thighs, and picked up the infant.

"You get to taste vanilla frosting this morning, Charlie. What do you think of that? Oh, mercy. The man has a way of leaving the really stinky ones to me. Do you know that?" She kissed the baby's cheeks, and blew each one a raspberry. "Yes, you've got some deadly stuff going on in that diaper. Talk about a witch ward."

She changed Charlie and then checked on the cinnamon rolls. They were done, so she pulled them from the oven and took the frosting she'd made last night out of the fridge. In ten minutes the rolls would be the perfect temperature to frost, then she'd bring them out to Lars.

But she didn't hear any hammering, so she decided to see what he was up to.

"Maybe Daddy is trying to be quiet," she said to Charlie as she skipped down the front steps with the infant propped at her hip. "We'll let him know we're up, then he can go to town with making you a new bedroom. What do you think about that? You're going to have your own room. And I'm going to make sure the other room becomes our bedroom. Lars!"

He wasn't in the framed rooms, so she scanned around the backyard and when she didn't see him, she frowned. "Maybe he went for a run?"

Her vision soared over the meadow, dappled by the rising sunlight and then she spied the opened bee shed. And lying on the ground before it—

Breaths chuffing from her as if she'd been thumped in the chest, Mireio gasped. "Oh, goddess!"

Running toward her husband, who lay on the ground, she called out to him. Charlie bounced at her hip so she clutched him tightly.

Plunging to the ground, she set the baby down as she realized her husband was not moving. He lay there as if he'd decided to take a nap on the summer grass, but...

Panicking, she pressed her fingers to his wrist, seeking a pulse. Mireio moaned. Her throat tightened. And her heartbeats thundered.

"No. Not now. This cannot happen! Lars!" She shook him at the shoulders but he did not rouse.

Why was he on the ground? Had he had a heart attack? He was a young, healthy man. Who'd been on a fast track to death until she and her friends had worked their witchy magic.

Or had they?

"No, the spell had to have worked! Come on! Lars!"

Charlie rolled over and caught his arms on one of Lars's legs. Mireio kept the infant in sight and didn't want to alarm him, but she didn't know what to do. Lars wasn't breathing.

"No, no, no no." Pressing her palms to his chest, she remembered the CPR training she and her friends had taken in case they ever needed it at the brewery. She pumped his chest with both hands. "This can't be happening!"

She had to call for help. Her cell phone was in the cabin. She didn't want to leave Lars.

She bent and pinched his nose. Tilting back his head, she breathed into his mouth. No reaction. She pumped at his chest again. Now she shouted his name and kept repeating "no," aware that Charlie was becoming agitated, but unable to stop her actions. She pumped hard, then breathed into her husband's mouth.

"Please! By the goddess!"

What spell could she work to bring him around? She had none. Had exercised the most powerful spell she could find to give him life… To dissuade death. And it had not worked.

Now Charlie's wails cut the air. Mireio turned to lift the infant. She pressed him against her thundering heartbeats, wishing it were Lars who was reacting, moving, hugging up against her for reassurance. It couldn't end this way.

It couldn't end.

How could it end?

"No!" she shouted and her tears spilled out as she rocked with Charlie before Lars. On her knees, she cried to the rising sun, to the trees and the flowers. And to the bees. "Please, don't take him like this. Not from his family. Not from…me."

A whisk of wind whipped her hair about her face and then the air stilled. Charlie's cries softened, as did Mireio's. She looked about, feeling a weird tingling in the atmosphere. As if magic, but not something she had invoked.

"What's happening? Please don't take him. Please?"

And then she noticed the dark swarm that rose up from the hives. It was thick and wide and buzzed loudly with the flutter of thousands of wings. The susurration of bees moved over their heads and hovered there like a black cloud. Strangely fearful of the swarm, she gripped Charlie closer and shuffled away from Lars's side. Yet, she was also curious. What would cause the bees to act so?

Charlie stopped crying and pointed up at the bees. He babbled something that sounded like "Baa."

"Yes, bees," she said on a tearful sniffle. "What do you think they're doing? Are they flying over your daddy?"

The swarm congregated over Lars's body, lowering as if it was a single entity. Some of them landed on him, crawling over his face and skin. And then Mireio noticed the ones that had landed on him were falling away, dead. Bees didn't just die like that. Not unless they stung someone.

"They're stinging him? No," she pleaded, but it came out as a whisper.

Bees would not sting unless provoked. What were they doing?

A rain of dark droplets began to fall over Lars's body. Mireio thought it could be honey, or perhaps the waxy propolis that the bees exuded after they'd processed the pollen in their bodies. Whatever it was, it was stained red, almost as if it were blood.

Instinctively, she glanced to the place where she'd knelt weeks earlier, sickened after her cruel act, which had served to give her immortality. Or had it? Had she expelled so much vampire blood that she'd never had immortality? And the blood that could have given that to her...

Had the bees taken it up and somehow alchemized it into their honey?

Now watching the bees with awe, she held Charlie as he stood in her arms and pointed at the swarm. The infant was in as much awe as she. If the bees had consumed the vampire's blood, could they possibly have taken on the immortality spell?

Whatever was happening, she had no intention of interfering. Lars had tended those bees with love and care over the years. He had spoken to them, telling him his trials, adventures and about the good times. Surely, he'd confided to them about the bad times. Had he spoken of her to the bees?

Were they now honoring their fallen keeper?

It was a beautiful thing to witness. Lars's body dripped with the blood-tinged substance. Bees crawled over him, fluttering their wings where he'd been stung. They were forcing it to permeate his skin, making it enter his bloodstream. Amazing.

"Baa?" Charlie looked to Mireio. The boy stretched out an arm and a bee landed on his fingers. The infant giggled as the insect walked along his skin.

She didn't shoo it away. As long as Charlie was curious, she was too.

"Thank you," she felt compelled to say to the insect. "For all the love you have given Lars. You bless us all."

The bee alighted, flew above her head so she could feel the hair move against her forehead a little, then soared back into the swarm. In its wake the swarm lifted and followed their leader back to the hives until finally the sun shone across Lars's body.

Making sure that there were no work tools lying about, Mireio set Charlie down and slowly crawled on her hands and knees toward Lars. Her husband's clothing was soaked from the bees' mysterious honey bath, and while she'd been certain he'd been stung—dozens of dead bees lay around him—she didn't see any swollen stings on his skin.

She dared to touch his cheek, then smoothed her fingers along his beard, thinking this might be the last opportunity she had to touch him so intimately. Her tears dropped onto his chest and she plunged forward to hug him. Drawing in the sweet taint from the sticky substance the bees had left behind, she sniffled and listened as behind her Charlie burbled gaily.

She must remember this moment with joy and give thanks for the short time they had had together, and hope for a future with Lars's son. He'd given her something special. She would honor his wishes and raise his child as her own.

So when the body beneath her suddenly jerked, Mireio let out a chirp and shot upright. "Lars?"

The werewolf groaned and his eyelids fluttered. Bee substance dripped from his lashes as he opened his eyes and looked at her. "Mireio, I love you."

Epilogue

Four months later...

The first storm of the season dropped six inches of snow in the first week of December. The day was bright and the air crisp. Lars clapped his gloved hands together while he waited for Mireio to situate herself on the big red plastic sled with Charlie in her lap. She'd bundled him up in a puffy blue snowsuit that made him look like a ball of dyed wool, but his little eyes gleefully beamed up at Lars.

"You ready, Charlie?" he asked.

"Onward!" Mireio called.

Lars gave a tug and headed down the path that cut through the forest. Snow crystals fell from the tree branches, clattering softly against one another. A red fox darted ahead of them. And life had never been better.

With Mireio's encouragement, he had returned to the doctor for another battery of tests a week after the amazing rescue mission performed by his bees. And...the doctor had been speechless. He'd pronounced him healthy, with no signs of the degenerative failings he'd previously shown. Though he'd warned him that something like this could return, he'd told him to leave and live life.

Which was exactly what Lars intended to do. He'd been given a second chance. He wasn't going to waste a single moment.

The cabin's addition had been completed three weeks earlier, and Charlie's room was currently being furnished. Mireio had talked him into making the other room their bedroom, which he could totally get behind. And with a makeshift hallway connecting the new addition to the bathroom, he had big plans to make Mireio the biggest most awesome bathroom ever come spring. Then they could sell her house in town.

Snowflakes sprayed up in his wake and Charlie giggled. The boy was walking now, with help, and Lars already thought he was growing up too quickly. Good thing he planned to be around for a long time to watch that lightning-fast growth.

The bees had saved him by dripping the vampire blood-infused honey substance over him. He knew that to his very bones. And so did Mireio. Not a day went by that they didn't thank the bees, even as they now hibernated for the winter.

And Mireio. His gorgeous witchy wife with a smile that truly gave him life. There was a reason he'd run through her yard that night so many months ago and had seen her standing there naked. The universe had known they belonged to one another. And now as a threesome, they intended to live, love and hopefully make the family bigger.

Life is filled with challenges, struggles, trials and

hardships. We can never know when we will die, only that it will happen someday. Live now. Live for every moment. And bless the bees.

* * * * *

Award-winning and bestselling author
Deborah LeBlanc is a business owner, a licensed
death-scene investigator and an active member of
two national paranormal investigation teams. She's
the president of the Horror Writers Association,
Mystery Writers of America's Southwest chapter
and the Writers' Guild of Acadiana. Deborah is also
the creator of the LeBlanc Literacy Challenge, an
annual national campaign designed to encourage
more people to read, and Literacy, Inc., a nonprofit
organization with a mission to fight illiteracy
in America's teens. For more information go to
deborahleblanc.com and literacyinc.com.

Books by Deborah LeBlanc

Harlequin Nocturne

The Wolven
The Fright Before Christmas
Witch's Hunger
The Witch's Thirst

Visit the Author Profile page
at Harlequin.com for more titles.

THE WITCH'S THIRST
Deborah LeBlanc

My heartfelt thanks to Rich, Meme and Roe—
you help make so much happen!

Chapter 1

Evette—Evee—François watched as black and pus-yellow liquid flowed from Bailey's arm when Daven clawed through it. Both were Nosferatu and hell-bent on destroying each other. Aside from Bailey and Daven, six more Nosferatu had paired off, each viciously attacking the other. Her head captain, Pierre, supposedly in charge of the two-hundred-plus Nosferatu they forced to remain in the catacombs and allowed out only for feedings, did his best to stop the fighting. He'd stretched his bulk of a body to its full eight feet, had morphed into his natural state—bald head with a large, throbbing vein that started at his forehead and then extended over the crown of his scalp like tree branches. His fangs, the longest and most lethal of all the teeth possessed by the Nosferatu within the catacombs, were bared. His hands had balled into fists. And when he shouted, the walls seemed to vibrate with the fierceness of his voice.

"Enough! As leader of this clan, I say enough! Return to your assigned spaces at once!"

Instead of listening to Pierre, more Nosferatu began to fight. They hissed and shrieked, and Evee let out a heavy sigh. She noticed that the Nosferatu who weren't fighting were either hiding behind a crypt or had rolled onto a grave shelf, seemingly content to watch, but not wanting to engage in any brawl.

"We've got to get them under control before they kill one another," Lucien Hyland said emphatically. He took hold of the two steel bars from a floor-to-ceiling gate that separated the outside world from the catacombs of St. John's Cathedral. He shook them, then pulled the thick chain and padlock that secured the gates. Neither gate nor padlock budged.

"Cousin, get your hands away from the bars—" Before Ronan Hyland could finish his warning, two Nosferatu slammed into the gate. Both reached for Lucien.

Lucien sprang backward, away from the gate, then looked from his cousin to Evee, who was leaning against a stone column, arms crossed over her chest.

"Why aren't you doing something?" Lucien asked Evee, his emerald green eyes ablaze with anger. "You're acting rather nonchalant over this ordeal. Why? Can't you see they're going to kill each other? Can't you see all the…blood?"

"No one's going to die—unless you stick your hands back there again," Evee said. "They're fighting, yes, but it's not to kill one another. It's out of boredom. They're not used to being cooped up at night."

Ronan, who Evee had learned was the more serious of the cousins who'd been assigned to her, shook his head. "I don't understand. The Nosferatu aren't senseless beings. Don't they know that keeping them here is for their own protection?"

Evee tossed him an exhausted look. "Imagine a room full of children and a huge storm is blowing outside. The children know the storm is dangerous, but that doesn't stop them from getting antsy and squabbling with one another when they're forced to stay indoors."

Ronan cocked his head as if considering her words.

Lucien let out a huff of frustration.

Evee closed her eyes for a few seconds. She'd felt exhaustion before, but never to this degree. She wished she had the power to turn back time. Two weeks of time at least.

Two weeks ago, things had flowed normally in her life. Well, as normal as life went when you were the middle sister from a set of triplets, and the triplets happened to be witches. The fact that she and her sisters, Vivienne and Abigail, were responsible for the Originals, those being the Nosferatu, the Loup Garous and the Chenilles, twisted the definition of normal all the more. By human standards, of course.

Along with the Originals, throughout the centuries, sprouted their offshoots, like vampires, werewolves, and zombies, etc., each created from either crossbreeding, malicious intent by some sorcerer with a wicked streak, or possibly an off-the-radar, wayward coven. Fortunately, others were in charge of the netherworld offshoots.

Evee and her sisters only tended to the Originals. She and her sisters were known as a Triad, which were triplet witches born from a triplet witch. The first set had been born in the 1500s, somewhere in France. According to legend, the first Originals and the chaos that went with them occurred when the first set of triplets got pissed off at the men they were supposed to marry. Evidently, the night before the triplets were to wed, they found their betrothed fooling around with other women.

Women scorned, men be warned, Evee thought. She supposed that creed existed even back in the 1500s because the anger of the first Triad played a huge part in creating the Originals. This caused the Elders from their sect, known as the Circle of Sisters, to punish the first Triad and the punishment carried to each generation of Triads that followed.

Evee thought cursing whole generations of Triads for something someone had done long ago was bullshit. She and her sisters had nothing to do with what had happened in the past with the first Triad. To her, it was simple. If a puppy peed on its owner's carpet, the owner might bop the pup on the snout with a newspaper to teach him "no." However, that didn't give that owner the right to go popping every pup born thereafter because the first one tinkled on a carpet.

Regardless, the creation of the Originals by her ancestors way back when must have been equated with peeing an ocean on a Persian rug, because Triads were still paying for the deed to this day. And there wasn't a damn thing she or her sisters could do about it.

So they'd simply lived with it. The Originals were assigned—Vivienne, or Viv as everyone called her, and the oldest of the three by ten minutes, took care of the Loup Garous; she, or Evee as she preferred being called, handled the Nosferatu; and Abigail, whom everyone called Gilly, managed the Chenilles. Once their routines had been established, life hadn't been so bad. Complex at times. But not terrible.

Until now.

For the last couple of weeks, they'd been stuck in a

nightmare that wouldn't go away, that no one seemed capable of waking them up from.

It wasn't like they hadn't run into issues with their broods before. Odd incidents were the norm when dealing with those from the netherworld. But for some reason, when the cousins—Lucien, Ronan, Gavril and Nikoli Hyland—arrived, all hell seemed to break loose.

They'd appeared at the Triad's front door, four extraordinarily handsome men, claiming to be cousins—although only two were with her right now—and swearing to protect the sisters and the Originals with their lives. They called themselves Benders and claimed their purpose was to save the Originals from monstrous creatures that hid in dimensional folds. They called the creatures Cartesians and said these were bent on annihilating the entire netherworld, especially the Originals and the Triad. With each netherworld creature's death, a Cartesian absorbed the powers of the creature it destroyed, then brought the essence of the kill to its leader, allowing the leader to grow stronger, which empowered him to create more Cartesians.

According to the Benders, the Cartesian leader meant to be the sole power of the netherworld, and once he had completed the task of absorbing the powers of every netherworld creature, humans were the next target. In essence, the Cartesians—specifically their leader—meant to control the very universe.

When Evee first heard the Benders' claims, she thought all four of them were a few cards short of a full deck. But in the days that followed their arrival, she'd seen much more than she needed to for truth to set in. Cartesians and the danger they presented were very, very real. She'd yet to see one of the creatures for herself, but her sisters Viv and Gilly had, and their descriptions had been all too vivid. Huge beings that appeared to be at least ten feet tall and had the expanse of body to match their height. They were covered with matted brown, gray and black fur, which hid thick scales like armor beneath it. Their teeth were all needlepoint incisors, and their claws were none like they'd seen before on any creature. At least four inches in length and razor-sharp. And the worst part was that they seemingly appeared out of nowhere.

The Cartesians' entry into this world came from rifts in the sky. The initial rifts were caused by natural disasters, odd cosmic alliances or an erred declaration. Their first experience with the Cartesians came after Viv, responsible for the Loup Garous, had told her brood in frustration that "she quit." She hadn't meant what she'd said, but exasperation could cause a person to throw caution to the wind. Once she'd uttered those two words, a small rift had occurred, and the Cartesians had gnawed, clawed and forced their hideous bodies through the opening and into this dimension.

So far, Viv had lost many Loup Garous to the Cartesians, and Gilly, some Chenilles. As if that wasn't bad enough, even stranger occurrences added to the Triad's terror. Something they couldn't understand, much less keep from occurring. Some of the Originals had gone missing. Simply vanished from their safe zones, from places that she and her sisters had controlled with border spells for years with great success. To date, Viv had nearly one hundred and fifty Loup Garous dead or missing; Evee had ten Nosferatu on the loose; and Gilly, fifteen missing Chenilles, plus two dead.

The missing Originals planted their current situation in the dirt of dire straits. Humans were now in danger. If they couldn't find the missing Originals and bring them over to the feeding grounds located at the North Compound in Algiers at their regular feeding time, which occurred in the wee hours of morning, they'd be seeking food elsewhere. They'd be looking at humans to satiate their hunger.

Adding to the dilemma, the wayward Nosferatu, Chenilles and Loup Garous were now open targets for the Cartesians. Evee had to find her brood so they could be watched over and kept safe from the enemy.

You would think that she and her sisters being witches could easily defuse the situation. But such wasn't the case. Along with the mayhem and confusion they faced, their powers and natural abilities like clairvoyance, channeling and mirroring seemed to be diminishing or worked haphazardly. Even the Triad's Elders, Arabella, Taka and Vanessa, appeared to be at a loss and utterly useless in helping them through the situation.

The only people they had to count on now were each other and the Benders, whom they'd decided to pair off with in order to cover more territory. Viv with Nikoli, she with Lucien and Ronan, and Gilly with Gavril.

So far the misfit teams seemed to be barely holding their own. At last count, Viv had located one of Evee's Nosferatu, whom she had Pierre fetch and return to the catacombs. Viv had also located at least twenty of her Loup Garous, whom she'd teleported to the North Compound, where Viv had them encamped.

Without question, the François sisters were torn in far too many directions. The missing Originals had to be located before humans were attacked, and the Originals who were already confined needed protection from the Cartesians. It didn't take a world of common sense to realize they couldn't be everywhere at once.

To aid in the matter, the Benders had established a

plan and built an electric field charged by their scabiors, the weapons they carried. The field, which the Cartesians couldn't penetrate, canopied each location where the Originals were kept. The North Compound for the Loup Garous, the Louis I Cemetery for the Chenilles, and, of course, the catacombs beneath St. John's Cathedral for the Nosferatu. The idea was to keep the Originals they now had safe within these electric domes, which would give each team time to search for the Originals who'd gone MIA.

The first time Evee witnessed the Benders' scabiors in action, she'd been nothing short of amazed. Alone, a scabior appeared toylike. A steel rod approximately eight inches long, its circumference about a half inch. A quarter-size bloodstone capped one end. But handled by a Bender, that which initially appeared benign turned into a weapon like no other Evee had ever witnessed.

A quick flip of the Bender's wrist, and the steel rod twirled between their fingers with a speed that seemed to defy the laws of physics. Once the scabior was charged and aimed at a Cartesian, it shot a bolt of electricity that pushed the monstrosity back into the rift, out of one dimension and into the next. The Benders' goal was to push the Cartesian back to as many dimensions as possible. The farther the dimension, the longer it took the Cartesian to find its way back.

With the electric dome charged, they could search for missing Nosferatu again.

It was dark outside, but barely, which meant she, Lucien and Ronan had plenty of time to search for the missing Nosferatu before feeding time arrived.

Suddenly, someone took Evee by the shoulders and gave her a gentle shake, breaking her reverie. It was Lucien.

"Evee, you have to do something to get the Nosferatu

under control," Lucien said. "I realize they're impatient and want freedom, but keeping them under the scabior dome's protection is crucial. Do something. A calming spell, anything that will keep them from destroying one another."

Evee took her time responding. She was overtaken by the depth of Lucien's green eyes bearing into hers, his shoulder-length hair the color of a black stallion's mane, his neatly trimmed beard and mustache that barely hid two prominent dimples that appeared whenever he smiled, something he definitely was not doing now. Evee guessed Lucien to be in his midthirties. He stood about six foot three and weighed maybe one seventy-five. Since she was only five foot seven, Evee had to look up at him, which she did feeling hypnotized. She couldn't help it. It made her feel like a slug, ogling him despite the fighting going on inside the catacombs, but it seemed beyond her control. She wanted nothing more than to breathe in Lucien's scent, a mixture of earth and musk doused by a fresh summer shower.

She was about to answer Lucien when Ronan suddenly appeared at her side. Another over-the-top hunk of a man who made it hard to concentrate on the task at hand.

"Evee, whatever malaise has overtaken you, you really need to snap out of it," Ronan said. "I know things may seem hopeless to you right now, but if the Nosferatu continue fighting this way, I'm concerned it will weaken the electric dome over the catacombs again."

"What makes you think that?" Lucien asked.

Ronan pointed to the dome. "Look."

Sure enough, the sparks of electricity that came from the four bloodstone-attached steel rods in four different directions had begun to flicker.

"We must calm them down," Ronan said.

Evee studied him for a moment. His collar-length black hair combed just so, his five o'clock shadow that accented a square jaw. His black eyes held such an intensity in them he could have melted a gold bar simply by staring at it and concentrating. Although he appeared a few years younger than Lucien, his height and build were similar to his cousin's. The biggest difference between the two men was Ronan's serious nature and the ease with which Lucien smiled.

Because there had been four cousins and three of the Triad, Evee had been paired with two Benders. Although they were two of the most handsome men she'd ever had the pleasure to meet, her initial intention had been to not allow attraction to enter into the serious business at hand. She'd never wanted to be drawn to either of the two men, although their good looks were second to none and each possessed unique qualities. But slowly and surely something other than the electric dome they'd created with their scabiors had begun to pulsate. Every time she looked at Lucien, she felt a jolt of electricity flow through her. When she studied Ronan, she felt sparks flutter through her, but not with the same intensity as she felt with Lucien.

Not that either mattered. They were men. They were human. She had no choice but to stay at arm's length.

Lucien pulled Evee away from the pillar she'd been leaning against and stood her upright, facing him.

"Please do something now, Evee," Lucien said.

Evee shook her head slightly as if just waking from a deep sleep. "I don't even know if my spells will work. Even my sisters seem to have problems with theirs."

"You have to at least try," Ronan said. "It's the only thing I can think of that's causing the dome to fade."

"What thing are you talking about?" Evee asked.

"The energy coming from the fighting Nosferatu."

"That can affect the dome?" she asked.

Ronan pointed to the arcs over the catacombs. "What else could it be?"

With a sigh of resignation, Evee went to the gates of the catacombs, pressed her body against it and raised her arms up by her sides and began to chant.

"Quiet now, ye creatures' mind,
Let thy actions turn from rage to kind.
See thy angst, fear and pain in vain,
So it is said.
So shall it be."

No sooner had Evee finished speaking the words than the Nosferatu that had been ripping into one another broke apart. They looked about, seemingly confused, as if unable to comprehend what they had just been doing. Each shuffled off to a corner and sat licking wounds, which immediately healed. A quiet hum soon filled the catacombs, except for an occasional impatient grumble from one of the Nosferatu.

At least the fighting had stopped.

"Why didn't you do that earlier?" Lucien asked.

"I—I don't know," Evee said. "I guess I was afraid it wouldn't work. Just another failure."

Lucien took hold of her chin with a thumb and forefinger and turned her head so she faced him. She had no choice but to look into his eyes.

"None of this is your fault. Whatever is causing the sporadic instabilities of your spells is not your fault. The Cartesians are powerful creatures, and their intention is to create havoc, to destroy the Originals and the Triad. Don't give up on your powers. Don't let the Cartesians see or feel your weakness, because that's what they'll focus on. We need to make sure you and your sisters stay safe, and the way you can help make that happen is to remain strong."

Evee nodded, reprimanding herself silently for having succumbed to complacency. There was no room for it when it came to protecting her Nosferatu, for it was her job to keep them safe.

Ronan nudged Lucien. "We need to strengthen the canopy again, then go hunting for more Nosferatu before it gets any later. It'll be feeding time before we know it, and the ones that are missing are going to be looking for food. That could mean attacks on humans if we don't find them and bring them into the fold."

Without a word, Lucien pulled his scabior from its sheath, which was attached to his belt, and Ronan followed suit. Together they did a quick flick of their wrists, twirled their scabiors around their fingers with lightning speed, then aimed them at the opposing poles. From the bloodstones that sat atop their scabiors shot a fierce bolt of lightning into the poles. They did the same with the remaining two poles, setting them alight until the catacombs lit up like a football field at game time.

Nosferatu scattered from the brilliance of the light, hiding behind crypts or crawling onto death shelves.

"Looks like that should hold them for now," Lucien said.

Evee nodded and then motioned Pierre, her overseer, to the catacomb gates. She told him what they had in mind, and that he was to keep tabs on all the Nosferatu within the catacombs just as he had been doing prior to them getting out of control.

Although Evee trusted Pierre with her life, she feared that if they didn't hurry and collect the missing Nosferatu and get all of them to the North Compound for feeding time, more fights would break out. Then they might lose the protection of the scabior canopy, and the Cartesians would find her Originals and annihilate them. Then it wouldn't be long before humans throughout the city would die senseless, useless deaths.

Evee feared that might be going on even now with her Nosferatu. She felt in her gut that somewhere in the city more deaths had already taken place. She could only hope she and her sisters wouldn't be next.

The Benders seemed very confident in their abilities and seemed to have a solid plan in place, or as solid as one might have in such a situation.

Evee, on the other hand, had not known this much fear—ever.

Chapter 2

Lucien didn't like the idea of leaving the catacombs to hunt for the missing Nosferatu. Although he knew that finding them was a task that had to be taken care of, he worried about the scabior dome flickering out again. If it happened once, it might happen again. Despite what he had told Evee about the energy generated by the squabbling Nosferatu making the dome less effective, Lucien wasn't convinced of that. That was just an assumption. He had no idea what had really caused the dome to weaken. The truth was that no Bender ever before had created a large-scale electrical barrier that locked in any creature. Having run out of options when so many Originals went missing, the cousins had found their task upon arriving in New Orleans more than overwhelming, and had opted to give it a try.

The first attempt had been at the North Compound to protect Viv's Loup Garous. When that had proven successful, he and his cousins had used the same technique to protect the Chenilles in the Louis I Cemetery, then here in the catacombs under St. John's Cathedral. The waning of power here concerned him greatly. Whatever hunting was needed must be done quickly and with specific directives so they wouldn't be chasing their tails as he felt they had been doing for the last day or two.

As Lucien considered a game plan, he noticed that Evee had moved closer and was now standing between him and Ronan.

"I know we have to look for the missing," Evee said. "But I want to apologize for zeroing out on the two of you earlier. All of the Nosferatu are my charge. You are here to help, which is much appreciated, and I had no business zoning out on you the way I did."

Lucien put a hand on Evee's shoulder and felt his pulse quicken when he touched her. Although Evee was dressed casually in jeans and a light blue T-shirt, she might as well have been dressed in a ball gown and tiara for all he cared. She was astonishingly beautiful no matter what she wore, and the simple act of touching her made his insides quiver.

"Don't beat yourself up over that," he said to her. "With all that's going on, I think you're handling yourself quite well. We just need to keep our heads about us." He gave her a soft smile. "For all you know, I might be the next one to 'zero out,' like you said, so I'll have to count on you and Ronan reining me back in." He squeezed her shoulder gently. "Don't worry, if you go to la-la land again, I promise to be there to bring you back."

He saw a flash of gratitude in Evee's eyes, and he felt his smile broaden. He forced himself to look away from her and down at his watch. "Time's pushing. If we're going to do any hunting for missing Nosferatu before feeding time, we'd better get started."

Evee nodded, took a step back and squared her shoulders. "If we're going to get this done," she said, "we'll need to split up. I know the two of you are here to protect me and my Originals, but look at what we're dealing with now. Too many missing Nosferatu, and humans, innocent humans, unwittingly waiting to be an Original's next meal. The closer we get to feeding time, the hungrier the Nosferatu will become. Humans will definitely be their target. So splitting up and hitting different directions only makes sense."

Lucien held up a hand. "No way are we splitting up."

"That would put you in too much danger," Ronan said, the frown on his face deepening.

"That would make us utterly irresponsible in our task to protect and defend," Lucien said.

Evee's eyes narrowed. "So are you saying that going off on your own, knowing there are loose Nosferatu, Loup Garous and Chenilles, any of which could slaughter you within seconds, is irresponsible?" she asked Lucien.

"Yes," Lucien said defiantly. "The bottom line is splitting more than we already have is ludicrous. We'd be asking for disaster."

"Yes," Ronan said. "Like we don't have enough to deal with now. I think we should stick together."

"Of course," Evee said. "Any wuss would want to play the safe card. Look, if the two of you would just stop yammering and get to searching, we might actually get the job done."

Lucien had to bite the inside of his cheeks to keep from laughing. If anything, Evee was not short on piss and vinegar once she had her mind set on something.

Ronan, on the other hand, evidently felt different. Appearing dumbstruck, he looked away, his cheeks turning a shade of pink.

"Look," Evee said to Lucien and Ronan. "I didn't mean for that to come out so…bitchy. I apologize."

Lucien looked up at her with a stoic expression. "Apology accepted."

With a sigh of relief, Evee looked from Ronan to Lucien. "We have to be levelheaded about this. I know what to look for where my Nosferatu are concerned. And believe me, as far as rifts are concerned, if I see so much as a deformed cloud in the sky, I'll be running to find you guys quicker than you can blink."

Lucien blew out a breath and glanced from Evee to Ronan. In his mind, Lucien knew Evee was right. They'd be able to cover much more ground if they separated. But his heart refused to let the words out of his mouth. He feared for her life and couldn't stand the thought of Evee heading anywhere alone.

Finally, Ronan said, "I hate to admit it, but what she's saying makes sense. I can head north into the Quarter and search there." He looked at Evee. "You'll have to tell me what to look for, though. Since it's already dark out, the Originals will have taken human form to blend in. They certainly won't have bald heads with thick veins and sharp fangs like the ones here. How do I tell what human is truly Nosferatu?"

"Good question," Evee said. "You can typically spot them easily if you know what you're looking for. I can usually locate a Nosferatu by scent. In your and Lucien's case, look for anyone standing about simply watching people, either an individual or a small crowd. If interest sparks, the Nosferatu will start following that person or crowd, keeping tabs on their every move. Also their skin will be much paler than the average human's. Some have eyes that are extremely light-sensitive, so they'll be wearing sunglasses inside buildings, even at night."

"What about clothing?" Lucien asked.

"No different than anyone else around them. Remember, they're trying to fit in and go unnoticed so they can scout out their next victim. And remember, too, the both of you are in as much danger as any human out there. I'm the only one who can control the Nosferatu. Don't confront them head-on or you might wind up being a meal. Should you find one, you need to come and get me or call for me. You can't fight them alone. They're too strong."

"This is sounding worse by the moment," Ronan said, sweeping his hands through his hair. "I've changed my mind. I really don't like the idea about splitting up."

"I know," Evee said. "And I agree that this plan is putting us a bit out there, raising the stakes and ratcheting up the danger, but think of what might happen if we don't do it. Let's at least give it a try. We can go in separate directions, hunt for half an hour, then meet back here in front of St. John's. That way we can report on what we've seen, then go our own ways again, each of us taking a different direction. At least that way we won't be apart for hours at a time. Thirty minutes, not that long, and if one of us doesn't show up, the others will know the direction to head to look for him...or her."

Lucien bit his bottom lip, rubbed a hand across his chin. "I don't think what I have to say about the plan matters. You're going to do what you want to do, right?"

Evee gave him a lopsided grin. "Pretty much."

"I figured as much," Ronan said.

"Fine, Ms. François, we'll do it your way," Lucien said with a half smile, which was the best he had to offer. He still thought the entire plan was a mistake. "Let's get it done and over with, then. Ronan, you head north to the Quarter. I'll take the riverbank west."

"Guess that leaves me with the east riverbank," Evee said.

"All right," Lucien said. "But what if something comes up and one of us needs help? We don't carry cell phones because they interfere with your spells and our scabiors. We have no way of contacting one another. You may have telepathic abilities with your sisters, but I don't have that ability with Ronan, Gavril or Nikoli. We have to find a method to reach out for help if we need it."

"Can you whistle?" Evee asked.

Lucien looked at her quizzically.

"Simple question," Evee said. "Can you whistle?"

Lucien pressed his bottom lip against his bottom teeth and let out a loud, ear-piercing whistle.

Evee clamped her hands over her ears until he finished, then said, "Sounds good to me." She turned to Ronan. "How about you?"

Without preamble, Ronan pressed two fingers against his bottom lip and let out a whistle just as shrill as Lucien's, if not louder.

"Good," Evee said. "If either one of you gets into trouble, whistle long and loud, and I'll come for you right away."

"No matter where we are?" Lucien asked. "Your hearing's that good?"

"Better than a hound's," Evee said.

"What about you?" Lucien asked. "What if you get into trouble? You plan to whistle, as well?"

Evee gave him a small smile. "Nope, sorry. I can't whistle my way out of a bucket. If I find my Nosferatu, I'll take care of them myself. I know how to deal with them. And if I run into a Cartesian, trust me, I'll run like hell and find you."

"You can't outrun a Cartesian," Lucien said. "If you see a rift appear, the best thing for you to do is hightail it into the nearest building. Stay out of sight. When the half hour mark comes around, and you don't show, we'll at least know what direction to head to find you."

"What exactly does a rift look like?"

Lucien thought for a moment, stroked his beard. "Think of it as a black wound, one blacker than black. You can see it even on a moonless, starless night. When it first appears it's like a black strip, a stitched wound in the sky. Then, as the Cartesians work their way through it, it begins to widen, like the stitches are being ripped away from the wound."

Evee shivered at the thought. "Believe me," she said. "Any of those ugly mothers won't have a chance to get a hand out of a rift before I haul ass. Don't worry. I'll keep my eyes peeled for anything odd in the sky."

"Doesn't sound like much of a plan," Lucien said.

"I agree," Ronan said, shifting nervously from foot to foot.

"Suppose you're so focused on finding the Nosferatu that you don't notice a Cartesian until it's halfway through a rift and reaching for you?" Lucien asked.

Evee gave him a stern look. "I'm not stupid."

"I in no way assumed or meant to imply you were," Lucien said, and arched a brow.

"I'll be alert," Evee said.

"But how can you look for your Nosferatu *and* watch for rifts overhead?" Ronan asked.

Evee scrubbed a hand over her face as if to wipe away frustration. "Remember, I have a slight advantage over the two of you. I can sense my Nosferatu. I'll keep my Spidey senses tuned to them while watching overhead."

It took another fifteen minutes before the three of them finally agreed to the divide-and-conquer method Evee had proposed.

When they finally left the catacombs, Ronan immediately headed for the French Quarter and Lucien started walking west, down the riverwalk. He watched Evee take off for the east bank of the river, watched her long, lean body stride with confidence, her shoulder-length black hair blown back by the wind. He remembered how her copper-colored eyes glinted with determination as they'd discussed their search-and-rescue plan. Lucien worried about her, more so now than ever.

Although the Triad looked similar, they weren't identical. Their eyes told different stories, as did their personalities. Evee always seemed to be the peacemaker, the one to handle things more logically than her sisters. She was also more apt to follow than lead. At this point, Lucien feared Evee had reached the point of desperation. That was why she had suggested they split up to search for her Nosferatu. He still felt like it was a big mistake.

As Lucien watched Evee's body fade off into the distance, his pace slowed. He continued heading west but kept looking back for her every few seconds. She continued heading east, and when he could barely make out her silhouette, Lucien suddenly felt like he was trudging through knee-deep mud.

He wasn't as worried about Ronan. His cousin was sharp and knew how to fight no matter what he faced. Ronan could easily take care of himself. But if a Cartesian attacked Evee, she'd be helpless. All the bravado she'd displayed in their conversation in the catacombs was one thing, but Lucien feared that dealing with a Cartesian, especially the unreliability of a Cartesian, would be far beyond her powers.

As crucial as it was to find the missing Nosferatu before any humans were attacked, he felt it was a greater priority to keep the Cartesians away from the Originals and especially the Triad he was responsible for. He would never be able to live with himself if something happened to Evee.

Lucien trudged another block west before suddenly doing an about-face and beginning to head east, in Evee's direction.

Something about the woman drew him, called to him. Lucien couldn't quite put his finger on it, but he just knew that he had to take care of her above all else.

He picked up his pace, almost to a run, wanting to at least catch sight of Evee as soon as possible. He heard the calliope of a steamboat in the distance as it chugged along the river. He smelled burgers and fries, pizza and pralines, all of which made his stomach rumble. He couldn't remember the last time he'd eaten.

The farther he headed east, the more the crowds began to dissipate, and the cacophony of music, talking and laughter muted to a distant hum.

It felt like he'd walked five miles before he finally spotted Evee walking along the river's edge, just as she had been before. He noticed her gaze shifting from left to right, then up, obviously trying to sense her Nosferatu and watching for Cartesians at the same time.

Suddenly Evee came to an abrupt stop, and even from where Lucien stood he saw a quizzical look cross her face. She looked up again, turned her head to one side, and Lucien saw her mouth drop open. He followed her gaze and saw it—a widening rift in the sky right above her. A Cartesian was hanging out from it at the waist.

"Run!" Lucien shouted to Evee, then yanked his scabior out of its sheath.

The Cartesian, evidently hearing Lucien's yell, threw Lucien a piercing, evil look, narrowing its monstrous eyes.

Obviously determined to complete the task before it, the Cartesian turned away from Lucien, stuck one of its long, furry arms tipped with four-inch razor-sharp talons out of the rift, then lifted its arm up and out, aiming for Evee.

It wasn't hard to determine that Evee had seen the same, for she let out a heart-stopping scream, then took off running—right into the river.

Lucien charged his scabior and shot a bolt of lightning at the Cartesian, hitting it square in the head. It shrieked and flew backward into the rift, and Lucien heard a distinct pop that indicated he'd shoved the monstrosity into the next dimension. The rift remained open, however, and Lucien kept his scabior aimed there, pushing the Cartesian farther and farther back.

By the time Lucien was able to sound off two more pops, a more crucial sound reached his ear. Evee screaming for help.

Like a wild man, Lucien spun about on his heels, tracking the sound of her voice. Evee was still in the river, her head bobbing up and then going under the murky water. Each time her head poked out of the water, less and less of it appeared. She flailed her arms frantically, coughed and sputtered whenever her mouth broke the surface of the water.

Lucien was now stuck between a rock and a hard place. It was obvious Evee needed to be pulled out of the river, but the rift overhead was still open. If he ignored it and went after Evee, another Cartesian could easily make its way through the rift and take her.

Praying Evee could at least dog-paddle, Lucien put all his energy into the open rift and held on to his scabior with two hands. Although only seconds passed before he heard yet another explosive sound, which meant the Cartesian had been pushed into another dimension and the rift was finally closed, it felt like hours.

For the entire time he fought the Cartesian, all Lucien heard was Evee sputtering and screaming, "H-help! I c-can't swim!"

Chapter 3

Evee knew she was about to die. Panic-stricken, she paddled with hands and feet as hard as she could to stay afloat in the water, but it was only enough to get her nose and mouth to break surface—every once in a while. Each time she got sucked down below the surface, her mouth and nose filled with muddy silt from the river. Bad enough she couldn't breathe, it made her want to throw up. The few seconds she broke the surface of the water she spent coughing, gagging, trying to capture as much oxygen as she could before slipping helplessly downward.

She tried moving her arms like she'd seen swimmers do, out and down, kicking furiously, desperate to move up and forward. But her body refused to stay horizontal. It felt weighted with stones and determined to pull her feetfirst down into the depths of the Mississippi.

Evee didn't know what scared her more: the realization that she was about to drown or having seen the Cartesian take aim for her. Either way, she didn't plan to go quietly into any dark night. All she knew to do was to keep fighting, struggling, hoping.

For the life of her, Evee had no idea why she'd run into the river instead of in the opposite direction toward land and buildings. Surely she would have found a safe, dry place to hide. But something seemed to overtake her logical brain as soon as she saw the Cartesian's arm cock and aim. Her brain immediately screamed, RUN! And in that horrifying moment, the only direction that made sense to her was away.

Even as she bobbed up and then underwater, fighting for air, for her life, she still saw the gruesome face of the Cartesian in her mind's eye. Monstrously huge head covered with scraggly fur. Long, pointed ears that flapped over at the tips. A flat nose with no bridge, and nostrils that looked canyon-size. Eyes solid black, without pupils, and the size of saucers. And its teeth, the most horrible of all—each tooth a thick pointed incisor, a mouth equipped to shred and masticate anything it got hold of. She shuddered, thinking about it.

Trying to keep her wits about her and forcing herself to think of the water, the enemy trying to destroy her now, Evee kicked harder, moved her arms and hands overhead, then down one at a time, hoping for progress. She heard herself crying out for help, but the voice sounded like it came from far away and from someone else. She didn't know which was worse: drowning or being chewed to death by a Cartesian. Both carried the same weight of fear in her heart.

Exhaustion sat atop her like concrete blocks, forcing her lower into the water. She barely had the energy to care anymore.

As she sank lower into the dark water, Evee suddenly

felt an arm wrap around her waist. Freaked, she twisted and turned, trying to get away. Opened her mouth to scream, only to have it fill with silt. She only had a few seconds of breath left in her lungs, and she used it to struggle all the more. The more she fought, the tighter the grip grew on her waist.

Finally, after what seemed to take an eternity, her head surfaced above water. Evee coughed, spat and gasped. When her lungs filled with air, her brain suddenly went into overdrive. She screamed, looking left and right, then up, searching for the Cartesian. Then the pressure around her waist registered once again, and all she saw in her mind's eye were long black talons ready to gut her from stem to stern. She screamed, whirling about, shoving her elbows backward, trying to pummel whatever held her.

"Stop, it's me, Evee. It's me."

Evee heard the voice, but her fear overrode recognition. She tried frantically to get away. "Let go, you ugly son of a bitch! Let me go!"

Arms wrapped around her waist tighter, and she felt her back pressed against...a man?

"It's me, Evee. Lucien. You're safe. It's okay. You're okay."

Startled, Evee turned her head sharply to the left. Lucien's face loomed beside her. A whimper of gratitude escaped her.

"The C-Cartesian," Evee said. "I—I...it..." Before any more words could form, she burst into tears that quickly turned into sobs, her body shivering against Lucien.

"I know," he said softly against her ear. "But you're safe now. I've got you. The Cartesian is gone. You're safe."

Evee put her arms around his neck, and Lucien swam

closer to shore. Before long, he stood upright, leaned over and scooped her into his arms.

Without another thought, she wrapped both of her arms around his neck as he walked onto shore, and buried her face in the crook of his neck. She shivered as if she'd just been dunked into a tub of ice water.

"I'm taking you home so you can get into some dry clothes," Lucien said matter-of-factly.

"I—I can walk from here," Evee said through chattering teeth. She removed her arms from around his neck, and Lucien set her tentatively, seemingly reluctantly, on her feet.

The minute her feet touched the ground, it felt like every muscle in Evee's body suddenly turned to mush. She felt her body go limp, but before she hit the ground, Lucien had her back in his arms again.

Neither of them spoke as Lucien walked the long distance to her home. She clung to him once more, buried her face against his chest. She felt safe in his arms, as if the bulging muscles in his arms and chest, his soft breath against her hair and face, was the safest place on earth. He never once broke stride or panted for breath as he cradled her.

It wasn't until they'd crossed the threshold of the three-story Victorian that Evee and her sisters called home, which they'd inherited from their mother, that Lucien set her feet back on the ground. He held on to her arm, as if making sure she'd stand steady before fully releasing her.

Evee had no sooner leaned against the kitchen table to catch her breath than Hoot, her horned owl familiar, came flying into the room at full speed. He flew straight toward Lucien, swooped down onto his left shoulder and dug his talons into him.

"Let go of him now!" Evee shouted hoarsely at Hoot, shooing him away.

"He has no business being here, Evette. Make him leave," Hoot demanded.

Evee was grateful that she was the only one, besides the Elders, who could understand her familiar. Everyone else, including Lucien, only heard squawks, squeals and chirps. She shooed at Hoot again. He remained on Lucien's shoulder, talons digging in deeper until Lucien grimaced.

"You had no business bringing him here alone," Hoot said. "And look at you. Just look at you. Soaking wet. What did he do to you? Did he hurt you? Are you bleeding anywhere? Have you been bruised? Damaged?"

Unable to answer Hoot's questions without sounding like a loon, Evee said sternly, "No! Let go of him right this minute or I'll put you in your cage."

With a shrill shriek of anger, Hoot finally released Lucien's shoulder and took flight, leaving the kitchen and heading for the foyer.

"That's some pet you have there," Lucien said, rubbing the shoulder that Hoot had dug into.

Evee sighed. "He's my familiar and overprotective."

"What exactly does a familiar do? Does every witch have one?"

"Most of the witches I know do. Familiars are supposed to be our eyes and ears when we're not around. Their purpose is mostly to warn us of pending danger. Hoot does that for me, but he's also bossy and gets carried away at times."

Lucien gave her a small smile. "It's nice to know you have someone looking after you."

Their eyes locked for a moment, and Evee felt her knees grow weak. Not from exhaustion this time, but from desire. It felt like desire, anyway, but could have been the aftermath of shock from the Cartesian attack and near drowning. She shook her head slightly, trying to clear her thoughts. It was then she noticed that she and Lucien were both soaking wet and dripping water all over the floor.

"There's a shower down here if you'd like to use it," Evee said. She pointed past the kitchen toward the front of the house. "Just past the foyer and living area is a hallway. Take a left there and you'll find a bathroom. Last door on the right. I'll use the one on the second floor." As an afterthought she put a finger to her lips, then said, "I'm sorry I don't have any dry clothes to offer you. House full of women, you know. But there's a robe hanging on the back of the bathroom door that you're welcome to use. And back here…" Evee led him to a small room located at the far end of the kitchen near the back door. The room held a washer and dryer, utility sink and folding table. "You can just toss your clothes in the dryer while you shower."

"Thanks," Lucien said. "Dry sounds like a great plan. I'll wait to shower when I go back to the hotel."

"Y-you're going back to the hotel?" Evee asked, then mentally admonished herself for sounding so needy.

They stood so close together in the small room that she felt Lucien's breath as he spoke. Just being this close to him calmed her. She forgot about the wet clothes on her own body and the chill that had her shaking since Lucien pulled her from the river. His presence sent heat radiating through her body, chasing away any semblance of cold.

"If you don't mind," Lucien said, "I'll dry my shirt first so you can direct me on the dryer settings." He grinned. "Too many buttons and gadgets on that machine. Left to myself, I'd probably shrink my shirt down two sizes or nuke it into ashes."

"No problem," Evee said, then held her breath as Lucien reached behind his head with both hands, grabbed the back of his T-shirt and pulled it over his head.

Seeing him bare-chested with rippled abs and sculpted, muscular arms stole what little breath Evee had left. She gasped to refill her lungs. An embarrassing sound at such a wrong time.

"Are you okay?" Lucien asked, his brow knitting.

"Huh?" Evee had been so absorbed with the sight and scent of Lucien so close to her, she hadn't heard what he'd said.

He handed her his wet shirt. "I asked if you were okay. You gasped. I was concerned it might have come from residual water from the river in your lungs."

"No, no, I'm fine." She took his shirt, threw it into the dryer and set the dryer on its gentle cycle so the T wouldn't shrink, then pressed the start button.

Evee glanced back at Lucien, trying not to focus on his chest. "Your jeans are heavier material, so set the dryer on time-dry for them." She pointed to the appropriate knob. "Both shirt and jeans will be dry before you know it." Evee didn't tell him what cycle would be best for his underwear. For all she knew, Lucien might be flying commando. Either way, she felt confident he'd figure it out.

Since the incident with the Cartesians and the near drowning, Evee felt out of sorts and confused. She found herself wanting, aching to feel the safety of Lucien. Just like when he'd carried her home.

She felt heat radiating from Lucien's chest, which was lightly matted with dark brown and black hair that formed a narrow path to the top of his jeans.

Evee felt awkward as she watched him remove his watch and set it on the washer. She had no business standing here. She had to shower and dress, as well, yet felt glued to where she stood. Unable to take her eyes off him.

Lucien turned to her, and she studied his strong, chiseled face, his eyes greener than the depths of the Pacific Ocean. An unspoken question flickered across his face, and Evee fumbled for something to say.

As Lucien stared at her, his eyes soft yet piercing, she said, "I—I'm sorry about earlier."

"Sorry about what? You didn't do anything wrong."

Evee glanced down for a few seconds before looking back up at him. "I forgot to say thank-you."

"For?"

"Saving my life. You know, from the Cartesian, from drowning."

"My pleasure, I assure you." Lucien tilted his head slightly. "If you don't mind me asking, don't you control the element of water?"

Evee nodded.

"Yet it frightens you. Why is that?"

She shook her head. "To tell you the truth, I don't know what the water thing is all about. I never did get it. I'm supposed to control the element of water, and I can, but from a distance. I don't know why I have such a fear of it. All I think about is drowning. Maybe it's a former life thing. Maybe I drowned in some other life and hold repressed memories about it. Then again, it could just be a weird phobia." She shrugged, feeling all the more uncomfortable. She was rambling like an idiot. She felt her cheeks grow warm. "I think not understanding it frightens me most of all."

"Life has a lot of unanswered questions," Lucien said, his voice low and husky.

She nodded and watched as his amazing eyes turned to a smoldering forest green.

"Whatever the reason," Evee said, trying to get her wits about her, "please accept my gratitude for your help."

"Accepted," Lucien said with a soft smile.

Something inside Evee told her to move on. To go upstairs and shower as she'd proposed earlier. Instead, she stood staring at him. Neither of them said a word.

Before she knew it, Evee sensed what almost felt like human hands push her closer to Lucien, seemingly without her consent. Suddenly, she found her lips on Lucien's, kissing him fiercely. His hands cupped the sides of her face and he returned the kiss, matching her ferocity.

The moment her lips touched Lucien's, Evee felt such a thirst overtake her, it was like every ounce of moisture in her body had been depleted, her body suddenly dehydrated. So much so she could have drunk the entire Mississippi River and would still be craving more.

His full lips, so delicious, succulent.

Lucien's lips moved over her chin, down the side of her neck.

A moan escaped Evee's lips, and she whispered, "Don't let me go...don't." She tangled her fingers into his collar-length black hair and pulled him closer.

Without warning and in one fell swoop, Lucien dropped his hands to Evee's waist, then lifted her up onto the dryer. He cupped the back of her head and kissed her long and deep.

Evee wrapped her arms around his neck, tangled her fingers into his hair. Her hair and clothes were still soaked from the river, but neither seemed to notice or care.

Lucien's hands moved at what felt like an infinitesimally slow pace, from her waist to the top of her thighs.

She groaned reflexively, and Lucien broke their kiss, studied her face, his eyes smoldering green, hypnotic.

Their eyes remained locked, their faces only a few inches away from each other. Lucien's eyes seemed to call on something deep inside her.

Locked in that moment, Lucien moved his hands to rest near the top of her thighs. He placed his thumbs between her legs, and she felt heat roll from her with the fierceness of a bonfire. He pressed his thumbs down a bit harder and began to rub his right thumb left and his left thumb right in the center of her legs.

Evee gasped loudly. She heard a loud humming in her ears and suspected the sound to be her own blood rushing hot and fast through her body. She arched her back, pushed her hips toward him.

Evee's mouth found Lucien's again and she took his tongue into her mouth and sucked hard as his thumbs moved faster, pressed harder against her.

Fire roared through her until Evee broke their kiss and arched her back, crying out, "Yes! Lucien, yes!" And in that moment a tsunami of all orgasms overtook her, washing away the fear that had held her captive earlier, shoving away every insecure thought, every inhibition she'd ever known. Shaking, she clung to Lucien once more.

"I need you," she said unabashedly. "I need you inside me."

Lucien took her face into his hands. "There's nothing I want more. You're one of the most beautiful women I've ever known, Evee. But taking you now, after all you've just gone through, would make me feel…" He smoothed her hair with a hand. "Not now. Trust me. We'll have our time together. When and if it's right. I promise."

With that, Lucien gently moved his hands from between her legs, wrapped them around her waist and lifted her off the dryer and placed her on the floor.

Evee wobbled once, and he caught her. He held on to her arms until her feet felt steady beneath her.

"Go now," Lucien whispered in her ear. "Shower. Get into some dry clothes. I'll let Ronan know what happened—except for this part, of course. We'll regroup."

Evee nodded slowly, then made her way clumsily back into the kitchen and through the foyer. As she headed up the stairs, her body still humming from Lucien's touch, she was grateful Hoot had made himself scarce. The last thing she needed was her familiar giving her a morality lesson and killing her buzz.

Three steps up the stairway Evee suddenly realized she'd stepped into a huge pile of shit. For it was then that she felt just how badly she wanted Lucien.

She walked slowly. Each step brought different emotions. The need for Lucien. God, he must think her a slut. She'd all but attacked him. All but begged him to screw her right there on top of the dryer.

Evee started to feel ashamed of herself. She should have shown more restraint. She had no business wanting any of the Benders. They were human, and her body hungered for more than a one-time fuck. That Evee could make happen at any time. But the Benders were different. Not only were they handsome, intelligent and powerful, but any woman would be stupid not to desire their heart along with their body.

And there lay her downfall.

No Triad shall marry or live intimately with a human.

The curse of the ages. If it was broken, they were assured it would cause the destruction of the world. That was the purpose for the mirrors inside their Grimoires.

They replayed each day since they were created, scenes of Armageddon.

Except as of late. Over the last week, the mirrors inside their Grimoires had stopped replaying the destruction of the world. All three showed nothing but swirls of gray smoke. And no one, including their Elders, had any idea as to why. When Evee stared at the mirror in her Grimoire, she felt hopelessness, helplessness. As far as any of them knew, the end of the world might already have begun.

Heaven help her if she had had sex with Lucien. It might have been the match that lit the fuse to a bomb that would blow the hell out of everything.

Herself included.

Chapter 4

Once his clothes were dry enough for him not to look like a drenched rat, Lucien quickly dressed while Evee was in the shower. He felt guilty for leaving without saying goodbye, but after the incident on the dryer, he thought it best to be on his way—quickly.

Lucien couldn't quite wrap his brain around what exactly had happened on Evee's dryer. One moment they were staring at each other, and the next her lips were on his. Her body so close to his sent more messages than he'd been able to sort through. He sensed passion pent up like a pressure cooker without a release valve inside her. So he'd provided one. Anything beyond that, and he'd have forever considered himself a schmuck. It had taken what felt like superhuman strength to control the need he had for her. Sending her off to shower while he waited for his clothes to at least half-ass dry, then leave, made him feel like chicken shit. But he figured better chicken shit than regret.

Instead of going to the hotel to shower as he'd told Evee he would, Lucien decided to scout for Ronan first and give him a heads-up on the Cartesian attack. With that in mind and visions of Evee burned into his brain, Lucien automatically reached for his left wrist to initiate the locator implanted in his watch. It took a second for him to realize it wasn't on his wrist.

Lucien stopped abruptly. "What the hell...?" Then he remembered. He'd taken it off at Evee's, right before tugging his shirt off and tossing it into the dryer. Why the hell did he remove it in the first place? The only time Lucien ever removed his watch was before stepping into the shower, even though the watch was waterproof.

Habit, he assumed. Clothes came off to shower, thus off with the watch. But now his butt was in a sling. He couldn't just walk back to Evee's after what had happened a short time ago. She might view his return as an excuse, get the wrong message. Not that she'd have gotten the message wrong. Not completely anyway.

Hell, who was he kidding? He was the one who'd have the problem if he had her alone right now. How was he going to get his watch back without it being awkward for either of them?

Nikoli, the oldest of his cousins, always reminded them of the Benders' mantra whenever they headed out on a mission. *Keep your dick in your pants and your mind on the mission.*

Normally that wasn't an issue for Lucien. Women flirted certainly, and, occasionally, he'd reciprocate. But that was as far as it went until the mission was over and all they'd gone there to accomplish had been completed.

This was different, though. The mission wasn't "normal," as it involved the Triad, whom they'd never protected before. It slid off the normal scale with the number of Cartesians they'd encountered so far and the Originals they had to find and protect. All new challenges for them.

As Evee was for him. What he felt for her whenever he was near her was far from normal. She was an extraordinary woman who always smelled like gardenias and daffodils. Her smile melted his heart, and her copper-colored eyes grew so bright when she got excited they could've lit up a quarter of the universe. Evee might have come across as the gentlest and quietest of the Triad, but she carried an innate strength that was unmistakable.

"Hey, what're you doing here?" a man asked, yanking Lucien from his thoughts. The voice came from behind Lucien, which caused him to clap a hand on the sheath of his scabior and spin about.

It was Ronan.

"Aren't you supposed to be hunting the west side of the riverbank?" Ronan asked.

Lucien slapped a hand over his thudding heart. "Man, don't you know better than to sneak up on me like that? I could've fried you."

Ronan gave him a lopsided grin. "Nah, your reflexes are too sharp for you to make that kind of mistake. So, what are you doing here?" He took a step closer to Lucien and sniffed. "And why do you smell like...fish and dirty gym socks?"

Uncomfortable with the number of people milling about Toulouse Street, Lucien motioned for Ronan to follow him into an alley just off Dauphine.

"What's going on?" Ronan asked. "You're acting weird."

In the muted silence of the alley, Lucien relayed to Ronan what he and Evee had gone through on the east bank. As he wound down the telling of the incident, even

The Witch's Thirst

in the faint glow of streetlamps, Lucien saw Ronan's face turn beet red.

"I told you!" Ronan said. "Didn't I tell you it was a bad idea to split up? Evee could have died. On our watch, she could have died!"

"Shh," Lucien warned. "If your voice gets any louder, we'll start attracting a crowd."

"Shh, my ass," Ronan said. "The Cartesian, the water…" He ran a hand through his charcoal-black hair and started pacing in a tight circle. He stopped abruptly. "Where is Evee now?"

"Still at her home, as far as I know," Lucien said, shoving his hands in his pockets.

Ronan stepped closer to Lucien. "Hang on a minute. What were you doing on the east bank when you were supposed to be scouting the west?"

Lucien lowered his eyes for a second, then shrugged. "Instinct more than anything. I just got a sudden urge to follow her. I'm glad I did."

Ronan's eyes narrowed. "So you saved her from the Cartesian?"

"Yes."

"And from drowning?"

"Yes."

"Then what?" Ronan asked.

"What do you mean?"

"What happened after you pulled her out of the river?"

Lucien glanced away for a millisecond. "I carried her home. She was in shock, shivering. Couldn't stand on her own two feet."

"Then what?" Ronan asked, taking another step closer to Lucien. "What did you do when you brought her home? Just drop her at the front door? Make her tea? Get her a warm, fuzzy blanket to wrap around her shoulders?"

Lucien stared at the fury evident on his cousin's face. "What's with the twenty questions and why are you so pissed?"

Ronan turned away, folding his arms across his chest. "You broke protocol. It's not like things aren't screwed up enough here. Breaking protocol confuses things all the more."

Lucien frowned. "Protocol for what? Rescuing a woman from a Cartesian and then from drowning?"

"Splitting up in the first place," Ronan said, pounding a fist into the palm of his hand. "I could have saved her from that Cartesian and from the water."

A neon light suddenly went off in Lucien's head. It answered a lot of questions and made him sick to his stomach at the same time.

"Ronan?" Lucien said.

"What?" Ronan turned to face him, his expression roiling with anger.

"You like her, don't you?"

"Who? What the shit are you talking about?"

"Evee. You like her, don't you?"

Lucien saw Ronan's shoulders slowly relax from their defense position. He unfolded his arms and shoved his hands into his pants pockets. "Keep your dick in your pants and your mind on the mission," Ronan said, his voice low, resigned as he stated the Benders' mantra.

Even in the darkness of the alley, Lucien saw defeat dull his cousin's large black eyes. In all the years they'd known each other, not once had Lucien ever seen Ronan make such a fuss over a woman.

It broke Lucien's heart to see his cousin look so dejected. The words that came out of his own mouth milliseconds later rattled him to his core.

"If—if you're interested in Evee," Lucien said, "you

should let her know. Eventually this mission will come to an end and so will the Benders' mantra. So, good, bad or indifferent, at least Evee will know how you feel."

Ronan blew out a breath. "I can't. I'm not good with women the way you are."

"Well," Lucien said, "you can either let your shyness rule your heart or take a chance and tell her how you feel."

Ronan looked him in the eye. "And what if she rejects me?"

"Then she rejects you, and you'll move on," Lucien said. "But you'll never know where you stand or *if* you can stand beside her unless you try."

Ronan slowly nodded, yet remained silent.

Now that he'd offered his heart up for slaughter, Lucien squared his shoulders and said, "Let's make another run through the Quarter, and then we'll go to the hotel so I can shower."

Ronan nodded again, still silent.

Although he hadn't uttered a word, Lucien knew his cousin well enough to know he was pondering what they'd discussed about Evee. Even now he was probably formulating a plan.

With a heavy heart, Lucien steeled his jaw and reminded himself that he was a Bender. He had to find the missing Originals, watch for Cartesians and take care of the Triad. That was his purpose, his innate ability.

And that's all there was to it.

Squaring his shoulders, he began walking again, and Ronan followed him. They moved along the streets of the Quarter, Lucien using hand signals to guide Ronan in one direction or another.

Lucien looked over the faces of the people on the streets. Surveyed those who stood or sat in the bars and restaurants he strolled into and out of. He tried to remember the things Evee told them to watch for. The whiteness of the Nosferatu's skin, sunglasses in the dark because some couldn't tolerate any form of light. The problem was, after much searching, everyone started to look the same. Men—women—drunk.

After an hour of looking, they still hadn't turned up anything. Lucien tried thinking like a Nosferatu, one hungry, away from its clan, not knowing where its next meal would come from or how it would get back to the catacombs. Maybe the missing Nosferatu didn't want to connect with its clan again. Maybe it wanted the newly found freedom.

Lucien clearly remembered what Evee had said about the lost Nosferatu. If they weren't reunited with their clan for feeding time at the compound, they'd find something or someone to drain of blood.

Once again, putting himself in the shoes of a Nosferatu, Lucien knew he'd go to a place with the most noise, the biggest cluster of people it could find. Once it defined its prey, it'd probably lead them down some dark alley.

The one place Lucien knew that fit this compilation, with many offshoots and empty, dark alleys, was Bourbon Street. First they had to study the street with the beat—Bourbon. A place whose streets and sidewalks held the footsteps, vomit or piss of some of the most rich and famous people from around the world.

Following that logic, Lucien signaled Ronan to his side, told him his game plan. Then they parted, each man taking a side of Bourbon.

Just as Lucien expected, as they walked the crowded street, glancing down one alley after another, they were faced with large groups of people laughing, talking, cramming the bars. How were he and Ronan supposed to identify a Nosferatu in this cluster? It felt like an impossibility.

An idea struck Lucien and gave him pause as he allowed himself back into the mind-set of a Nosferatu. He knew it would find an alley to make the kill. Its prey might be found in the crowded streets, but the kill would be done in seclusion. Not public.

So what made sense to Lucien was to walk Royal Street, which ran parallel to Bourbon, then straight ahead, checking out every alley between Iberville to Esplanade, which crossed the parallel streets. He signaled for Ronan, told him to focus on the alleys between the streets he felt were the likeliest place a Nosferatu would strike. They'd walk in tandem as much as possible.

It wasn't until Lucien reached Barracks Street that something caught his attention. Sucking sounds, mouth to flesh. He looked across the street for Ronan and saw he was ahead, near Esplanade, dodging into yet another alley. He didn't want to call out to him and warn whatever he'd have to face in his own alley.

Lucien removed his scabior from its sheath and made his way toward the sounds he'd heard.

The only streetlights he had to work with were the weak streaks shooting from pole lamps on Royal and Bourbon. So the farther he walked down Barracks, the darker it became.

He heard a woman moan. "Oh, baby, yes! Put it in now!"

Lucien walked faster, zeroing in on the woman's voice. As he made his way toward the voice, a skinny, haggard-faced woman approached him, a hooker looking for a john, wanting a good time, a night's wage. He ignored her and had walked another half block when a drunk stumbled out of a side alley and bumped into him. The drunk threw a punch at Lucien as if he was the reason he'd misstepped.

Lucien dodged the fist and quickened his pace, his ear still tuned to the woman's voice.

"Oh, yeah, baby. Give me more. I want more."

By the sound of her voice, Lucien suspected she was already copulating, or was about to, with whatever man she'd picked up on the street. From where he stood, Lucien noticed the woman had her back to him in an alley that grew darker with every step he took.

Even in the darkness, however, Lucien noticed something white just over the woman's left shoulder. No question, it was a Nosferatu in midtransformation.

"What the f-fuck?" the woman said.

There was no mistaking the balding white head, the large vein that bulged from its forehead. Quite noticeable even in the dark.

Despite her slurred speech, a testament to heavy alcohol consumption, the woman evidently didn't care for what she witnessed, either. That white bald head, the cauliflower ears, the pointed fangs that should have been front teeth. Her screams, when they came, told Lucien she had suddenly turned stone-cold sober. But her cries for help were drowned out by revelers shouting, laughing, talking up in the Quarter, where the action was at an all-time high.

Lucien remembered what Evee said he should do if he spotted a Nosferatu. Yet he stood mesmerized, watching the Nosferatu's clawlike hands wrap around the woman's arm, holding tight. Its head tilted back, fangs showing, ready to strike.

Suddenly snapping out of his stupor, Lucien placed

two fingers against his bottom lip and let out a loud, shrill whistle.

So far, the only thing his whistle did was create a diversion for the creature. It turned to Lucien, hissed, then sank its fangs into the woman's throat. Its eyes rolled back in its head as it drank, sucked, consumed the meal before him. As much as he wanted to do something to save her, Lucien knew he was no match for a Nosferatu. He didn't have the weapons or the magic to send it to its knees.

In what felt like the blink of an eye, he found Ronan at his side.

"Son of a bitch," Ronan said, looking at the Nosferatu feasting on the woman.

"No shit," Lucien said.

Evidently irritated by the sound of Lucien's and Ronan's voices, the Nosferatu abruptly threw the woman it had been feeding on to one side. And a second later, it stood right in front of the Benders, a hand on each of their throats.

"You stupid, little men. What were you whistling for? Your dinner or mine?" the creature said.

Its grip on Lucien's neck felt like a band of steel. Its fangs were exposed, twisted and yellow, and dripping with blood.

In a flash, Lucien did the only thing he knew to do. He kneed the Nosferatu in the groin. He didn't know if it would have the same effect as it would've had on a human, but he didn't care. In that moment, he had to do something.

Fortunately, Lucien's effort threw the creature off balance, which caused it to release Ronan and Lucien, giving them time to unsheathe their scabiors.

Although he had his weapon in hand, Lucien wasn't

quite sure what to do with it. There'd be no pushing the creature back into another dimension, because it belonged in this one.

When the Nosferatu regained its balance, it grabbed for Lucien again. Instinct kicked in, and Lucien used the bottom, steel part of the scabior and quickly skewered the Nosferatu's right eye. Lightning fast, as if on the same brain frequency, Ronan jumped into the fray and jabbed the steel rod of his scabior into the creature's left eye.

The figure wailed and screeched, clawing at its own face. Lucien knew the Nosferatu would heal itself soon enough, and its eyes would be as good as new or better than before they'd been destroyed.

Although pus ran from its eye sockets, Lucien and Ronan witnessed the regeneration process firsthand. The Nosferatu's eyes grew larger. Empty sockets at first; then new orbs appeared, black pupils. As suspected, the creature was regaining its sight.

Not knowing what else to do, Lucien prepared to attack the eyes again, once it got a bead on him. He held his breath, waiting.

Suddenly, the Nosferatu jerked backward as if bashed with a two-by-four from behind. It fell on its side onto the ground, and Lucien saw a long, ornate silver dagger jammed into its back and extending out of its chest, right through the heart.

Shocked, Lucien looked about in the darkness and spotted Pierre, Evee's head Nosferatu. He stood beside his felled creature, brushed his hands together and shook his head.

"Such a waste," Pierre said. "He should have followed orders and stayed with the group in the catacombs."

As Pierre spoke, Lucien heard the voices of people gathering at the intersection of Barracks and Bourbon.

The sound of sirens wailed in the distance, and in a flash, Pierre disappeared into the night, leaving Lucien and Ronan to face the crowd, the dead woman, the dead Nosferatu who, in death, had reverted to human form, and the police, whose sirens Lucien heard in the distance.

Lucien felt like a mouse stuck in a trap. He heard chatter coming from the crowd, each telling a different story, yet carrying the same theme. Lucien and Ronan were going to be fingered as murderers.

How the hell was he supposed to explain this to the police? And where was Evee? She'd specifically said to whistle for her and she'd come. Pierre had shown up instead. And although Lucien was grateful that he'd arrived in time to save them from the Nosferatu, it infuriated him that they'd been left alone to face the consequences of something and the someones they'd been sent here to protect.

Chapter 5

After showering, Evee threw on a pair of jeans, a maroon scoop-neck sweater and work boots. The entire time she'd stood under the water, Lucien had been on her mind. Although she really didn't want him to leave when he did, Lucien had been strong enough to stop things before they'd gotten out of hand. He would probably have blamed himself for taking advantage of her under duress—and he wouldn't have been that far off the mark. She'd been so petrified, had felt so vulnerable that more than anything she'd needed to feel strength and a sense of someone being in control. Lucien provided both in spades.

Knowing that didn't keep Evee's body from shivering as she went to her closet for a light jacket. The cold didn't cause her shivering. The need for Lucien did.

A short, loud screech had Evee spinning about on the balls of her feet and her heart racing up to her throat.

It was Hoot, her familiar, who stood perched at the foot of her bed frame.

Evee slapped a hand to her chest. "Don't do that!" she said. "You scared the hell out of me."

The horned owl's large eyes blinked slowly. "Good," he said.

Evee scowled at him. "What do you mean good?"

"At least I have your attention now."

"What the hell is your problem?" Evee asked, slipping on her jacket.

"Problem? I'm not the one with the problem, Evette François. You are." He blinked, turned his head around at a ninety-degree angle, then whipped it back in her direction.

"I'm fine," Evee said. "So how about you mind your own business for once?"

"That's not my job, and you know it."

Evee sighed and glared at Hoot. "Then spit it out. I've got things to tend to."

"Spit it out? Have you no brains left in your head?" Hoot asked. "You damn near get killed by one of those hideous monster things, jump into the river when you can't swim for shit, then not only lead but encourage that Bender guy to put his hands on your privates."

"I don't need you riding my ass about any of it right now." The last thing Evee wanted or needed was Hoot giving her some type of moral-code lesson when all she wanted to think about was Lucien. The musky, wet smell of him. How his hands had felt on her body. How even through her wet clothes she'd felt their heat burst into a furnace so hot it would have melted an eighteen-wheeler loaded with rebar.

"As your familiar, I'm allowed to ride whatever the

hell I want to protect you," Hoot declared. "You had no business being with him in that intimate way."

"How do you know there was any intimate anything?" Evee asked. "You disappeared. If you were so against me being with him, why didn't you do what you always do—stick your beak in where it doesn't belong?"

The owl let out a short, angry screech. "Unlike you, I've been out searching for the Nosferatu."

Evee put a hand on her hip. "And what do you think I've been doing? Playing solitaire all this time? I've been looking for them, too."

"You weren't while you were playing touchy, feely with that Bender."

"How can you make that claim when you weren't even here?" Evee asked.

"Oh, I was here," Hoot said, whipping his head about as if checking for intruders behind him.

He turned back to her. "Here just in time to see the games you two were playing."

"Oh, shut up," Evee said. "Nothing happened."

"From the groaning and moaning you were doing, that sure was some kind of nothing." Hoot chirped.

"Enough," Evee warned.

"What're you going to do, tape my beak shut?" Hoot asked. "Look here, missy. You've got a lot on your plate right now. You may be paired with him, which is a ridiculous idea in my opinion, but that doesn't give you the right to act like a harlot."

"Stop," Evee warned again. "Or I'll not only tape your beak but clip your wings."

Hoot squawked. "Liar, liar, pants on fire."

"What good are you as a familiar if all you're going to do is chew me out for every little thing I do?" Evee said.

"My job is to help you see straight in case you go

crosswise, and you, Ms. François, have gone crosswise big time."

"What part of 'enough' don't you understand?" Evee said, heading for the foyer.

"The part where I tell you humans are dying," Hoot said, and blinked twice. "And one of your Nosferatu."

Evee froze in place, and her body temperature suddenly felt like it had dropped twenty degrees. She turned slowly to face Hoot, who was now roosting on the stairs' newel post.

"What humans? Where? Which Nosferatu?" Evee asked, her questions coming out rapid-fire.

Hoot fluttered his wings as if ready to take flight, then settled back into place. "Two humans in Chalmette. One in the Quarter."

Evee felt her mouth drop open. She snapped it shut and swiped a hand over her face. "Chalmette? You mean the Nosferatu have gone beyond the city proper?" She leaned against the front door for support.

The bird gave her an affirmative squawk. "Not only that, it seems like some of the missing Loups, Nosferatu and Chenilles are attempting to form their own feeding pattern."

Evee held her breath as he continued.

"Some of the Nosferatu, in human form, of course, lured a couple out to one of the abandoned areas in the ninth ward. Sucked them dry, then left. The Loup must have been hiding in wait. As soon as the Nosferatu left, two Loups ran in and devoured the corpses, leaving nothing but bone, which, of course, the Chenille finished off. Every drop of marrow."

"You're sure about this?" Evee asked.

Hoot blinked twice. "Witnessed it myself."

"Any other witnesses?"

"For the woman in the Quarter, yes. Chalmette, no. Sooner or later somebody is going to find those bodies back there, though. Police are going to get involved. There won't be much of the bodies left to identify, but still…"

Evee felt tears suddenly burn against her eyelids. The Triad's problems had just multiplied a hundredfold. If the Originals had trekked all the way to Chalmette, they could, for all intents and purposes, travel into another state. That wasn't something she and her sisters had considered. The Originals had been cared for and fed for years in the same way, the same place. Dealing with that, the Triad used logic and assumed they'd remain close.

So much for logic.

"What about the Nosferatu?" Evee asked.

"Which one?"

Evee let out an exasperated sigh. "The one you said was dead, damn it."

"Don't be snapping at me," Hoot warned. "I'm just the messenger. The Nosferatu was Chank. You know, the redhead when he's in human form. He lured a drunk woman into an alley in the Quarter. Two of those Benders and Pierre stopped it, but not before the kill. The drunk woman didn't stand a chance. And if those Benders keep sticking their noses where they don't belong, they'll wind up sucked dry and chewed through to their fingernails. Lucky for them, Pierre came around and rescued them. Had to run a silver dagger through Chank. From the looks of things, no other way to stop him."

"Which Benders were involved?" Evee asked, worry suddenly flooding over her. She thought of Lucien.

"What does it matter which? They're all nosy busybodies who have no business here."

"Which ones?" She all but yelled the question this time.

Hoot screeched loudly. "How the hell do I know? The one with the short black hair. The quiet one. And the one you were playing house with earlier."

Ronan, Lucien, Evee thought, grateful they were safe, but still feeling like she needed to throw up.

She felt her brow knit and glared at her familiar. "If you knew…saw all this going on, why didn't you summon me?"

Hoot screeched loudly. "Summon you? I tried when I saw what was happening in Chalmette! But you were obviously too busy playing hussy with one of the Benders to hear me. That's why I had to come back here, hoping to find you!"

Evee rubbed her forehead, left the foyer and went into the kitchen. Feeling lost, she shrugged off her jacket and tossed it over a kitchen chair. She grabbed the kettle from the stove and without thinking brought it over to the sink and filled it with water. She placed the kettle on the counter, not bothering to bring it back to the stove for heating. Instead, she sat at the kitchen table and placed her hands over her face. Shook her head. Her world had become an impossible place in which to function, to live, to think.

"Evette, you have to listen to me," Hoot said.

Evee lowered her hands and looked up. Saw her familiar perched on top of the kitchen chair opposite her.

"I think I've heard enough from you for one day," Evee said, forcing back tears, fury and uncertainty.

"Too bad," Hoot said. "You're going to listen."

"I don't have to listen to shit. You're not my boss or my father." Evee scowled.

"No, but I am your familiar. Same thing. And you're going to listen." Not waiting for Evee to respond, Hoot hurried through his words. "You're heading off a cliff with that Bender. And it has little to do with sex and you know it. What you have to guard is your heart. You have Nosferatu missing, others killed, and the rest locked in the catacombs. You keep hunting for your missing Nosferatu, just like your sisters are looking for their Originals, and none of you are being successful at it. I don't know why you can't hone in on your brood like you usually do."

Evee swiped a strand of hair out of her eyes. "You think I don't know that? I feel like I've been running in circles and don't know how to straighten any of this out. And for your information, you horny-eared copperhead, don't you think if I could hone in on my brood I'd have done it days ago?"

"Okay, given, but you have to admit, this has gotten way out of hand. Much bigger than anyone suspected." The bird blinked and bobbed his head. "You're going to have to devise some other system to feed your brood."

"Another system?" Evee looked at her familiar with incredulity. "It took years to set up the one we have now."

"Maybe so, but how are you going to get the Nosferatu out of the catacombs and safely to the North Compound with so much going awry? They'll be out in the open. Have you forgotten about the Cartesians? And now humans are being killed. Police are going to get involved soon. You and your sisters could be found out."

"No shit."

"Just saying."

"So what's the answer?" Evee asked, feeling her cheeks heat with anger. "You're sitting on top of that chair spouting all that verbiage like you're high and mighty. Do you have an answer for these problems?"

Hoot turned his head until he nearly faced backward, then turned back to Evee and blinked without saying a word.

"I didn't think so." Evee scowled. "Don't you think that if I knew how to stop all this crap, how to get my Nosferatu back and turn things back to normal, I wouldn't have done it by now? And as far as the Benders are concerned, forget it. We've got to worry about humans now. *Dead* humans."

"Have you considered that what you're doing with that Bender might have something to do with what's happening?" Hoot asked.

"I didn't *do* anything with the Bender," Evee said, knowing she was bordering on a technicality. "Look, give me time to think, will you? Go. Leave me."

Hoot squawked, and without another word, left his perch on the kitchen chair and flew out of the room.

Evee dropped her head back into her hands. She felt guilty about having been here, in this house with Lucien, experiencing his touch, her explosive orgasm. All the while humans died by the Originals, and one of her Nosferatu had to be taken down.

Wearily, she got out of her chair and was about to head to the bathroom to wash her face when the back kitchen door opened with a bang.

Elvis, Gilly's ferret familiar, scurried into the house followed by Socrates, Viv's Bombay cat and familiar. Both ran around the kitchen table, claws clicking on the wooden floor. As they skittered to a stop near Evee, Hoot evidently decided to join the party because he swooped into the kitchen from wherever he'd been roosting moments earlier. He settled onto the kitchen counter and eyed the other two familiars. Within seconds, Hoot started shrieking and squawking at the top of his lungs. Elvis responded with loud chitters and chirps, and Socrates began to caterwaul so loudly it hurt Evee's ears.

No sooner had Evee put her hands over her ears than

Gilly and Viv hurried into the house behind their familiars. Viv closed the door behind them, and both turned to Evee wide-eyed.

Evee felt her heart skip a beat, fearing by the look on her sisters' faces that something more had come to torture them.

Dropping her hands from her ears, Evee yelled over the brash symphony of animals, "What's wrong?"

"What?" Gilly shouted, obviously having a difficult time hearing over the noise.

"What's wrong?" Evee asked again over the cacophony of animal noises.

Gilly looked over at Viv questioningly.

Frustrated, Evee held both hands out, glared at the familiars and shouted, "Y'all shut the hell up now!"

Elvis gave one last titter, Hoot a short squawk, and Socrates let out one innocent meow.

When all was quiet, Evee asked once more, "What's wrong?" She swiped a strand of wet hair out of her face. She hadn't had time to dry it after her shower.

"You haven't heard?" Viv asked.

Evee frowned.

"About the humans," Gilly said, then stomped a foot. "The *dead* ones, Evee."

"Yeah," Evee said, looking away. "Hoot filled me in a few minutes ago. He saw the whole thing."

Viv did a double take. "What? He saw it? What about Pierre and Chank?"

Evee nodded. "That, too."

"You mean your familiar saw all this going on and didn't summon you?" Gilly asked, putting a hand on her hip.

"He claims he tried, but I didn't hear him, didn't feel

him," Evee said. "I didn't know about the humans or Chank until Hoot came here to tell me."

Gilly eyed her. "How can you not pick up an emergency summons from your familiar? What were you doing while all that was going on? And why is your hair wet?"

"Shower," Evee said, feeling her cheeks flush. "Didn't have time to dry it." Before her sisters pummeled her with more questions, she shot out her own. "Why are the two of you here? Aren't you supposed to be looking for Chenilles and Loup Garous?"

"We were," Gilly snapped. "Found out about the humans and Chank and have been racing around like fools trying to find you. Wanted to make sure that you knew and that you were okay. Is that a crime?"

"I didn't say it was," Evee said. "Why are you being so bitchy?"

Gilly held her arms out. "This isn't bitchy. It's pissed. We've been out there busting our humps and you've been here taking a shower."

Evee turned away from her sisters and went to the counter, picked up the kettle she'd filled with water earlier and headed for the stove. She didn't want to explain to them that she'd needed a shower after the whole Cartesian and river ordeal. She feared if she did, she'd spill the beans about Lucien, as well. As upset as they appeared now, even dropping a hint about her sexual encounter with Lucien, albeit one-sided, would have thrown both of her sisters into cardiac arrest.

"Well?" Viv said. "Explanation please." She pursed her lips.

Ignoring her, Evee put the kettle on the stove and turned on the burner. She really didn't want tea, but at least this gave her something to do.

"Evee, you know the death of the humans and the witnessing of the Nosferatu takes our situation to a whole new level," Viv said. "The police will get involved, which is going to make this catastrophic. This situation is bigger than I think even the Benders realize. We need to figure out some kind of workable game plan. All we've been doing is chasing our tails, looking for Nosferatu, Chenilles and Loups."

Gilly nodded. "Agreed. Dead humans. We're way over our heads...wait a sec. What's up with that?" Gilly walked over to Evee and touched her right shoulder, just near the edge of her scoop-necked sweater, and tugged it down an inch.

"What?" Evee asked. She felt Gilly pull the back of her shirt lower.

"What the hell?" Viv said, and hurried over to Gilly's side.

Evee tried looking over her right shoulder to see what her sisters were gawking at. She couldn't see anything. "What? What, damn it?"

"Your *absolutus infinitus*," Viv said quietly.

All Triads since the 1500s were born with a black *absolutus infinitus* birthmark on a certain part of their body. Evee's was on her right shoulder, Gilly's on her right ankle, and Viv's on her right hip. The mark was part of the curse carried by all Triads.

"What about it?" Evee asked, still trying to look over her shoulder.

"It...it's gray," Gilly said, her voice soft with astonishment.

"Get the hell out," Evee said, and took off to look in the foyer mirror.

When she reached the mirror, she turned sideways, reached back and tugged on her shirt. Her sisters stood beside her, silent. Frustrated, Evee yanked her sweater up and over her head, not caring that she stood only in her bra and jeans. She turned sideways again, and felt her mouth drop open. She saw it, plain as the nose on her face. Her once charcoal-black *absolutus infinitus* had faded to an ashen gray.

"What happened to it?" Viv asked.

"I don't know," Evee said, still staring at her shoulder in the mirror. "I never felt anything, never noticed any change to it until you mentioned a minute ago." She turned to Gilly. "What does it mean? The color change?"

Gilly glanced over at Viv and they both shrugged.

"It's gray, like the mirrors in our Grimoires," Gilly said. "Maybe they're tied together somehow."

The Grimoires were books of spells that had been handed down from one Triad generation to another. As part of their punishment, the first set of Triad had been forced to write every spell known to the Circle of Sisters and the Triad, along with the purpose of each spell, and the consequence of each spell once cast. The spells had been written on parchment paper and bound in elderwood. Inside the front cover of each Grimoire, a notch had been cut out of the elderwood, just big enough to hold a fist-size mirror. The mirror had been purposely set into each Grimoire so that whenever a Triad opened her book, the first thing she saw was the reflection of an apocalyptic destruction of the world. A reminder of what would happen should a Triad shirk her responsibilities and duties of the Originals assigned to her. It showed blood and gore, and the world as a wasteland. Viv, Gilly and Evee read their Grimoires daily, right before a feeding, noting new spells that might be needed should something go awry with their Originals.

Only a few days ago, when they opened their Grimoires, the sisters had been shocked to find that the mirrors no longer showed the apocalyptic vision. They only reflected gray swirls. Nothing more.

"When did your *absolutus* turn gray?" Gilly asked.

"I told you," Evee snapped. "I don't know. I'd probably still be oblivious of it if you hadn't noticed it. It's not like I check on it every day."

Gilly turned to Viv. "What about yours?"

Viv glanced around the foyer as if to confirm that no one was around but her sisters. Then she unbuttoned and unzipped her jeans. She wiggled her jeans down just enough to bare her right hip, where she carried her *absolutus infinitus*.

It, too, had turned gray. Viv's hands shook as she pulled up her pants, zipped and buttoned them back into place.

"What the fuck?" Gilly blurted. "It's gray, too."

"You think I didn't notice?" Viv snapped.

"You didn't notice the change before?" Gilly asked.

"No." Viv looked up at her sisters blankly.

"But you shower every day, right?" Gilly said. "Wouldn't you have seen it in the mirror?"

"Well, I didn't," Viv said. "This is the first I've seen it like this."

Evee and Viv looked at Gilly simultaneously. "What about yours?"

Gilly's eyes widened, and then she nodded. She leaned over and lifted the right leg of her linen pants and twisted her right foot slightly inward. Her *absolutus infinitus* sat right above her right ankle as usual, its color unchanged—charcoal black.

"I don't understand what's going on," Evee said. She shivered. "I'm freezing here. I've got to dry my hair before I get pneumonia. You two go back to the kitchen.

Get something to eat. I'll dry my hair and meet you back there in a few."

When Evee got to her bathroom, she saw Hoot perched on the counter near the bathroom sink.

"I told you," Hoot said.

Ignoring him, Evee opened a vanity drawer and pulled out her blow-dryer. She plugged it in, turned it on and aimed a blast of warm air at her familiar.

Hoot screeched and flew off the counter and out of the bathroom, all the while yelling, "Told you, told you. See what you get for being a hussy?"

"Shut up," Evee said, aiming the blow-dryer at her hair. If Hoot snapped back a reply, she didn't hear it. Blessed be the dryer.

By the time she finished with her hair and made it back into the kitchen, her sisters were seated around the small kitchen table, each with a steaming bowl of gumbo in front of her and a cup of tea.

Gilly motioned for Evee to sit next to her, where another bowl of gumbo and cup of tea had been set out for her.

Evee sat and picked up a spoon, ready to dig into her food. The first bite drew a sigh from her. "This is so good," she said, and quickly dug in for another spoonful.

"Thanks," Viv said. "Made it a couple weeks ago. Put it in the freezer for a rainy day. Or shitty day, whatever works." She shrugged.

"Uh, by the way," Gilly said to Evee. "Before I forget to tell you. We've been summoned by the Elders. I'm sure they've heard about the humans and want an update from us."

Evee felt her shoulders droop. "When?"

"This evening. Before the feeding."

"That late?" Evee said. "Don't they usually go to bed around seven or something ridiculously early like that?"

Viv shrugged. "It's not usual times right now."

"Oh, and something else," Gilly said. "We were wondering…" She looked at Viv.

Viv arched a brow at her sister while spooning more gumbo into her mouth.

"What were you doing here showering when you were supposed to be out looking for your Nosferatu earlier?" Gilly asked.

Evee stared down into the bowl in front of her. "I, uh… I had a situation with a Cartesian."

Viv and Gilly dropped their spoons into their bowls simultaneously.

"When? Where?" Viv asked.

"What did you do?" Gilly asked.

"Were you hurt?" Viv asked anxiously. "You don't look hurt."

Evee held up a hand to stave their questions. Ate one more bite of chicken and sausage gumbo, then readied herself for the inquisition.

Finally, she said, "We split up. Me, Ronan and Lucien each went separate ways to cover more ground and look for Nosferatu. I was headed downriver, Lucien upriver, and Ronan took the Quarter."

Her sisters stared at her bug-eyed.

"Anyway, I was walking riverside when a rift opened in the sky out of nowhere and a Cartesian hung out of it so low it could have scooped me up in one grasp. Luckily I caught him out of the corner of my eye and took off running. Only ran the wrong way. Right into the river until I couldn't feel the bottom anymore."

Gilly gasped. "You can't even swim."

Viv reached out and touched Evee's arm. "You must have been terrified."

Evee nodded, her eyes brimming with tears again as she recalled the event. "I didn't know what was going to happen first. The Cartesian attacking me, or me drowning."

"Obviously neither happened, since you're sitting right here," Gilly said, sounding grateful. "What did happen? The Cartesian, you stuck in the water…?"

"Lucien showed up," Evee said. "Must have doubled back, because the next thing I knew the Cartesian was gone, and Lucien was pulling me out of the water."

Gilly cocked her head. "And did he bring you back here to the house?"

Evee swirled bits of chicken and sausage around in her gumbo with a spoon, knew what was coming next. Finally, she said. "Yes, he brought me here."

"What about Ronan?" Viv asked. "Where was he during all this?"

"I told you," Evee said. "In the Quarter. He wasn't anywhere near the river."

"Where are they now?" Gilly asked.

"Who?"

Gilly rolled her eyes. "Lucien and Ronan."

"Far as I know, Ronan's still in the Quarter," Evee said. "Lucien may have gone after him, I'm not sure."

"In soaked clothes?" Viv asked.

"Yeah," Gilly chimed in. "You said he pulled you out of the river. Surely he'd have gotten soaked doing that, right?" Suddenly, Gilly's head popped up and she sniffed the air, turning her head slowly from left to right, sniffing the entire time, like a cat tracking a mouse. A few seconds later, she got up from her chair, following her nose into the utility room at the back of the kitchen.

"Well, I'll be damned," Gilly said, which caused Viv to jump up from her seat and head to the utility room.

Evee took off right behind them.

"What's wrong?" Evee asked when she finally caught up with her sisters.

Gilly twirled about and faced her. "You had sex in here, didn't you? I can smell it."

Evee felt her cheeks burn with embarrassment. "I did not have sex," she proclaimed.

"Oh, yeah?" Gilly said, then reached for an object on the washer and handed it to Evee. "Then what's this doing here?"

Evee turned Lucien's watch over in her hand, wondering how it had gotten there. Then suddenly remembering him taking it off before stripping out of his shirt.

"Fess up," Viv said. "What happened?"

There were too many other things going wrong now for Evee to start playing fifty questions with her sisters. "Okay, all right, but I didn't have, like, real sex with Lucien. He helped me home so I could shower and get into dry clothes. We happened to kiss. He sat me on top of the dryer, then put his hands…his thumbs between my legs, and before I knew it fireworks happened."

Gilly's mouth dropped open, as did Viv's.

"What were you thinking?" Gilly asked. "We barely know these men, and you let one of them touch you like that? You should know better—"

"I knew better," Viv interrupted. "But it still happened."

Now it was Evee and Gilly's turn to stare at their older sister.

"Except we went all the way. Nikoli didn't just touch me."

"You mean like the real deal?" Evee asked, feeling a bit envious.

"Yeah." Viv nodded, and a small grin spread across her face. "And more than one time."

Gilly placed a hand on her forehead and groaned.

"What?" Viv said to her. "You mean nothing's happened between you and Gavril?"

"No," Gilly said gruffly. "Nothing."

Viv looked over at Evee. "Why Lucien? Why not Ronan? Convenience?"

"Not really," Evee said, feeling slightly offended that her sister had made the question sound like she screwed everything in sight every chance she got. "I mean Ronan is a really nice guy. Good-looking, too. But there's something about Lucien that…well, draws me to him. I couldn't have stopped that first kiss even if I'd have wanted to. Couldn't have stopped him touching me."

Gilly slapped her hands on the table. "Maybe that's why your and Viv's *absolutus infinitus* turned gray. Because of what happened between you and Lucien, Viv and Nikoli. You know the curse says we can't marry or live intimately with any human."

Evee and Viv looked at Gilly simultaneously before Evee said, "I didn't marry Lucien."

"And I'm not living intimately with Nikoli," Viv shot back. "We simply had sex."

Gilly sat back in her chair. "I think the both of you are working with semantics here. It's all in the interpretation of what the curse actually meant. Do we know that for sure? I mean, we're talking the 1500s here, when the curse was cast. What if the original Elders considered living intimately together to mean just having plain old sex? Back in that day and age, the only women who screwed just to screw were harlots in bordellos. If that's the case, wouldn't that mean that just having sex without being married was part of the curse, as well? What if the two of you having sexual encounters with those Benders caused all this chaos to happen? The missing Originals, the attacks on humans?"

Viv scowled at her. "Man, oh, man, you really stretched that one out of your butt. Regardless, it's not like I can take it back now, right? We didn't oppose the curse. We didn't defy it by marrying those men, and we're not living intimately with them. Period."

"As I said," Gilly said. "Semantics."

Despite the reprimand coming out of Gilly's mouth, Evee could've sworn she saw envy and longing in her sister's eyes. Had she had the chance, she'd have slept with Gavril. Evee knew it as well as she knew her own name.

"Not," Viv retorted.

Evee put the tips of her fingers from her right hand against the palm of her left, calling for a time-out. Viv and Gilly stared at her, anger still popping in their eyes.

"Who did what, when and where is not what's important right now. Dying humans are. We've got to find our missing Originals and get them confined, and the ones who are confined need to be protected from the Cartesians."

"That's all we've been trying to do," Viv said. "With not much success, I might add."

"Maybe once we fill the Elders in, they'll have some ideas. Especially about why our spells are weakening. Hell, we can't track our own behinds, much less our own broods. We need backup. Serious backup."

"No way on the Elders," Evee said. "The sex part with the Benders will come out, and that's the last thing we need."

Elvis, Gilly's familiar, suddenly raced into the kitchen, tittered, then let out a short screech as if in agreement.

"Hush," Gilly told him, then turned to Viv. "I don't

think it's going to do us any good to go back to the Elders. They were supposed to contact the others from the Circle of Sisters to help with spells from different locations. If they did, I certainly haven't seen any evidence of it. Have you?"

Viv and Evee shook their heads.

"Look," Evee said, "we have to keep our heads and hands about us, and no more panty play with the Benders." Even to her own ear, the last part of what she'd just said sounded flat, unconvincing and regretful. "I think one of the biggest challenges we've got coming up is feeding time. It'll be here before we know it, and I have a feeling that the Cartesians are going to attempt a strike while we're transporting our broods to the North Compound." She turned to Viv. "Your Loup Garous are already there, but I don't know how we're going to get the Nosferatu and Chenilles out there without a Cartesian attack."

"Maybe there's a different way for us to set up the feedings," Viv said. "What if I had my ranch hands drain the cattle's blood and then we can pick it up and bring it to the Nosferatu instead of bringing the Nosferatu to the compound? The corpses will be there for the Loup Garous, who are already in the compound to eat. When they're done, I can have my ranch hands, Charlie, Bootstrap and Kale, gather up the bones…damn, never mind. I've never allowed the ranch hands to go into the North Compound, and I can't have them go there now. Too big a risk. Can't chance a Loup attacking any one of them."

"Seems like the only part we're short on," Gilly said, "is getting the bones collected and brought to the Chenilles in the Louis I Cemetery. And since Viv is the only one who can control the Loups, we'd have to count on her to collect the bones and transport them over here."

She shook her head. "No way I can see you doing that by yourself."

The three sisters looked down at the floor, then up at the dryer, all three sighing in unison.

Still holding Lucien's watch, Evee fingered it. The watch seemed so apropos. Their spells, ideas and time were running out.

As hard as she tried to stop the thought, it floated loud and strong in Evee's mind. Unbidden, unwanted.

Soon they could be facing the total destruction of the Originals and the Triad.

Chapter 6

The safest—and only place—Lucien and Ronan could think of to ride out the storm of the deaths in the Quarter was their hotel room.

Ronan turned on the television, watching for any updated news reports, and Lucien went straight for the shower that he'd been needing for some time.

After undressing, Lucien turned the shower on hot and the knobs to full jet. He stepped into the spray and leaned forward against the wall of the shower. He closed his eyes and let the jets of hot water soak his hair, pelt against his body.

He tried emptying his mind of the vision of the murdered woman, of the merciless Nosferatu, the gawkers and hecklers. It was then Lucien felt the weight of the entire mission abruptly settle on his shoulders. This was far bigger than anything they'd ever faced before. And with certainty, he knew it would get a lot worse before it got better.

Despite the weight and horrible images fleeting in and out of his mind, Lucien suddenly found himself thinking about Evee.

Evee's explosive reaction to his touch surprised him, and it had taken Lucien every molecule of will he possessed to send her off to shower and for him to leave her home.

Lucien was anything but a prude when it came to women. He'd known many of them over the years. but no one like Evee François. She was tall and slender, with black hair that fell soft and straight to her shoulders. Her eyes were the color of shiny copper pennies, her nose small and perfect. Her lips, so full, luscious, they held the power to drop any man to his knees to beg for one more kiss, one more touch. Her mouth had ravaged his as if she meant to pour the very essence of all she was into him. Oh, how she'd clung to him, kissed him, wanted him.

Although all the triplets were beautiful, there was something about Evee that stuck to Lucien like dried lavender. And he refused to let it fade away. Maybe it was the softness of her voice, the pureness of her heart, how easily she stood up for what was right. Evee took her responsibilities so seriously, yet, at the same time, she held the essence of a certain type of woman Lucien had always craved for and never found. Until now.

The problem was he'd not only found what seemed like the perfect woman, he'd wound up shooting himself in the foot at the same time. He'd all but offered Evee up to Ronan on a silver platter. But he hadn't been able to help himself. He'd never seen his cousin so enamored by a woman before. And despite what he felt, Lucien always had believed that blood was thicker than water. He'd suggested Ronan pursue Evee. And Lucien had no plans to counter or one-up anything his cousin did. In the end, the decision would be Evee's.

Once he finished showering, Lucien got out of the tub, dried off with a white, fluffy towel provided by the hotel, then tried to get dressed. The problem was his pants. All the thinking he'd done about Evee had left him with a hard-on. Even the idea of possibly losing her to Ronan had not squelched his desire for her.

Lucien had to wonder if something wasn't wrong with his own head. How could he feel such sexual desire right now? They'd just witnessed a woman's murder and blinded a Nosferatu.

Groaning, Lucien lightly slapped the front of his pants. It did nothing but bring Evee even closer to mind. How just the slightest touch of his thumbs between her thighs had sent her into an explosive orgasm that left her shaking. He had never known a woman to be so responsive to his touch, and he thirsted for more. What man in his right mind wouldn't?

With one last grunt, and envisioning an impossible geometrical equation that needed to be solved before the room exploded, Lucien was finally able to zip his pants. The bulge behind the zipper was still evident so he quickly threw on a black T long enough to cover it.

No sooner had he put himself in order and stepped out of the bathroom than the hotel room door burst open, and Nikoli and Gavril stormed in. Gavril gently kicked the door closed behind him.

Ronan, who'd already showered and dressed, lay across one of the beds with an arm over his eyes. The commotion with the door had him out of bed and standing military straight.

"Where have you been?" Nikoli demanded, glaring at Lucien.

Taken aback, Lucien glared at his cousin. "What the hell's wrong with you? I just finished showering."

"How convenient," Nikoli said, then turned on his heels and walked over to the window on the other side of the bed and stared out of it.

Lucien glanced from Ronan to Gavril, then aimed his chin at Nikoli. "What's with the attitude?"

"We've been summoning you by satellite for over an hour," Gavril said, pointing to the watch on his left wrist.

All the Benders wore the same gadget. It looked like a watch only with more buttons and tiny knobs along its perimeter than any NASA gismo. It operated as a watch, compass and homing device and emitted a red beacon in the center when one Bender summoned another. And that was only activated if one of them stood in deep shit.

Puzzled, Lucien shook his head. "If you summoned me, I never—" He looked down at his wrist, saw nothing and did a double take. He'd forgotten he'd left his watch at Evee's.

"Where's your locator?" Gavril asked, frowning. "You never take it off."

Lucien's mind went on pause for a moment. It was true. He never took it off, except to shower, which was something none of his cousins knew. The watch was waterproof, shatterproof, but obviously not dumb-ass proof, for he'd left it on Evee's washer. For some reason he couldn't explain at the moment, or possibly ever, he'd removed it in Evee's utility room and placed it on the washer before they'd…well, before.

"Yo, cuz, you've gone deaf, too?" Gavril asked, plopping down in an overstuffed chair. "Where is it? You get robbed?"

"No," Lucien said, feeling awkward. "I didn't get robbed. Must have left it at the François house."

At the mention of the Françoises, Nikoli turned away from the window and joined his circle of cousins.

Ronan stormed toward Lucien, his black eyes growing darker by the second. "You had no business being over there in the first place. The two of you were supposed to be hunting Nosferatu at opposite ends of the river."

Lucien scowled. "Since when did you become my father? Did you not hear what I told you earlier? Nothing happened. The ball in this game is in your court."

Ronan stood and faced him, his jaw muscles working furiously.

Nikoli stepped between Ronan and Lucien and held a hand on their chests, nudging them farther away from each other.

"Chill," Nikoli said to Ronan. He turned to Lucien. "Now, what fucking ball are you talking about? 'Cause this sure ain't no game, cuz."

"I know it isn't a game," Lucien said. "Just something between Ronan and me."

"So he left it at the François home, what's the big deal?" Gavril asked. "We all know Lucien's been working as hard as the rest of us. Cut him some slack."

"You're taking his side?" Ronan asked Gavril.

Gavril snorted back a laugh. "Cuz, you sound like a five-year-old."

"Are you kidding me?" Ronan fumed. "You're actually pulling sides."

Nikoli dropped his hands. "Everybody shut the hell up and get a grip. This isn't about sides. We're a team. Benders. We're not here to piss in each other's boots. We've got enough problems to deal with." He turned to Lucien. "And you, no taking off your transmitter again. You had us worried."

"Sorry," Lucien said, and sat on the couch. "I don't

know why I took it off. Just muddled in the head at the time, I guess. We had a Cartesian attack out on the east bank. It nearly got Evee. I yelled to divert it, and it gave Evee time to run away. Problem was, she ran right into the river, and she can't swim. Had to pop the Cartesian, then rush into the water to get Evee before she drowned."

Nikoli looked at Ronan. "Where were you when all this was going on?"

"In the Quarter, searching for Originals."

"You mean to tell me that the three of you split up?"

Lucien looked down, feeling ashamed for a moment. "Yeah. It's all me, though, cuz. Sounded like a decent plan at the time. Split up and cover more ground."

"If the three of you were headed in different directions," Nikoli said, "how did you wind up where Evee was?"

Lucien shrugged. "Instinct told me to follow her. Good thing I did."

Gavril tilted his head, his brow knitted. "Isn't Evee the one who's supposed to have power over the element of water?"

"Yes," Ronan said.

"Then I'm lost," Gavril said. "If she has the power over water, how did she wind up nearly drowning?"

"I don't know," Lucien said. "She said she has power over water from a distance but is deathly afraid of going into it."

"Aside from controlling it, how does anyone not know how to swim?" Nikoli asked.

"A lot of people don't know how to swim," Lucien said. "And it really is none of our business as to why Evee can't. All I know is that she couldn't get her feet under her and someone had to get her out. Now, if we can put that issue behind us for a minute, you might want to hear about another problem that needs attention."

Nikoli scratched his chin and sighed. "More?"

"You talking about the scabior canopy?" Ronan asked Lucien.

"Yeah."

"What about it?" Nikoli asked.

"The one we set up in the catacombs started to wane," Ronan said. "We had to recharge it."

"Crap," Nikoli said, and leaned against the wall nearest him and swiped a hand through his hair. "Man, if those canopies go out, we've got nothing to keep the Originals that the Triad still have under their control... controlled."

The scabior canopies had been Nikoli and Viv's brainchild. The first one had been formed around the North Compound to keep the Loup Garous in check and the Cartesians out. It didn't take a genius to figure out that the Benders, with their four scabiors combined, couldn't watch over all the Originals at the same time and search for the ones who'd gone missing. To remedy some of the problem, Viv had used one of her Loup Garous to bend four steel poles that cornered the five-hundred-acre property at forty-five-degree angles. Each pole had a bloodstone placed at the top of it, just like the Benders' scabiors. The bent poles were aimed toward the center of the property, pointed at one another, then charged with Nikoli's scabior. That charge created an electrical dome over the entire North Compound, which kept the Cartesians from dropping down out of a rift into the compound. With the contained Loups protected, Nikoli and Viv were free to hunt for the ones that had gone missing.

The same protocol was used at the Louis I Cemetery,

where the Chenilles were kept, and the catacombs at St. John's Cathedral, where Evee kept her Nosferatu.

The fact that one of the domes had to be recharged worried Lucien, as it did his cousins. The others would have to be watched over closely to make sure they wouldn't need the same boost. That was all they needed. More to watch over.

As if reading his thoughts, Nikoli stood upright and stuck his hands in his back pockets. "Something else we're going to have to keep an eye on. I'll do a check on the compound before the feeding."

"Same here at the cemetery," Gavril said.

The room went silent for a moment, each cousin lost in his own thoughts.

Finally, Ronan cleared his throat. "There's more, guys."

Gavril's eyebrows arched. "More?"

Ronan nodded. "Earlier, when Lucien and me were in the Quarter, looking for Originals, we heard a woman screaming down one of the streets that branches off Bourbon. At first, she was making sounds like she wanted whoever was with her to fu…have his way with her. We checked to make sure she was all right, and saw one of the Nosferatu with her, transforming right there. Right in front of her. She started screaming so loudly I worried that people in the next parish might hear her."

"Man, oh, man," Gavril said, shaking his head in disbelief. "Don't blame her. What'd y'all do?"

"Jumped the Nosferatu. Gouged his eyes out with the back end of our scabiors. Unfortunately, we didn't make it there in time to save the woman."

"But Nosferatu heal themselves pretty quickly, don't they?" Nikoli asked.

"Oh, yeah," Lucien said. "And that one was regrouping double time. We were planning our next attack. I mean, the Nosferatu already knew we could get to its eyes, so I'm figuring it'd probably hit us from another direction, right?"

"Makes sense," Nikoli said.

"So what'd you do?" Gavril asked.

"Nothing," Lucien said. "Didn't have time. The next thing I knew, the Original jerked back, then fell over dead."

Gavril and Nikoli looked from Lucien to Ronan, waiting for a follow-up explanation. It wasn't like either to play a suspense card when relaying an incident.

Nikoli motioned with a hand for Ronan to continue.

"It was Pierre. Evee's head Nosferatu. He stabbed the rogue Original in the back with some kind of dagger. It went right through the Original. Came out the front of his chest, right through the heart."

Nikoli blew out a loud breath. "Bad for the Nosferatu, but good for us. Don't know how we'd have dealt with that one."

"You mean a Nosferatu has the ability to purposely kill its own?" Gavril asked.

"I'm no expert," Lucien said, "but I believe they do, if doing so serves a higher purpose. I know the Triad take the safety of humans seriously when it comes to the Originals. Guess that situation merited a higher purpose."

"There's more," Ronan said, and began to pace the room.

"Shit," Gavril said. "What?"

"There were witnesses, human witnesses. They saw the death and then the transformation of the Nosferatu to human after it died," Ronan said, frowning.

Lucien nodded. "And the police were summoned."

Gavril gawked at him. "You talked to the police? Were you interrogated? Did they consider you a suspect?"

Ronan and Lucien shrugged simultaneously.

"I have no idea what they thought or suspected," Lucien said. "As soon as we heard the sirens, Ronan and I took off for the hotel. How could we have possibly explained to the police what happened? They'd have thought we were totally drugged out or had some wires loose in our heads."

"Do the Triad know all this?" Lucien asked.

"Ten to one they do," Gavril said. "I was with Gilly looking for Chenilles when she suddenly said, 'Something's come up. I've got to go.'"

"She didn't tell you what the 'up' was?" Nikoli asked.

Gavril shook his head. "She just took off. Said we'd meet later at the docks when it's time to take the ferry to the compound for feeding."

Lucien got to his feet. "If the Triad know, surely they're together right now. Probably going to see their Elders for help, call in reinforcements."

Nikoli tapped the tips of his fingers together. "Maybe we should be doing the same thing."

Lucien, Gavril, and Ronan looked at him in unison.

Nikoli held out his hands, palm up. "You know, call for backup."

"Have you lost your—" Ronan began.

Gavril shook his head.

"I know, I know," Nikoli said. "But hear me out. There comes a time when we've got to suck it up, put pride on the shelf and call in our own cavalry. I mean, really. Look at where we are, for heaven's sake. I don't know about you three, but I feel like we've achieved little to nothing. We're being reactive instead of proactive."

"Our setting up the electrical canopies to create safe places for the Originals *was* proactive," Lucien said.

"True," Nikoli agreed. "But you said it yourself. The scabior canopy at the catacombs had to be recharged. What if something happens to the other two? What if they go out? Humans died, Lucien. Police are going to start crawling all over this."

Ronan rolled his left hand into a fist and punched it into the palm of his right. "No other Bender in our history has ever called for backup, and I, for one, am not about to start now. We've got to work the plans we've already set in motion." He turned to Lucien. "No more splitting apart more than we already have. It was stupid to allow Evee to go off on her own."

"Allow?" Lucien said with incredulity. "Evee is not a child. She's a strong and intelligent woman with a mind of her own. Just like her sisters. I don't believe any of them would allow anyone to force them in any given direction."

"Including yours?" Ronan snapped.

"My what?" Lucien asked, taken aback by Ronan's anger.

Without another word, Ronan stormed out of the hotel room.

Nikoli winced as the hotel door slammed behind his cousin.

"Who stuck a broom up his butt?" Gavril asked.

Lucien shook his head, indicating that he didn't have a clue. But he knew. Ronan cared for Evee. Wanted to protect her at all costs. Lucien understood that all too well.

Unfortunately, there was nothing Lucien could do about Ronan's feelings. He had given his cousin leeway to pursue his interest in her, and he planned to keep himself away until Evee either rebuffed Ronan or forced all of them out of New Orleans.

The only feelings Lucien had control over were his own. Whether he experienced guilt or fear, anger or frustration, the one thing he knew was that for now, he had to lay down what he felt for Evee and give Ronan space. Maybe even coach him a bit on how to approach Evee.

Even as he thought about it, Lucien looked down at the floor and shook his head slightly. Goddamn, he felt like an idiot. He wanted to be the one to pursue her, the one she'd run to whenever she was afraid or uncertain.

As stupid as it sounded, all he knew to do was play fair, help Ronan gain a bit of an edge and let nature take it course.

And for now, that had to be enough.

Chapter 7

It was nearing 10:00 p.m., and Arabella, Taka and Vanessa, the three Elders responsible for the Circle of Sisters and the Triad, were in their nightgowns huddled over cups of tea at the kitchen table. They lived in the Garden District of New Orleans, in an old Victorian about four or five blocks from the Triad.

"When did you hear about the humans being attacked, about the Nosferatu and the witnesses?" Taka asked. "Who told you?"

"Earlier," Arabella said. "About an hour ago and then a half hour later from Brunedee, a Circle sister from Plaquemine."

"Aw," Taka said, waving a dismissive hand. "I wouldn't lose sleep over that. Brunedee is a gossip magnet. Last I heard, she'd spread word that Brad Pitt met her at a gas station in Metairie, and he was so enamored with her, he up and left Angelina."

"And you believed that?" Vanessa asked.

Taka gave her a stern look. "What do you think I am, brainless? No way Brad would leave Angelina and all their kids for Brunedee. Nicholas Cage, maybe. But Brad, uh-uh."

"Everything, including the Nosferatu and witnesses, checks out," Arabella said quietly. "It's been confirmed twice."

"How on earth did Brunedee hear about it before us, especially with her living almost a hundred miles away?" Vanessa asked.

Arabella shrugged. "You know how the Circle of Sisters works. News travels fast. And news like this…" She shook her head. "Sisters in Argentina are probably hearing about it by now."

The Elders sat silent for a moment, each staring inside her teacup as if waiting for some apparition to appear.

"We lost three humans, too," Arabella said. "In case you hadn't heard."

Vanessa and Taka drew in deep breaths in unison.

"When? Where?" Taka asked.

"One in the Quarter, earlier this evening. The other two in Chalmette."

Taka gasped. "Chalmette? They're out of the city? Mother Earth, that means the Originals can go anywhere!"

"I know," Arabella said quietly.

"What happened to the human in the Quarter?" Vanessa asked.

"Word has it that a Nosferatu attacked her in some back alley. Two of the Benders were nearby, attempted to stop it."

"Well, that was stupid," Taka said.

"At least they tried," Vanessa snapped.

Arabella kept staring at her tea. "Got the Nosferatu

in the eyes. At least it served as a diversion. Too late for the poor woman, though."

"Yeah," Taka said, "but the Nosferatu heal themselves, like, super fast."

Arabella nodded. "That's what happened. Then it went after the Benders. Pierre had to take it down."

"Evee's lead guy at the catacombs?" Vanessa asked.

"Yes."

Taka shook her head. "Had to be bad for him to kill one of his own."

"Killing humans is serious business," Arabella said. "Pierre did the right thing. If he couldn't call the Nosferatu back into the fold, he had no other choice. That's just how it goes."

"Which Nosferatu got it?" Taka asked. "Sabrina? She's always been a hardheaded Original. Always liked to stir up trouble."

Arabella shook her head. "It was Chank."

"Aw, man, the redheaded one?" Taka said. "I always thought he was a sweetheart. Had great hair. Good-looking, too."

Vanessa gave Arabella an eye roll, which evidently wasn't missed by Taka.

"Well, he was," Taka said. With a look of frustration, she got up from the table and started to pace about the kitchen. Her open-back slippers slapped against her heels with each step.

"Arabella, you did contact everyone in the Circle about what's been going on here, right?" Taka asked. "I don't mean what just, just happened with the humans. I mean the deaths of Viv's Loups, the missing Originals?"

"Of course I did. I've summoned the Triad, too, to come this evening so we can discuss all this mess."

"And nothing's happened? The entire clan gets involved and nothing? Why have we suddenly become so ineffective?" Taka demanded. "It's as if we've become nothing more than three old ladies living in a shoe."

"Stop talking like a nut job," Vanessa said with a huff.

"Nut job, huh?" Taka retorted. "The cops have already been here twice, and twice we ignored them. With witnesses to the Nosferatu death and transformation, who do you think will be knocking on our door next? Probably the FBI. The CIA. The IRS. Who the heck knows? News might travel fast among the Circle, but it flies like lightning through New Orleans. The city is going to be in an uproar. We could be looking at lynchings, like they did way back in the day. Witch hangings, burnings." The more Taka spoke the faster she walked, and the harder her slippers slapped against her heels.

"Stop being so melodramatic and working yourself up to a frenzy," Vanessa said. "We need to quit speculating and come up with a better plan. Isn't that right, Arabella?"

Arabella finally glanced up from her teacup, looked over at Taka, then Vanessa. "I'm concerned that Taka might not be exaggerating."

Vanessa did a double take at Arabella, and her brow furrowed. "What do you mean?"

Scratching the hives suddenly covering her arms, Arabella shook her head. "I'm concerned. Seriously concerned. If spells from the entire clan of the Circle of Sisters haven't helped, I don't know what else to do."

"No ideas at all?" Taka asked, fear creasing her face.

Arabella looked back down at her teacup. "Well... okay, maybe one, but the two of you won't like it."

"Spill it," Vanessa said. "We can't afford for things to get any worse."

Sighing, Arabella looked up. "You know how I said

I'd heard about the recent event earlier, then again from Brunedee?"

"Yeah," Taka said warily.

"Well, the first I heard of it was from Gunner Stern."

Vanessa gasped. "What were you doing talking to that stupid sorcerer? You know the rules. No collaborating with those idiots."

"Gunner isn't an idiot," Arabella said.

"He is if he hangs out with Trey Cottle and Shandor Black, the other two sorcerers in New Orleans," Vanessa said. "You may be sweet on Gunner, but he's still a sorcerer, and he may be a nice guy, but hanging out with those other two scumbags makes him a scumbag by association."

"Yeah," Taka said. "But he is a nice guy. I've got to admit, he's not like the other two."

"Oh, hush," Vanessa said. "You don't know any more about Gunner than you know where your reading glasses are right now."

Taka tsked. "Do, too. They're right here." She patted the top of her head and frowned when she didn't feel them perched there. She stuck her hands in her nightgown pockets. Empty. "Well, they're somewhere."

Vanessa rolled her eyes.

Arabella took a sip of tea, then said, "I happen to think that out of all three sorcerers in the city, Gunner is the most levelheaded. And for your information, I'm not sweet on him."

"But he is on you," Taka said.

"That's for sure," Vanessa agreed. "The way he looks at you…" She fanned her face with a hand. "Hot, hot, hot."

"Oh, please," Arabella said. "You're acting like a pubescent teen. I think Gunner has integrity, that's all. Now both of you stop with the attraction comments. We have to stay on track."

The three Elders fell silent for a moment, Taka still pacing, Vanessa sipping tea.

Arabella thought about Gunner, who lived in New Orleans proper. He'd called her in confidence to tell her about the incident with the Nosferatu and the human witnesses. During their conversation, he'd said that Trey and Shandor were out having dinner with a client.

Out of all the sorcerers, Gunner was the one Arabella trusted. Trey Cottle was a sorcerer whose entire world revolved around him, and him alone. He was a selfish twit. Overweight, sweaty, plump-faced with a band of gray, thinning hair that wrapped around the back of his head. And he wore thick black glasses that constantly slid down the bridge of his nose. Arabella guessed him to be in his late sixties, early seventies.

Shandor Black was Trey's partner at their law firm and his indomitable yes-man. He had a long, pinched face, a long beak of a nose, and if he ever had an opinion about any issue, he made sure it mirrored Trey's.

Gunner, although often seen in Trey and Shandor's company, carried himself quite differently. He appeared to be in his midsixties, had a strong, handsome face and blue eyes that twinkled whenever he spoke to Arabella.

When Gunner had called Arabella with the news, he'd offered to help in any way he could. And, oh, how she wanted to say yes. But keeping protocol in mind, especially being an Elder, she had to get a vote on the issue with the other two Elders and the Triad.

"It's late," Taka said, then yawned. "Are you sure the triplets are coming tonight? Can't they come in the morning, and we can discuss everything then? It's way past my bedtime. My brain works better in the morning." She ran her hands through her short white hair, making it poke up in untidy spikes.

"They'll be here," Arabella said. "I'm sure with all that's going on, they're trying to get their ducks in a row before coming here and then heading out again to take care of their feeding."

Taka suddenly stopped in midpace. "What if the cops come knocking at our door while the triplets are here?"

"Stop," Vanessa said. "Don't wind this up any tighter than it already is. We'll deal with that issue if it comes up. Until then, don't add it to our pile of worries."

Arabella nodded in agreement and took another sip of tea, noticed the cup shaking slightly in her hand. Of course she was nervous, anxious. Who wouldn't be under these conditions? Something was way off in their world of spells and ancient tried-and-true incantations. Most appeared to be useless. She had contacted each leader of the Circle of Sisters around the country and beyond, invoking their help. And for the first time ever, to Arabella's knowledge anyway, their powers combined seemed to have little to no effect on the situation here, regarding the Cartesians or the missing Originals.

Taka suddenly walked over to the kitchen table and slapped a hand onto it. "I think Arabella's right," she blurted. "We need some serious backup. I vote we bring the sorcerers in on this deal."

"Are you crazy?" Vanessa said. "The only thing they've ever provided us is trouble. They're into their own incantations and spells, and they're always having to do with benefiting themselves. When have you ever seen them use their powers for the good of others?"

"I think Gunner would," Arabella said, seeing in Taka's words an opportunity to create a slight opening in the door of impossibility. She had begun to give up hope that Gunner could ever be recruited in their mission. "He did offer to help."

Vanessa snorted. "Get real, old girl. You're only saying that because he's sweet on—"

"Stop it," Arabella said. "It's not about that."

"Bullshit it's not," Vanessa said.

Taka gasped. "You used the B word!"

"Oh, grow up," Vanessa said to Taka, then turned to Arabella. "You want us to be realistic and get back on track, then you have to admit that Gunner's got a thing for you. Whenever that man's around you he smiles so big that if he wore false teeth, they'd fall out."

"He's the only one I'd really trust," Arabella said. "Not only is he sensible, but I've seen him do good for others."

"When and for whom?" Vanessa asked.

Now Arabella rolled her eyes. "I don't remember the exact time, place or person, but he has helped."

"But what could only one sorcerer do to assist us when the entire clan of Circle of Sisters can't make a difference?" Taka asked. "I say we just roll the dice, bring all three in and make something serious happen. We can't deny that something's out of alignment here. I don't know if it's the cosmos or something with the thinning ozone layer, whichever, whatever, we're in serious trouble."

Vanessa tsked. "Whether Gunner is sweet on you or not, Arabella, I seriously don't think one sorcerer can do the trick. And I sure as hell don't want those other two snot-ball sorcerers mixed up with us."

"How do you know one wouldn't make a difference?" Arabella said. "All you keep saying is, 'no, no, no, don't involve the sorcerers.' But seriously, look how deep things have gotten. The Triad and Benders haven't found any more missing Originals. Now humans are being attacked, they've witnessed the death of a Nosferatu, and more Cartesians are finding their way into our dimension. If we don't do something, and quickly, things are just going to get worse. Missing Originals means more humans are in danger, especially now. Feeding time is coming soon. The missing ones will be hungry and look for the first source of food they can find. And in this city, you know what that's going to be. Humans."

Taka raised her right hand. "I vote we start with Gunner, see what happens. He might at least offer some advice. Maybe there's a spell he can cast that is blocked from us."

"I think the whole idea is stupid," Vanessa said. "I understand the seriousness of this matter, but I think bringing in the sorcerers, even one, will only make things worse. That's what happens when you bring the devil into your ranks."

"Oh, for earth, water, air and fire's sake," Arabella said. "Gunner is not the devil."

"Maybe not, but he hangs out with Trey and Shandor. And you know what they say—if you mess with crap, you're going to get some on you."

"That's not true," Taka said. "I've smelled Gunner before. He smells real good. Not like poop at all."

"We'll discuss this in more detail when the Triad arrive," Arabella said. "I'm sure with all that's been going on, they'll have more to tell us. Once we get an update from them, we'll fill them in on what we've heard from this end, then take a vote regarding the sorcerers. One or all three, it doesn't matter. We just need everybody's input and vote. Otherwise, things remain just as they are."

"You mean in the shitter?" Vanessa said.

"Pretty much, from the sound of it," Taka said, and shook her head. "In all my years, I've never known things to be this bad. Maybe that's why we suck at this now. We've never been through it before."

"Experience has nothing to do with our spells not

working," Arabella said. "The fact that they're not working is my greatest concern."

In that moment, a knock sounded from their front door. The three women froze, staring at one another.

"We're getting way too jumpy," Arabella said. "I'm sure it's the Triad."

"Check the peephole before you open the door," Taka whispered.

Another knock sounded on the door, and Arabella rose from the table and headed out of the kitchen, through the living room and into the foyer. She put her hand to the doorknob, felt a shiver run up her spin and decided to do as Taka suggested. She looked through the security peephole in the door.

Outside, standing near the door on their front porch, were two police officers. Both stood with hands on hips, heads slightly lowered, faces grim.

Hearing shuffling sounds behind her, Arabella turned about quickly and saw Taka and Vanessa standing at the end of the foyer.

"Who is it?" Vanessa mouthed.

Arabella held a finger to her lips.

"I knew it," Taka said, a little too loudly. "It's the cops, right?"

Arabella scowled at her and pressed her finger to her lips harder. Maybe if they didn't make any noise, the officers would go away. Hopefully they'd think no one was home.

Then a thought struck Arabella, sending another shiver up her spine. She could only pray that the Triad didn't decide to show up at this moment with the police standing right outside their door.

Chapter 8

After meeting up with Evee, Gilly and Viv had chosen to go and check on their Originals to make certain the scabior canopies were still in working order. They'd agreed to reconvene at the house in a couple of hours, and then, just before feeding time, go and see the Elders who'd summoned them. It was Gilly's idea to extend the meeting time with the Elders by those few hours. The later it got, the more tired the Elders would be. The more tired they were, the better the chances were that the triplets wouldn't get their butts chewed out for one thing or another.

Although Evee wanted to check on her Nosferatu, she knew she had to get Lucien's watch, with all its buttons and gizmos, back to him as soon as possible. She had no idea if he remembered that he'd taken it off and left it on her washer. She had an inkling the fancy watch that also looked like a compass and some type of homing and navigational device, all rolled into one, had to be important to him. His cousins also wore the same device. If nothing else, bringing Lucien his watch was as good an excuse as any to see him now instead of later.

Evee left the house and took the trolley from the Garden District to the Canal Street intersection. She thought she remembered Lucien saying that they were staying at the Hotel Monteleone, and crossed her fingers that she was right.

When the trolley came to a stop on Canal, she hopped off and made her way down Royal Street. The Monteleone was barely a half block down Royal.

The hotel had been built back in the late 1800s, and time did nothing but add to the majesty of the structure, a favorite haunt of distinguished Southern authors. Its infamous Carousel Bar was a popular hangout in the city. Although Evee had been in the hotel more than once, she still took a moment to stare at its grandeur when she stepped inside. People milled about the lobby, and she heard laughter, music and the clinking of glasses in the Carousel Bar that sat just inside the lobby on the right.

After a moment, it suddenly dawned on her that Gavril, Nikoli and Ronan might be in the same hotel room as Lucien. If so, how was she going to explain why she had possession of Lucien's watch?

Feeling a few jitters settling in, she made her way to the registration desk and waited behind a pudgy, elderly gentleman as he spoke to the redheaded woman behind the desk.

When the woman finally handed the man his room key, Evee stepped up to the desk.

"Welcome to the Hotel Monteleone," the receptionist said. "How may I help you?"

"I'd like to speak to Lucien Hyland. I believe he's staying here," Evee said.

"Do you know his room number?"

Evee bit her bottom lip. "No, sorry. Maybe you could just ring his room and let him know I'm here? My name's Evee François."

The woman eyed Evee for a moment, then tapped some keys on her computer. "Hmm, are you sure he's staying at this hotel? I don't show a Lucien Hyland listed here."

"He's staying here with his cousins, so the room may be under one of their names. Either Nikoli, Gavril or Ronan Hyland."

The woman nodded, pressed more keys on her computer. Evee saw her right eyebrow arch ever so slightly before she picked up a phone and discreetly tapped in four numbers. She turned her back to Evee, and whispered into the phone. Her voice wasn't low enough for Evee not to hear her.

"Mr. Hyland? Yes…of course. There's a young lady here who'd like to speak to Mr. Lucien Hyland." A short pause; then the woman said, "Evee François." Another pause, this one shorter. "Yes, sir, I certainly will."

She turned back to Evee, hung up the phone and gave her a big smile. "Mr. Hyland asks that you please go right on up to his room. Number 1215."

Feeling awkward, Evee leaned closer to the registration table. "Would you happen to know which Hyland answered the phone?"

Not breaking her smile, the woman said, "No, I'm sorry." She glanced over Evee's shoulder. "May I help the next guest, please?"

Feeling dismissed, Evee turned to get a lay of the land and spot the elevators.

"Ms. François?" the receptionist called to her while tapping away on her computer. She stopped tapping long enough to point two, well-manicured fingers at a bank of elevators that stood beside the bar. "Those elevators will take you to the twelfth floor. Take a right out of the elevator and the room will be four doors down on the left."

"Thank you," Evee said, then hurried for the designated elevator bank. For some reason she felt skittish, wanting to bolt out of the hotel. What if Lucien's cousins were in that room? How was she to explain why she had Lucien's watch?

The elevator doors whisked open, and after taking a deep breath, Evee stepped inside and pressed the button for the twelfth floor. As the cubicle bumped its way higher and higher, Evee had to admit that her jitters had more to do with Lucien than his cousins. What if she went to the room and found him alone in there? That gave her more to worry about. His magnetism went through her like nothing Evee had ever felt before. In the short, intimate time they'd been together, it was as if Lucien knew how to read her mind, body and soul. Such a dangerous, erotic triathlon.

As the elevator came to a halt, dinging an announcement that it had reached the twelfth floor, Evee reprimanded herself. She wasn't a child. She was in control of her actions. All she had to do was return the watch, then confirm when and where she, Lucien and Ronan would meet for feeding time or hunt for Nosferatu. Simple.

She stepped out of the elevator and felt sweat beading on her forehead. If this was supposed to be as simple as she'd just tried to convince herself it was, why had she broken into a cold sweat?

It was then she realized she was standing in front of Ronan Hyland.

Evee hurried to hold the elevator door open for him.

"Thanks, but no need," Ronan said, swiping a hand through his hair. He gave her a gentle smile. "I forgot something in the hotel room, so I have to go back there anyway. What brings you out this way?"

Evee hesitated for a beat, then decided the truth was never hard to cover. "Lucien forgot his watch at our house. I noticed the four of you always have them on, so I figured it must be important. Decided to bring it to him right away."

A dark shadow flitted across Ronan's face. It was quickly replaced by a warm expression, which suited the rest of him. His black hair, collar-length, was combed away from his angular face, save for a few strands that lay against his forehead. His seemingly constant five-o'clock shadow only highlighted the deep black of his eyes. He had a perfect nose that sat above full lips. No question Ronan was a handsome man. Any woman would be crazy not to want him, chase him relentlessly.

"No problem," Ronan said. "Come on. I'll take you to the room."

Chewing on her bottom lip, Evee followed Ronan, taking a right and heading down a maroon-and-gold swirled carpeted hallway until they reached room 1215.

She squared her shoulders and had lifted a hand to knock when Ronan produced a key card for the door. Without a word, he slipped the card into the door slot and pushed the door open.

Standing in the studio area of the suite was Lucien, all six feet three inches of him, wearing jeans and an olive green, button-down shirt. The color complemented his beautiful green eyes and his Mediterranean, caramel-colored skin. If his eyes had been a pool of water, Evee would gladly have dived into them, despite her fear of water, and not cared if she ever resurfaced.

For a moment, Evee wished she had taken a little more time putting on a bit of makeup. She had just slipped into a pair of jeans, sneakers and a blue pullover. She suddenly felt self-conscious of her hair, which she'd pulled back into a half-hearted ponytail.

Evee heard the click of the suite door softly closing.

Lucien smiled when he saw her, and she stood transfixed, studying his full lips and straight white teeth. She would have given anything to have his mouth on her again.

"You okay?" Lucien asked, his smile fading. "Anything new come up?" He threw Ronan a questioning look.

"Uh…yes… I mean no." Evee held out his watch. "I thought you might need this before we hooked up again."

Lucien stared at her for a long moment before reaching for his watch and attaching it to his left wrist. "Thank you for bringing it. That was very thoughtful of you. My cousins gave me hell about not having it earlier."

At the mention of his cousins, Evee threw a slight glance around the sitting area of the suite, trying to see if anyone else was inside.

"Are Gavril and Nikoli here?" Evee asked.

A soft smile played around Lucien's lips. "No. Gavril went to meet Gilly to check on the scabior dome over the cemetery, where she's keeping the Chenilles, and Nikoli went for Viv. They're going to the North Compound to make sure things are set up for the feeding. I was about to go and check the catacombs."

"Is that where you were headed when we met by the elevator?" Evee asked Ronan.

He shook his head. "Had other business to tend to first."

Evee saw a look pass between Ronan and Lucien that she couldn't read.

Ronan cleared his throat. "Please excuse our rudeness. Make yourself comfortable."

Although Evee's mind said, *Time to leave, woman. NOW!* she ignored it. "Please don't let me stop you from whatever business you have to take care of," she said to Ronan.

"It can wait a bit longer," Ronan said, smiling softly.

Seemingly out of nowhere, Lucien grabbed a MagLite flashlight from the desk near the room's east windows, then quickly attached his sheath and scabior to the belt of his pants. His expression had turned hard, almost purposely so. Even worse, he avoided eye contact with Evee.

"I'll check the catacombs, cuz," Lucien said to Ronan. "Why don't you take some time to explain to Evee exactly how our watches work? I think it'll help her understand my deep appreciation for returning it to me so quickly. I'll meet the two of you at the docks later for the feeding."

With that said, and with no more preamble than a stiff nod at Evee, Lucien left the room so quickly you'd have thought a bomb had been set to go off in the hotel at any moment.

Once the door closed, and not so softly this time, Evee gave Ronan a questioning look. "What was that all about? Did I do or say anything to anger him?"

"Of course not," Ronan assured her. "Worry does that to him occasionally."

Evee felt Ronan's statement to be true, but it was the reason for his worry that concerned her.

Ronan motioned her to a couch in the living area of the suite. "Would you like a soda? Water? Something a bit harder perhaps?"

Evee gave him a shy smile. "No, thanks." She sat on

the couch, not knowing what to do with her hands, feet or legs for that matter. She finally crossed her legs and held her hands in her lap. "I didn't mean to come here and interrupt whatever you're working on. Just wanted to return Lucien's watch, see if we were going to meet up later for the feeding."

"What would make you wonder that?" Ronan asked. "Of course we'll be there for the feeding."

Evee nodded and felt like a mentally challenged bobblehead. There was no way in hell she'd ever tell Ronan about the sexual experience she'd had with Lucien on the dryer. The question had actually been meant for Lucien, who'd already vanished. He'd left her house so quickly she wasn't sure if he even wanted to be around her anymore.

Ronan sat beside her and placed one of his large hands over both of hers. "I know there's a lot going on right now, Evee, but I swear we'll get to the bottom of it and bring your world back to order."

Evee blinked. Her thoughts and Ronan's words seemed to cross paths, which left her befuddled. She felt her cheeks go from warm to hot. "Thank you," she said quietly.

She glanced down and just then noticed that Ronan's hand covered both of hers. His touch was gentle, his large hands reassuring. He smelled of Coast soap with a hint of musk.

Holding her breath, Evee purposely turned away and surveyed the living room. "I'm sure you've heard about the attack on the human and the Nosferatu, right?" she asked, then immediately felt stupid. Of course he knew. He'd been there along with Lucien.

"Yes." Ronan sat back on the couch. "I was there. So was Lucien. We were able to slow the Nosferatu down, but not before he'd made his kill. He had to be taken down by your lead guy. What's his name? Pierre?"

Evee nodded.

"That's what sent my cousins here. They'd already heard about the incident and wanted to tell Lucien and me about it. They were able to reach me." He tapped the face of the watch on his left wrist. "This has a geo node in it that allows us to summon one another if an emergency comes up. Since Lucien wasn't wearing his, he never got the signal."

Evee chanced a glance his way. "I'm sorry about the watch. If I hadn't been so stupid and jumped into the river, Lucien wouldn't have gotten wet and—"

Unexpectedly, Ronan placed a hand to her cheek and gently turned it so she faced him. "Nothing was your fault, Evee. I don't know why Lucien took his watch off in the first place, and knowing now is pretty irrelevant. It was his responsibility. Not yours. Please hear me when I tell you, nothing was your fault. Do you hear me?"

She nodded ever so slowly.

"Why are you shaking?" he asked, his voice soft. "I can feel you trembling. Tell me. What's wrong? Besides the obvious, of course."

She looked up at him. "I—I guess I'm afraid that so much has gotten out of control that we won't be able to fix it. Nothing will ever be normal again, will it?"

In response, Ronan pulled her close to him. Evee stiffened slightly, then made a half-hearted effort to allow his lead.

Ronan kissed the top of her head, as a brother would a sister. "Evee, I know we're facing hell and damnation with all that's going on, and I don't want to add more to your plate."

Evee glanced up at him, steeling herself for more bad news. "What is it?"

"When…when this is over," Ronan said, "would you like to have dinner with me?"

Evee's eyes widened. "You mean like a dinner date?"

Ronan nodded, and he released her body as if bracing himself for the worst. A rejection.

His eyes were so expectant that Evee nearly felt sorry for him. Without question she would have given up half her powers to have Lucien sitting here, asking her the same question. She didn't know how the extreme attraction she felt toward Lucien started or why it was there, for all four Benders were drop-dead hunks.

Thinking about it now, Evee started to feel like a fool. Lucien hadn't asked her to dinner. There had been some odd sexual explosion that he seemed to know she physically needed and gave it to her. Ronan, on the other hand, was handling her like she was a lady. Maybe a bit too prim and proper for her taste, but at least she knew where she stood with him.

As for Lucien, she had no clue. Especially when she'd arrived at the hotel. He couldn't have left fast enough.

Evee smiled at Ronan. "I'd love to have dinner with you when this is over, and we can all breathe again."

A look of surprise flashed in Ronan's eyes, and then the smile he gave her lit up his entire face.

Ronan jumped to his feet. "I'll look forward to it."

Evee rose from the couch, as well. "As will I." She smiled at Ronan, but her heart didn't feel what her face expressed. Despite all the logic in the world, Lucien was the one man who filled her thoughts constantly. It was almost like they were two halves of one piece, only Lucien hadn't figured it out yet. And she couldn't have explained it if her life depended on it.

Regardless, without provocation or impetus, as far as Evee knew, she rowed alone in her make-believe Lucien-and-Evee boat.

She *would* look forward to dinner with Ronan, and to prove it, she gave him a small kiss on his cheek.

Smiling, yet seemingly flustered, Ronan began grabbing things from the suite. His belt, his scabior… "I'll go and meet up with Lucien to make sure he doesn't need help at the catacombs. See you at the docks later?"

"Absolutely," Evee said, and grinned. All the while, all she could do was wonder why her smiles and grins and dinner date agreement felt fake. Like she was someone else making the promises. Giving out what was so desperately sought after by a wonderful, albeit quiet, thoughtful man.

No matter how many tongue-lashings she gave herself mentally, or how many logical explanations she forced into her brain about agreeing to date Ronan, Evee still couldn't help feeling like an asshole.

Chapter 9

Having been summoned by the Elders earlier, Evee, Gilly and Viv had little choice but to make an appearance. They'd put off the meeting as long as possible, but the inevitable had to happen.

They'd met up at an agreed-upon time about a block from the Elders' home. Surprisingly, each of their familiars had been there, waiting for them, when they arrived. When ordered to go home, they refused. Being too tired to argue, Evee and her sisters simply walked to their destination in silence, familiars in tow.

After a quick welcome, they'd been escorted into the dining room and motioned to sit at the table, which they did. The room had an old Victorian air about it, but felt comfortably lived in. The dining room contained a beautiful oblong oak table held upright by a large, claw-footed pedestal. Eight oak chairs surrounded the table, each covered with soft, albeit worn, pastel fabric. Against one wall stood a huge china hutch that held more bric-a-brac than china, and beside it sat a small oak table draped with crisp white linen. Atop the linen sat a blue, antique washbowl and pitcher.

Even at this hour, it was evident the Elders had taken the time to dress for the meeting. Vanessa, who appeared to be in her midsixties, the same age as Arabella, wore a black polyester pantsuit printed with red and yellow flowers, and pink slippers, the only type of shoe Vanessa ever wore. She was a constant worrier and often forgetful. Her hair had been dyed auburn, and she wore it in a chin-length sweep-over. Her aquiline nose sat perfectly between bright brown eyes, and wine-red lipstick covered her thin lips. Vanessa loved costume jewelry and a lot of it. Her ears weren't pierced, so she had black and white baubles, the same size and color of her necklace, clamped to her earlobes.

Taka, on the other hand, wore an electric blue overshirt on top of a black blouse and had accessorized it with a string of pearls and a turquoise necklace. Her earrings were turquoise, as well, but about the size of brooches. She was a week shy of sixty-nine, had snow-white hair, which she wore in a tousled pixie cut, blue eyes and a snub nose. Arabella had evidently chosen to dress a little more conservatively for the meeting. She wore a light lavender, silk blouse and white linen pants, and her makeup had been perfectly applied to her heart-shaped face. Her blond-white hair sat on her shoulders, curling under slightly. A classic look for a classy lady.

Arabella began the meeting by telling them about Gunner, Brunedee and more than Evee wanted to hear.

When Arabella finished her report, they sat around the table silent, the mood somber.

"So, let me get this straight," Evee said to Arabella,

finally breaking the silence. "You originally found out about the human attack from Gunner Stern, one of the sorcerers?"

"Yes," Arabella said.

"How did he find out about it?" Gilly asked.

"Word travels," Arabella said. "And the sorcerers get around a lot more than we do."

"How can you trust anything any one of the sorcerers has to say?" Viv asked. "They've always been out for themselves. Since when have they ever shown the want or need to help the Triad or any member of the Circle of Sisters?"

Arabella held up a hand. "I know, but for some reason, I think we can trust Gunner."

"What makes you say that?" Evee asked. "He's always hanging around with Trey Cottle and Shandor Black. Both are snakes in the grass, in my opinion. Their power belongs to them and them alone. They use it to their advantage, and they very rarely, if ever, use their spells or incantations or whatever the hell else they do to better mankind."

"Gunner's not like that," Arabella insisted.

"Why are you so set on defending him?" Evee persisted.

"Well, first of all, he didn't have to share any information with me. He could have kept it to himself and gloated over it. In fact, we should have gotten the information from you before hearing it from any sorcerer or a sister who lives a hundred miles away."

"What sister?" Gilly asked.

"Brunedee."

Gilly sighed, and then everyone fell silent.

Evee sat with Hoot perched on her right shoulder, quiet for once, and felt anger start to bubble up in her chest.

To her, having the sorcerers know about their problems just made things worse. She stole a glance at her sisters. Both sat, staring at the table, apparently deep in thought. Elvis, Gilly's ferret, had wrapped himself around his mistress's shoulders and Socrates, Viv's Bombay cat, lay across her lap.

"If it helps," Taka said, breaking the silence, "we only found out about the human and Original a relatively short time ago."

"Hours ago," Vanessa corrected. "Hours."

Taka glared at her and tsked.

"Okay," Evee said. "Gunner and Brunedee told you. What happened after that? I don't understand what's going on here." She looked from Arabella to Taka, then at Vanessa. These were their Elders, the women the Triad were supposed to go to when all else failed. Right now they simply looked like three tired old women.

"Weren't you supposed to contact all the leaders in the Circle of Sisters and ask for their assistance?" Evee asked Arabella. "Weren't they supposed to put out a collective protection spell around this city? A binding spell to protect us against the Cartesians and the disappearance of more Originals?"

"I did," Arabella said. "All of it. I can't explain why the spells have been ineffective. Occasionally, the three of us can get a spell to work. Then at other times they don't."

"Maybe it's the ozone layer," Taka said. "Or global warming. Probably both, since we have so much pollution, and glaciers are melting, you know."

"What the hell does that have to do with their spells?" Vanessa snapped.

"Well, if it can affect glaciers and the heating pattern of the earth, don't you think both or at least one can affect spells?" Taka said.

"I don't believe it's either," Arabella said. "Something else is going on. We just haven't been able to put a finger on it. Tell us what's been going on with the three of you. What problems are you running into? How are the Originals?"

"I have the Nosferatu together in the catacombs," Evee said. "The Benders created this electrical dome with their scabiors to keep any Cartesians from getting to them. Seems to be working."

"Same with the Loup Garous," Viv said. "I've got them all together in the North Compound."

"The Chenilles are together in the Louis I Cemetery," Gilly said.

Arabella frowned. "How can you keep them cooped up like that without infighting?"

"Oh, we have infighting," Evee said. "At least I do. But so far, my calming spells seem to keep them under control."

"So your spells work?" Vanessa asked.

"Sometimes," Evee said. "Fortunately, the calming one did."

"Hmm," Arabella mused. "I guess those Benders know what they're doing. Electrical domes. Who'd have thought of that?"

"Yeah, it was a good idea," Evee said, "but we ran into a problem with the one in the catacombs earlier today. Its power began to wane. It had to be recharged. I'm concerned that whatever's affecting our spells will wind up dousing those domes until they're out and can't be recharged. We're taking advantage of them while they're still live. Keeping the Originals we have protected beneath the domes while we search for the missing ones."

"My word," Arabella said, the furrows in her brow deepening.

"Global warming," Taka said. "I'm telling you. Global warming."

"Oh, shut up with your global warming," Vanessa snapped.

"Stop, both of you," Arabella said to Vanessa and Taka. "We've got some serious issues to work through, and the problem is that I don't have a clue about what to do about them. I do know that we have to get this under control and fast. The police have already been here twice. They showed up not long after we heard about the human and the Nosferatu."

Evee felt her blood run cold. "What did you tell them?"

"Nothing," Arabella said. "I didn't even answer the door. We just stayed really still and quiet and waited until they left."

"They'll be back," Vanessa said. "I feel it."

"Why would they come here?" Gilly asked. "Why would they tie you to the Nosferatu or any of the Originals? We've spent years protecting the city from any knowledge of the Originals and of us. I mean who we were…are."

"I think our cover's blown," Taka said. "They're going to be hunting us like dogs. You wait and see. It'll be like back in the day. Lynchings, burning at the stake, the whole enchilada."

"Stop. You're overreacting," Arabella said.

"Oh, yeah?" Taka replied. "Then how come you refused to answer the door? I'm telling you, we're going to be riding the flashback train. People are going to come after us, wanting to burn the devil out of us."

Vanessa huffed. "You're going over the deep end, Taka. We have enough to deal with without your imagination jumping onto an express train to never-never land."

"I'm not on any train," Taka insisted. "It's the truth."

Gilly huffed. "Look, instead of spending so much time

arguing, explain to me why an entire clan of the Circle of Sisters can't affect change in this situation. We're talking at least, what, fifteen to seventeen hundred witches around the country, all of them focused on our situation, but more are being added every day."

Gilly turned to Arabella, her expression hard with fury. "Why is that, Arabella? I mean, you're the head of this group of Elders. Why are spells from around this country turning out to be so ineffective? Why are ours useless, for the most part? What the hell are we supposed to do?"

Arabella returned her hard stare. "The first thing we have to figure out is why they're not working."

"And how are we supposed to do that?" Evee asked. "Anybody have a functioning crystal ball here?"

"Oh, crystal balls are so passé," Taka said.

Arabella suddenly sat upright in her chair. "Evee, have you tried channeling?"

"Huh?" Evee said, the question catching her unawares.

"Channeling. Maybe you can contact one of the dead Originals, some of the Loup Garous that were slaughtered or the Chenille that's passed on. Even Chank, your Nosferatu. Maybe they can see more from the other side than what we're seeing here. They might have some idea about what we can do with this."

Evee pursed her lips. She considered Arabella's suggestion. Thought it might have some merit.

Just as she was about to voice her agreement to try the channeling, Hoot began to flap a wing. He hopped off Evee's shoulder and landed on the dining room table and walked rapidly from one end of the table to the other, squawking the entire time. Among the Triad, Evee was the only one who understood what Hoot was shouting about. Unfortunately, she knew the Elders could understand him, as well.

"What?" Arabella asked, staring at Hoot.

The owl flapped his wings, and screeched until Evee thought he'd lose his voice. Hoot was ratting her out about her intimacy with Lucien. She wanted to duck under the table and hide from embarrassment.

Evidently deciding to join the rat wagon, Socrates scrambled off Viv's lap and jumped onto the table, along with Hoot. He began to meow, then caterwaul.

Although Evee couldn't understand what Socrates was saying, judging from the red blotches blooming on Viv's cheeks, it wasn't a good thing. She had a feeling Viv was being snitched on by her familiar, as well.

Knowing it would be useless to try and quiet Hoot, Evee had to wait until he ran out of steam. When both owl and cat finally stood quietly on the table, Arabella, Taka and Vanessa stared at the Triad with shocked expressions.

"Is—is it true?" Arabella asked. "They're saying the two of you have been intimate with the Benders. Those *human* Benders."

Elvis, Gilly's ferret, let out a small chitter and snuggled closer to his mistress.

Evee looked from Viv to Gilly, then back to Arabella. Words refused to come out of her mouth.

"I'm going to ask you one more time," Arabella said to Evee and Viv. "Have you two been intimate with the Benders?"

Evee wanted to take Hoot by the neck and pluck every feather from his body. After a long moment, she finally faced Arabella and said, "Yes, I have."

"Me, too," Viv said, her voice just above a whisper.

"In the name of all gods, are you kidding?" Taka said. "Oh, this is bad. Very not good."

Vanessa threw her hands up. "Figures. Hell, it might not be good, but at least we're getting closer to solving our spell problems."

"What do you mean we're getting closer to solving them?" Viv asked.

Arabella aimed her chin at Evee. "Your familiar claims you've been intimate with Lucien, and you," she aimed her chin at Viv, "with Nikoli." She looked at Gilly. "Your familiar has given us no indication of any transgression on your part, so I'm assuming you have not, as of yet, been intimate with the human Bender you're paired with?"

"Don't be ridiculous," Gilly said. "I have not."

Arabella leaned into the dining table. "I think we've found the problem as to why some of our spells aren't working. Why we're being inundated with such chaos and mayhem." Her voice rose an octave, and her eyes sparked with anger. "You know the rules about humans, do you not, Vivienne and Evette?"

"Yes, I do," Evee said. "But the Triad curse says that we're not to marry a human or live intimately with one. Neither Viv nor I have married a Bender, nor are we living intimately with them."

"That may not make a difference," Taka said. "It's all in the interpretation. It's possible that sleeping…no, having sex with a human counts, as well. For all we know, it could be the reason why the ozone layer is thinning."

"Drop the damn ozone layer," Vanessa snapped.

"Yet it could be enough to cause our spells to not work," Arabella said solemnly.

"But not all of our spells are ineffective. Remember, I told you my calming spell worked on the Nosferatu," Evee pointed out.

"Were you intimate with the Bender before or after you cast that spell?" Arabella asked.

Evee glanced away and chewed her bottom lip. She remembered how Lucien had touched her as she sat on the dryer, still soaking wet after having jumped into the river. How his thumbs found their way between her legs, crisscrossing, circling, rubbing across her jeans until she'd exploded beneath his hand.

"Before or after?" Arabella asked again.

"I didn't have sex with him before or after the spell," Evee said, feeling a tinge of guilt. It wasn't like she lied. They really hadn't had sex. Not yet, anyway.

Arabella narrowed her eyes. "But were you intimate with him in any way?"

Evee threw up her hands, hating the interrogation. "Yes, yes, we were intimate. No sex, but intimate, yes. And I wanted more, damn it!" She wanted to grab the blue pitcher perched inside its matching washbowl and throw it across the room.

The Elders turned to Viv.

"Yes, we had sex," Viv said, anger in her voice. "Lots of sex. Good sex. The I-want-more-of-it kind of sex. The three of you happy now?"

With her back ramrod straight, Arabella placed both of her hands, palm down, on the table. "It's not enough that we're having to fight these Cartesians, who are becoming more numerous by the day. Yes, we have the Benders to ward them off, but this electrified canopy they supposedly set over your Originals has begun to weaken. Your own words. I have a feeling that the growth in the number of Cartesians and the weakness of our spells are directly related to your intimacy with the Benders. We must regroup, re-empower ourselves so we're up for the struggle. This means no more intimacy with the Benders, do you understand?"

"Yes," Gilly said.

Arabella ignored her. "Vivienne, Evette, do the two of you understand?"

Evee gave her a half-hearted nod.

"Vivienne?" Arabella said.

"Yeah, I'm not deaf. I understand."

"If the two of you don't take this seriously, we will lose this battle and probably all of the Originals. And trust me, it's not hard to figure out that if the Cartesians plan to take out the Originals, they plan on taking you, as well. This is bigger than the six of us. Bigger than the entire clan of the Circle of Sisters. The Cartesians mean to control the entire netherworld. I can see that as clearly as I see my own hands. How any of you can think of sex at a time when so much turmoil surrounds us is beyond me. You should be ashamed of yourselves."

Tired of the harangue, Evee finally spoke up. "I'm not ashamed. I have nothing to be ashamed of. I broke no mandate of the curse. I haven't married Lucien, and I'm not living with him intimately."

"But you almost had sex with him," Taka said. "I'm sure that counts for something. Maybe it's just a part of the curse the first Elders didn't clarify. Maybe that's part of it and why things have gone so haywire."

Evee rolled her eyes, then looked down at the table.

Seemingly satisfied that he'd done his job appropriately, Hoot hopped across the table and jumped back on Evee's shoulder. She shooed him off, and he landed on the floor beside the table, squawking.

Socrates attempted to settle back into Viv's lap, and she swatted him off and onto the floor alongside Hoot.

Evee and Viv looked at each other simultaneously and

nodded. Their familiars were supposed to protect them and be loyal. There obviously was a clause in the familiar journal, because Hoot and Socrates had just betrayed them.

Evee had never felt so lonely as she did in that moment. Except for her two sisters, she was utterly alone and lost. She didn't know what to do next, which wasn't like her. She had thought herself to be levelheaded, and been sure that she could always see the next step that needed to be taken. Now all that seemed visible to her was a vat of mud that gave no direction as to what they should do next.

Arabella looked around solemnly. "Now that everything's out on the table, so to speak, we're going to fix this. So much has gotten out of hand that I'm considering having one of the sorcerers help us."

Evee felt her mouth drop open. "The sorcerers? Are you kidding?"

"You can't!" Gilly said, alarm making her voice shrill. "Those men aren't interested in anyone but themselves."

"Gunner's different," Arabella said.

"That's because he's sweet on you," Taka said.

Gilly's head snapped to attention. "Is that why you want to bring that sorcerer into our circle? You hammer Viv and Evee about the Benders, yet you want to bring in a sorcerer who has the hots for you?"

"Watch your mouth, young lady," Arabella warned. "Gunner is not like Trey or Shandor. They may be together often, but I think it's simply because like hangs about like. Gunner was the one who warned me about the humans and the death of the Nosferatu. He told me on the QT, not when Trey and Shandor were around. He might be able to offer some form of advice, have some spell that isn't used by the Circle of Sisters. His viewpoint will be once removed, clearer, which in and of itself may be of help."

Evee lightly tapped a fist on the table. "I refuse to let the sorcerers get involved with my Originals. They'll make it worse. I don't trust any of them. I don't know how you can even suggest it, Arabella. Ever since I can remember, you've drilled into us that we take care of our own problems."

Arabella clicked her tongue against her palate and turned her head to one side.

"I think Arabella's idea has some merit," Taka said. "We've lost our footing, even if it's because you two were doing the dirty with the Benders, and we have to find a way to stand up again."

Evee sighed and looked at Vanessa. "And you? Do you feel the same way?"

"I'm on the fence about it."

Evee looked at Arabella, who turned back to face her. "Look, we are the ones out there fighting these Cartesians with the Benders, despite any sexual events. They have saved many Originals since they've been here. We're out there constantly, with little sleep, forgetting to eat, hunting for the missing Originals. Fighting to keep the other Originals safe. All I ask is that you don't add to our chaos by bringing any sorcerers into our situation. We don't need any more problems."

Arabella studied Evee's face, and from the look in Arabella's eyes, Evee knew the Elder was considering all she'd just said.

"You know the rules in matters like this," Arabella said. "Majority vote determines the decision. However, since you and Vivienne were intimate with your Benders, I'm releasing the majority vote. I'll take full responsibility for what should be done."

"Good thing because you already have my vote," Gilly said, not breaking eye contact. "Hell no on the sorcerers."

Arabella gave her an infinitesimal nod. "I will think on this. I know it's getting close to feeding time, and that the three of you have to go."

"Promise me," Evee said. "Promise me you won't bring a sorcerer into our circle."

"All I can promise you, Evette, is that I will think on it and let you know my decision, which will be soon."

"Why not now?" Gilly asked.

"Enough," Arabella said. "I said I'd think on it, and I will. End of discussion."

"What will you do if the police show up here again?" Viv asked, diverting everyone's attention. "Keep hiding?"

"Of course not," Arabella said. "We're going to have to eventually face them."

"Does facing them mean you tell them we're witches?" Gilly asked. "That we're responsible for the Originals that are running about the city?"

Evee squirmed in her seat, grateful she hadn't told the Elders about the Cartesian that tried grabbing her by the river.

"No way would Arabella tell the police that," Taka said. "All we have to tell them is that we're three old ladies living here in the Garden District and have no idea about what they're saying."

"So you plan to bold-face lie to them," Gilly said.

"Absolutely," Taka said. "That way they'll move on, look in a different direction."

"I don't understand what would cause the police to come here in the first place," Viv said. "Do you think they suspect we're witches?"

"No way, Jose," Taka said. "We've kept that secret under wraps forever."

"What if the sorcerers said something to them, directed them here?" Evee said. "Why else would they be way out here in the Garden District? It happened in the Quarter and Chalmette. Why aren't they searching out there?"

"We can what-if until dawn," Arabella said. "Don't worry about the police. I'll take care of that situation. Now go about your feeding."

As Evee, Viv and Gilly left the Elders' home, Evee couldn't help wondering if they were the ones being fed—to the police, to the Cartesians, to annihilation.

Chapter 10

Lucien stood outside St. John's Cathedral, pacing in front of the massive structure, waiting for Evee. Every time he spotted a person with bold black hair, he felt his heart stop and then kick-start again. He had to admit he was absolutely smitten by the woman, and he feared his feelings for her might cloud his judgment. He'd all but handed her over to Ronan, for heaven's sake. What business did he have wishing, wanting anything regarding Evette François? Still, Lucien couldn't help wondering what had happened between Ronan and Evette. What did he say? What did she say?

As if the cosmos had been listening and chose to answer, Lucien spotted Ronan a block away.

Lucien felt his jaw tighten reflexively.

"All clear?" Ronan asked when he reached Lucien on the steps of the cathedral.

"So far. Scabior dome is still holding up."

Ronan checked his watch. "Evee's running a little late," he said more to himself than to Lucien.

"Mmm," Lucien said, trying to sound offhand. "We've still got plenty of time." What he really wanted to know was what had happened between Ronan and Evee once they'd been left alone. Knowing Ronan, however, that information would never pass his lips unless someone directly asked. So he did.

After checking both sides of the vast concrete walkway that fronted the cathedral, and still not spotting Evee, Lucien asked, "So, how'd it go?"

At first Ronan looked at him questioningly, as if he had no idea what his cousin meant. When realization dawned on him, a slow smile brightened his face. "You were right."

"About?"

"You know, being more assertive. Telling Evee how I felt and sort of letting the chips fall where they may."

Lucien felt nausea wash over him. "And where did they fall?"

Ronan gave him a small shrug. "I didn't bring up how I really felt about her. You know, it seemed too brash, too soon. Hell, I've barely spoken to Evee. But I did ask her to go on a dinner date once this was all done."

Lucien watched him expectantly.

"She said, yes, cuz. She really did. Even gave me a small kiss on my cheek." Ronan looked down at the ground and tapped the toe of his boot against one of the concrete steps of St. John's.

Every bone in Lucien's body felt like it went limp at one time. "Sh-she kissed you?"

"Yeah. Nothing big, you know. A kiss on the cheek isn't like a whole French job, but it was sweet. Perfect, in fact. Thing is… I don't know… I could be overthinking things, but she didn't seem really thrilled about the prospect."

"What do you mean?"

"You know, it came across kind of…plastic. Almost like she was doing me a favor."

"You are overthinking it. Evee's not like that. If she said she'd have dinner with you, then you've got a dinner date."

Forcing a smile, Lucien fist-bumped Ronan's fist. "You go, big man."

Something inside Lucien felt like it wanted to explode. He was anxious to see Evee again, especially after the last time they'd been together. There was no question as to what he felt for her, and it was more than sexual. All of who she was consumed him, body, mind and soul. All he could think about was her. And he had no idea when those feelings started or how they grew so intense so quickly.

Lucien paced nervously up and down the cathedral steps, needing to work off excess energy. He feared that the moment Evee appeared, he'd take her into his arms, as he thirsted so much for her full, luscious lips. He needed to kiss her, to feel her skin against his. He hated being away from her, even for a moment. And that frightened him. He had no business feeling this way. Now he had no choice but to wait until time passed and the dinner date between Ronan and Evee occurred. Only then would she be able to fairly compare.

Lucien chewed the inside of his right cheek. He'd never felt this way about any other woman before. The ones he'd had before Evee had been easy to let go. Too easy. Most of the time he'd found them too clingy, which made him all the more anxious to be on his way. Lucien didn't consider himself a cad. He was a realist. Why lead a woman on, allowing her to believe there was more be-tween them than what he felt? He couldn't, wouldn't toy with a woman that way.

With Evee, Lucien felt like he wore a new pair of shoes, ones that felt a little snug around the toes, but be-came more comfortable with each time he put them on.

"Where should I take her?" Ronan asked. "There're so many great places to eat—"

"Three o'clock," Lucien said suddenly, and motioned with his eyes for Ronan to look to his right.

Evee was on her way to them.

Ronan's face broke out into a huge smile when he saw her. Lucien's heart skipped two beats.

As usual, during feeding time, Evee was dressed in black jeans, a pullover T and sneakers, with her hair pulled back into a ponytail.

When she met Ronan and Lucien at the upper step of the cathedral, Lucien frowned. There was something in her eyes that bothered him. A hard, dismissive look.

She nodded at him, then at Ronan. The action couldn't have been more aloof.

"What's wrong?" Lucien asked.

"Nothing." Evee's voice had an angry snap to it. "Let's get to work."

Lucien took Evee's arm, turned her toward him. She pulled away.

"What's wrong with you?" Lucien asked. "Have I done something to upset you?"

Evee sighed, her eyes softening a little. "You haven't done anything. I have."

"What are you talking about?" Ronan asked.

She eyed Lucien, her expression serious. "All the chaos we're going through—more Cartesians coming out of seemingly everywhere, human attacks, human witnesses, the deaths of some of the Originals, the missing of many more… The only thing we can figure out is that all of it has to do with our being…" She glanced at Ronan, then seemed to check herself. "With the two of you being human. It has to stop. We can't handle everything that's going on now. What the hell are we going to do as things get progressively worse?"

"I'm a bit confused," Ronan said. "What has to stop? Our helping you?"

Evee threw a dismissive hand in the air as if to encompass the entire vocabulary of the English language. "Anything other than business," she finally said. "Nothing intimate, like talks about dinner or dates. It's business at hand or nothing. Everything else clouds our judgment."

Lucien felt his heart thud painfully in his chest. He knew she'd meant to say that their being intimate in her home had caused most of this, and he knew in his heart of hearts that it couldn't be further from the truth. He couldn't lose this woman. But as soon as he had thought, he wanted to flog himself for even thinking it. Not only was Ronan looking forward to spending time with her, but Lucien had never "pined" for any woman. And especially not over some stupid curse, whether real or exaggerated. He needed Evee in his life. The admission of that, even in his own mind, caused his breathing to grow labored.

"You and your sisters met with the Elders, haven't you?" Lucien said.

"Yes, but what does that matter?"

"Were the Elders the ones who came to this conclusion? That you're to stay away from us? I mean, in any capacity other than business? No small talk, nothing off topic?"

Evee turned and gave him a hard look. "Not in those

exact words, but yes. They were adamant about focusing on one thing. The problems facing us now. They already knew about the human attack and death in the Quarter and the killing of the Nosferatu by its leader. The police even came to their house. Twice."

Ronan's head jerked up. "What did the Elders tell them?"

"Nothing," Evee said. "They ignored them. Didn't even answer the door." She shook her head. "I just don't get what the police were doing all the way out there. How they knew where the Elders lived."

Setting the police issue on a back burner, Lucien took Evee's arm again, and though she tried to pull away once more, her effort felt half-hearted. He pulled her closer to him, touched her chin with a finger and turned her head so she faced him. Peripherally he saw Ronan bristle.

"Evee, you didn't do anything wrong," Lucien assured her. "As I've known and you've reiterated, the curse of the Triad is that they were not to marry a human or live intimately with one. I haven't done either with you, nor has Ronan."

"Yeah, well, according to the Elders, there surely had to be a clarification error with the original Triad and first Elders. I spouted the curse as I'd been taught it, verbatim, to the Elders, but they're convinced an error of omission occurred back then. They're convinced that our—any intimacy, however small, creates more chaos, despite what the curse specifically states."

Frustrated, Lucien looked from Evee to Ronan. "It'll soon be time to leave for the feeding. Cuz, would you mind doing one final check in the catacombs?"

Ronan stared at him. It didn't take much for Lucien to read the expression on his cousin's face.

Dude, if I'm supposed to try and get closer to Evee

why don't you *check the catacombs so I can be alone with her?*

Ignoring the blatant glare, Lucien said, "We'll head over to the docks. Make sure everything's good to go. Once you check the catacombs, you can meet us there."

With a scowl, Ronan turned on his heel and headed into the cathedral.

As soon as they were alone, Lucien asked Evee, "How did the Elders find out about you and me, anyway?"

"My familiar ratted me out. So did Viv's."

Lucien did a double take. "Viv's been with... Nikoli?"

"Evidently, because Socrates, Viv's familiar, sang like a canary, telling the Elders all he knew about the two of them. Same thing with Hoot regarding you and me. I swear I wanted to pluck that owl bald."

"Evee, you have to hear me out here," Lucien said. "I realize there's a Triad curse, and that it's real and significant. But I think something as serious as that curse set by the first Elders wouldn't have been left to interpretation. It was stated in the way they meant for it to be understood. They wouldn't have carelessly thrown out any curse that could be misread. It would have been direct. I honestly believe that our small sexual encounter doesn't have a doggone thing to do with the turmoil that seems to be growing daily."

"How can you know that for sure?"

"Because I know the Cartesians, and they're the ones responsible for all this. Viv may have brought the Originals and the Triad to the Cartesians' attention when she offhandedly and in anger said she'd quit caring for her Loups. But I know the rest of it, everything we're experiencing now, has to do with the Cartesians. You have to remember that they have a leader, and that the leader has an agenda. It wants to be the sole power in the netherworld, then of the entire universe. It wants to control the stars, the weather, inhabit the earth and populate any other planet with Cartesians. In order to do that, it has to control and take all the Originals to absorb their power. It wants the Triad for the same reason. Then it'll take possession of all the power of every creature in the netherworld, those that are the offspring of the Originals. And the way that leader plans on accomplishing this is to create chaos and turmoil. To confuse us and have us running in circles so it can accomplish that goal. Don't you get it? This is much bigger than anything you or I could have created by what happened on the dryer."

Evee stared at him, eyes wide, blinking back tears. "Who's this leader? Why aren't we looking for it? If we take the leader out, wouldn't the rest of them scatter?"

"I've always believed the same thing," Lucien said. "The problem is we don't have a clue as to who or where this leader is. It never makes an appearance. Always sends its minions to do its dirty work."

"Then how do you know what to look for?" Evee asked. "Shouldn't that be our focus, finding the leader?"

Lucien nodded. "Of course. But, Evee, we've been looking for the leader for ten generations. Right now our priorities have to be caring for the Originals you have and finding the ones that are missing. Killing Cartesians along the way will be a given. Hopefully, we'll luck out and find the bastard that leads them."

A tear slid down Evee's cheek. "This so-called leader has to be the first Cartesian created by the original Triads. The ones who took certain matters into their own hands and turned their betrothed into the Originals, and did it out of spite and anger." She sighed heavily. "Regardless, I can't take any more chances. We have to get this straightened out. I don't know if the curse regarding

Triads and humans was misinterpreted or not. Whether something was misquoted as it was handed down from generation to generation or not, I just can't take any more chances. It can't simply be coincidence that after we became intimate, things seemed to jump further out of control. So, please, let's drop this for now and get to work. Like you said, it's getting close to feeding time, and I need to get the Nosferatu ready. Make sure they're not trying to massacre each other again."

Lucien took a deep breath, nodded, and let go of her arm. He had so much more he wanted to say to her. He longed to tell her how much he needed her. But he said nothing. Only led the way to the docks.

They hadn't walked a hundred feet when Lucien suddenly grabbed her arm.

"Wait," he said, catching a whiff of clove in the air.

"What?"

"A rift," he said, looking up at the sky. The first hint that a Cartesian was nearby was the scent of clove, followed by the smell of sulfur as it worked its way through a rift.

He suddenly felt Evee at his side, holding on to his arm. She looked up, seemingly searching the sky, as well.

"Where?" Evee whispered. "I don't see anything."

"Clove. I smelled it as we were leaving the cathedral. That scent is the first sign a Cartesian has found a rift and is working its way through it." He felt Evee's grip tighten on his arm.

"Do you see anything?" she asked, still looking skyward.

"No. But it's close. Just hasn't broken through the rift yet. Once it does, I'll smell sulfur along with the clove." Lucien wished he had a giant spotlight to aim at the sky. Stars were out, but every black distance between the Big

Dipper and the next cluster of stars seemed darker than the one above it. All of them looked like rifts.

Just then, Lucien heard the sound of pounding, running feet behind them. He swirled about and saw Ronan headed their way.

As Ronan pulled up alongside Lucien, he said, "I smelled it from the catacombs. Clove."

"Yeah," Lucien said. "I just caught a whiff of it a moment ago."

Lucien was about to tell Evee to go into the cathedral for safekeeping when a loud boom sounded from overhead. It was immediately followed by the overwhelming stink of sulfur.

In that moment, three rifts opened up overhead. A Cartesian hung from each rift, leaning over by its waist. Each had a massive, matted fur head, huge black eyes with no pupils. Mouths open, every tooth a lethally sharp incisor. Their claws, long, sharp talons, all of them reaching, searching, clawing.

Lucien shouted for Evee to go into the cathedral and into the catacombs. He and Ronan simultaneously pulled their scabiors from their sheaths, snapped their wrists once, then twirled the scabiors between their fingers faster than even Evee's eyes could track.

Lucien aimed it at one of the Cartesians, and for the first time since he could remember, he missed. Ronan aimed the electrical beam from his scabior at the same Cartesian and caught it right between the eyes. He kept his scabior aimed at it until the rift from which it came closed up as neatly as a zipper.

In that moment, another rift suddenly tore through the sky, then another and another, with Cartesians worming their long arms through each opening. Within seconds, their massive heads poked through the rift, and like their counterparts, they began to stretch and swing their long arms and claws toward them.

"Go into the catacombs," Lucien shouted again at Evee. "Hide out there with the Nosferatu!"

"Bullshit!" Evee shouted back. "I'm not about to leave you and Ronan out here by yourselves."

"Go!" Ronan insisted. "There're too many out right now. Stop being stubborn, damn it. Go! You don't have anything out here to use for protection."

Lucien palmed the handle of his scabior once more, snapped his wrist once, then twirled the scabior at breakneck speed between his fingers. He took aim at the Cartesian closest to them. Lightning exploded from the bloodstone atop the scabior and, this time, struck the Cartesian in the forehead. With an ear-piercing howl, the Cartesian flew back, and Lucien heard a loud pop, an indicator that he'd pushed the Cartesian back one dimension.

Keeping his aim steady, Lucien shot again, then again. After a third sound of explosion, the rift that had held that Cartesian zipped closed.

Just when he thought he was down to three Cartesians, another boom sounded and another rift appeared overhead, farther to the left. The Cartesian coming from this rift obviously didn't plan on wasting any time. It immediately thrust itself from the rift to waist level and swung an arm at Evee.

One thing with Cartesians, they were so massive that they had no need to fully leave the rift. Half of them hung out, vulnerable, while the other half stayed safely out of sight. They didn't need to make a full body appearance, however. Their arms were so long and their talons so sharp that they simply had to swipe at their victims and could easily gore, grab, kill anything they desired.

"Now!" Lucien yelled at Evee. "For heaven's sake, go!"

"I'm not leaving the two of you," she insisted.

Lucien couldn't take his eyes off the sky to argue with her, reason with her. Cartesians seemed to be dangling from every corner of the night. Long yellow incisors bared, talons spread and reaching, reaching.

A feeling ran up the back of Lucien's back, and it took a second for his brain to register it as concern, a sense of being overwhelmed, overpowered.

It surprised Lucien when he'd missed the first shot at one of the Cartesians because it'd never happened to him before. But what surprised him even more at the moment were the feelings oppressing him. They all balled up into one emotion. Fear. Too many Cartesians, not enough scabiors. Evee.

Before Lucien knew it, Evee suddenly appeared between him and Ronan. He opened his mouth, planning to scold her for being so hardheaded, but snapped it shut when he saw her hold out her hands, palms up, aimed at the sky.

"Double, thrice, by tens ye shall see.

No longer one to be seen by thee.

Thine eyes shall fully confuse thy mind.

Making all evil intentions blind.

Blunder thee, blunder now.

I call upon Poseidon, Tiamat and Apsu, bring strength to my command.

So it is said.

So shall it be."

When Evee was done, Lucien stood dumbstruck, watching as the Cartesians who had been aiming directly for them were now swinging wildly in every direction but theirs.

A look of confusion filled the Cartesians' grossly huge

black eyes. Each looked from right to left, up and down, and swung its arms in random directions.

From what Lucien saw, it was as if either the Cartesians had lost their eyesight or Evee's incantation had performed Cartesian lobotomies.

"Shoot," Evee shouted at Lucien and Ronan, snapping both out of a stupor.

Lucien aimed at another Cartesian, shot it back four dimensions. Ronan targeted one, and managed to push it back five. Finally, Lucien took aim at another and sent it back three, which he gladly settled for because it was the last Cartesian and all the rifts had vanished.

Drawing in an exhausted breath, Lucien replaced his scabior in its sheath, then turned to Evee, who appeared to be mildly shaken by all she'd just witnessed.

"What did you do?" Ronan asked. "They looked confused, like they'd gone blind or something. Is that what your spell did? Cause them to go blind?"

Evee grinned. "Something a little better. I did an illusion spell. Instead of the Cartesians seeing just one of you, me and Lucien, I made them see twenty of all three of us, running in different directions. They couldn't tell what was real from illusion. That's what caused the confusion. That's why they were swinging in every direction. Because they saw us everywhere."

Lucien shook his head in disbelief and took Evee's arm. She didn't resist this time. He walked her slowly toward the docks. Ronan took hold of her other arm as though it took two to steady her walk. She didn't protest.

When they reached the dock, Ronan said, "I'll pull anchor and slip-tie the mooring rope."

"I'll have a look at the motor," Lucien said. "Don't want to run out of fuel."

Lucien kept one eye on Evee as she stood a few yards

away from the dock. There was amusement on her face. He figured she knew that at the end of a crisis, men had to do something, anything, to calm their nerves. Which was exactly what he and Ronan were doing.

Suddenly, catching a strong scent of cloves and sulfur that seemingly came out of nowhere and without preamble, Lucien and Ronan froze in the middle of their nerve-calming work and looked up and about.

Evee was looking, as well, into a rift that had formed right over her head. She seemed frozen in place.

"Evee, run!" Lucien yelled.

"To the cathedral," Ronan added. "Get inside the cathedral!"

As Lucien and Ronan scrambled off the ferry, reached for their scabiors, the Cartesian that had managed to sneak up on them was hanging from his waist, his large arm and claws swinging back, ready to strike Evee.

Running and trying to aim a scabior so it hit the right spot were two things that didn't work well together.

Lucien saw Evee's hair brush across her face as the Cartesian reached but missed her. It quickly swung back, wiggled over the rift until it was nearly below waist level, and aimed at Evee once more.

Lucien's brain kicked into overdrive. It might take a scabior to rid a Cartesian from this dimension, but they wouldn't stand a chance with this one. It was too close to Evee. He had to get her out of the way.

Evidently realizing the same thing, both Lucien and Ronan sprinted and ran as fast as their legs could carry them toward Evee. Lucien saw Evee's mouth move, but no words came out and she remained glued to her spot. Only now she looked over at Lucien and Ronan running at full speed toward her. Lucien saw the resignation on her face.

Just as the Cartesian drew his arm and claws up from his back swing, Lucien and Ronan reached Evee at the same time. Lucien tackled her to the ground even as the creature's claws raked through her ponytail, yanking out a bit of hair. Lucien kept his body covering hers as he worked his scabior out of its sheath.

It was then Lucien heard an ear-piercing scream.

"No!"

Lucien rolled over in time to see the Cartesian lifting Ronan into the rift. After the Cartesian had missed Evee, it had found Ronan in midrun toward Evee, right in its target area. It had skewered Ronan in the head. In one temple and out of the other. There was no mistaking, Lucien's cousin was dead.

Lucien stumbled to his feet, and this time he was the one screaming, "No! No!" He aimed his scabior at the Cartesian. Blasts of lightning shot the creature in the forehead, in the chest, which caused it to howl in pain and fold back into another dimension. No matter how many times Lucien struck the beast with the scabior, Ronan remained stuck to its claws.

Roaring with fury and shooting the Cartesian again and again, Lucien knew he must have looked like a wild man ready to take on the world.

But the world soon came to an end.

For the rift closed, taking the Cartesian and Ronan with it.

Chapter 11

It had taken Evee some time to convince Lucien to leave the docks and the cathedral. He kept looking up at the sky, as if hoping by some miracle Ronan would drop out of it, and he'd be there to catch him. She couldn't blame Lucien for not wanting to leave. Had the Cartesian taken one of her sisters, Evee would probably have spent the rest of her life in the spot she'd disappeared from, waiting for her return.

Aside from Ronan's death, the worst part now was the lack of closure. There was no body to return to his cousins or his family back home. All Lucien had was a story to tell and memories to live with. Evee couldn't imagine how difficult that must be for him. Her heart ached, not only for Lucien but for Ronan. The man had died so she might live. She'd never have the chance to thank him, to offer gratitude or restitution.

Just before they left the docks, Lucien signaled for his

cousins from the geo node on his watch. He gave them the coordinates to Evee's café, which sat only a few blocks away in the Quarter. Evee also summoned her sisters, using special signals they'd refined since they were children. Whenever any of them found trouble, they'd summon the other two by using the distress calls innate to their familiars. For Evee, it was a high-pitched screech, the same sound Hoot made when he was afraid or sensed mortal danger. They'd refined the calls, making each sound so natural that another human would never associate the sound with them. Evee had no coordinates to give Viv and Gilly, but having gone through this drill on more than one occasion, they knew the first place to look for her was the café.

Evee held Lucien's hand as they walked the few blocks to their destination. The café would be closed at this hour. A good, private place to break the news to the other Benders and her sisters.

When they reached Bon Appétit, Evee unlocked the door, switched on the lights and motioned Lucien to sit anywhere he pleased. He chose a table, sat and remained mute, only shaking his head to turn down the drink Evee offered him. She wanted to sit by his side, to hold him and ease some of the pain he carried. But she felt that at this moment, the one thing he needed was to be alone with his thoughts. He'd be forced to talk soon enough. Forced to relive that horrible moment when the Cartesian had taken his cousin. For now, the most helpful thing Evee could do for him would be to leave him with the solitude he seemed to desire.

As she went behind the counter to prepare drinks for Gavril, Nikoli and her sisters, a thought suddenly struck Evee. What if Lucien blamed her for Ronan's death? Had it not been for her, there would have been no reason for him to run in that direction or block anyone from danger. The Cartesian would never have reached him.

Just thinking about that made Evee feel weak in the knees. She pulled up a stool near the register, kept one eye on Lucien, who sat with his head bowed so low it nearly touched the table. Tears welled up in Evee's eyes. The truth had been staring her in the face all along and either shock or shame had kept her from seeing it. And that truth was Ronan would still be alive this very minute had it not been for her. If she'd only listened when Lucien told her to run. But fear had kept her frozen in place. What kind of Triad did that make her? To freeze up in the face of danger?

A stupid and useless Triad, that was what it made her.

Evee felt shame and remorse consume her and felt tears flow down her cheeks. The only sounds within the café were the coffeepot brewing, the ice machine dropping a fresh load of ice into its bin, Lucien drawing in a deep, ragged breath from time to time and the occasional creak of a floorboard. Evee kept her tears silent.

Over the next twenty minutes, the only thing that changed in the café was the smell. It was now filled with the scent of freshly brewed, dark-roast, chicory coffee. Evee had remained seated on the stool and Lucien at the table he'd chosen when he first walked in. He'd yet to raise his head or speak since they arrived.

Evee was debating on whether or not to offer him coffee when the front door of the café opened and the rest of their troupe stormed in. Gavril, Gilly, Viv and Nikoli. Out of habit, Evee found herself waiting for Ronan to bring up the rear, then felt fresh tears fill her eyes.

"What's wrong?" Gilly and Viv asked simultaneously, both staring at Evee.

Instead of answering, Evee motioned to Lucien with her eyes.

Obviously catching the signal, Gavril and Nikoli walked over to Lucien, each standing on either side of him.

Nikoli placed a hand on Lucien's shoulder, which caused him to finally lift his head.

The look on Lucien's face was one of a man whose soul had just been ripped in two. His eyes were red-rimmed, yet no tear tracks ran down his cheeks. It broke Evee's heart to see him this way.

"What's going on, cousin?" Gavril asked, squatting next to Lucien.

Lucien looked at him, opened his mouth to speak, then shook his head.

"Hey," Nikoli said. "Where's Ronan?" He looked at Evee. "Is he in the restroom?"

She shook her head.

Gavril got to his feet, pulled out the chair beside Lucien and sat. Nikoli walked over and sat opposite them at the same table.

"Would somebody tell us what the hell is going on?" Gilly said. "We're here because you sent out an emergency call. The same goes for Gavril and Nikoli. The four of us nearly broke our asses getting here as quickly as we could. Now we're here. So somebody say something."

Lucien opened his mouth, looked from Gavril to Nikoli, then snapped his mouth shut and shook his head.

Nikoli reached over and put a hand on Lucien's arm. "Cousin?"

Gavril suddenly drew in a sharp breath and sat bolt upright in his chair. "It's Ronan, isn't it? Something's happened to him?"

Viv and Gilly looked over at Evee, the same question in their eyes. She didn't signal a confirmation or a denial. She felt it was up to Lucien to break the news to his cousins first.

Lucien lifted his head, placed both hands on the table, looked from Gavril to Nikoli. "Yes," he said, his voice hoarse and hollow.

Gilly and Viv, both frowning, went over to a second table, grabbed two chairs, then brought them over to the table to sit near the Benders.

"What happened? Where is he?" Gilly asked.

"Dead," Lucien said.

Evee worked hard at keeping her tears in check. Lucien had to be the one to break the news. If she started crying, her sisters would pounce on her with a hundred questions.

Everyone around the table stared at Lucien, their expressions ranging from disbelief to confusion, as if they hadn't heard correctly.

"Ronan is dead?" Nikoli asked, his voice holding a note of incredulity. "Where is he? What happened?"

"How'd it happen?" Gavril asked.

"When did this happen?" Viv asked.

Seemingly at a loss for words, Lucien looked over at Evee, his eyes begging for help.

"A Cartesian attack," Evee said. "About an hour ago. The three of us were waiting until it was time to send the Nosferatu to the North Compound on the ferry when all hell broke loose. Lucien and Ronan were fighting a shitload of Cartesians. Then just when we thought it was over, a rift appeared over my head, literally."

"Holy Mother Earth," Viv said. "What did you do?"

"I couldn't do anything," Evee said. "The moment I spotted it I froze. Like some half-brained ass, I froze. It was as if every muscle in my body tensed up and held me in place. The Cartesian took a swing at me, so close I felt the wind from its movement ruffle my hair. Lucien yelled for me to run, but I couldn't. It was as if the Cartesian had me mesmerized."

Viv frowned. "That so doesn't sound like you," she said. "Freezing up, I mean. If anything, you'd usually be the first to react. Go for the jugular."

"I can't explain why I couldn't move. Maybe it was shock. I truly don't know. The Cartesian kept swinging for me, and I felt it getting closer to me each time. I actually watched it pull back for another strike and knew I'd be a goner with that one."

"You knew that and still didn't move, run, anything?" Gilly asked.

"Yeah," Evee said. "I was actually contemplating what it might feel like to die as the Cartesian started a downward swipe with its horrible claws. Then, out of nowhere, I felt myself being shoved down to the ground by a flying tackle. It was Lucien. He knocked me down and away just in time. For me, but not for Ronan. He must have been only inches behind Lucien, because he caught the downswing from the Cartesian just as Lucien tackled me."

Everyone around the table gawked at her, except for Lucien. He was looking in her direction, but Evee knew it wasn't she he saw. The faraway look in his eye told her he was reliving Ronan's death.

"Is that what happened?" Gavril asked Lucien. "Ronan isn't…wasn't that stupid to get caught in a Cartesian's backlash."

Evee looked over at Lucien, whose focus seemed to be back, front and center.

"Yeah, that's how it happened. Just like Evee said. I knocked Evee down so she was out of harm's way. I think Ronan was following too close to have it come down any other way. In a matter of seconds, the Cartesian swung out again. It—it skewered Ronan in the head. Its claws went into one temple and out of the other."

"Jesus," Gavril said, and then both he and Nikoli got up from the table and began to pace the dining area.

Except for the sound of Gavril's and Nikoli's footsteps, the only other thing Evee heard was sniffling. Her sisters were crying openly.

"Wh-where's his body?" Nikoli asked, breaking the silence.

"The Cartesian never released him," Lucien said. "I blasted it with my scabior, hoping to shake Ronan loose from its grip, but it wouldn't or couldn't let go. I struck it again and again, mostly missing. I was too shaken up that it had Ronan. Before I had a chance to figure out any other way to get it to release him, the Cartesian disappeared into the rift, taking Ronan with it."

Evee felt tears well up in her eyes. "Ronan was doing the same thing Lucien was doing. Trying to save my life. If it hadn't been for me, none of this would have happened."

"Suck up the self-pity, Evee," Gilly said matter-of-factly. "There's enough going around this café to last a lifetime. It went down the way it was supposed to go down. There are no coincidences."

"Where were you when all this was going on?" Nikoli asked Lucien.

"Lying on top of Evee on the ground, trying to keep my body over hers to protect her. When I heard Ronan scream—"

"Jesus, he screamed…" Nikoli said as if trying to envision the incident in his mind's eye.

"I rolled over and fought the Cartesian, trying to get it to release Ronan, but it wouldn't or couldn't let go. Man, had all those Cartesians showed up while Evee was crossing the Nosferatu, there'd have been a serious bloodbath. They'd have been wide-open targets in the water. Easy pickings for the Cartesians." Lucien's eyes suddenly brimmed with tears. "Before I knew it, Ronan… it all happened so fast, I didn't have time to close the rift in time to help him."

With tears still streaming down her face, Evee said, "It's my fault Ronan got killed."

"Why the hell do you keep saying that?" Viv asked.

"Because Lucien had yelled for me to run for safety, and all I did was freeze in place. If I had done as he asked, Ronan would probably still be alive right now. I'm so, so sorry. I should have listened."

"Stop beating yourself up," Lucien said. "As Benders, we put our lives on the line every time we confront and attempt to destroy a Cartesian."

"Yeah," Evee said, "but if it hadn't been for me freezing in place like an idiot, Ronan would still be alive."

"Stop. It's not your fault," Lucien insisted. "Ronan chose to be there to help you, to run after you and knock you out of the way. I was only seconds earlier. There truly is no blame here. Those ugly Cartesian bastards are determined to kill whatever and whomever they please. That Cartesian was already in midswing, aiming for you. Ronan acted quickly, but unfortunately couldn't get out of the way fast enough. That Cartesian was aiming for you, not Ronan. Pushing you down to safety was both Ronan's and my choice. I simply reached you first."

It broke Evee's heart to see so much pain in Lucien's eyes. Nikoli and Gavril seemed to be at a loss for words.

Despite Lucien claiming it wasn't Evee's fault, she couldn't help feeling a ton of guilt resting on her shoulders.

She was trying to find the right words to offer her

condolences when Gilly suddenly sat bolt upright in her chair.

"The feeding," Gilly exclaimed. "What time is it?"

"We have a couple hours yet," Evee said.

Viv nodded after glancing at her watch.

Gilly pushed himself away from the table. "With all this Cartesian talk, I'm going to look in on my Chenilles. Hang out there until it's time to get them to the docks."

Gavril got to his feet. "I'm going with you."

A look of surprise crossed Gilly's face. "There's no need for you to come, Gavril. What with Ronan and all. I'm sure you have family to tend to and notify. I'll be fine on my own."

"I said I'm going with you," Gavril said, and walked over to her.

Viv rose from the table. "I hate that business has to take precedence at such a horrible time, but the Loup Garous need to be set up in the back of the property and kept there until the Nosferatu are done feeding. We're going to have to do this quickly. If there are as many Cartesians as Evee and Lucien are saying, all the Originals taken out from under those electric domes will be sitting ducks."

Lucien nodded. "I understand."

"We—we're so sorry for your loss," Viv said. "And I'm sorry that we were the cause of it. I know you think otherwise, but had it not been for me saying I quit to my Loups in the first place, none of this would be happening."

"No need for anyone here to assume any responsibility for Ronan's death," Lucien said. "He was a Bender through and through. Sometimes braver than all of us put together. But in reality, as with all things, there's a time to live and a time to die. I suppose Ronan's time here was done. If it hadn't been here, fighting to protect the Triad and the Originals, it probably would have been somewhere else."

Nikoli shook his head slowly. "It's not going to be the same without Ronan. But he would have wanted us to keep fighting. To bring back order and safety to the Originals and Triad." Nikoli turned to Lucien. "I hate to leave right now, cuz, but duty calls. I need to make sure Viv doesn't run into any Cartesian problems while she moves her Loups out from under the dome in the North Compound."

Although Gavril, Gilly, Viv and Nikoli spoke their piece about having to leave, not one of them moved toward the café's front door.

Lucien looked from one to the other. "You need to go and tend to your broods, and, cousins, you need to make sure they don't run into problems with the Cartesians. Make sure they stay safe. I'll go back to the hotel and contact Uncle Charles, Ronan's dad, and let him know what's happened."

"Maybe we should simply pack things up and head to Buffalo Grove and be with the family," Gavril said, his voice doing an occasional hitch. "They may need our support. This is a big loss. Not just because Ronan was a Bender. We grew up together. We were like brothers."

"I know," Lucien said. "This will not only hurt Uncle Charles, but it'll affect all of our families. But neither Ronan, Uncles Charles, nor our own fathers would want us to head back. We're Benders, and we have to stay and complete what we've set out to accomplish. That's been a given oath since we arrived here."

Gavril nodded hesitantly. "You're right, cuz. Neither Ronan nor Benders before us would want us to bail right now."

Lucien nodded.

With nothing left to say, Viv, Gilly, Nikoli and Gavril were about to leave the café to tend to the business at hand when Lucien suddenly said, "Wait!"

Everyone turned in his direction.

"I just thought of a way to get the Nosferatu and Chenilles to the compound without having them exposed to the Cartesians."

"What?" Gavril asked.

"How?" Evee asked.

Lucien stood from his place at the table and tapped a finger to his lips. "Viv, can you and Nikoli chance exposing one of your largest Loups for a project?"

"What project?" Nikoli asked.

"Yes," Evee said, not waiting for Lucien to answer Nikoli's question. "If it'll help the rest of the Originals get safely to the feeding grounds, we can make it happen." She looked at Nikoli. "You'll be there with your scabior, right?"

Nikoli nodded, then turned and frowned at Lucien. "What project are you talking about?"

"If we can build electrical domes over the safe zones for the Originals, nothing says we can't build one over the ferry, right?"

"Oh, great call, cuz," Gavril said. "That narrows the kill zones to a much shorter distance. Their safe place to the ferry, then off the ferry into the compound. Same on the return."

"That should work," Nikoli said.

"But can it be done in such a short time?" Gilly asked.

"My Loups can make anything happen," Viv said proudly. She turned to Lucien. "We'll get started now. I still have steel pipe from the other domes we created, and we still have plenty bloodstones to anchor to the top ends of the pipes."

Gavril nodded. "Mission on," he said, and he, Nikoli, Viv and Gilly high-stepped out of the café like a troupe on a mission.

When the café had emptied, save for Lucien and Evee, Evee walked over to Lucien and took his hand. "Great call on the dome for the ferry."

Lucien abruptly let go of her hand. "I have to go to the hotel now and make that call to my uncle."

His abruptness confused Evee. She stood and went to his side. "I—I'm so sorry for your loss. If I hadn't defied the curse on the Triad, this probably wouldn't have happened. I've been trying since you arrived to brainwash myself into thinking it was all right to sidestep the curse, because I allowed myself to use semantics, taking the curse verbatim. Since then, so much has escalated, worsened, I can't afford myself the luxury of thinking I'd found a way to circumvent the curse. I haven't." Evee felt tears fill her eyes again. "I can only be responsible for my actions, which means we can't be together anymore. Ronan's death is proof of that. If it hadn't been for me, in more ways than one, Ronan would still be alive."

"You don't know that," Lucien said.

Evee glanced down at the floor for a minute, then looked into Lucien's pure green eyes. She stood on tiptoe and kissed him on the cheek. "I care for you more than you'll ever know. That's the biggest reason why I can't allow 'us' to happen."

Lucien studied her face, and she saw that his eyes had grown flat, expressionless. "Ronan cared for you, too."

Without saying another word, Lucien left the café.

Evee stared at the closing door, and her heart felt like it had split wide open within her chest, leaving sharp edges that stabbed her with each thought.

He'd left without saying goodbye. Nothing.

Evee sat down heavily on one of the chairs at the table. There was no holding back tears this time. She sobbed openly for Ronan, for the pain his death had caused so many. And no matter how many times the Benders had said otherwise, she still felt responsible for Ronan's death.

Now she was experiencing a death of her own. A life without Lucien. The thought consumed her with so much pain she didn't think she'd have the wherewithal to leave her chair and stand on her own two feet.

Much less stand for anything again.

Chapter 12

Score!

Well, almost.

The target had been the Triad, which his Cartesian missed completely. He still couldn't believe it. How close his Cartesian had come to grabbing such a choice morsel and wound up missing again and again.

The only thing that saved the creature from receiving severe punishment at his hand was the kill it did manage. The Bender.

A Bender wasn't exactly what he'd hoped for, but taking one out of commission had a significant benefit. One less to worry about. One less running around with his little baton-twirling act that somehow managed to shove his Cartesians to other dimensions.

He wished he knew where the power of the Benders' batons came from. Oddly enough, for as long as they'd pestered him, it was a wonder he'd never considered that before. Someone or something had to give those little batons power. Did they have a leader with powers who made those batons deadly? If so, that was someone he needed to add to his list. He must find the answer to that. The answer might come from the next Bender.

If he instructed his Cartesians properly, they'd capture a Bender without killing him. He didn't know if a human could survive a dimensional change without harm, but it was worth a shot. If a Bender did survive the change, he'd make certain to interrogate him at length. Torture him if necessary to find out who had infused their batons with power.

Now that all was said and done, he reviewed his initial plan to see where'd he'd gone wrong and how he might get better results next time.

He'd meant to take out the Triad near the church while she waited to cross her Originals over the river by boat. With her out of the way, the Nosferatu would reach the shore of the compound with no one there to remove them—except him. Permanently. With that in mind, he'd aligned part of his army along rifts that he'd already had them working on for some time. It was to be a rush, surprise attack. The Benders had taught the Triad about the rifts, how they slowly opened. How the Cartesians wormed their way through the rifts. The last thing they'd expect was an immediate opening and Cartesian drop.

The surprise attack had worked as expected, but, alas, he didn't wind up with the prize he'd craved.

Regardless, there had been a kill.

And it meant at least one lesson had been learned, although it needed refinement, for the underling Cartesian had brought the essence of the Bender to him. Had dropped his lifeless body at his feet, as all Cartesians were expected to do after any kill, and then he'd opened his mouth and sucked the essence from him just as he did with every kill.

The taste of the Bender initially was too sweet, like sugar melting into rotten tooth. The aftertaste was bitter like lemons, so much so it made his lips pucker.

He wasn't sure what the sweet and bitter meant. He'd never eaten anything with such contradicting tastes.

After pondering it awhile, he'd waited to see if it might make him sick. Or maybe the Benders had been created so that if they were captured and killed by a Cartesian, their very essence might kill him. Had he been the leader of the Benders, that would have been his plan.

But after a while, when nothing happened and he had only the bad aftertaste left in his mouth, he'd shrugged it off. Maybe all humans tasted that way. Sweet and sour. Maybe it depended on who they'd been in life. What they'd accomplished. What purpose they'd served. Despite the taste, he hadn't felt any measure of additional power transferred to him. If he felt anything at all, it had been remnants of the man's brave heart, which did him no good. His heart was already the bravest heart he knew in existence. For whom or what else in existence would have the wherewithal to not only create and grow the most vicious beings in the universe, but lead them?

He supposed he could get used to the taste if he had to… and he would. For after all, once the Triad and Originals were taken care of, humans were next on his list.

After he'd emptied the Bender and tossed the shell of his body away, he made a point of gathering his Cartesians, all of them, to instruct them once more on their method of attack.

Earlier he'd noticed that one Cartesian had literally pushed one of his legs through the rift, which made it all the more vulnerable to the Benders. Of course, the action that followed only confirmed his orders, for the overzealous Cartesian had been one of the first to get zapped by the Benders.

Not wanting to take anything for granted, he planned on going over how his Cartesians should attack so there wouldn't be any further errors.

So far, none of his Cartesians had dared to lean over the edge of a rift far enough to cause them to fall out. For one thing the Benders did not know, and if it was up to him, would never know, was that if a Cartesian fell from a rift to earth, it became nothing more than an animal. Its protective scales would shed like that of a snake, only its scales would never return. Covered only in fur, it would be vulnerable to any form of death. A bullet, an arrow, a hammer blow to the head. Once on the ground, a Cartesian couldn't make its way back to any dimension. It was doomed to fight out its remaining days on earth, hiding from any and all who hunted its kind.

His army needed to be reminded that the rifts were their haven, their protection. From a rift, a Cartesian had all the power it needed to conquer anything.

Reviewing the mistakes made in the recent kill, he couldn't help thinking of the Bender who'd been skewered instead of the Triad. A look of shock had been the man's death mask. The kill had been so instantaneous, had happened so quickly and unexpectedly that the Bender never uttered a sound, save for one scream before he was impaled. Nothing followed. No more screams. No yells for help. Black and white, immediate death.

That had left him with some regret. He would have liked to hear the gurgle of death, screams of pain, to have seen the Bender attempt to fight his way free of the Cartesian, and then, when that was unsuccessful, watch him writhe in the throes of death. But he'd been denied it all. The only screams and cries he'd heard had come from the Bender left behind.

He knew to expect one of two things to happen. When an enemy lost one of their own, the rest of its team either dispersed from the weakness of having lost one member, or they grew stronger and became more vengeful. Determination on steroids to annihilate whoever or whatever had killed one of their own.

Unsure yet as to which to expect from the Benders, he could only wait and see. Of course, he hoped the former would happen and not the latter. If weakened by the death of their team member, the Triad and Originals would be left to their own devices.

He'd think positively. Sadness, extreme sadness had a way of eating away at humans until they were little more than shells of their former selves. If that happened to the remaining Benders, he'd have much to rejoice over. They might remain in the city, but their grief might cause them to become lax, which was perfect, as far as he was concerned. There'd be no more hunting, searching for missing Originals. He'd simply collect them all and take their powers unto himself. Once the missing ones were consumed, it wouldn't take much effort to collect the rest. The weakened Benders would weaken the Triad who'd become dependent on them.

Now that he thought about it, the Cartesian who'd missed the Triad and killed the Bender instead had done him a favor. The process would speed up now.

He already had big notions and big plans. Much bigger than anything the small Bender lying like a ragdoll at his feet drained of life, of the essence of anything and everything he once was, might have come up with.

Oh, yes, this death, although regrettably not a Triad's,

would more than likely give him what he craved with his whole being faster than he could ever have hoped for.

He'd bet on it.

He was getting closer, so close to his goal. It took all of his mental powers to keep his excitement in check. He knew the Triad faced serious roadblocks, were at a total loss regarding any plan of action, especially now that humans had been brought into the picture. He couldn't have been more excited.

It had been his plan all along. Well, not the summation of the plan, but the journey toward it.

He was pleased with his work and the work of his evergrowing army. Create chaos, mayhem and destruction. And all was happening gloriously, independently and collectively. It created more rifts, more opportunities to get to the Originals and the Triad.

He had to admit that he carried a tinge of disappointment with one of his soldiers. The one who'd come inches from grabbing a Triad. That soldier had been stupid, allowing itself to get distracted and let the Triad slip away. Oddly enough, the stupid wench had all but killed herself after that. Running into a muddy river without a clue of how she'd retreat from its depths.

He'd watched in amusement as she thrashed, flailed, yelled, her head dunking into the water again and again. Each time she managed to surface, less of her head appeared.

Then, of course, the Bender who took out the distracted Cartesian, the one that had come so close to capturing his prize, jumped into the water to save her, protect her, take her away. He couldn't think of a son of a bitch he hated more, except the other Benders keeping him from realizing success faster than it was occurring.

Except for the river incident, the Benders had kept the

Triad so far up their asses his army hadn't been able to squeeze in for a shot, a taste of any of them.

The Originals, though, were a different story—sort of. His soldiers, his pets, his creations had managed to get some of the Originals. And the taste of the first Original capture had created such a feeding frenzy among his creatures, it had taken him some time to get them back on track—in line.

As always, his Cartesians were allowed a taste, a small morsel of their captures as a reward before the capture was brought to him to devour. He alone absorbed every ounce of energy that the victim possessed. It not only caused him to grow in his own power but also allowed him to create new Cartesians. That was how he'd grown his army, one new Cartesian at a time. And now they stood at the ready, eagerly awaiting his command. Hundreds of them developed, molded by his own hand. His beloved creations.

After centuries of trial and error, he'd perfected their looks and abilities. Their appearance, in many ways, mimicked his own. He wanted his creatures to create such fear and a sense of foreboding that the sight of them alone would stop a prey's heartbeat, leave it motionless and easy to capture.

For the most part, that strategy had worked, but mostly with the subspecies of the Originals. Vampires, werewolves and the like. But the fear factor had proved useless when it came to Benders. Those meddling infidels had been meticulously trained to purposely seek out his Cartesians, not avoid them. Not once, in ten generations of Benders, had he seen any Bender freeze or hesitate at the sight of his hideous beauties.

In fact, the opposite seemed to occur. The Benders seemed to glory in the sight of the Cartesians, anxious, heart racing with excitement as they aimed what looked like toy batons at his creations and pushed them out of this world's dimension.

To make matters worse, the Benders appeared competitive, all eager to be the first to send a Cartesian to the farthest dimension possible.

So far, this generation of Benders had managed, on one occasion, to send two of his Cartesians back seven dimensions. This meant it would take decades for them to make their way back to him. They'd have to claw, tear, rip through the tiniest hole in each dimension to return. Since other dimensions were not as active and restless as the one now containing the Originals and Triad, rifts were more difficult to locate. This problem alone caused a severe time lapse for the Cartesians that had been pushed back that far.

Fortunately, no Bender, thus far, had accomplished the ultimate goal—shoving the Cartesians back to the eleventh dimension from which there would be no return. The eleventh dimension contained nothing but a void, a place that had no rift potential whatsoever.

And the Benders' second goal, capturing him, the leader of the Cartesians, had always been an act of futility. His army made sure of that. He was their leader— the master and god of his glorious monstrosities.

Capturing him and pushing a Cartesian to the eleventh dimension hadn't happened in the past Bender generations, and he sure as hell wouldn't allow it to happen with this one.

The current Benders assigned to protect the Triad and Originals were proving to be quite ingenious, however. Much more so than the ones who'd fought before them. Enemies though they were, he had to give credit where credit was due. The electrical domes the Benders had created to protect the Originals in their safe places had been a well-thought-out plan and, for a while anyway, an effective barrier.

Ingenious as it was, however, he'd discovered, albeit by happenstance, that the electrical currents of the domes could be affected, minimized. And the key to doing so was simply to allow nature to take its course.

The sexual distraction of the Triad owing to the Benders seemed to be one catalyst, and the second was allowing the Originals that had gone missing to do what they did best when left to themselves—attack humans.

The Nosferatu that had thirsted for the drunken harlot in that dark alley could have been easy pickings for his Cartesians. For a while, the Nosferatu had been left to its own meanderings. He'd watched as it found its prey and had lured her into the alley.

In that moment, he'd been torn between having his soldiers snatch the Original then and there and watching the kill of the human. Then, once the Nosferatu was engorged with the woman's blood, he'd have his Cartesian snatch it from the same dark alley.

His curiosity had won the coin toss. He wanted to watch the kill, thinking that once it was glutted with blood, capturing that particular Nosferatu might prove to boost its overall power, thus allowing him a bigger bang for the capture.

Sadly, neither had occurred.

Once again, the opportunity had been lost at the hands of a Bender. As disappointing as that had been, it did wind up being quite the fascinating show. Nosferatu against Bender—then watching an Original leader kill one of its own. He'd watched with glee as humans gathered, witnessing the event—creating more chaos. More problems.

It was then he realized that the increase of chaos somehow affected the electrical domes, causing their power to wane. That had been an unexpected bonus.

And now that humans were involved, he anticipated all hell to break loose. He couldn't have asked for anything more perfect.

Now the Triad, who had already been running from pillar to post, protecting their sequestered Originals, hunting for the ones who'd gone missing, which had been his master plan, would come unglued. This was one way he would get all he wanted, demanded, which was supreme power over all. To do so, he had to set the stage to make it happen. Create turmoil, weaken and distract the Triad, confuse the Benders.

With humans thrown into the mix, one having seen a Nosferatu in all its glory, many witnessing the death of that Nosferatu by its leader, soon the entire city would be in a state of commotion.

Man would wind up killing man. Original would kill Original.

Once that mayhem heightened, all would be his for the taking. All the Originals, the Triad, every bastard offspring hiding beneath the Originals' skirt—vampires, werewolves, the rest of the netherworld. He'd even cleanse his palate between consumptions with a sorcerer or two. No, he'd definitely take all three. And, of course, the Triad Elders were on his checklist.

Finally, he'd have it all. After all the years of working, waiting, his plan was coming to fruition.

Oddly enough, the closer he came to accomplishing his goal, the more bittersweet if felt to him. He so enjoyed watching the Triad and Benders running in circles, chasing their own tails, accomplishing little more than adding to their own frustration.

As he often did, he wondered what pleasure he'd experience when consuming a Triad. He imagined the taste to be as exquisite as the finest chocolate, something to be savored on the tongue. He'd allow it to melt slowly so every morsel would be experienced to its fullest extent. He'd take his time, let the sensation wash over him. Allow the scent of it to fill his nostrils, his lungs.

Even now he could almost feel it on the flat of his tongue, washing through him, rolling over all his senses. And once that time came, which he knew would be oh-so-soon, he imagined the height of the sensation to be greater than any human orgasm ever experienced.

The completion of it, the longing and desire he'd carried for it, finally meeting. How could anything compare to such glory?

No human emotion, need or desire could possibly match something of that magnitude.

And the culmination of it was so close, just within reach now.

In the meantime, he still had work to do. More heartache, worry and desperation to create for the Triad and the foolish Benders who followed them like puppies.

He anxiously awaited the perfume of their terror, their uncertainty to waft over him like the fragrance of an entire field of summer flowers.

Little did the Triad or Benders know that their own fears and indecisiveness, their own questioning of themselves as the Triad's powers continued to diminish—all of it was their own worst enemy.

Soon there would no longer be the waving of hands, lighting of candles, useless charms and incantations. All would belong to him.

Once again, feeling as giddy as a child awaiting a

much-desired treasure, he forced himself to stay in check. To remain stoic, strong.

He'd only allow his Cartesians to see him as a pillar of strength, a force never to be questioned. Whose orders were to be followed without a second's hesitation.

He must always be seen as their master, not a foolish twit who succumbed to emotion.

And soon, very, very soon, the world would view him the same way. Master of all that existed.

And every knee would bend at his feet.

Chapter 13

Taka Burnside knew she was going to be in big trouble with the other two Elders, Arabella and Vanessa, but she couldn't just sit around doing nothing anymore. The police had returned to their house not long after the Triad left. And once again, they'd stood in silence, hiding, not answering when the police beat on the door over and over, seemingly forever, trying to get someone to answer.

That had scared Taka. She didn't want to go to jail. She didn't want to be hanged by the neck in a tree or burned at the stake. And it would happen, she was sure of it. The past would revisit the world of witches.

Despite what Vanessa and Arabella told her about being overly dramatic, Taka knew better, and she knew what needed to be done. Arabella and Vanessa just didn't have the courage she did.

Taka had to wait quite some time after the triplets left before Arabella and Vanessa had gone to bed. It was about two in the morning before Taka felt it safe enough to move around without stirring the two awake. She'd quickly dressed in a pink polyester pantsuit and white orthopedic shoes. She'd slicked her hair down with a comb, then grabbed her white faux leather purse and sneaked out of the house. She'd gone through the back door, since it didn't squeak as loudly as the front door did when opened.

Her mission was clear, her steps sure. She intended to find Gunner Stern, the sorcerer that Arabella claimed they could trust. If Arabella trusted him, then they had a real possibility for help. At least there was some merit in finding out. Arabella's word counted for something. She wasn't an airhead.

Taka knew that if Vanessa and Arabella thought anyone in their group to be an airhead, they'd point to her. But nothing was further from the truth, as far as she was concerned.

It was true that occasionally words kind of slipped out of Taka's mouth before she'd thought them through. And sometimes she had an issue with expressing what she meant in the right order. But she had a brain. A good one. And she planned to use it to do what must be done.

As she made her way through the Garden District, counting on streetlamps and moonlight for direction, she hoped her knees wouldn't give out from the long walk ahead. The trolleys didn't run at this hour of the day.

Keeping her head up and her attitude positive, Taka kept a single mantra running through her head. *Feet, don't fail me now!*

She planned to find Gunner, explain that their issues were much bigger than the problem he'd reported to Arabella, then ask for his help.

She knew that in doing so, she was spitting right in

the eye of the Elders' protocol, the one that insisted on a majority vote when faced with a decision of this magnitude. And she knew that asking a sorcerer for help was no small matter. Taka had little doubt that Vanessa and Arabella would be furious with her. They might even consider dismissing her from the order of Elders.

Right now Taka didn't care what they did to her. Arabella was taking far too much time to make a decision. Something needed to be done now before all they knew and loved was destroyed. The Triad, the Originals, the humans in this city.

How long could they stand in silence in their home, hiding like mice from a cat, every time a police officer pounded on the door?

As far as Taka was concerned, everything they'd attempted so far to help the Triad and the Originals had failed miserably. They couldn't simply sit around wishing, hoping something would change.

The one thing that had really set Taka on this quest was the fact that all the leaders in the Circle of Sisters around the country had collectively set a spell in motion to help them, and nothing had happened.

Arabella had made a point about Gunner. Having someone outside the Circle of Sisters might be able to bring a new perspective to their problems. Being a master of his own incantations and spells, Gunner just might have an idea on how to help them.

Taka kept reminding herself about Arabella's point as she walked, seemingly forever. When she finally reached Canal Street, there were very few people milling about. A few homeless men sleeping near door stoops, a couple of drunks singing nonsensical songs.

When she reached Evee's café, Bon Appétit, which, of course, was closed at this hour, she stood near its front door and studied the lay of the land. From here, she at least had a sense of direction. Trey Cottle's law office was across the street, and she knew he lived in an apartment right above the office. Shandor Black lived in an apartment about a block away. Although she didn't know Shandor's exact apartment name or number, it wouldn't have taken much to find him. A few knocks on a few doors, some irritated people having been roused from sleep. No big deal.

It was then that Taka realized she didn't have a clue as to where Gunner lived. She'd just assumed he lived next to Trey and Shandor since they were together so often.

Yet, in that moment, Taka remembered that she'd never heard Gunner mention where he lived.

She sat on the stoop of the café, clutched her purse to her breasts, and slapped herself on the forehead. She was a damn airhead. She should have thought this out more thoroughly before taking off. For all she knew, Gunner could live in Baton Rouge, a city over an hour away. Many people commuted to work in New Orleans from surrounding cities.

What was she supposed to do now? Taka sighed heavily, her feet throbbing from having walked so far. The Elders made a habit of walking the Garden District area from time to time for exercise and fresh air. But at her age, Taka's brain had lied to her, convincing her that her body could easily make the walk to the Quarter.

She sat, staring at Trey Cottle's office, at the apartment windows above it. They were dark, which meant Trey was either asleep or out for the night. As she stared, an idea struck her. The only way she'd be able to find out where Gunner lived was to ask one of the two sorcerers that the other two Elders didn't trust.

As far as Trey was concerned, Taka held no opinion

one way or the other, except that she considered him ugly with his round belly, triple chins and the snooty nose with glasses always resting at its tip. Then there was his balding, sweaty head. But looks weren't what she was after. She needed information, and if anyone knew where to find Gunner, Trey would certainly know.

If Trey was up there in his apartment, sleeping, she could wake him and at least ask for Gunner's address. Certainly he wouldn't get upset for that small bother. All he'd have to do was give her the address and go right back to sleep.

Taka got to her feet and crossed the street to Trey's office. Alongside the building was a wrought-iron gate, which was locked. Beyond it, down a short alley, she spotted a stairwell and landing that obviously led to Trey's apartment. The fence stood at least eight feet tall. No way she'd be able to climb it and jump over.

Standing back a few feet, Taka studied the darkened apartment windows again. With the gate in her way, how could she get Trey's attention? Knocking on his office door wouldn't do any good, as it also had a wrought-iron security door over the mahogany one that led into the office.

Frustrated, Taka looked down both sides of Canal. Only a straggler or two walking on the opposite side of the street. She paced for a moment, head lowered, rubbing her chin between a thumb and finger.

That was when she happened upon a pebble…then a second, slightly larger one. She picked them up, rolled them over in her palm. In the movies, when a boy wanted to get a girl's attention in an upstairs bedroom without her parents knowing, he'd toss pebbles at her window until he got her attention.

Excited that she might have found a way to reach Trey,

Taka took the smallest pebble and threw it at one of the upstairs windows. She missed by a foot, hitting the brick siding of the building instead.

Sticking her tongue between her teeth, she took the larger pebble, closed her left eye to get a better sight on her target, then threw it as hard as she could.

The rock not only hit the window but shattered it.

Gasping, Taka jumped left, then right, not knowing whether to run away or just wait out the tongue-lashing she was sure she'd get from Trey.

Within seconds Trey Cottle's face appeared at the window. From the streetlamps that lined Canal, Taka could easily see the fury on the man's face. When he looked down and saw her, however, his expression changed.

It went from anger to surprise to oddly soft and curious.

"Why, Ms. Burnside, were you the one who broke my window?" Trey called down to her.

Taka began to wring her hands, her purse swinging in the crook of her right arm. "Y-yes. I—I'm so sorry. I didn't mean to throw it that hard. I wanted to get your attention because I need some help with something."

Trey lifted an eyebrow and said, "Wait. Wait right there. I'll come down and let you in."

"No, no, that's not necessary," Taka said, anxiety riding her body like a bull just let out of a chute.

Before she could say more, Trey had already disappeared from the window, and she saw lights flooding the rooms upstairs.

Taka stood on the sidewalk, shifting nervously from foot to foot, needing to pee. She shouldn't have come here. Something in her gut told her that coming to Trey Cottle's place had been a big mistake. Then again, it could just be her paranoia running amok. The only other option she'd had was to find Shandor, which would have meant knocking on more doors, waking more people. She took long, deep breaths, trying to remember the bigger purpose as to why she was here. That all she planned to get from Trey was an address. Gunner's address.

The longer Taka waited, the more she needed to pee. She crossed her legs to keep from letting go right there on the sidewalk in her pink pantsuit.

Trey suddenly appeared to her left, at the wrought-iron gate that closed off the short alley. He wore a maroon silk robe over maroon pajamas. Their pant legs clung to his chunky thighs.

He quickly unlocked the gate and motioned Taka inside.

She hesitated. "I—I really don't need to go inside. I hate to bother you. I know it's late or rather very early morning, but I'm a little desperate. I need Gunner Stern's address. Do you know where he lives? I really need to contact him."

Trey cocked his head to one side and shoved his glasses up the bridge of his nose. "Why would you be looking for Gunner at this hour?" he asked.

"I need… I just need to talk to him," Taka said, being careful about what she relayed to Trey.

Trey sighed. "He lives out by the Causeway, Ms. Burnside, which is quite the distance from here." He looked down both sides of the street. "I don't see any vehicle nearby. May I call you a cab? And while I do so, I'll write down Gunner's address for you."

Taka was about to say yes, please, then remembered she hadn't taken any money with her. All she carried in her purse was tissue, a compact, a hairbrush and a can of pepper spray. She hadn't thought about bringing money.

"I appreciate you offering to call a cab for me, but it seems like I left home without any money. I know the

Causeway's a long way from here, but I'll figure out a way to get there. If you would be so kind as to just give me his address."

Trey tsked and said, "I know you said it's important, but if you can't physically make it to him, you're certainly welcome to use my telephone and call him. I have his number, and I'll most certainly give you as much privacy as you need while you speak to him."

Taka thought about it for a moment, feeling out Trey, trying to get a sense of whether he was sincere or not.

Remembering her initial mission, Taka squared her shoulders and walked past the gate, which Trey closed behind them. She then followed him down the short alley and up the stairs into his apartment.

As he ushered her inside and led her through the apartment, Taka saw a neatly kept kitchen and a living room decorated with mahogany and leather furniture.

Trey motioned to a room on the right, just past the living room. "My phone is right in there. It's my home office." He opened a pair of French doors and led her into a large room that held a circular desk, two wingback chairs in front of the desk and a tall leather-back chair behind it. The desk itself held a computer, a telephone and mountains of paperwork. Bookshelves lined every wall of the room, each overflowing with books.

Trey pointed to the telephone. "There you go. You're welcome to it." He leaned across the desk, picked up a pen and wrote a set of numbers on a yellow Post-it note. He handed the note to Taka. "This is Gunner's number. He's probably asleep right now, so just let it ring. I'm sure he'll eventually answer. I'll be out in the kitchen if you need me for anything."

"Thank you," Taka said, feeling a bit uneasy as soon as Trey left the room and closed the door behind him.

She listened to his footsteps as he made his way down the hallway. When his footsteps finally faded to nothing, Taka picked up the receiver of the phone and punched in the number Trey had written down for her.

On the fifth ring, a man answered the phone. "H-hello?" His voice sounded thick with sleep.

"Is this Gunner Stern?" Taka asked quietly.

"Who is this?" he asked.

"Taka Burnside. I'm one of the Elders, you know, along with Arabella. I've met you a few times at the Bon Appétit Café."

The man cleared his throat. "Oh, yes, Ms. Burnside, I know who you are. I apologize that it took me a while to recognize your voice. It's a bit early in the morning."

"I—I know," Taka said. "I'm so sorry for waking you, but we desperately need your help."

Taka heard shuffling on the other end of the phone, and when Gunner finally responded, his voice sounded strong and alert.

"How may I be of help?" he asked.

"I'm not sure," Taka confessed. "I was hoping you might have some ideas."

"Regarding…?"

Taka glanced around the room, making sure she was alone. She cupped the mouthpiece of the receiver and lowered her voice even more. "Mr. Stern, the Elders need you. Things have gotten out of control for us. We're losing some of the Originals, and humans are being attacked. We've had the entire clan of Sisters casting spells to help us, but their incantations don't seem to be working. You're the only one of the sorcerers I trust to ask for help. Arabella trusts you, too. At first no one wanted any sorcerer involved, but we're running out of options, and if we don't do something soon, I'm afraid we'll lose everything. The Originals, the Triad, the people in this city." Taka stopped her blabbering and listened for a response from Gunner.

A few seconds passed before he said, "You are in quite the fix, aren't you? Is there somewhere we can meet to discuss this in person?"

"I—I don't know." Taka fretted that if she waited to meet him face to face, went over the entire story again, the other Elders would wake and find her missing.

"Where are you now?" Gunner asked.

Taka whispered into the mouthpiece while eyeing the room. "At Trey Cottle's apartment."

"What are you doing there?" Gunner asked quite loudly.

"I didn't know where you lived. I wasn't sure where Shandor lived, either. I just knew Trey's apartment was on top of his office, so it was easy to find. I figured he'd know your address, so I got his attention. Sort of in a bad way, though. I threw a rock at his window and it shattered. Trey was nice about it. He didn't get angry at me or anything. He told me you lived out by the Causeway, and I wasn't able to make it there by cab because I forgot to bring cash with me. I didn't know you lived that far away. So Trey offered to let me use his phone. Gave me your phone number."

"Listen carefully," Gunner said. "Don't say anything more. Just hang up the phone, leave Trey's apartment and head straight to your house. I'll meet you there."

"No, I can't meet there," Taka said frantically. "The other two Elders don't know I'm out here. Can we meet at Evee's café? The Bon Appétit? It's not open now. No one will be there."

"Can you get inside the café?"

"No, I don't have a key."

There was a moment of silence before Gunner said, "I don't like the idea of you standing out in front of the café at this time of night…morning."

"I'll be fine," Taka said. "I've got Mace with me."

Another moment of silence, then Gunner said, "All right. Just leave that apartment this minute and go to the café. I'll be there as quickly as I can."

Taka nodded, then realized he couldn't see the gesture. "Yes, I will. Thank you. Thank you so much for speaking with me."

"Leave now," Gunner insisted. "I'll be looking for you, and I promise I won't keep you waiting long."

"Thank you."

A second of silence made Taka wonder if she should hang up now. Before she did, Gunner's voice came to her ear. "Taka?"

"Yes?"

"Before we meet, I want to give you an important piece of advice."

"Certainly. What is it?"

"Don't ever return to Trey's apartment again. Understand?"

Now it was Taka's turn to bleed silence into the line. Only when she finally said, "Yes. I understand," did Gunner hang up his phone.

She hung up, sitting behind Trey's desk in the large leather chair. Taka had a sinking feeling in the pit of her stomach that she'd just crossed a line she'd never be able to return from. Not only had she contacted a sorcerer, but she done it from Trey Cottle's apartment.

Something inside her didn't feel right. She did as instructed, leaving the apartment as quickly as possible.

Taka ran into Trey as she followed the route he'd used

to bring her to his home office. He stood near the stove with a kettle of water he placed on a burner.

"Ah, Ms. Burnside, just in time. Would you care for a cup of tea?" Trey asked. His brow furrowed slightly. "You seem a bit rattled. I hope all is well. Maybe some chamomile tea will help settle your nerves."

"No, thank you," Taka said quickly. She noticed Trey's eyes grow darker. "I appreciate the use of your phone. And I do apologize again about your window."

"Then please do me the courtesy of allowing me to help calm your nerves. You don't have to talk about whatever's bothering you if you don't want to."

Taka felt the hair on the back of her neck stand on end, and her body tensed, ready for fight or flight.

"I'd love to, really, but I can't. Arabella and Vanessa will be worried about me. I need to head back home. So, thank you. Thank you again for your kindness," Taka said while making her way to the kitchen door. When she opened it, ready to fly down the stairs, Trey called out to her.

"Wait a moment," he said, and followed her to the door. Taka felt her insides tremble and prayed it wasn't obvious to Trey. "I'll need to unlock the alleyway gate so you can leave."

"Ah." Taka forced a smile. "Of course. I'm sorry to inconvenience you again."

"No problem, Ms. Burnside."

They made it to the gate, and Trey unlocked it, then opened it wide so Taka could leave.

As she squeezed past him and felt she could breathe again now that a fence separated them, Taka said, "Thank you again. And I'll be happy to pay for your window, Mr. Cottle."

Trey tsked. "No need, Ms. Burnside. I understand emergencies. The window's on me. Have a good evening." He smiled at her, and the look came across more like a smirk.

Taka hurried away, wanting to throw up and wishing more than ever that she'd never gone to Cottle's apartment.

Chapter 14

After Lucien left the café without saying goodbye, Evee had sat there for a while. And then, finally managing to pull herself out of her despondency, she went home to dress for the feeding. She put on a fresh pair of black slacks and a black pullover sweater and brushed her hair back into a ponytail.

She left the house weary but also somewhat cautiously. Her illusion spell with the Cartesians had worked. But to what end? Ronan had died anyway. Why did that spell work and not others? She didn't have a clue. She was only grateful that it had worked.

She'd never seen so many Cartesians hanging from the sky, roaring, clawing, all of them like vultures starving for fresh meat. Although Lucien and Ronan had faced them bravely, Evee didn't have to be a Bender to realize they were seriously outnumbered. Evee had been certain that through their years of experience as Benders, Lucien and

Ronan would have figured their way out of the calamity. But despite her confidence, Evee had refused to leave them out in the open, alone, with so many enemies eager to kill.

The illusion spell had come to mind unbidden, and although she had had issues with previous spells going south or simply fizzling out altogether, she hadn't hesitated to stand by Lucien's side and speak her incantation.

Oddly enough, she wasn't surprised that it had worked. She didn't know if the ferocity she'd felt to help Lucien and Ronan had given the spell the extra kick it needed to work. For all intents and purposes, the reason the spell worked really didn't matter now. What mattered was that it had worked. Only too little too late. If only it had saved Ronan's life, as well.

After leaving her house, Evee decided to look in on the Nosferatu in the catacombs once more before she checked on the ferry and the electrical dome they'd discussed building over it to protect the Originals en route to the compound.

The walk to St. John's was a long one, but it gave her time to think.

The Elders had given her and Viv hell when the Triad's familiars had ratted them out about Evee's intimacy with Lucien and Viv's with Nikoli. They'd reprimanded the sisters, and warned them to forgo all intimacy with the Benders.

She and Viv had given the Elders a half-hearted agreement that they'd stay hands off, but that didn't do a damn thing to keep her from thinking about Lucien. The man could wear an Eskimo coat and hood over an armored bodysuit, and Evee would still be able to feel the strength of all that made up the man. The bulk of his muscular arms, the ripples of muscles that ran down his chest and stomach. The width of his hands. The length of his fingers. How he towered over her, a gentle, protective giant that turned her insides into mush.

After meeting with the Elders and all but being blamed along with Viv for the turmoil and suffering unleashed in the city, Evee had tried to stay resolute.

She'd met Lucien at the cathedral as they'd agreed upon, and attempted to keep her distance from him. Remain aloof. Her resolve had vanished, however, the moment she saw his strong, finely chiseled face and the fierce emerald of his eyes. Every time Lucien had spoken to her, Evee had trouble concentrating on his words. She'd watched his lips, which made her thirst for him in the worst way. She wanted to kiss his full, beautiful lips again.

The fight with the Cartesians had been fierce, and it had terrified her. But for the first time since they'd been paired together, along with Ronan, she felt they'd operated as a team. It made Evee feel good to contribute the way she did.

Still feeling a sense of remorse over Ronan's death and with Lucien on her mind, Evee soon found herself on Canal Street before she knew it. She took a right on Chartres, then made her way to the cathedral and into the catacombs.

The electric canopy that Lucien and Ronan had recharged with their scabiors was still intact. The Nosferatu beneath it paced restlessly. They all looked over at her questioningly, and Evee could almost hear their collective mental questions.

Now? Is feeding time now? Will you release us from here—now?

The only one Evee made eye contact with was Pierre, her lead Nosferatu. Evee mouthed to him, "Very soon."

Pierre gave her an almost imperceptible nod, then went about his business.

With that, Evee quickly left the catacombs and cathedral and headed for the docks to check on the ferry.

Evee had barely walked fifty feet when she heard someone call her name. A man.

"Miss François."

She froze, then turned slowly in the direction of the man's voice.

Standing about a half block away was Shandor Black, one of the three sorcerers who lived in New Orleans. He walked in her direction, his tall, lanky body stiff in motion, a body that appeared more comfortable settled in a chair than chasing a Triad in the wee hours of morning.

Shandor was one of the sorcerers that the Elders had mentioned often. One they didn't trust any more than they trusted Trey Cottle, Shandor's usual sidekick.

As he drew closer, Shandor pushed his eyeglasses up on his long, hooked nose, closer to his beady eyes. The glasses did little to enhance the man's thin, drawn face that carried a perpetual scowl.

"How lovely to meet you out here, Miss François," Shandor said when he finally reached Evee.

Evee nodded politely. "Mr. Black. What brings you out at such an early hour?"

"Well, actually," he said, pressing his glasses against his eyes again, "I was looking for you."

Evee felt her head jerk up in surprise. "What on earth would you want with me?"

"I hear that you and your sisters were facing quite a dilemma," Shandor said. His voice held a nasal stuffiness to it. "I wanted to offer my assistance."

"Where did you hear about this so-called dilemma?" Evee asked, eyes narrowing.

"Oh, you know," Shandor said, absently rubbing his chin. "Word gets around rather quickly in this city. Well, the Quarter, anyway." He attempted a smile, but the gesture appeared to make his face hurt.

"So," Evee said, and put a fist on her hip. "If I understand you correctly, you've heard a rumor about me and my sisters and decided to seek me out at what…two thirty in the morning?"

Shandor shrugged. "I don't sleep well these days. Insomnia. I often walk the city at night when I can't sleep."

"And what made you think I'd be out here this early?"

"Oh, I've seen you out in this area this early from time to time on nights when I can't sleep. Figured it'd be worth a shot, looking for you here, I mean."

Evee felt gooseflesh rush along her arms just thinking that Shandor had been watching her without her knowledge. And now confronting her here.

Stiffening her spine, Evee said, "Tell me what it is you think you know."

"I'd be happy to," Shandor said. He pointed to a stoop near a darkened building. "Why don't we sit over there for a chat? I'll tell you what I've heard, and you can decide whether or not my services might come in handy."

They walked the few steps to the stoop, which was little more than three cracked brick steps, and Evee said, "Feel free to sit. I'm fine standing right here."

Shandor shrugged again and sat on the stoop with a grunt, then drummed his fingers on his knees. "Aging is no fun, I've got to tell you. These old knees have seen better days."

Anxious to get to the ferry and wanting to rid herself of Shandor, Evee put her hands on her hips. "Please get to the point. I have business to take care of."

Shandor squinted up at her. "Oh, of course, of course."

He looked down, continued to drum his fingers against his knees. "Well, let's see. I've heard that the Originals, not all of them, but some, have gone missing. I've also heard about the human and the Nosferatu killed. Plenty of human witnesses from what I was told. Plenty."

Evee felt fury roil through her body. "When did you hear such things?"

"Today."

"From whom?"

"As I said, word travels, and my source for the information is very reliable."

"Bullshit!"

Shandor stopped drumming his fingers and peered up at Evee. "Why, Miss François, such language from a nice young lady like yourself. I must say, it's not very becoming."

Evee's hands rolled into fists on her hips. "Tough tits, Shandor. Your 'word travels fast' excuse is bullshit. We both know it. You had to get that information from someone specific, and I want to know who."

Shandor held up an indignant chin. "Who gave me the information is truly irrelevant, especially with the problems all of you are experiencing now. And really, Evette, I truly believe I can be of service to all of you."

Evee remembered the discussion she and her sisters had had with the Elders. How they'd argued back and forth about getting any of the sorcerers involved. Evee had felt strongly about not allowing them into their lives.

She glared at Shandor, who still sat on the stoop, his back resting against the building behind it. He crossed his arms and placed them in his lap. As relaxed as a man waiting for the city bus.

"Hypothetically," Evee finally said, "suppose what you heard was true—and I'm not saying it is. What do you possibly have to offer anyone who might be in such a state?"

Shandor let out a snort of laughter. "We have many spells and incantations that are different from yours. And since we're sorcerers and not witches—and I'm not meaning that in any sexist way or implying any inferiority of one to the other," Shandor assured her, "we might add some extra punch."

Evee opened her mouth, ready to ream out Shandor, but he blabbered on before she was able to get a word in edgewise.

"Just hear me out," Shandor said. "Don't think that me, Trey or Gunner don't know how the Triad feels about sorcerers. No matter those feelings, wouldn't calmer heads prevail? I know that collectively we can put a stop to all this. No more deaths. No human deaths. You, once again, in full control of all that's yours. I'm quite confident we can help make that happen."

"We *are* in control of our Originals and each other," Evee said through clenched teeth. "Thank you very much for your concern, but I assure you it's unwarranted. Your information and whatever reliable source you think you have are wrong."

"You're only saying that because I won't reveal my source," Shandor said, then struggled to his feet. "Let me assure you, Miss François, despite what you think, my information source is as reliable as your familiar."

Evee frowned. "What about my familiar?"

Shandor held out a hand. "Nothing, really. Only a point of reference. Think about what you're asking. It would be quite crass of me to divulge the name of my source who specifically asked to remain anonymous. I'm only here to offer my help, and I don't know how my revealing that information, thus breaking my promise, would cause you to trust me more. In fact, the opposite would be true, would it not? It would cause you to mistrust me all the more."

"You're right," Evee said. "I don't trust you. Any of you. Why should I? All I've ever seen from you and Trey are spells and incantations that served no one but yourselves. Not once have I seen either of you open up to help other people in the community. Your motives have always been self-serving. Why come to me now if you think there are issues? What would you gain out of this, Shandor?"

"Truthfully," Shandor said, looking wistfully down the street, "to save this city, the one we both love. Look, Evette, we both play baseball, so to speak, only we play in separate fields. It only makes sense that if one team winds up in trouble, trouble big enough to affect both playing fields, both teams should merge to conquer the problem."

Evee sighed, noting time getting further and further away from her. "I appreciate your metaphor and offer to help, Mr. Black, but I assure you that we have things firmly in hand."

Shandor pursed his lips and studied Evee for a few seconds. "Do you plan on assuring the police officers who've made numerous trips to the Elders' home in the same way?"

Evee felt her brows lift in surprise. She didn't allow herself to give Shandor the satisfaction of asking how he knew about the police.

Shandor clicked his tongue against his crooked front teeth. "What do you think the Elders will tell them when they finally do decide to open the door? Or worse, if the officers obtain a warrant and force their way inside?"

Evee only stared at him, working hard to remain expressionless.

"If we join forces, Miss François, we can certainly have the police officers turn the other cheek, so to speak. Point them in a completely different direction. The Triad and Elders remain safe that way."

Unable to stop herself, Evee huffed. "Trust me. Whatever you think you can do with your powers, we can do three times as much. The Triad is not a simple cluster of witches. We have our own ways and powers."

"So I've heard," Shandor said. "But from what I've heard recently, those powers seem to be slipping, for whatever reason. If that's true, then imagine you having the help of the sorcerers in this war you're fighting. You would be able to conquer these problems in a day, two at the most. Think of it. No more sleepless nights. No more having to watch the catacombs, where you're keeping the Nosferatu cloistered."

"How do you know where my Nosferatu are?" Evee demanded.

"Oh, there are many things I know. I'm aware that the Chenilles are collected in the Louis I Cemetery, and the Loup Garous have been gathered in the North Compound out in Algiers."

Without a second thought, Evee spat, hitting the ground and missing Shandor's shoes by a couple inches. "I'm going to ask you once more, Black. Where are you getting your information?"

"And once more, I have to reiterate that I cannot divulge that information. But all of it's true, isn't it?"

Evee heard a low growl come from the bowels of her throat. "In a million years, how can you possibly expect me to ever trust the likes of you?"

Shandor eyed her. A glint in his milky brown eyes.

"Because you have no one else to turn to. Because you're at a loss and afraid. Because we're your only hope. There's no one else who could possibly understand where you're coming from or how the challenges you face affect you."

"Except the opposite sex of witches?" Evee nearly shouted. She leaned into Shandor to make certain he heard every word she said, and that he wouldn't miss the determination in her eyes. "This is the last time I'm going to repeat this. I don't know what you've heard or who you've heard it from, but it's all bullshit. We take care of our own. It's not like sorcerers don't ever run into challenges of their own. When was the last time you called on any of us for help? Never! Whatever situation we may face, we'll conquer it as a Triad with our Elders."

"And your new friends?" Shandor smirked.

"What the hell are you talking about?"

"Oh, we see more in this city than you give us credit for. I've seen those four handsome young men following the Triad's every footstep."

"Who told you about the Benders? Your fastidious, reliable source?" Evee taunted.

"What was there to tell? Who could possibly miss those handsome men in this city? They truly stand out, and I've personally seen two of them following you through the Quarter. Their appearance here is certainly no secret. They're—"

Evee finally held up both hands, stopping his rant. "As I stated before, Black, I have business to tend to. I would ask that you mind your own business, and we'll take care of our own."

With that, Evee turned on her heel and stormed away from Shandor Black. She had to let her sisters, the Elders and the Benders know that word was on the street, and worse, in the hands of the sorcerers. That was a problem they certainly didn't need. For this one held the potential to turn things a lot uglier than they were now or make them far worse than anyone expected.

Chapter 15

After making his call to Ronan's father and the rest of his family regarding his cousin's death, Lucien paced about the hotel room, unable to think. All his brain focused on was the sight of Ronan, the long black claw that had been shoved into his left temple and came out of his right. His face bloody, eyes open and void of expression, mouth slightly open from the shock.

The only comfort Lucien had to offer Ronan's family and his own was that Ronan's death had been quick. There'd been no struggle, no death throes. Lucien's cousin had simply hung from that goddamn claw like a ragdoll.

Aside from his cousin's death, the worst part would be the lack of closure for Ronan's family. They'd have no body to bury. Only memories, which they planned to share in a memorial mass to be held as soon as the Benders' mission was over.

Gavril and Nikoli had been right. Although he was grieving, Ronan's father had insisted that the other Benders carry on with their tasks despite this horrid event. He specifically said Ronan would have wanted it that way, as well. When Lucien had spoken to his father about the news, he also reminded his son to complete their mission. It was the Benders' way. Always had been. Always would be. They'd make time for emotions later.

Still, Lucien couldn't help remembering the huge smile Ronan had had on his face when he'd announced that Evee would have dinner with him once the mission was over. Lucien wished Ronan had spoken up sooner, at least to show Evee he was interested in her. The problem was, and aways had been, that doing so wasn't Ronan's style. He wasn't like the rest of his cousins. He looked at life much more seriously and quietly than they did.

Shaking off the thoughts of Ronan and women, Evee specifically, Lucien began to feel like a caged animal in the hotel suite. He left the room and the hotel.

Since the front of the hotel emptied out onto Royal Street, he had but a block to walk before he reached Bourbon. Not that he felt like looking for Originals. He simply needed to hear people right now. Normal people. Laughing, singing, talking, all of them seemingly without a care in the world.

Lucien couldn't remember ever feeling that way. Not only did he go about life with many cares, but sometimes it felt like the entire world rested on his shoulders. Feeling the stirrings of self-pity, he frowned and forced himself to study the streets. He walked down alleys, peered behind buildings, looking for any of the missing Originals.

It was eerily quiet in the Quarter at this time of morning. Aside from a handful of drunks, some singing while staggering along the sidewalk, a couple of others puking in the middle of the street, the streets were all but empty. The air smelled of garbage, booze, vomit and urine. Not a place anyone would care to hang around in for very long.

As hard as he tried to keep Evee off his mind, she popped back in without his permission, and this time, Lucien couldn't shake her off.

He wished he could turn back time and do things differently. Instead of playing the martyr and suggesting that Ronan ask her out, Lucien should have shot his own gun straight and on target. He really liked Evee, thought she was one of the most beautiful women he'd ever known.

Lucien knew that Ronan's slow approach to women was due to fear. Fear of rejection. He had easily faced Cartesians, one of the most dangerous creatures in the netherworld. Yet when it came to speaking his mind to a woman, he froze. Out of all the other cousins, Lucien was probably the only one who knew that Ronan had been more afraid of being rebuffed by a woman than of getting attacked by the monstrous creatures the Benders had hunted for years.

Some years ago, Ronan had told Lucien in confidence that he felt something had to be wrong with him. Some trauma he couldn't remember that made him so slow and uneasy about even asking a woman on a date. He'd been raised on the same street as his cousins, all four of them damn near connected at the hip since they could walk and talk. You would have thought that some of their bravado, their fearlessness with women had rubbed off on him. But it hadn't. He'd always seemed to be the odd man out.

Fortunately, regardless of all the odd theories Ronan had ruminated on regarding women, he'd known he served a purpose. Ronan had been good at his job, a job that was serious. It saved people's lives. Kept the universe in sync, and preserved the harmony between the humans and netherworld. The importance of that mission had to mean more to him than losing out on any woman. Including Evette François.

As logical and stoic as that sounded in his own head, it didn't stop Lucien's heart from aching. And he knew it would do so for some time.

Suddenly, a scream broke through Lucien's musings.

It sounded like a woman, and her screams seemed to be coming from a couple blocks away. Possibly down St. Ann Street.

Lucien broke into a run, taking a right on Ursuline, a quick right on Dauphine, then two blocks onto St. Ann.

Just as he turned onto the street, he saw a dark-haired, petite woman running out into the street, her face bloody, her clothes shredded. And right behind her was a Nosferatu in full natural form.

Although the streetlamps on St. Ann's were few, there was no mistaking the Nosferatu's lanky form, his large white bald head with the large vein across its forehead.

Lucien took off for the woman, meaning to shove her to safety and distract the Nosferatu. But the Original was gaining ground quickly, which meant it was actually toying with the woman. A Nosferatu had the ability to easily move from place to place in the blink of an eye. The fact that he allowed the woman to run and he simply trotted after her proved the creature planned to toy with its prey before taking her.

"Hey!" Lucien yelled, attempting to get the Nosferatu's attention. He suddenly had a sense of déjà vu, remembering how he'd had to do the same with two Loup Garous. Although he'd distracted the Loups by yelling at them, he'd failed to rescue their prey. However, he had managed to blind the Loups, keeping them from easily hunting other prey.

The Nosferatu was different, though. Even if Lucien blinded the bastard, a Nosferatu healed itself quickly, and it would only take a matter of minutes before it would regain its sight.

When he failed to get the Nosferatu's attention, Lucien yelled again. "Hey, you ugly fuck. Over here!"

This time the Nosferatu stopped and looked over at him. He stood, hunched over, looking from the woman to Lucien. Probably trying to figure out which would be an easier target.

Unfortunately, the woman won the Nosferatu's coin toss. He spun about and knocked her down to the ground before Lucien had time to blink.

Lucien took out his scabior. It was all he knew to do. Without question, the Nosferatu had ten times more strength than he had, but if he caught it by surprise, he might be able to do enough damage, cause enough of a distraction for the woman to escape.

At that moment, Lucien heard voices behind him. A shriek, gasps, curses.

He glanced back and saw that three people now stood at the corner of St. Ann and Bourbon, watching the action.

The Nosferatu looked back at them and let out a guttural growl. Its long fangs bared, its face twisted with fury.

Lucien turned to the three onlookers. A chubby man wearing a Who Dat T-shirt and stained jeans, an average-size man with glasses and no teeth, and an elderly woman in a very short skirt and halter top.

"Get back!" Lucien yelled at them. "Get out of here!"

Instead of listening to him and dispersing, the crowd seemed to grow thicker with onlookers. Five or six more people had joined the original three to watch the show.

Even with the crowd watching, Lucien feared that if he

didn't get the Nosferatu away from the woman, she'd have no hope of survival. Worse, if the Nosferatu did manage the kill, it would go after the next human in line. That could be him or anyone standing in the growing crowd.

"Get out of here, damn it!" Lucien shouted at the on-lookers.

No one moved. They stood, mouths agape, watching the events unfold. Lucien heard bits and pieces of their conversation, their words jumbling over each other.

"What's going—"

"What is that ugly—"

"—at that ugly son of a bitch!"

"—some kind of monster."

"Somebody call—"

"He's going to murder her! Stop—I—"

"—the police! Somebody call the—"

"Shit, look at—"

"Somebody help her!"

"Fuck me—"

"—not going over there! Look at that thing!"

"—like a horror story."

As people continued talking over one another, Lucien decided to take the Nosferatu by surprise as it had the woman on the ground and its fangs bared, ready to latch on to her neck.

Just as Lucien was about to make the leap for the Original, he suddenly caught a strong scent of clove and sulfur.

Instinctively, he looked up at the sky, and right over where the Nosferatu and woman struggled, Lucien saw a rift open up wide, which surprised him. Usually a rift appeared as a slit in the sky, and it took a bit of time for a Cartesian to work its way through the opening. This one, however, seemed to burst open like a pustulant wound, and within seconds, a Cartesian's fur-matted head appeared. It didn't take long for it to hang from the rift by the waist, lower its massive arms and swipe down with its claws toward the Nosferatu, who was already draining the woman of her blood.

With scabior already in hand, Lucien found himself in a conundrum. He had been willing to put his life on the line to save the woman from the Nosferatu, but now with a Cartesian aiming for a Nosferatu he had to choose. Get the human to safety or blast the Cartesian back into other dimensions.

Choices, always choices. And never easy ones.

Although it hurt his heart, Lucien had little choice but to choose the bigger cause. He had to get rid of the bigger danger. The Cartesian.

Despite the crowd of onlookers still whispering, squealing, gasping, now shouting at the sight of the Cartesian overhead, Lucien held on to his scabior, gave a quick flick of his wrist, then twirled the scabior lightning fast between his fingers. He heard comments from the crowd growing louder.

"What's that guy doing?"

"What's that thing in his hand?"

"What—"

Lucien forced himself to tune out their blabbering and focus on the task at hand. With the scabior charged, he aimed it at the Cartesian and hit it square in the face. It shrieked and jerked backward. A loud noise followed its retreat.

With the rift still open, Lucien kept his scabior aimed at it, concentrated only on the Cartesian, then heard a second and third pop, which meant he'd been able to push the Cartesian back two more dimensions. Only then did the rift in the sky disappear. It closed so quickly, it was as if someone had zippered it shut in one fell swoop.

With that done, the sounds from the crowd reached Lucien's ear once more. Some women were crying, men were cursing, yet not one of them stepped a foot closer to the Nosferatu, who was now draining the woman on the ground dry. Lucien had only to look at the locked expression of terror in her open eyes to know she was already dead.

Evidently oblivious of the Cartesian who'd come so close to attacking it, the Nosferatu had chosen to finish its meal with gusto.

With the Cartesian taken care of, Lucien knew he still had to deal with the Nosferatu. The gawking crowd had refused to disperse, and he feared that once the Original finished with the woman, it would spring lightning-fast for yet another victim.

The problem was he wasn't sure how to effectively stop the Nosferatu. Not with its ability to heal so quickly.

Instead of taking the chance of riling the Original while it fed and have it focus on the others in the crowd, Lucien took one more shot at getting the gawkers to move on.

"Get the hell out of here," Lucien shouted at them. "I can't stop this creature. And when it's done, there's a good chance it'll come after one of you. Go! For the love of God, get the hell out!"

This time, at the sound of Lucien's voice, the Nosferatu looked up from its prey and screeched a warning to Lucien. Its mouth was covered with blood, which dripped down its chin. The sight of that alone sent the men and women crowded near the end of the alley screaming and running off in different directions.

Lucien stood his ground, scabior in hand, waiting for the Nosferatu to turn on him.

Oddly enough, the Original didn't. It turned back to the woman, attached its fangs to her neck, obviously determined to drain every drop of blood from her body.

Although Lucien had managed to get rid of the Cartesian, he still felt like a failure. A woman had died because he hadn't been able to handle both the Nosferatu and Cartesian at the same time.

Knowing there was nothing he could do to permanently stop the Nosferatu without Evee's help, Lucien started to head for the docks, where he knew a dome was being built to transfer the Originals across the river to feed. He'd make sure to let Evee know of the sighting. With any luck, she'd be able to reach the Nosferatu and bring him back into her fold.

Turning away from the sickening sight and the sucking, licking sounds coming from the Nosferatu as it fed, Lucien started for the docks.

That was when he heard the wail of sirens and horns. Evidently, someone had called the police. And once again, just as he'd had to do when tackling the Loup Garous and the Nosferatu with Ronan, Lucien quickly left the site. For there was no way in hell any explanation of what truly happened would satisfy the police. They'd take him in for questioning, wasting time he didn't have to spare.

Hurrying down St. Ann to Chartres, Lucien started to feel like a pathetic loser. A wuss.

Always running. Away from love, away from himself, away from the police.

Chapter 16

Instead of going to the docks as she had initially intended to do once she left Shandor, Evee chose to detour. She turned off Dumaine, then onto Bourbon. Fury still roared through her from her confrontation with Shandor. She had to let her sisters and the Benders know about the sorcerers.

She was sure Viv was already at the North Compound, getting the cattle set up for the feeding. But Evee knew Gilly would be at Snaps, the bar-and-grill she owned off Bourbon. She counted on Gavril being with Gilly. If that proved true, then Gavril would be able to summon the other Benders, hopefully. That way everyone except Viv and Nikoli, who had to remain at the compound, would be able to huddle up at Snaps and discuss the new challenge facing them.

When Evee arrived at Snaps, she found it packed with people, even at this hour of the morning. Drunken laughter echoed off the walls of the building, and loud music pounded from the jukebox.

Evee spotted Gilly at the far end of the bar, taking an order from an already too drunk customer, as the other two barmaids hustled from one end of the bar to the other.

When Gilly saw Evee she sent her a wave, pointed to the customer in front of her, then held up a finger, signaling for her to wait.

As soon as Gilly served a Crown and Coke to the man, she rounded the corner of the counter and went over to her sister.

Gilly leaned in close to Evee's ear, obviously wanting to be heard above all the ruckus of yelling, laughing, music and talking. "I was just getting ready to leave for the docks. We're slammed tonight, and I wanted to make sure my people had a handle on this crowd."

Evee turned so her mouth was next to Gilly's ear. "I have something to tell you before we go to the docks. Where's Gavril?"

Gilly aimed a thumb over her right shoulder. "Back in my office. Guess the noise in here was getting to him."

"We need to include him in this conversation," Evee said.

"What's up?" Gilly asked, frowning.

"Can we go somewhere quieter?"

Gilly nodded, took Evee's hand and led her through the crowd, down a short hallway, past the men's and women's restrooms, to her office, which was at the end of the hall. Gilly opened the door, motioned Evee inside.

The office was basically a ten-by-twelve-foot room that held a desk and two chairs. Paperwork overflowed on a small credenza.

Gavril sat behind the desk and smiled when he spotted Evee. His smile quickly faded, however, and Evee suspected it had something to do with her expression, which probably read "urgent and ugly."

Sitting upright, Gavril asked, "What's wrong?"

"I need for you to use the watch thingy that you and your cousins wear and contact Lucien. Have him meet us here ASAP," Evee said.

"What about Nikoli?" Gavril asked.

"Nix him. I'm sure he's with Viv at the compound, and we need them there to get the cattle ready. I'll fill Viv in on the news when we get to the compound."

Instead of questioning her further, Gavril immediately punched two buttons on his watch, then looked at Evee. "Done. He should be here any minute."

From what Evee had gathered after Lucien had left his watch on the dryer at her house and she'd returned it to him, the Benders' watches contained geo nodes that emitted a signal. Whenever one of the Benders was in dire straits and needed help from the cousins, he activated the geo node. Once the signal was emitted, the Benders who received the signal were to drop whatever they were doing and go to the signaling Bender's aid.

Gilly sat in one of the chairs, swiped a hand over her face. She seemed utterly exhausted, which made Evee feel a bit guilty about bringing her more bad news.

"What's going on?" Gilly asked, then held up a hand. "Yeah, yeah, I know you want to wait until everybody gets here, so never mind. But really, Evee, with all that's going on right now, I can't take much more." She narrowed her eyes. "You didn't…you know…" Gilly threw Gavril a quick glance before turning back to Evee. "Do anything that the Elders told us to stay away from?"

"I don't have anything to do with this one," Evee said. "It just popped up, and I think it's important that we all know about it. It could be a game changer."

"Good changer?" Gavril asked.

Evee shook her head. "I wish."

"Man, oh, man, oh, crap, fuck, shit," Gilly said in one long breath. Then put her head in her hands.

"You mean like more missing Originals?" Gavril asked. "Dead ones?"

"I don't know," Evee said. "Something's come up that might very well twist us way off track."

"How's that possible when we're off track now?" Gilly asked.

Evee studied her sister's face. "We may not have solved the problem yet, but we're working hard to get a handle on it. The problem is that somebody else has suddenly got their hand on the wheel and is trying to steer."

"Who?" Gilly asked.

Before she had a chance to say more, the office door opened and Lucien hurried inside.

"What's the emergency?" Lucien asked, anxiously looking about the room.

Evee closed the door behind them.

"Why did you summon me?" Lucien asked Gavril. His eyes suddenly grew wide. "Where's Nikoli? Is he hurt? Is he okay?"

Gavril held up a hand and patted the air, signaling for Lucien to bring his anxiety down a few notches. "Nikoli is fine. I purposely didn't signal him because he and Viv, along with one of her Loup Garous, are building a dome over the ferry. It's getting closer to feeding time. I didn't want to take him away from the task. We'll fill him in on whatever news Evee has as soon as we see him."

"Evee?" Lucien looked at her questioningly.

"Evee has some news she feels we all need to hear," Gavril said. "According to her, there's company intending to join us in the troubles we're trying to work through."

"What are you talking about?" Lucien asked, still looking at Evee.

"I'd ask all of you to sit," Evee said, then held out a hand, indicating the shortage of chairs.

"We're fine standing," Lucien said. "Please, continue."

Evee nodded. "Earlier, I was headed to the docks to check on the progress of the dome when I heard someone call my name. It was Shandor Black."

"No frigging way," Gilly said.

"Yes, way. He claimed he had been looking for me. Had seen me walk the route to the ferry on many occasions."

"What?" Gilly said, her brow furrowing deeply. "You mean that son of a bitch has been stalking you?"

"Claims he suffers from insomnia and often walks the streets in and around the Quarter when he can't sleep."

Gilly bared her teeth as if she meant to attack and gnaw through the first thing in sight.

"Was that the emergency?" Lucien asked. "That you'd been followed?"

"No," Evee said. "It's what Shandor said."

Everyone remained quiet, waiting for Evee to continue.

"He claims that he heard from someone that we were having issues with the Originals," Evee said. "He knew about the human attack, the Nosferatu death, about the missing Chenilles, Nosferatu and Loup Garous. He even knew about the police going to the Elders."

"The police have been to see your Elders?" Lucien asked. "This puts a whole new twist on things. We'll have to do double time on discretion. I mean, I couldn't help what happened in the Quarter, when Pierre had to put down one of the Nosferatu, but with the police snooping around, that means we'll have to limit our exposure during the day. If we don't, I'm sure we'll be spotted by one of the witnesses, who'll wind up going to the police. They'll ask difficult questions. To the Triad and the Benders. What did the Elders tell them?"

"Nothing," Evee said, a bit put off with Lucien's pessimism, although it had reason. "When the police knock on their door, they don't answer. So nothing's been said... yet."

Lucien nodded, his lips a thin line of worry.

"Anyway," Evee said, "the bottom line of all this is that Shandor knew too much." She looked from face to face. "Did any of you tell him anything?"

"Of course not," Lucien said. "I don't even know the man."

"As if!" Gilly exclaimed, pounding a fist on the chair arm.

"I don't even know who Shandor Black is," Gavril said. "So I know it wasn't me and would bet my life that none of the Benders have said a word to anyone. We're here to help you, not spread gossip to people we don't even know."

"Who exactly is this Shandor Black?" Lucien asked.

"One of the three sorcerers who live in New Orleans," Evee said. "He's partners in a law firm with Trey Cottle, one of the other sorcerers."

"And neither of them can be trusted for shit," Gilly said. "Both of them have only done spells and incantations to serve their own needs. I've never known either of them to reach out and help anyone else."

"Who's the third sorcerer?" Lucien asked.

"Gunner Stern," Evee said. "He's not a business partner with Trey or Shandor, but he seems to hang around them pretty often, so there's a question about him there. He seems like a genuinely nice guy, and our Elders, well, at least one of them appears to trust him. But Shandor is Trey's yes-man and his right hand. And for the exact reasons Gilly just mentioned, there was no reason for Shandor to approach me. Too out of character. Claimed he wanted to help us. Join forces for the sake of the city."

"Bullshit," Gilly said.

"My words to him exactly," Evee said. "But despite Shandor, it seems we now have someone on the streets spreading rumors about us."

"Do you think it might have been the Elders?" Gilly asked.

"With the fight we had with them earlier about the sorcerers, I seriously doubt it," Evee said. "And you know Arabella. When she says she's going to think on something and then get back to us, that's exactly what she's going to do. There's no pushing a go-button with her until she's ready."

"So, I assume you haven't heard from her yet?" Gilly said.

"Right. No update."

"Me, either. Maybe it was one of the other Elders," Gilly said, then stuck her thumbnail into her mouth and chewed on it.

"You know they don't do anything without Arabella's approval. Even without that, Vanessa hates all of the sorcerers. She'd rather cut off her head than run to one for help. As for Taka, well, she's a few crayons short of a box. I just don't see her having the wherewithal to simply take to the streets and start spreading rumors. Besides, you know how fearful she is about being found out. She's probably having nightmares about being hanged, then burned at the stake."

"Then someone else has to be watching us…closely," Gilly said.

Evee shuddered at the thought.

"Just how big is the threat if the sorcerers do get involved?" Nikoli asked.

"It's a trust issue," Evee said. "There's no telling what kind of spell or incantation they'd cast. Remember, Trey and Shandor are infamous for only using their powers for their benefit. Anything that gives them more power, more control over the world of magic. It's always seemed like they were in competition with the Triad or anyone from the Circle of Sisters. They jump in, screw things up so it turns bad for us and looks good for them. I swore I saw a smirk cross Shandor's face. I wanted to spit on him. He tried to sound nonchalant, of course, even look worried, concerned about us. I didn't bite."

"We need to keep a close eye out for those guys," Gavril said. "What do they look like?"

Gilly snorted. "One looks like a pig, the other a rotting twig with glasses."

Evee couldn't help grinning at Gilly's short, but relatively accurate, description. She filled in the blanks for the Benders. "Trey's kind of short and dumpy. Balding head, gray hair wrapped around the back of his head. He wears glasses that always sit near the tip of his nose. Always wears a suit. Except for wearing a suit and glasses, Shandor is Trey's mirror opposite. Tall, lanky, thinning gray hair that he combs back, away from his forehead. And he has a thin face that holds a perpetual scowl. Both in their late sixties, early seventies. As for Gunner, he's a white-haired gentleman, late sixties, I'd guess. Pretty average in appearance, except for his eyes. They're bright blue. Average height and build. Nice face. Very different from Trey and Shandor."

"Different doesn't always mean different in a good way," Lucien said. "For all we know, this fellow, Gunner, because he's so different from the other two, might be the one finding out information and spreading rumors. If he's as different from the other two as you say, it would be easier for him to collect data. You know, nice guy, no one suspects a thing."

"Maybe we do have to look at what seems least obvious," Evee said. "Honestly, though, right now we don't have time to hammer through this. We've got a feeding to do. I just wanted to warn all of you. Give you a heads-up. It's not like it's not tough enough that some of our spells don't work, but now we've got to watch out for spies."

"But your spell did work," Lucien said. "Remember the illusion spell earlier?"

"You did an illusion spell?" Gilly asked, gawking at Evee. "Wow, I haven't seen you do one of those in years. How'd it go?"

"She saved my life," Lucien said with no hesitation. "We'd just come out of the catacombs when it seemed like the entire sky opened up with Cartesians. I tried to get Evee to go back into the catacombs, but, being who she is, she was determined to stay and help. That's when she did the illusion spell. Confusing those Cartesians was brilliance in the making. They didn't know where to aim. It gave us time to push all the ones who'd crawled through rifts back."

"You go, girl!" Gilly said, giving a little clap of congratulations.

"Just something that had to be done," Evee said. "I'm thankful it worked. Now let's get ready for the feeding. I'm sure the dome's done, since the ferry isn't that big, and Viv's probably getting the cattle ready."

Gavril put a hand on Gilly's shoulder. "Guess we'd better get our lineup ready for the Chenilles."

She nodded.

Lucien grabbed the doorknob to leave, then turned to Evee. "I know this sorcerer thing has everyone concerned. We just have to take this slow. I don't mean in speed, but slow as in being mindful of every decision we make, so it's the right one. And, of course, keep an eye peeled and look over our shoulders from time to time. Don't worry. I've got your back, and I know Nikoli has Viv's."

"And I've got Gilly's," Gavril said.

"Glad we're all up to speed," Evee said. "Hopefully things will start heading in the right direction and quick."

With that, everyone left the office single file.

Evee felt Lucien's body close behind hers as they made it into the main room and squeezed through the crowd of people. A six-foot transvestite, wearing black fishnet stockings and a shorter than short red glitter dress with accompanying four-inch red glitter heels, and one of Gilly's waitresses were walking at a furious pace. The waitress carried a tray filled with nachos smothered in cheese and jalapenos, three margaritas and two glasses of beer. Evee came to an abrupt halt to let her hurry by. Lucien pulled up short right behind her, and in that moment, a drunk sideswiped the waitress, and her tray flipped out of her hand, its contents landing all over Evee.

With a gasp, Evee stood stock-still, feeling melted cheese slide from her hair down to her cheeks, the front of her clothes. She felt like a garbage dump and smelled like a margarita gone bad.

"Oh, God, I'm so sorry!" the waitress said. "Somebody bumped into me and…please let me help. Get something to clean you up."

"I've got it, Darnelle," Gilly said, and turned to Evee.

"Is it as bad as it feels?" Evee asked.

"Worse," Gilly said. "You look like a walking disaster. I've got a clean pair of jeans and shirt in my office that I keep there for emergencies. You can use those. We wear the same size, so no problem there. No way you're going to get all that goop out of your hair in the bathroom sink, though."

"You know the Monteleone's just a block away," Lucien said. "You're welcome to shower in our room."

"Plan," Gilly said. "I'll go get the clothes. Then Gavril and me will head out to do our thing." With that, Gilly hurried off to her office.

Evee felt like an idiot, standing there with cheese and booze dripping all over her body. She refused to look at Lucien. Too many people were staring at her and laughing as it was.

Within minutes, Gilly was back with jeans and a green-striped sweater. She handed them to Evee. "Here. Go, shower."

Thinking about taking a shower in Lucien's hotel room gave Evee pause. But only for a moment as another glob of cheese dripped down from her hair and slid down the middle of her face.

Holding the clean clothes at arm's length, Evee gave Gilly a look, which she hoped her sister could read. *You know this shower thing is sending me into dangerous territory, right?*

Gilly lifted an eyebrow, and the hint of a smile played around the corners of her mouth. "Shower, then off to the docks, right?"

"Right."

"A little cheese and booze isn't so bad, considering," Gilly said. "What else could possibly go wrong between here and the hotel?"

It wasn't the distance between Snaps and the Monteleone that Evee worried about. It was the distance between her and Lucien in the hotel. She made a mental note to re-mind her bright-eyed sister to lose the words "What else could possibly go wrong?" from her vocabulary.

Evee knew all too well that many things could go wrong...and probably would.

Chapter 17

Lucien led Evee down Bourbon Street, then Royal toward the hotel. Unfortunately, she'd suffered a few catcalls along the way. A drunken jerk yelled, "Hey, lady, watch out for the big-ass birds out here! Oops, too late. One already gotcha!"

Lucien had to hold back his temper because he'd wanted so badly to punch the guy out. And anyone else who made a negative comment. He knew how embarrassed the remarks made Evee because she stayed close behind him, nearly pasted to his back, trying to stay out of sight as much as possible.

When they finally reached the hotel, Lucien went straight to the bank of elevators, placing Evee in front of him so she was sandwiched between him and the elevator door. As they waited for the elevator to ding open, Evee wrung her hands every time someone walked in or out of the lobby.

As hard as he tried to give Evee some sort of safe refuge, inevitably somebody would walk by, do a double take at her, then move on with a laugh. He couldn't blame them for staring, really. She was quite the sight. Cheese covered most of her head, and her face was smeared with it despite the many napkins she'd used to try and clean her face. Her clothes were a lost cause. Her black pants and shirt had been doused with alcohol and dribbled cheese.

Lucien kept his fingers crossed that there'd be no one else in the elevator when it opened.

Two seconds later, he found that his luck held out. The doors whispered open with not a soul inside.

He hustled Evee into the elevator, hit the button for the twelfth floor and jabbed the close button numerous times, wanting the doors to close before anyone else stepped inside.

Lucien let out a sigh of relief as the doors closed, with him and Evee the only riders. Only then did Evee take a step away from him.

"This has got to be one of the most humiliating things I've ever been through. I smell like a bar and garbage dump all mixed together," she said, and for a moment, Lucien thought she'd start crying. Instead, she lifted her chin and stared at the floor numbers illuminated one by one over the elevator door.

As the tiny cubicle began moving upward, Evee kept her eyes on the floor number lights.

"It's not so bad," Lucien said, and swiped a string of nacho cheese off her left cheek, then licked the cheese from his finger. "Doesn't taste bad, either."

Evee gave him a light punch in the arm, and the smallest of grins.

He smiled softly, and held the clothes Gilly had given Evee to change into closer to his chest. The conversation about the sorcerers in Gilly's office played over in his mind, but, for some reason, it didn't concern him as much as it seemed to bother the Triad. Of course, he didn't know the sorcerers as well as they did, so his radar on the matter could be way off. Right now his thoughts were on Evee. How close she was to him, no matter the cheese and booze. The thought of Ronan tumbled across his mind, causing Lucien to remember how enamored Ronan had been with her. It saddened him that Ronan would never experience the dinner date he'd made with Evee.

Fate had taken Ronan out of Evee's life. And although guilt over Ronan pressed against his heart, he had a choice to make. Either mourn what might have or could have been between Ronan and Evee or wait for fate to deal a double hand. His last choice was to make certain this woman would always be by his side, safe, protected… loved. A word that felt strange to Lucien even when he thought about it. He'd never uttered the L word to any woman before, and although he'd yet to say it to Evee, there was no denying that somehow, in the midst of all they'd gone and were still going through, he'd managed to fall in love with her.

As the elevator took its time making its way to the twelfth floor, he noticed that Evee had her fingers of both hands crossed at her sides. He guessed that she was hoping that the elevator wouldn't stop on another floor before it made it to the twelfth.

To break the silence, Lucien asked, "You really think those sorcerers are a threat to us?"

"I do. Just don't know how big. I don't know what their agenda is, but I know that two of them for sure are trouble."

"The Trey and Shandor duo?"

"Yeah."

The elevator finally bounced to a stop, and the doors swished open. Lucien stuck his head out to check for people and gave Evee a thumbs-up, indicating the coast was clear.

Evee grabbed on to the back of Lucien's shirt and clung tight as they left the elevator, hung a right in the hallway, then all but ran fifty feet before Lucien came to a stop. He dug into his back pants pocket, pulled out a key card, then stuck it into the appropriate door slot and pushed the door open. He hoped the maids had already taken care of business for the day. Not that he and his cousins were slobs, but Gavril had been the last to use the shower, which usually meant towels strewn all over the floor and toothpaste spit in the sink.

Lucien breathed a sigh of relief when he walked in and saw the beds neatly made, and everything smelled lemony fresh and dust-free.

He pointed to a room on the left. "Bathroom's right in there. Help yourself."

"Thanks," Evee said, then grabbed the clothes out of his hands and hurried off to the bathroom, closing the door behind her.

Half expecting it, Lucien thought it a bit odd when he didn't hear the lock click on the bathroom door.

Not knowing what else to do with himself, he walked over to one of the beds and sat on the edge of it. He ran his fingers through his hair, hearing the sound of water now coming from the bathroom. The sound made him fidget. He wasn't sure what all the sorcerer information really meant, but if Evee considered them worrisome, then he'd trust her judgment. Enough to see them as another part of an equation, which only meant more trouble. The last thing they needed.

Growing more restless by the second, Lucien got off

the bed and went into the sitting area of the suite. He picked up a magazine that highlighted the have-to-see locations in New Orleans, then sat on the couch and flipped through the magazine, not paying attention to any of the pictures or articles. He couldn't stop thinking about Evee in the next room.

He imagined her in the shower, wanted more than anything to be in there with her. Touch her, hold her, reassure her. He just needed to be near her; cheese or no cheese, booze or no booze, it made no difference to him. Beneath it all was the essence of Evee, and that always filled him with need and desire. It made his heart grow so huge it felt like it wanted to burst from his chest.

Lucien continued to flip through the magazine. First forward, then backward, still not seeing a damn thing on its pages.

Suddenly, unexpectedly, Lucien heard Evee call out to him.

"Lucien, do you have any shampoo? I don't see any in here."

He jumped to his feet, went to his travel bag and grabbed the shampoo he normally carried with him when traveling. Hotels rarely handed out enough shampoo and cream rinse to handle four grown men sharing a suite.

Lucien stepped up to the bathroom door and said loudly, "I have some here. Do you want me to leave it outside the bathroom door?"

A moment of silence followed before Evee said. "The bathroom's pretty big and cold. Is there a way you could, like, bring it in here?"

Surprised with her answer and confused by the hesitation in her voice, he asked, "Do you have the shower curtain closed?"

"Of course I do," she said.

He waited a beat, then said, "Do you want me to bring it to you?"

A hesitant moment passed before Evee said tentatively, "If you don't mind, you can just sort of stick your hand around the curtain and hand it to me."

"Sure," Lucien said, then wondered who in the hell had taken over his body and mind. Like it would be no big deal for him to be but a curtain's distance away from her, hand out shampoo, then leave. Sure, no problem.

Biting the inside of his cheek, Lucien opened the bathroom door. The room was filled with steam.

Obviously hearing the door open, Evee said, "I tried using soap, but it didn't work. Now my hair's caked with clumpy soap and cheese goo."

"I'm sure the shampoo will help," Lucien said. He pushed the bottle around the edge of the shower curtain. "Here you go."

Lucien saw her silhouette move in the shower, behind the white, translucent shower curtain. Seeing the outline of her naked body took his breath away.

She took the shampoo bottle from him, and in the translucent glory he'd found as his window, Lucien saw her bring the bottle up to her nose.

"Smells good. Thank you."

Not wanting to leave, Lucien tried to think of something, anything to say so she wouldn't send him immediately away.

"Glad you like the shampoo," he said, and wanted to slap himself for how ridiculous he sounded. Now all he could do was follow up the asinine statement with more stupidity. "I usually carry that brand with me whenever we travel. Can't ever have too much shampoo when you're traveling with three other guys."

"I'm sure," she said absently, and Lucien saw the silhouette of her tilting the shampoo bottle into her hand, then leaning over and placing the bottle on the side of the tub. The sight of her heart-shaped ass became clearer as it moved closer to the shower curtain, and Lucien thought he'd have a heart attack. He stifled a groan.

He watched arm shadows move to her head, hands folding up shoulder-length hair, scrubbing, scrubbing.

"Are you still in here?" Evee suddenly asked.

"Oh…uh, yes, sorry. I'll leave you to your shower."

"Wait. Before you go, could I bother you for a comb? I don't think I'm getting all the cheese out. Combing it out might help. I promise to clean the comb when I'm done."

"No problem," Lucien said, then reached for his comb, which happened to be sitting on the counter near the bathroom sink.

With comb in hand, Lucien slipped it around the edge of the shower curtain. "Here you go. Hope it helps."

He saw the shadow of her hand reaching blindly for the comb.

"Sorry. I've got shampoo in my eyes. Can't quite make out where your hand is."

Lucien stretched his arm in farther. She finally latched on to his hand.

"Got it," she said, probably more to herself than to him.

Figuring he'd either go into the living area of the suite and die a slow death or take a chance while he had it and remain by the shower.

"Do you need any help in there?" Lucien asked. "Do you want me to check your hair? Make sure all the cheese is out?"

"Do you have any cream rinse?" Evee asked, evidently avoiding his indirect lead.

"I think so," Lucien said. Reluctantly, he turned to the

vanity and checked the small hotel bottles neatly lined up on a narrow silver tray. He found one labeled conditioner and grabbed it.

He stuck his hand with the conditioner back behind the shower curtain. "Here you go. It's the hotel's brand. Sorry I don't have anything better."

"Thanks," Evee said. "Trying to get this comb through my mop of hair without conditioner is hell." Once again her hand reached blindly for his. As her hand wandered along the shower curtain, it pushed the curtain aside a bit more. Lucien stood transfixed, seeing her naked body standing before him, her eyes closed, her hand searching. He aimed the bottle of conditioner at her hand, and she grabbed it.

Out of respect, Lucien backed away, allowing himself only a shadow's view once more. He watched her bathe her hair with conditioner, work it through with her fingers, then lean over again for the comb she'd placed on the edge of the tub. As soon as she touched it, the comb fell into the tub.

"Shit," she said softly.

Reflexively, Lucien reached into the shower. "I'll get it." He didn't think about what he'd just done until he looked up and saw her looking down at him.

They stared at each other for a long moment, neither uttering a word. Water still pelting her body.

Lucien silently handed her the comb.

Evee took it from him, her eyes never leaving his face. He saw her lips move, heard her whisper his name. Fire seemed to melt the copper color of her beautiful eyes. Need was written in the expression on her face. He allowed his eyes to move slowly, blatantly down her body. Watching water splash over her breasts, her stomach, her thighs…between her thighs.

Determined not to give it a second thought, Lucien took a step back from the shower and removed his clothes in record time.

Before either of them had a chance to say a word, Lucien stepped into the shower, picked up the bar of soap that sat at the bottom of the tub, and rubbed it between his hands. When his hands were completely lathered, he dropped the soap, put his hands on Evee's naked shoulders and turned her so she faced the shower wall.

She moved without hesitation, and Lucien began to caress her shoulders and back with his soapy hands. He worked down to her buttocks, taking his time, moving his fingers over and in every private part of her. He heard her groan with desire, which only flared his need to white-hot.

Lucien lathered his hands again and began to work his fingers down her legs, reached her right ankle, then moved to the left and worked his way back up, his fingers kneading, fluttering over her. When he reached the top of her thigh, Lucien pressed against both of her thighs ever so gently, and Evee immediately placed her hands on the back shower wall, threw her head back, and spread her legs slightly. Enough for Lucien's fingers to work their way between them.

He brushed his fingers lightly between her legs, barely touching the mound that emitted so much heat even in the shower that it sent a shiver of pleasure through Lucien's own body. As his fingers slid across the slit of her heat, Lucien knelt in the midst of the shower spray and placed his lips on her beautiful, heart-shaped ass. He kissed and licked one cheek, then the other, nipping occasionally, which caused her to moan.

When he press a finger inside her, only a knuckle's depth, she called his name.

"Lucien…yes, more!"

Her body began to shake, and once again, Lucien was amazed at how responsive she was to his touch.

He slowly moved one hand around her waist so it rested between her legs only from the front. Then in one fell swoop, Lucien ran the finger he'd been teasing her with from behind deep inside her, captured her clitoris between the thumb and forefinger of the hand now in front of her, then nipped one cheek of her ass.

Evee cried out, and shuddered, and as she shook with the force of her orgasm, he bit down harder. The bite seemed to hit a reset button in her body, because Evee screamed his name and rode his fingers like her life depended on it.

As the waves of her pleasure began to wane, Lucien gently ran his hands over her ass, especially over the bite mark he'd placed there.

He heard her breathing, still labored, her head now down, hair hanging like black curtains along the sides of her face. Lucien grabbed the soap once more, lathered his hands, then stood.

He stood and turned Evee so she faced him. The look in her eyes lay softly on his face, and he brushed the hair away from her cheeks with a finger.

Looking her in the eye, Lucien moved his lathered hands over her breasts, taking her nipples between his thumbs and forefingers, squeezing gently, pulling gently. Evee's eyes closed and she moaned loudly, always a signal for Lucien.

With no further preamble, Lucien grabbed her around the waist and lifted her. Evee's legs automatically wrapped around his waist. Moving his hands to her ass, holding her in place, Lucien pressed the hard length of him into the swollen, open, ready and eager mouth between her legs.

Throwing her head back, Evee, groaned. "More, God, Lucien, more!"

Lucien gave her what she craved. He thrust the full length of his manhood into her body, holding her up and thrusting her forward, matching his every thrust. He lowered his head to her right breast, put her nipple in his mouth, ran his tongue around its stiffness, then bit down ever so gently.

Once more the bite seemed to trigger an inner animal that hid within Evee, for she grabbed handfuls of his hair, urging him to move harder, faster within her.

Lucien didn't hesitate to oblige. He lowered his head, bit his bottom lip to control the explosion teetering within his body.

"Yes! Yes!" Evee cried, and hot lava soon bathed him. Lucien felt it overflow from her, sending warm rivulets down his own legs.

"All of it," Lucien demanded. "Give me all of it… now."

With a wail of pleasure, Evee's body bucked again, and more flowed from her body. Only then did Lucien allow himself to let go, and the force of his orgasm was so powerful Lucien felt his legs weaken. He fought to stay upright, still holding Evee up and against him.

When they were both spent, Lucien lowered Evee slowly, carefully to her feet, still holding her close to him. She rested her head against his chest, and he cupped the back of her head, pressing her in closer.

They stood there, holding tight to each other, so many emotions flooding Lucien that he couldn't name them all. He kissed the top of her head. Kissed it again.

Evee lifted her head, brought her hands to the sides of

his face and drew his lips to hers. It took seconds before the kiss became as ravishing as the sex they'd just had.

Knowing they had responsibilities to tend to, Lucien reluctantly took her face in his hands and moved it a micro inch away. He kissed her cheek, her chin, nuzzled her neck. Then he simply held her, feeling the heat of the shower beating into his back for a moment longer. He'd never felt such satisfaction or any of the other rumble of emotions inside him with any other woman. He'd always—always been able to walk away without regret.

But this time—this time, Lucien feared this was one woman he'd never be able to walk away from...ever.

Chapter 18

Arabella paced the length of her foyer, waiting, waiting. Vanessa stood nearby, at the bottom landing of the stairs, holding on to a newel post, tapping a slippered foot against the floor.

"Where could she have gone?" Arabella asked Vanessa.

"Maybe somebody kidnapped her," Vanessa said.

"Stop talking like that," Arabella said.

Vanessa tsked. "You're right. We wouldn't be that lucky anyway. The kidnapper would bring her back."

Arabella shot her an angry look, then glanced over at the old grandfather clock ticking at the end of the foyer.

"She's never gone out this late before," Arabella said.

"Well, we are talking about Taka. Something doesn't have to make sense for her to do it. We both know she's a little loose in the goose," Vanessa said. "For all we know, she might have simply gotten bored and gone for a walk through the District. You know how she loves to make new friends."

"At three in the morning?" Arabella said. "I don't think so."

Arabella shook her head and paced the foyer again.

Suddenly a noise that sounded like a creaky hinge echoed from the back of the house, near the kitchen.

Arabella froze, listening intently, and heard the unmistakable sound of a door gently closing. She took off for the kitchen.

"What is it?" Vanessa asked.

"Can't you hear the back door?" Arabella said. "I just heard it close."

"Well, that little sneak," Vanessa said.

"We don't know that it's her," Arabella said. "Somebody could be breaking into the house."

"Oh, for the love of earth, get a hold of yourself. It has to be Taka. She's the only one besides us with a key. We'd have heard glass shattering. A window breaking, and remember, the door doesn't have a window. The only windows are over the kitchen sink. So, see? It has to be Taka."

Arabella and Vanessa took off, nearly colliding into each other as they turned the corner into the kitchen. Both came to a sliding stop as the kitchen lights flickered on.

There stood Taka, right inside the back door, her eyes deer-in-the-headlights wide. "Oh…hey. What are you two doing up?"

Arabella put a hand on her hip, felt a huge flood of relief flow through her. "Where have you been?"

"No," Vanessa said. "Where the hell have you been? Do you have any idea what time it is?"

"I couldn't sleep," Taka said. "So I went for a walk."

"At this hour, in this city?" Arabella said. "Are you crazy? You could have been murdered or kidnapped."

"Oh, I wasn't worried about that one bit," Taka said, patting the patent leather purse she had clutched to her chest. "I took Mace. Got it right here, in my purse."

Vanessa snorted. "By the time you'd have dug through all the junk you keep in there, anybody could have hauled you over a shoulder and shoved you into a van before you managed one squirt. Think about it. You could be on your way to Missouri right now and not even know it."

Taka rolled her eyes. "Really, so melodramatic. I went for a walk. That's it."

Arabella pointed to the kitchen table. "Sit."

Sighing, Taka did as she was told.

When they were all seated around the table, Arabella jabbed the tabletop with a finger. "We deserve an explanation," she said to Taka. "You had us worried sick. You didn't put on a pantsuit to stroll the District. And you never do that alone. We always go together."

Vanessa nodded. "Safety in numbers."

"I've already told you," Taka insisted. "I couldn't sleep and needed some air."

"And I can tell you're lying," Arabella said, leaning back in her chair.

Taka blinked at her. "What do you mean you can tell?"

"When you lie, your left eye twitches," Vanessa said. "And right now it's twitching to beat the band."

Taka glanced over at Arabella. "What band is she talking about? I didn't see any band out there."

"Oh, quit acting like you're innocent," Vanessa said. "You know that your left eye twitches when you lie. Stop acting like you're senile or trying to make us think you're stupid, because you're not."

Taka huffed and hugged her purse closer to her chest.

"Neither of you are my parents or guardians. I'm quite old enough to choose when I want to go out and take a walk outside or not."

"Not in this city, especially with all that's been going on lately," Arabella said. "That was a stupid move, Taka. You could've been seriously hurt out there. So I want the truth now. What did you do?"

"Walked," Taka said.

Arabella sighed. "Where?"

"Through the District."

"And?" Vanessa asked.

Taka looked down at the table. "And then I sorta found myself down on Canal."

"Oh, mother of marbles. Canal Street!" Vanessa slapped a hand against her forehead. "All right, it's official. You *are* senile! Nobody but the homeless roam that street at this hour."

"Not true," Taka said. "Had a great time people-watching."

"How long were you out there?" Arabella asked.

"What's it matter? I'm back."

"Because we've been so damn worried about you all night, all right?" Vanessa said.

"Baloney," Taka said. "I wasn't out there all night."

"You two stop bickering," Arabella demanded, then studied Taka. "I woke up about half an hour ago from a bad dream. I got up and checked on Vanessa, then looked in on you, saw you were gone. So I woke up Vanessa, and we've been pacing the floor ever since, sick with worry. Now you're telling us you were out on Canal Street."

Arabella gave Taka a stern look. "Walking out there this late is bad enough, but why do I get the feeling that there's more to this than you're letting on?"

Taka pursed her lips and looked nonchalantly around the kitchen.

"Taka Burnside, you either spill everything or else," Arabella said.

"Or else what?" Taka asked, a defiant tone to her voice. "What're you going to do? Put me over your knee and spank me like I was a kid?"

"Don't be ridiculous," Vanessa said. "I'd be the one to do that."

Arabella shot Vanessa a warning look to shut up.

"Taka," Arabella said, as calmly as she could, "as Elders, we have a responsibility to take care of the Triad and the Originals they care for. We also have a responsibility to each other. Which means no lies between us. Whatever it is you did, wherever it is you went, we'll figure it out. And if anything happened, we'll figure out a way to fix it."

"Nothing happened," Taka insisted.

"Then why won't you tell us where you went and what you did?"

"I already did."

Letting out a loud sigh of frustration, Arabella leaned farther into the table. "Okay, you want to play this game? Where on Canal did you stop? Did you happen to go into any shops or buildings when you were done there?"

Taka looked away, a sure sign she was hiding something. "I might have made a stop along Canal," she admitted, still not looking Arabella in the eye.

Arabella let a moment of silence pass before she finally said, "Just spit it out, Taka."

Taka let out a loud breath of frustration, slammed her purse down on the table and placed her hands on top of it. "Okay...okay. I went to Trey Cottle's apartment."

Arabella and Vanessa let out a collective gasp.

"Lights were out in the apartment windows above his office, so I threw a rock against one. You know, like they do in the movies. Just meant to tap it, hoping the noise would wake him up. Only I must've thrown too hard because the window broke. It woke him up, though."

"You did what?" Arabella asked in disbelief.

"Why—" Vanessa said, then seemed to lose whatever else she meant to say.

"I wanted to find out where Gunner Stern lived," Taka said.

"Why on earth would you do that?" Arabella asked.

Taka looked at her with a dumbstruck expression. "You were the one who was always saying that Gunner might be able to help us. That you sort of trusted him." Her voice grew stronger, angrier. "We've been sitting around here with our fingers up our butts while everything's being destroyed around us. I thought you had a good idea about getting Gunner involved, and I wanted to act on it right away. The only problem was I didn't know where he lived. Trey's address was all I had to work with, since he lives above his law office."

"You broke his window?" Arabella said, mostly to herself.

"I didn't mean to break it," Taka said. "I'd planned on knocking on the door. The problem was the door to his apartment is up a flight of stairs down a short alleyway behind the law office. And the alleyway was closed off by a locked wrought-iron fence. That's when I thought of the rocks."

"Sweet Mother Earth," Vanessa said, slapping her hands over her face.

"What the hell were you thinking?" Arabella asked.

"Well, I figured if I could get Trey's attention, he would certainly know where Gunner lived. Once I had the address, I planned to go and talk to him about what's been going on, just like you suggested earlier, Arabella. This wasn't something I just pulled out of thin air. We've been talking and talking about this. I figured it was time to act on it. No disrespect, Arabella, but you always seem scared to do anything outside of the box. So I sorta took things into my own hands."

Arabella and Vanessa sat gaping at her, speechless.

Taka soon filled the void of silence. "Anyway, it wasn't so bad. Trey invited me inside, gave me Gunner's phone number and let me use his home office in private to call him."

Now it was Arabella's turn to slide her hands down her face, while Vanessa looked at Taka agape.

"You went into Trey's apartment?" Arabella asked.

"Yeah, I just told you that. Trey told me Gunner lived out by the Causeway, which was too far for me to walk, and I'd forgotten to bring money with me. Didn't think I'd need any. Anyway, Trey was the one who suggested I call Gunner if I really needed to speak to him that badly."

"You were in Trey Cottle's apartment...?" Vanessa said incredulously.

"Are you deaf?" Taka asked Vanessa. "I've already told the two of you a hundred times that I went there."

"You're an idiot, no question," Vanessa said.

"Oh, bite me," Taka said.

Arabella held up a finger, signaling for them to stop the quipping. "What happened while you were there?" she asked Taka.

"Had no problems at all...well, sort of. I didn't get Trey involved because I know how everyone hates him. He led me to his office, closed the door, and I waited to make sure I couldn't hear his footsteps anymore before I called Gunner."

"What did Gunner say?" Arabella asked.

"Told me not to go to Trey's anymore. Said not to talk about anything more over the phone, after I said we really needed to talk to him. Needed his help. He said he'd meet me at Bon Appétit Café to discuss anything we needed his help with."

"For the love of the elements," Arabella said. "Gunner tells you to meet him at Evee's café and you come back here?"

Taka shrugged. "Since the Causeway is some distance away, I figured I had time to come back here and fill you in so we could all meet with him."

"Then why the hell did you take so long playing word games with us?" Vanessa demanded. "Gunner does have a car, and if you asked for his help, I'm sure he jumped right into it and is probably waiting at the café for us now."

In the midst of Taka's news, Arabella found herself simply staring at the Elder. How could she have been so out of line? Taking it upon herself to track down a sorcerer without the consent or approval of her and Vanessa? That was so unlike Taka it boggled Arabella's mind.

Suddenly a cold chill of intuition ran down Arabella's spine. "Are you sure Trey didn't hear your conversation with Gunner?" she asked.

"I told you, I waited until I couldn't hear his footsteps walking down the hallway before I even called Gunner," Taka said. "Trey didn't hear anything. Couldn't have."

"Did you happen to notice if he had a second phone anywhere in the apartment when you went inside?" Arabella asked, suspecting the worst.

"I didn't see one," Taka said. "Why?"

"If someone has a phone in their home office, where they're not always located in their apartment, chances are there's another phone in the house. The living room or the kitchen maybe."

"Okay, so?" Taka said, looking at Arabella quizzically.

"If he has a second phone, and I'd bet my broom on it that he does, chances are that he was listening to your conversation with Gunner on the other line. Probably heard everything you said to him."

Taka frowned. "But I didn't hear anything but Gunner's voice on the phone. If Trey had picked up another line, wouldn't I have heard a click or at least heard him breathing?"

"Trey's slicker than oil on wet grass," Vanessa said. "And you're forgetting that he's a sorcerer. He could easily have muted any sound he made to make sure you didn't hear it. Basically, you just stuck your foot in the lion's den. No, make that all of our feet in the lion's den."

"You don't know that for sure," Taka said. "Besides, Gunner said he'd be glad to help any way he could. So despite what Trey did or didn't do, my vote is that we go over to Bon Appétit and see if Gunner's there. Find out what he may have to offer in order to help us."

"We may never know what he has to offer, because I guarantee you," Arabella said, "if you used a phone in Trey Cottle's apartment, he was listening to your conversation. He'll probably put a stop to Gunner showing up at the café."

"You screwed up big time, Taka," Vanessa said. "And we're in enough trouble as it is. We can't control what we have going on right now, and you've just turned up the heat a thousand degrees. And that fire is right under our feet. Now what are we supposed to do?"

"I don't think Trey can stop Gunner from helping if he really wants to," Taka said. "Gunner sounded really worried over the phone. I'm sure he'll show up and offer his support. I'm counting on it because you said you trusted him, Arabella, and that he was a nice guy."

"I also said that I needed time to think on it before we made a move."

"But you were taking too long," Taka said. "Something had to be done right away. So many Originals missing. We could lose more. Maybe even the Triad. I was only trying to help."

"I understand that," Arabella said. "But you can't just take things of such magnitude onto yourself. The three of us have to be in full agreement and understand what we're getting ourselves involved in."

"And because of your stupidity," Vanessa told Taka, "there's a good chance Trey Cottle has got his nose right in the middle of it all. He never has anything going on around him that he isn't aware of. That egomaniac has snitches around every corner."

"So why don't we just go talk to Gunner and let him know what's going on?" Taka said. "Even let him know we suspect that Trey may have overheard the conversation."

Vanessa shook her head. "Don't you get it, oh brainless one? If Trey overheard your conversation with Gunner, chances are high that he's going to be snooping around the café to overhear our conversation."

"I don't know about you," Arabella said to Taka, "but I don't have keys to Evee's café. Do you?"

Taka chewed her upper lip for a second. "No. I figured I'd meet Gunner in front of the café and talk to him there."

Vanessa groaned. "What were you thinking? Talking to Gunner out in the open? We might as well call Trey up and have him come right over and join in the party."

Arabella's frown deepened and she shook her head. "Oh, Taka, what were you thinking?"

Taka began to tear up. "But…but I was only trying to help."

"And I said I was going to take some time to think about it," Arabella said. "You blatantly went against my orders."

"Yeah, yeah, I know," Taka said, looking forlorn.

"Arabella may take some time to think things through," Vanessa said, "but once she has, her advice is always sound. You take off on your own, and you've completely tilted this wagon over, and now shit will spill out all the way down the street to Cottle."

"You've got to get this in your head, Taka," Arabella said. "Trey Cottle is not to be trusted in any way. If he finds out what's going on with us, he's going to take advantage of us in a time of weakness and make our lives more miserable than they are now. You know how he's always had his nose stuck in the Triad's business. Sneaking around, watching everything they did. Not out of curiosity's sake. It almost felt like he was trying to learn something from them."

"Why would he do that?" Taka asked.

"Because he's a damn sorcerer," Vanessa said. "And he has his own agenda. Most sorcerers feel they're above witches anyway. Trey's never wanted anything to do with witches, yet he keeps an eye on the Triad. The only reason I can figure he'd do that is to learn more spells."

Taka nodded. "I know the sorcerers have always felt they were above us."

"Then why did you go to him?" Vanessa said. "Why on earth did you go to Trey Cottle's?"

"I've already answered that a dozen times," Taka said. "Have you ever considered getting a hearing aid? You might need one. Now I'm going to bed. I'm extremely tired. I've done my good deed for the day. If you two don't want to meet Gunner, then I'd suggest calling him, so the poor man won't be standing out by the café wondering what the hell has happened to us."

"Do you still have Gunner's phone number?" Arabella asked.

Taka nodded, dug into her purse and pulled out the piece of paper Trey had given her with Gunner's number on it.

Arabella took the paper from her and got up from the table. "I'll give him a call now. Try to straighten this out."

"What if he's already at the café?" Taka asked.

Shoulders slumping, Arabella said, "If he doesn't answer the phone, then I'll have little choice but to go to the café. But I won't discuss anything with him there. I'll set up another place and time to meet. I only hope this ridiculous faux pas doesn't cause him to get angry with us. Then he might refuse to help."

"No way he'd get mad at you," Taka said. "He's sweet on you."

"That's true," Vanessa agreed.

"Why is it so hard for you to admit?" Taka said. "I think it's cute."

"He is not, so stop saying it," Arabella insisted.

"The fact that you won't admit it doesn't make it not so," Vanessa said.

"Right," Taka said. "At our age, you can't just throw that kind of man interest away."

Arabella scowled. "You march yourself on up to bed. I don't want you out of this house again until morning. I'll get in touch with Gunner one way or the other. Set up a meeting for tomorrow, at a more decent time and place. Maybe. I'm still not sure about getting any of the sorcerers involved."

"Why won't you give Gunner a chance to help?" Taka asked.

Arabella blew out an exasperated breath. "When I talk to him or see him and feel he has something legitimate to offer, I'll consider it. Until then, keep your behind in your bedroom. If I have to put a lock on the outside of your door, I will."

Taka lowered her head, trying to hide a look of disappointment, which Arabella caught.

"And one more thing, Ms. Taka Burnside, don't you ever leave this house like that again without letting us know. You could've gotten killed out there."

Vanessa snorted. "Killed? You might as well chalk her up for it. Because if Trey Cottle is involved with this in anyway, we might as well be dead."

"That's not true!" Taka said loudly, then looked at Arabella. "Is it?"

Arabella gave her a weary look. "I have no idea. All I can say is that you've really done it this time, Taka. You've put all three of us, the Triad and the Originals in more danger than you know. Trey is a force to be reckoned with, and I don't know if we have the wherewithal to deal with everything that sorcerer might decide to dish out."

Chapter 19

Something inside his chest pounded so hard he thought it was going to explode from his body at any moment. He didn't know if he had a heart, but that was what he associated the sensation with.

Everything was building up to such heights that he had to force himself to calm down.

He sent a legion of Cartesians, which were always at his side, away for a moment so that he'd have time to establish a direct plan.

He didn't want any mistakes.

Nothing going off half-cocked.

Everything was nearing a conclusion, and he had to make sure it went as smoothly as possible.

No mistakes. He had to get it right, if this was going to work.

He'd never used pen or paper before because he'd never had a need for them, as he kept mental notes. His memory held on to every form of minutia. Everything that had happened to him since it all began centuries ago. He made a checklist in his mind, which seemed apropos, for he knew how to check ideas off mentally, without missing one. Not even the nuance of one.

He planned on killing off the rest of the Originals very soon. Possibly as soon as tomorrow. From there, his ultimate goal would begin. He'd take the Originals, and before the Triad even had a moment to mourn their loss, he'd grab them, as well.

The Triad carried the most power in the city, which was why he craved them so. Third on his list were the Elders. Although they recently seemed to have become ineffective as witches, much less Elders, he believed they still had some measure of power despite their advancing years, because they were in charge of the Triad. Not only were they responsible for the Triad but they kept control over the entire clan of the Circle of Sisters as well. That had to count for something. Certainly, with that much responsibility, regardless of age, had to come great power.

Once the Originals, Triads and Elders were taken care of, he intended to sweep the city for all netherworld creatures—the vampires and werewolves, fae, leprechauns, anything that claimed a stake in the netherworld.

And then would come the humans, in order of power. Out with the voodoo priests and priestesses, for what minuscule powers they possessed. Then he'd go for the humans who controlled other humans. Not that they possessed supernatural powers of any kind, but their control and power over other humans carried its own weight.

The mayor of the city of New Orleans was definitely on his list. Then the police chief of every district in the city. He'd have his Cartesians destroy them all. Every councilman, judge, police officer, everyone in pecking order of power, all the way down to the principals of schools.

Then his plan was to take the rest of the population by economic order. The richest, the rich, the heads of companies, down to the blue-collar worker, housewives. Then, of course, the children.

He'd leave the city barren. Cleaned of all netherworld and human debris before he sent thousands of his Cartesians to reinhabit the city and restructure it to his specifications. New Orleans would be his flagship, then all other cities around the world part of his fleet.

Once he had proven what his army was capable of under his command, which he considered far beyond genius, all else would easily unfold.

After conquering this city, he'd no longer have to take baby steps. He'd race from city to city, country to country, as he had done for the past few decades, striking a clan of vampires in New Zealand, a horde of werewolves in New York City. Only this time, he'd have thousands more Cartesians at his disposal, and his own powers would be infinite.

As quickly as he planned to move, he wanted to save the very top of the human heap for last. A coup de grâce, so to speak.

He'd finish off the United States first, of course, for in and of itself, the country carried great power. His next directive would send his Cartesians to Washington, DC. First the netherworld creatures that inhabited the city, and then, of course, for any additional boost of power, he'd send them directly to the president of the US. Followed by the vice president, all of congress, the senate, even NASA. Every source of power that held up and led the entire country.

Once these entities were destroyed, he anticipated the

entire world to go into shock. Country after country, and all the powers who controlled them, would be shaking in their boots. Never having heard of such an enemy. And even better, not knowing how to destroy it.

He knew if he kept his wits about him, he'd soon be moving onto England, Japan, then country to country, continent to continent. All of it. Everything. Until he stood supreme.

And from the looks of things, he was well on his way to great success. Who would've thought it would come so easily?

A couple weeks ago, it had taken only one of the Triads to utter a handful of words to begin their demise. The oldest Triad, Vivienne François, in a moment of weakness, had made claim to her Originals that she'd quit. No longer wanted anything to do with them. Although those words might have been spoken in anger or frustration, it didn't matter. The words had been uttered, sent out into the universe and had called his name.

He'd heard it quite clearly, and sent his Cartesians racing in her direction before they lost compass of her. Wherever that Triad was, so were her Originals.

Prior to that, they had seemingly searched for the Originals, as well as the Triad, for what felt like forever. Then in one swoop of good fortune, the Triad had uttered her words of denying her brood, which opened the door for him so widely it allowed him to pursue his ultimate dreams.

Words indeed were powerful things. The Triad had simply been too naive to realize just how powerful. Now all was in his favor.

As much as he hungered to accomplish his goal, he couldn't help feeling a twinge of understanding for the wayward Triad. It had to be difficult, keeping track of the Originals day after day. Feeding them, maintaining them under the radar of the humans. It most certainly was a full-time job. It didn't allow them lives of their own.

Now that he thought about it, wasn't that in fact his case? He had spent centuries going after the subspecies, attacking wherever and whenever he could find them, gaining power so he might grow more Cartesians. His dream had always been to find the Originals and Triad, so wasn't his world, his so-called life, just as singular and linear as the Triad?

Their job was to protect, his was to destroy. Same singular lifestyle, only serving different purposes.

For now, while the Triad and their rogue companions, the Benders, attempted to protect the Originals they still had in their possession, he'd made sure to throw chaos their way to keep the ball in his court. In the meantime—and without the Triad's knowledge, he suspected—he'd had his Cartesians picking off subspecies in the city as often as possible.

He needed whatever power he could get right now. His army now counted well into the thousands, but to accomplish his ultimate goal of world and universal domination, it would take an army of millions.

Each netherworld creature gave him the power to create one new Cartesian. But an Original, the ones his Cartesians had tasted in what the Triad called the North Compound a couple of weeks ago, had allowed him to create a hundred in an instant. How could anyone blame him for wanting them all? They would produce an army beyond any number he might hope for.

And promised a far, far greater reward.

Chapter 20

Leaving the Hotel Monteleone in the clothes Gilly had lent her, Evee headed for the docks.

It was past time to get the family's ferry ready to cross her Nosferatu and Gilly's Chenilles over to the North Compound for the feeding. She imagined her sister Viv, pacing and cursing, wondering where the hell they were. On a regular day, her Nosferatu would already be in the compound by now.

But for the last hour, she'd been otherwise detained. Fully and completely and happily detained.

Although Evee and Viv had both been warned by the Elders to stay away from the Benders, Evee had been unable to do that with Lucien. She'd known from the get-go that going to his hotel room to shower was tempting fate. Asking him for shampoo, then instead of allowing him to place it outside the bathroom door for her to fetch, she'd all but coaxed him inside. She'd acted like a wounded female, not wanting to step out of the shower and face the cold. For Pete's sake, how pathetic.

The last person she had any nerve to lie to was herself. She'd wanted him to come into the bathroom, wanted him inside the shower with her...wanted him inside her. The Elders' warning had been the furthest thing from her mind. She was determined to hold on to her concrete belief that the curse attached to all Triads had been literal. They weren't to marry or live intimately with a human. She'd done neither. So what the hell?

It had been difficult leaving Lucien. She'd felt like a pool of melted butter, unable and unwilling to solidify to anything reasonably worthwhile. Evee had never felt so satiated, so...so complete. And, if truth be told, she needed, wanted more. In a way, it frightened her because she didn't think she'd ever have enough of Lucien.

Forced to bend to obligation, Evee walked toward the dock to ready the family ferry to cross the river to Algiers, where the cattle were kept at the North Compound. The compound was the standard feeding area, and the feeding order had been established for years.

Viv had three ranch hands, Charlie Zerangue, Bootstrap and Kale. Their primary job was to keep the front forty acres filled with cattle, sheep, pigs, etc., then send a designated number of animals down a chute that led them past the ranch to the feeding area, which had always been off-limits to the ranchers. As far as she knew, from what Viv had told her and Gilly, not once had the ranch hands ever asked about why the animals were sent through the chutes nightly but never returned. They simply did what they were told. Such a rarity in today's world.

Once the cattle were in place, the Nosferatu were sent in to feed first, since they drained the animals of blood. Once they had their fill, they were ferried back to the city, and then Viv allowed her Loup Garous in, to feed on the meat. When the Loups were sated, Viv moved them to a different area of the compound, then signaled for Gilly to ferry over her Chenilles. They completed the feeding by draining the bones of the animals of every drop of marrow.

Evee had warned Lucien to stay behind the back of the cathedral when the Nosferatu were led to the ferry. He was human, after all, and at this time of morning, the Nosferatu were beyond starving. Once they were on the ferry and on their way to the compound, it would be safe for him to come to the docks.

And Evee would be with him again. Because of her absolute fear of water—the fear had been bad enough before her near drowning earlier, but now she was positively petrified—she never rode the ferry with her Nosferatu. She had no idea where or when her phobia of water had come from. It was possibly from drowning in a former life, but regardless, the fear was as real as the nose on her face.

Even prepping the ferry made her nervous. It made her think of when she'd run into the river to escape the Cartesian. Had it not been for Lucien, she would surely have drowned.

The family ferry was moored near the east of the riverwalk, where it was dark and there was rarely any foot traffic. This morning, predawn, it lit the riverwalk like a thousand Christmas trees. Viv, her Loup, and Nikoli had accomplished what they'd promised to do. The ferry now had an electric dome on top of it to protect the Originals riding to or from a feeding. The relief that sent through Evee was huge and physical.

Evee checked the engine, then checked the gates along the sides of the ferry as well as the one in the back that closed the ferry, forming a sort of pen. This was to make sure the Nosferatu, no matter how rowdy they became, stayed safely aboard.

Once the Nosferatu were stacked onto the ferry, she usually started the engine and, by incantation, sent the ferry across river to the compound, where Pierre, Evee's lead Nosferatu, made sure they were off-loaded into yet another chute to keep them from running wild in the five-hundred-acre compound. Their chute led directly into the feeding area.

After the Nosferatu were fed, Viv invariably sent out a loud whistle and cawing sound, which let Evee know they were done feeding.

Pierre, having fed himself, usually brought the Nosferatu back onto the ferry and then signaled to Evee with a howl that the loaded ferry was ready to head back.

At Pierre's call, Evee usually issued an incantation to restart the ferry motor and lead it back to the city. When they returned, she would lead them back to the catacombs.

This time, however, she was concerned. With her incantations seemingly choosing when or whether to work, she feared things might not go so smoothly today.

Forcing herself to think more positively, Evee tried to limit her concerns to one issue. The Nosferatu had been cooped up for too long because of the Cartesian attacks. When things had been normal, many of them had worked jobs in the Quarter, in handsome or beautiful human form, serving as bartenders, dancers, street performers or hotel clerks. All of them, however, returned to the catacombs for feeding time, where they quickly transformed to their natural state. Tall, lanky, with a large white, bald head that had a large vein across their forehead. The vein led to the top of their heads, where it branched off to smaller yet still prominent veins. Their eyes bulged out, large and black and red-rimmed. Every one of them lashless. Their noses were long, the hooked end nearly meeting their upper lip. The fangs, the tools they used to puncture and feed with, were their two front teeth, both long, crooked and yellow. Their fingers were twice the length of an average man's, and their fingernails, yellow and twisted, extended at least three or four inches past their fingertips. They remained in their natural state after the feeding, when daylight shortly followed, and it was their time to sleep.

Lately, because of the Cartesians, Evee had kept all her Nosferatu in the catacombs even after dark, allowing them out only for feedings. This had caused them to become extremely restless. More than once, Evee or Pierre had had to break up territorial fights. She couldn't blame the Nosferatu. With nothing else to do, it was only natural that they got on each other's nerves.

She'd have to be hypervigilant in moving them from the catacombs to the ferry. The fact that they'd been stuck in the catacombs for too long might cause some of them to bolt. The lure of freedom might be too irresistible for some. That could mean more missing Nosferatu. More danger for the humans in the city. If any did bolt, the chances that she'd be able to call them back into tow would probably be slim to none. She hadn't been successful calling to the ones who were already missing. Although she'd tried more times than she could count, not one of them had responded and returned to her.

Finally, after triple-checking the ferry and starting its motor, Evee left the ferry and went to the catacombs, where she signaled Pierre it was time to bring them out.

With a simple nod, Pierre called to the Nosferatu, lining them up near the catacomb gates.

Before she opened the gates, Evee said a calming spell, hoping it would keep her Originals in tow, at least enough to get all of them onto the ferry.

"Quiet thee, oh creatures mine.
Let these words turn thy rage to soothing wine.
Angst and boredom, fear and pain.
Bring to thy mind now that 'tis all in vain.
So it is said.
So shall it be."

Once she was done, she peered through the gate and saw that the Nosferatu were still fidgeting nervously, refusing to follow Pierre's orders. Some had started yanking on the catacomb gates as if wanting to rip them open. Some snarled, others whimpered.

Evee glanced at Pierre, who appeared at a loss and just as concerned about opening the gates as she was.

"Once more," Pierre said. "The calming spell. Louder. More forceful maybe."

Nodding, Evee held her hands against the gate of the catacombs, ignoring those who were still pulling on them. She overlooked her brood. Staring each one in the eye, she hardened her expression. And this time she shouted, allowing fury to carry her voice.

"Quiet thee, oh creatures mine.
Let these words turn thy rage to soothing wine.
Angst and boredom, fear and pain.
Bring to thy mind now that 'tis all in vain.
So it is said.
SO SHALL IT BE!"

Evee spoke the last line of the spell so loudly her throat hurt.

Surprisingly, loud worked. The Nosferatu gathered as directed without another whimper or snarl.

Evee gave Pierre a nod, then opened the gate and led

the Nosferatu out of the catacombs. She walked quickly, with Pierre bringing up the rear, and steered her Originals to the ferry, where they boarded without hesitation.

Once Pierre stepped aboard, Evee closed the back gate of the ferry, latched it, then with a wave of her hand, sent it chugging across the water.

As she watched it creep along the muddy Mississippi, Evee thought about Viv. Viv always stayed on the feeding grounds until all the Originals had been fed. Although she knew to make herself scarce while the Nosferatu and Chenilles were off-loaded from the ferry to the chute that took them to the feeding area, Evee couldn't help worrying.

The calming spell had worked, but only after she'd used it twice. Evee hoped it would hold. She had no control over the Loup Garous or the Chenilles. Her brood consisted solely of the Nosferatu. If her Nosferatu suddenly decided to go rogue while on the compound, that would put Viv in danger. Not only her personally, but it would screw up the entire feeding process for the other Originals.

Evee tried desperately not to think that way, but the thought kept niggling at her brain. That and the thought of Viv and Nikoli.

When they'd met with the Elders, Viv had confessed, just as Evee had, to having been intimate with one of the Benders. Evee couldn't help wondering if her sister fought with the same constant desire for Nikoli that she did for Lucien.

Evee knew Nikoli was with Viv now, and wondered if Viv had gotten distracted like she had with Lucien. Not that Viv would shirk her responsibilities when it came to getting her ranchers to send food through the feeding chute. But as Viv waited for the Nosferatu to arrive, was she kissing Nikoli? Was he touching her? Did Nikoli touch Viv in the same way Lucien touched her? Did her sister crave being near her Bender?

Or had she listened to the Elders and, even at this moment, was keeping an arm's length away from Nikoli? Out of the three of them, Evee had to admit that Viv was the most levelheaded. But that didn't mean she was the strongest emotionally. Maybe Gilly was. She'd claimed nothing had yet happened between her and Gavril, which was hard to believe. Gilly was so out there. She always said what she meant and meant what she said. How on earth had she not slept with Gavril yet? His looks were exquisite, and Evee had seen the way he looked at Gilly, like she was a walking goddess. Evee had seen them laugh easily together, noticed how they always stood near each other. A team. A couple. Who'd yet to have sex? It was mind-boggling.

From birth the Triad had been taught that they had one and only one crucial task to tend to in their lifetime. To take care of their Originals. No one, not their mother before she died or the Elders as they trained them, had taught them to stay emotionless in the face of an impossible attraction. No matter how firmly the Elders' order had been hammered into them about staying away from the Benders, it seemed to Evee that the directive had slid off her like water off a duck's back.

She could no more deny what she needed or wanted from Lucien than she could deny she was one of the Triad. And, knowing her sister Viv, she seriously doubted she could deny what she felt for Nikoli.

What the hell were they supposed to do? What kind of Triad were they? Purposely defying their Elders' commands. Hearing that their attraction to the Benders might be causing the trauma happening with the Originals and

Cartesians just didn't seem to stave off their desire. If what the Elders had said was true, how could she simply not care? Why didn't she feel one ounce of guilt?

Evee figured, as the Elders had mentioned when they reamed them out, that it was all in the interpretation.

A member of the Triad wasn't to marry or live intimately with a human. And they weren't doing so.

All Evee had to do was keep repeating that to herself, and like a magic spell from some unknown source, guilt never stood a chance in her brain.

She wondered if the same was true with Viv.

Logic. It all had to do with logic.

The only problem Evee had with that bit of logic was the roller coaster she rode with Lucien. Would she ever be able to get off it?

What was she supposed to do once their mission was complete, and the Benders moved on to their next mission? How would she survive?

Would she survive?

No one and nothing had ever touched her, satisfied her in the way Lucien had. He'd not only touched her body as if he read her mind but he had grabbed her heart, her soul, without her permission and before she knew it was happening.

And although Evee wasn't sure what that exactly meant, she feared she wouldn't be able to do without it ever.

Which meant she'd truly have to break the rules of the Triad curse, and her Originals, all of them, would be lost to her forever.

Could she—would she…ever let it go that far?

Chapter 21

"Don't you ever ride the ferry with them?"

At the sound of a man's voice, Evee spun on her heels, terror in her eyes.

Lucien quickly walked up to her and put his hands on her shoulder. "I'm so sorry I frightened you. You're always so alert. I figured you'd seen me walking over to you."

Evee let out a shaky breath. "No problem. I was daydreaming while watching the ferry. Guess I was lost in thought."

"Good thoughts?"

She gave him an easy smile. "Started with some worrisome. Ended with very good ones."

Lucien returned her smile, still holding her shoulder. He'd been watching Evee at work from around the corner of St. John's Cathedral. Although she'd warned him to stay out of sight until the Nosferatu had been loaded onto the ferry, he'd already known to do so. Since he was human, it was far from wise to be within view of a group of hungry Nosferatu heading out to be fed. The last thing Lucien intended to be was a snack before they reached the compound.

So he'd stayed behind the far column of the cathedral, watching Evee at work. He'd been very impressed watching her control her Nosferatu. How she'd sent the ferry on its way with a wave of her hand. The moment Lucien had seen the ferry start puttering slowly across the river, he'd headed in her direction. Along the way, he'd noticed only one or two people at the far end of the riverwalk. He'd spotted a couple holding on to each other, kissing under the moonlight, in the fog that slowly settled over the city, and it made him yearn for Evee. Made him think about how she tasted when he kissed her.

He'd watched her for a while before approaching her. Taking in the beauty of her standing there, hands at her side, as she watched the ferry start across the river with her Nosferatu, watching the lights from the makeshift dome on the ferry get swallowed by fog as it moved slowly north. Some of the Nosferatu were grunting, grumbling, shifting about on the ferry so that it tilted from side to side. At one point Lucien had thought the ferry might tip over on its side, and had it not been for the buoys beneath it, it very well might have.

Lucien had seen for himself how anxious the Nosferatu had been, locked up in the catacombs. How they'd fought, bitten and grabbled for the smallest of territory below the cathedral. He didn't know how Evee'd done it, but he had to admire how calmly and methodically she had loaded them onto the ferry. And now they were on their way to be fed. Finally.

He trusted Nikoli was on the lookout over the North Compound for any Cartesians as the feeding transfers were made. With the dome now protecting the ferry, the only worry spots they had for the Cartesians were the transfers to the ferry and feeding area, then back again.

Evee blew out a breath, and Lucien released her shoulder.

"I didn't know what to expect here or on the feeding grounds. Things have been so crazy lately. I don't know what to look out for first anymore. Cartesians, more Nosferatu going missing because I'm keeping them caged up, or some stupid sorcerer who's decided he wants in on our territory. It's like you never know who'll show up or not, when or where. It's confusing as hell, don't you think?"

Lucien nodded. "A good way to put it. I don't know much about the sorcerers here, but judging by what you've told me, we certainly don't need any one of them, much less all three, involved in this."

Evee stood silently studying his face, the smile on her face soft.

Without giving it a second thought, Lucien took hold of her shoulders, gently turned her around, then wrapped his arms around her. They watched the ferry in silence as it chugged its way to its destination.

Lucien felt Evee lean back against him, pressing her back against his body. He leaned over and kissed the top of her head. She smelled of chamomile and freshly cut roses. His arms, encircling her waist, felt like they belonged there. Had always belonged there.

He ran his hands through her ponytail, then moved it aside and gently kissed the back of her neck. He felt her stiffen slightly, so Lucien reluctantly released her.

She turned to face him, a look of longing mixed with confusion on her face. "I... I..."

"It's all right," Lucien said. "No need to explain anything. I know that you feel guilty about us and think that everything that's going on is because of our intimate relationship. But what the curse mentions...that damn curse that was issued down from so many generations ago, is not what we're doing."

The very next thing that came to Lucien's mind, he didn't verbalize. *Not yet anyway.*

"This…" Evee touched her chest, then pressed a hand to his chest "…is difficult for me to process. I was given a direct order by my Elders to not be intimate again with you, even if that meant staying away for you altogether. My head heard and understood, but the rest of me doesn't seem to give a damn. I always want to be close to you."

Lucien breathed a silent sigh of relief. For a moment, he'd thought she'd turn from him and never look back. "Evee," he said, touching her right cheek lightly with his fingers, "I feel the same way. I want to be near you, help you, protect you, always."

"That's what scares me," Evee said. "The always part."

Lucien leaned over and kissed her cheek. "We're adults. We can slow the tempo to whatever pace makes you more comfortable. Make sure we…well, stay in compliance with the curse's rule. We truly can do whatever it is we need to do."

Evee nodded slowly, but she didn't look convinced. "As if now I can even turn this conversation back to business."

Closing his eyes, and drawing in a deep, exaggerated breath, Lucien held out his arms, crooked them at the elbow and forced his biceps to bulge significantly. "See?" he said. "I am man. Hear me roar."

That drew a large smile from Evee, which he treasured.

"Okay, so business…right now all we have to do is wait for the Nosferatu to get back and corral them back into the catacombs safely. When you know the ferry is heading back with them, I'll check the catacombs to make certain the dome doesn't need recharging. Then we'll tuck your brood under it, and they'll be safe and sound. Then maybe you can get some much-needed rest before we start another search. That sound like a plan?"

Evee touched one of his bulging biceps, and Lucien saw something hungry cross her face. She looked up at him. "Lucien, I don't know what I'd have done without you through all this. You saved me from drowning... you've been such a calming influence amid all the chaos. I—I just really want to thank you."

Lucien smiled and ran his fingers over her cheek, brushing stray strands of hair away from it. As he touched her, gently, slowly, Evee said, "You know, I have to confess something."

"What's that?" Lucien asked.

"When you and your cousins first got here, to be honest, I didn't trust you."

Lucien chuckled. "You don't think I knew that? I wouldn't have trusted me, either, if I had been you. Four men, showing up out of nowhere, claiming to be Benders, and that we're here to help you. All because some wacko creature you'd never even seen before was hell-bent on attacking you and your Originals. Taking possession of you. I would've considered myself facing four loonies."

Evee grinned. "Yeah, it was sort of like that." She glanced over the water, and Lucien watched it with her. Dark with a fecund scent, the sound of it lapping against the shore. All of it held an odd, calming effect.

Looking back up at Lucien, Evee finally broke the silence. "You know, I really don't know what to think and make of us. Just like I don't know what to think and make out of all that's going on with the Cartesians, our Originals, now the sorcerers."

Instead of letting Evee attempt to tie a knot between what they'd experienced together and what they fought outside their intimate circle, Lucien once again smoothed hair from her face and said, "As for what's happened between us, I don't know about you, but it felt as natural as breathing to me. The rest of it connected on its own. Like a hurricane during hurricane season. The Cartesians simply found a way to the Originals."

"I think that happened because of what Viv said to her Loup Garous," Evee said sadly. "When she told them she quit and didn't want anything more to do with them."

"You and I both know your sister didn't mean that in the truest sense of the word. Frustration does that to a person. Makes us say and do things we wouldn't do otherwise. We can't keep pressing that button, though. You know, pointing to Viv as the reason the Cartesians are here. The simple fact is that they're here. The Cartesians got a taste of an Original, who they'd been searching for for what seems like forever. Too many years, centuries even. When they finally realized where they were located, the Cartesians' entire focus turned here. That's not your fault. It isn't even Viv's."

Evee looked at him, listening intently, her copper eyes large and bright even in the darkness.

"The fact is that there's a leader of these Cartesians, and its agenda is to take over the entire netherworld, to take over the Triad, to take your power and that of the Originals and make it its own."

"So you've said."

"It's a fact, Evee. When he's done with you, the Originals, the others from the netherworld in this city, it'll go after the humans here. Then it'll move on to another city, another country, another continent, taking every ounce of power from any netherworld creature and living being so it can ultimately control the world, then the universe. That's its ultimate goal."

"But why?" Evee asked. "What purpose would that serve this so-called leader? No one would be left then, but the Cartesians."

"That's the point and what it wants. Think of every crazy leader from history," Lucien said.

"History has shown us that such insane leaders do appear from time to time, for whatever reason, as if to test our wherewithal as human beings. Take Hitler for instance. His goal was to rid the world of what he considered to be inferior humans and produce a super race that would be under his control. Who can make sense of such insanity? From Hitler to this Cartesian leader, they have their own sense of purpose. And that purpose makes no sense to anyone except the creatures or people who blindly follow them."

"Scary analogy," Evee said.

"Yes, but true," Lucien said. "The biggest difference between the two is that the leader of the Cartesians has a special ability. Every time one of its Cartesians makes a kill and brings the essence of that kill to its leader, that leader is able to create another Cartesian. That's how it's been able to grow its army over all these years."

"So, are you saying that this leader was at one time the only Cartesian alive? Then grew its own army by killing?"

"That about sums it up," Lucien said. "The original Cartesian was created many generations ago. It's had plenty of time to build its army with every kill of a netherworld creature. Unfortunately, the Benders only came onto the scene ten generations ago. By that time, the first Cartesian had plenty of time to grow its army. We followed them for ten generations but have only managed to get its minions. The leader stays well hidden."

"Do you even know what the leader looks like?" Evee asked.

"All I know is what we learned during our training as Benders. Supposedly, the leader is larger than any Cartesian any Bender has yet to face. And I'm not sure if it's rumor or not, since no Bender has admitted to actually seeing the leader, but supposedly its head is not covered with fur and scales, unlike its minions. I've heard that its head is humanlike. Only its body is covered in scales and matted fur."

"It almost sounds like you're chasing a shadow. A bogeyman," Evee said.

"Feels like that sometimes," Lucien admitted.

"Shadows or not, I'm in this with you," Evee said. "Remember, we're supposed to be a team."

Lucien gave her a long, tender look and even in the dark, he saw determination and longing in her eyes. It made his heart swell. No one, besides his cousin, had ever purposely chosen to stand by him during the midst of a fight with the Cartesians. Yet here was this beautiful, intelligent woman, offering herself to him. Offering to stand by his side when she just as easily could have left the bulk of the work to him.

Before Evee even realized what she was doing, she stood on tiptoe and kissed Lucien softly. His full, luscious lips set a fire to her own as they always did. The kiss was supposed to be one of gratitude. Gratitude for Lucien's help. For him being there for her. For standing by her side to protect her.

If truth be told, thinking a kiss of gratitude would be just that, a kiss of gratitude, was ridiculous. She'd only been fooling herself. All she had to do was be near him, and her body was immediately ablaze with need.

Lucien, obviously feeling her, sensing her need, took her into his arms and kissed her. He held her tight, putting a hand behind her head and pulling her closer. Their kiss deepened to a maddening dance of lips and tongues. Their tongues seemed to battle with a hunger neither could control. Sucking, longing, reaching for the farthest corner of their mouths.

Evee found herself breathing harder, faster. With her body pressed so close to Lucien's, she felt his heart galloping beneath his chest, and she was certain he could feel hers doing the same.

The need she felt for Lucien was so great she likened it to a pot of boiling water. The heat grew so great and so fast it overflowed its container, popping, splashing, sizzling.

She broke their kiss for only a moment, looked about, saw nothing but darkness. Not one person in sight. And it would be a while before the ferry would return with the Nosferatu.

Knowing they were alone, she reached for Lucien, wrapping her arms around him. Kissing him with a scalding fervor she didn't know she possessed. She moved her hands over his chest, wanting him, needing him. Wishing she could strip him naked. But being in a public area, although seemingly empty, she didn't think naked was a good idea.

She felt like she'd die of thirst if she didn't have him here and now, no matter where they were. Her body overtook her mind. Logic felt like nothing more than a nuisance. She grabbed hold of the front of his shirt with both hands and pulled him along with her to the nearest pier poles, where they moored the ferry.

Lucien followed her lead, silent, eyes smoldering with desire.

Evee leaned her back against one of the pier posts and pulled Lucien close, her hands fisting in his hair. She kissed him harder, deeper.

Suddenly, Lucien took both of Evee's arms in one of his hands and held them over her head, against the post.

His mouth moved down to her cheek, her neck, licked the lobe of her right ear.

Evee felt her breathing grow ragged, and the rest of the world seemed blind to her, save for Lucien.

"Take me," she whispered as he nipped the nape of her neck with his teeth. "N-now. Take me. Here. Now."

Lucien pulled away from Evee slowly, looking deeply into her eyes, his hand still locking her arms over her head against the pole. He glanced left and right so quickly it was barely noticeable. Evee was sure he was double-checking to make sure they didn't have an audience.

Evidently confident that they were alone, Lucien turned his full attention to her. He unbuttoned her slacks with his free hand and yanked them down and off without preamble.

No words were needed as Lucien released her arms, placed them around his neck, then lifted her into his arms as easy as if he were cradling a baby. He lifted her up, and her legs automatically wrapped around his waist. She heard the sound of the zipper on his jeans, and then before she knew it, Evee felt the hardness of him pressing between her legs. She was already wet and swollen, so ready for him. She wanted to cry out, scream, "Now! Now!" but there'd been no need.

As though reading her mind, Lucien entered her, slowly at first, then evidently feeling how wet and ready she was, drove his entire length into her deep and fast. He held on to her legs, lifting her higher, pushing into her deeper, pulling her legs up even higher so she felt every inch of him, so he reached that spot deep within her that caused her to lose control and flood him with her juices.

As he dived into her again and again, Evee bit her bottom lip, holding back a cry of pleasure, as she erupted with an orgasm so powerful her vision blurred.

"More, damn it," Lucien said. "Give me more." He arched his back, giving her all he had. Hard and deep. "Give it all to me, baby. Everything."

Evee didn't know how or why, but the sound of Lucien's command sent her immediately over the edge again, her body erupting and soaking him.

Lucien continued to ram his hardness into her, refusing to stop until she was completely drained. Evee had no idea how he maintained such control over his own orgasm as he hammered himself into her again and again, making sure she gave him all she had.

Evee felt her body grip around his hardness, pulling him in deeper, contracting over his stiffness, her body sucking on his hardness, milking him.

Lucien met her stroke for stroke, and although Evee's back was pressed against a large wooden piling, all she felt was him.

As she felt another orgasm begin to roll through her, Lucien held her legs up a bit higher, shoved harder, and this time Evee couldn't hold back her cry as she exploded over him.

Only then did she feel him tense, his release so close. He drove harder, his eyes never leaving her face. A moan suddenly fell from his lips, and she felt him empty himself into her.

Lucien shivered with the intensity of his orgasm that seemed to last forever. This woman was nothing short of phenomenal in all ways. Never had he come across anyone with such depth, such sexuality, such commitment and daring. All of it was the wonder of Evette François.

Reluctantly, slowly, Lucien pulled out of her, lowered her legs to the ground and tugged her trousers up. With deft fingers, he zipped and buttoned them into place.

Evee still leaned against the piling, seemingly spent. Lucien held on to her with one hand while zipping up his pants with the other.

Once they were fully clothed Lucien took Evee into his arms and held her close. He pressed her head against his chest, hoping she heard the thudding of his heart.

And she rested there so comfortably, as if leaning against a familiar place, a comforting place.

Lucien held her close, smoothing her hair with a hand, kissed the top of her head. In that moment, he felt a twinge of pain hit his heart.

Where were they to go from here?

Lucien knew deep in his soul that he could never be without this woman. Yet the curse that held the Triad captive had now become his curse.

He needed more than one-night stands and an occasional sexual encounter with Evee.

He knew deep in his soul that they were meant to be together…always. Lucien wondered if there was a way to break the curse that refused to let a Triad marry or live intimately with a human. He wondered if the Triad had even explored the option.

As he kissed the top of Evee's head again, he made a mental note to himself. Besides completing the mission he and his cousins had been sent here to accomplish, Lucien would do everything in his power to find out if there was a way around the Triad curse. Someway to break it.

For in his heart of hearts, Lucien knew he could not live without Evee beside him…ever.

Chapter 22

Evee didn't quite know what to think. She felt slightly embarrassed, like some wanton slut. Not in a million years would she ever have considered having sex outside in the middle of a public venue, where anyone might happen by.

Even though it was dark, and she'd not seen any other person even close to the docks, she could have, should have shown a bit more decorum. A little discretion at least.

The simple fact was that the moment Lucien had put his arms around her, her body took over her brain. In that moment, there could have been a circus act going on ten feet away with twenty thousand spectators, and she still would have craved him, wanted him…taken him.

Fortunately, there'd been no one around to see when she willingly gave up her privacy standards just to have Lucien inside her.

With clothes straightened, she looked out onto the water, afraid to face him. She wondered if he thought her to be too loose, too needy. She felt Lucien's hand rest on her shoulder and squeeze lightly. As if reading her mind, he leaned over and whispered in her ear.

"It's all right. No one saw us." He turned her to face him. "Evee, you're one of the most glorious women I've ever known. So open and honest in what you feel and the way you express it. Don't feel bad about any of this, please."

Evee gave him a half smile. "I'm trying."

She smoothed some wrinkles in his shirt with a hand. At least nothing on either of them looked out of the ordinary. As if nothing had occurred at all. It wasn't that she didn't want to think about the fact that they'd just had sex, but she'd be facing her sisters soon. The less they knew or suspected, the better.

In silence, Lucien and Evee stood side by side, looking over the water. Evee was waiting for Viv's special signal, the loud howl and squawk, that the Nosferatu were ready to return city side.

Evee stood with her arms folded against her chest. A cool night breeze washed over her, sending goose bumps up and down her arms. It might have been the breeze that sent a shiver through her or the fact that Lucien was still standing beside her.

Where he was concerned, Evee always felt like she was dying of thirst and no amount of having him seemed to fully quench it. Even if he stayed inside her for a month, Evee felt it still wouldn't be enough. In all her life, she had never needed anyone so desperately as she needed Lucien. And it wasn't all about the sex, which frightened and excited her at the same time.

Suddenly, Evee heard someone clear their throat behind them. She whirled about, her heart pounding in her chest. Lucien simply glanced over his shoulder.

Gavril had made it to the docks and was walking toward them.

When Evee saw him, she felt a slight flash of guilt. She'd just had sex with Lucien…again. Gavril's appearance reminded her of Ronan. She'd known by the way Ronan had looked at her from time to time that he'd been interested in her, wanted a relationship with her. They'd never have the dinner she'd promised. But that had been all she'd promised. She would never have led Ronan down a deceptive path. Her interest was in Lucien, and that was all there was to it. Although Ronan had been as handsome as the rest of his cousins, he had a seriousness and quietness about him that didn't quite call to Evee the way Lucien did.

"What's up?" Lucien asked Gavril.

"Wanted to check out the ferry before we brought out the Chenilles. How'd it work for the Nosferatu?" Gavil asked.

"So far so good, but we'll have a better handle on how it worked as soon as the ferry returns," Lucien said.

"Why aren't you with Gilly?" Evee asked, feeling her mood shift to angry and anxious.

"She's fine," Gavril assured her. "I triple-checked the dome over the cemetery before we left, but I didn't want to chance her getting hurt if the dome we set up over the ferry wasn't working. That's why I came to check on it."

Lucien narrowed his eyes. "What aren't you telling me?"

"Huh?" Gavril said.

"You know if anything had gone wrong with the dome on the ferry, we would've reached out to you with a warning."

Gavril shifted his eyes to Evee, then back to Lucien. "I hate when you're right, you know that?"

"What happened?" Evee asked. "Is Gilly really okay? You need to be back with her, watch over her."

"I will," Gavril said. "I just wanted to warn the both of you that we had a Cartesian attack right off Rampart Street. It was only one, nothing I couldn't handle, but there was something different about the way the Cartesian came through it."

"Different how?" Lucien asked.

"One second it wasn't there and the next, boom, there it was, hanging out of a rift by the waist. No warning at all. No scent of clove until the bastard shot out of the rift. Then it stank to high heaven with clove and sulfur. Their pattern is changing, and I don't like it one damn bit. No preamble. Just BAM and there they are, rift already open."

"I noticed the changes," Lucien said. "It happened the same way when Ronan…when Ronan and me fought them riverside."

"Hang on a minute, guys," Evee said, and cocked an ear toward the river. Clear yet faint, she heard Viv's whistle and caw, signaling that the Nosferatu had been fed and were heading back on the ferry.

"The Nosferatu are heading back," she told Lucien and Gavril. "The two of you need to leave before they get here."

"But we can't leave you and your Originals alone," Lucien said. "It's too dangerous. The Cartesians have become unpredictable, even more than usual."

"Then what the hell is Gavril doing here?" Evee demanded.

"He's here to warn us," Lucien said, his tone hardening.

Evee turned to Gavril. "Appreciate the heads-up on the Cartesian, but please go to my sister and don't leave her again."

"Ten-four," Gavril said, then took off for the cemetery and Gilly.

As soon as Gavril was out of sight, Lucien said, "He knows what he's doing, Evee. I'd trust Gavril with my life. He won't let anything happen to Gilly."

Evee wanted to say, *Right, like Ronan knew what he was doing?* But she didn't say it. It would have been unnecessary and harsh.

"There's the ferry," Evee said, pointing straight ahead at the calliope of lights floating in their direction.

She turned to Lucien. "Why don't you go and give Gavril a hand while I put the Nosferatu away?"

"I'm not leaving you," Lucien said firmly.

"But there really isn't much for you to do. They get off the ferry, and I've got only a couple hundred feet before I can stash them away. Gavril and Gilly have to lead the Chenilles much farther."

"I'll gladly give them a hand," Lucien said.

Evee blew out a breath of relief. She didn't know what to expect from the Nosferatu when they were off-loaded from the ferry. All she knew was she didn't want danger to smack Lucien in the face.

"I'll give them a hand as soon as you've put the Nosferatu back in their hidey-hole," Lucien said.

Evee threw him a scowl. "I don't have time to fight with you about this now. The ferry's mooring. You need to be in the back of the cathedral. Not the side of it like last time when I loaded them onto the ferry. The back."

"But weren't they just fed?" Lucien asked. "Shouldn't they be satiated now?"

"That's the point of me sending them to the feeding ground, so they can drink until they've had their fill," Evee said. "But you never can tell with a Nosferatu. One can see a human, and it might decide to make a pig of itself and go for more."

"We have a little time before they get here, don't we?" Lucien asked.

"A minute," Evee said. "They're already mooring."

In that moment, a crack of thunder sounded overhead. Since the night had been foggy, they'd had no warning of impending bad weather. Lucien and Evee immediately focused their attention on the sky.

"Smell it?" Lucien asked.

"Yeah, just the clove, though," Evee said, her voice trembling. Nothing good ever followed the scent of clove.

Evee looked out at the ferry. Pierre had already killed the motor and was headed for the back gate of the ferry.

"Don't let them out!" Evee shouted at Pierre. "Stay there. Stay!"

Pierre looked over at her, cocked his head as if unsure of what she'd said.

Evee ran halfway to the ferry and shouted again, "Don't let them out yet! Looks like we've got problems." She pointed up at the sky, in the same direction Lucien was focused.

Pierre frowned and nodded, his expression one of extreme worry.

Evee ran back to Lucien. "Where—"

"Oh, Christ on a cracker," Lucien said, pointing overhead and a bit to the left. "There."

Evee looked in the direction where Lucien pointed. She didn't see anything out of the ordinary, but suddenly smelled the rot of sulfur. Gagging, she covered her nose and mouth with a hand. "What the hell is that—"

Another crack of thunder, and in that moment, Lucien pulled his scabior out of its sheath.

That was when Evee saw it. A huge rift appeared

seemingly out of nowhere. Its maw was blacker than any black Evee had ever seen. The sky could have been painted white for the contrast it created overhead. The rift couldn't have been more obvious. It seemed to slice through the stars and part of the moon, and from it dangled three monstrous Cartesians. One actually had a leg sticking out of the rift, as if it planned to jump from the gap.

With scabior in hand, Lucien gave a quick twist of his wrist, twirled the scabior between his fingers and took aim.

He blasted the Cartesian who had the leg out of the rift, sending it tumbling back with a high-pitched screech.

Then he took aim at the one next to it, a Cartesian with arms that seemed long enough to reach the ground from the rift it hung from.

"Go to the catacombs!" Lucien shouted at Evee.

"No way."

"Goddamn it, stop being so hardheaded and go!"

"No fucking way."

And with that Evee held her hands out, palms up, aiming for the sky.

"*Double, thrice, by tens ye shall see.*

No longer one to be seen by thee.

Thine eyes shall fully confuse thy mind.

Making all evil intentions blind.

Blunder thee, blunder now.

I call upon Poseidon, Tiamat and Apsu, bring strength to my command.

So it is said.

So shall it be."

Just like the first time Evee had used that incantation for Lucien and Ronan, this time, too, her words produced the same results. The Cartesians started swinging blindly in all directions. Their snorts of fury sounded like thunder blasts.

"I'm at three," Lucien shouted, still aiming at one of the Cartesians.

"Three what?" Evee asked, terrified by what hung overhead. She wanted to take the question back. She felt stupid for having asked it while Lucien was in the middle of fighting for their lives. Her life. The Originals' lives.

"Dimensions," Lucien said. "We push them back to the farthest dimension before the rift closes. The farther we send them, the longer it takes for them to make it back to our dimension."

"I'm at six," Lucien said. "Rift's closed."

He aimed at the second Cartesian, whose arms seemed to do nothing more than dangle from the rift, as if it were tired of aiming for ghosts. "Four on this one," Lucien said. "Rift's still open."

Evee watched in wonder as the brightest lightning bolts she'd ever witnessed shot from the scabior. She suddenly bumped into something and turned to see she had stumbled over the first step in front of St. John's Cathedral. She'd never noticed she'd been moving backward as Lucien fought the Cartesians.

"Five," Lucien said. "Rift closed." He took aim at the last Cartesian, got two good shots to the head before the rift closed.

"Evee?"

The sound of Lucien's voice broke through Evee's numbness. She looked over at him, slowly, as if nothing out of the ordinary had just happened.

Lucien shoved his scabior in his sheath, then put an arm around her shoulder. Looked deep into her eyes.

"You did it again," Lucien said quietly.

"What?"

"Saved my life with your incantation." He leaned down to kiss her, but Evee put a hand to his chest to hold him back.

"Not with the Nosferatu watching. They might not understand and view you as a threat."

"But—"

"No buts," Evee said. "Let's just call it even. You saved me from a Cartesian and from drowning. I confused a few so you could work your magic. I'd say we're about even, don't you think?"

"Not even close," Lucien said with a grin. "But I'll leave that discussion for another time. You've got Nosferatu to get back into the catacombs. I'll be behind the cathedral if you need me. Just yell."

"Oh, don't worry, I will. Seems like I've become quite vocal these days." With that, Evee turned away from Lucien and headed for the ferry.

Even with the task ahead so uncertain, she couldn't help smiling.

Vocal indeed.

Chapter 23

This time Lucien did as he was told and remained behind the cathedral until all the Nosferatu were settled into the catacombs. He leaned against the massive building, chewed on a blade of grass and pondered all that had happened in the past few hours.

Without question, this was one of the most unusual missions he'd ever been involved in. He tried keeping his mind from settling on two of the most frightening experiences he'd had to date. The first being Ronan's death, and the second discovering Evee and how she affected him.

If he was a philosophical man, it'd be easy to see a new life beginning as one ended. The beginning being Evee and the ending Ronan, of course. But a new life interpretation involving a Triad was questionable at best.

So much for being philosophical.

Keeping one ear tuned to the grumbling and shuffling of the Nosferatu as they made their way into the catacombs, he heard Evee's soothing, lolling voice encouraging them inside. The sound of it made Lucien's heart feel bigger, and he also felt guilt creeping in.

So far the only thing they'd expressed between each other had to do with sex. Although Evee was sexually beyond any man's dream, she had captured more of him than just an erection. But what he felt for her went way beyond sex. The sound of her voice enamored him, as did the different expressions on her face. Whether she wore no makeup and a haphazard ponytail or dressed for a ball, it didn't matter. Lucien thought her to be the most beautiful woman he'd ever laid eyes on.

As hard as he tried, he couldn't help thinking of Ronan, how he had been interested in Evee. Lucien had honestly wanted to give him the opportunity to try to win her over despite what he felt for her himself. But that chance was gone forever. This left Lucien with two choices. Run as far away from Evee as possible and try to forget her, just out of courtesy to Ronan, or pursue her, hoping to fill her heart the way she filled his.

If he chose the first option, it meant building a steel cage inside himself that she couldn't get through, then leave as soon as the mission was completed, or possibly change partners with Gavril. As far as he knew, nothing physical had happened between his cousin and Gilly, so switching shouldn't make a difference.

As logical a man as Lucien was, just the thought of switching Triad made his stomach roil. He had to stay true to himself, which meant being with her and somehow doing so while keeping it a secret from everyone else but Evee. He had to tell her how he felt so she would not start thinking that he only wanted her for sex.

Even if he did run and hide behind one mission or another, how did a person reverse love? It wasn't like he'd meant for it to turn out that way. It had simply happened, Triad curse or not. And falling in love was like falling into a deep hole. You couldn't just fall out of love, like you couldn't fall out of a deep hole. You had to be pushed or pulled out, and Evee had done neither.

Lucien was in the middle of that thought when Evee appeared behind the cathedral. She gave him a soft smile.

"I think that instead of just having Viv call Gilly and let her know it's time for her Chenilles to go to the feeding ground, we go and meet with her and Gavril. That way if there are any problems with the Cartesians between the cemetery and the ferry, Gavril will have you for backup."

"Great idea," Lucien said.

Evee nodded. "Now that we have a dome over the ferry, the switchover at feeding time will be less stressful. But it doesn't change anything where the missing Originals are concerned. We have to really put our heads together and come up with a plan on how to find them. That's the only way we're going to be able to protect the humans in this city."

"Another good point," Lucien said.

Evee cocked her head to one side and grinned at him. "Are you always this easy, Mr. Hyland?"

Lucien started heading for the Louis I Cemetery and said in a stage whisper, "Far from it, Ms. François. Far, far from it."

By the time they reached Gilly and Gavril, the Chenilles were all gathered tightly together, piled up next to their mistress, who stood by the electric canopy at the front gate of the cemetery. The Chenilles wanted out, and now.

Judging from the frenzy on the Chenilles' faces, Lucien worried that once the cemetery gates opened, Gilly might be faced with a stampede. He hoped Gilly knew the same calming spells that Evee used on her Nosferatu.

No sooner had Lucien completed that thought than he saw Gilly hold out her hands, palm up, and begin to chant.

"Quiet thee, oh creatures mine.
Let these words soothe thy rage to wine.
Angst and boredom, fear and pain.
Lead thy mind to see now that 'tis all in vain.
So it is said.
So shall it be."

Lucien watched in amazement as the Chenilles that had been twitching, nipping, whining, shoving only seconds earlier now stood in an orderly line, knowing they were going to be fed.

Of all the Originals, the Chenilles could easily have passed for human, even in their natural state. Male and female alike stood between six feet five inches and seven feet tall. They all appeared to be around the same age, somewhere in their midtwenties. Some had beautiful long blond hair, some short and black—handsome men, exotic women. He supposed they used their beauty as bait to lure in a victim. If victims paid close attention, however, they'd be able to see the most telling sign on a Chenille. Its skin. It was more yellow than white, like each carried a different stage of liver failure. What the victims didn't know until it was too late was that a Chenille's incisors were long and threaded, like a screw, yet hollow in the center.

Once a Chenille latched on to bone, it drilled small holes through it to reach the marrow, and then used the same incisors to suck the marrow from the bone. Like sucking through a thick milk shake with a straw. Although they preferred the blood and meat to be neatly discarded, as they were used to in the North Compound, an overly hungry Chenille could certainly forgo that formality. It would use its incisors to rip through skin and flesh until it reached its prize. Bone. Lots of bone.

Just before Gilly opened the cemetery gates, she motioned to Gavril that it was time for him, Evee and Lucien to move out of sight.

Peering around the corner of the cathedral, Lucien was relieved to see the Chenilles following Gilly's orders to the letter. Gavril chose to follow behind the Chenille parade by at least two hundred feet. Lucien and Evee thought it best to watch over Gilly and Gavril, but do so by way of alleyways and around dark corners of buildings. The last thing Lucien wanted was to draw attention to himself. What if one of the witnesses who'd seen him and Ronan fighting the Nosferatu showed up and fingered him? It'd wind up being a circus show.

So, sticking to that plan, Lucien and Evee ducked and swerved through alleyways as they watched Gilly and Gavril make their way to the docks. With every step they took toward the docks, Lucien felt like it was one too many. He kept one eye on Gavril and kept watch over the sky.

It was eerily quiet when they arrived. Which made Lucien's and Evee's sneakers sound like hammers on concrete.

Gavril swiveled about on his heels. "Damn, cuz, give a guy a heads-up, will ya? Why are the two of you here, anyway?"

"Since the Nosferatu are put away," Lucien said, "and you and Gilly have the farthest to walk without protection over to the docks, we thought it might be a good idea to follow the two of you in case you needed backup."

Gavril pulled his long gingerbread-colored hair behind his head, reached into the front pocket of his jeans with his free hand and pulled out a rubber band, which he quickly wrapped around his hair. With that done, he moved his head from shoulder to shoulder, and Lucien heard vertebrae misalignments pop back into place.

"I appreciate your having our backs," Gavril said. He aimed his chin down Rampart toward a section of run-down shops. "Let's wait out there until Gilly has them off-loaded onto the ferry. Don't want them picking up our scents."

Now that they were at the docks, Lucien took Evee's hand and motioned for Gavril to follow them. He planned on positioning everyone along the side of the cathedral, just as he'd done earlier with Evee and the Nosferatu.

They watched as Gilly led the Chenilles onto the ferry, stepped in behind them, then closed the ferry's back gate. The look Gilly gave Gavril as she untied the ferry made Lucien wonder if there was more to their relationship than either was letting on.

Before the ferry took off, two men suddenly appeared out of the shadows and walked toward the ferry.

"What the hell?" Lucien said.

"Son of a bitch," Evee said. "That's Trey Cottle and Shandor Black, two of the sorcerers I told you about."

Now that the back gate of the ferry had been secured and the electric dome activated, Lucien all but jogged over to the men to see what they wanted. Evee was right at his heels and Gavril only two steps behind Evee.

As they drew even closer, Evee suddenly skidded to a stop. She signaled for Gilly to get the ferry moving as she confronted their unwanted company.

"What are you doing here?" Lucien asked.

"No," Evee said. "What the fuck are you two bastards doing here?" she demanded.

Lucien raised an eyebrow, quite impressed with Evee's

extensive, spur-of-the-moment vocabulary. "I'm assuming I'm having the pleasure of meeting Shandor Black and Trey Cottle?"

"Oh, yeah," Evee said. "I don't know about pleasure, but the short, fat, sweaty one is Cottle, and the one with the hooked nose and two-foot jowls is Black."

"Miss François," Trey Cottle said, "there is no reason for you to be so condescending, so harsh with your friends."

"You're no friends of mine," she retorted.

Almost as if she hadn't spoken, Cottle said, "Concerning us being here, our purpose is only to help."

"Yeah, I know how you're here to help. Shandor has already confronted me about it. What did he do? Go whining to you that I wouldn't let him anywhere near us?"

Trey harrumphed. "I knew before he did. I'm the one who sent him to you."

"So just tell me what the fuck it is you want with me," Evee said. Lucien placed a hand on the small of her back, which oddly enough calmed her considerably.

"We want to help," Trey said. "I think you're missing a very important element where the Originals are concerned. Why some of them have gone missing and those missing have already started to kill humans. Now you're having to take extra measures just to get your Originals from their holding areas to the ferry. I'm sure all of that is quite inconvenient."

Evee swiped a hand over her mouth. "Just what the hell do you think you can do that we haven't done? Are you standing here telling me that you have some special spell or potion that can make everything right again? That you can bring back every missing Original and return things to normal?"

Trey shrugged. "I don't know about back to normal.

You do have some Nosferatu who've died. That I can't undo." He turned slightly to face Lucien. "Death can have an odd effect on people. Some can move on as if nothing's changed in their lives. Others exist knowing their lives will never be the same."

Lucien felt fury raging in his head, thundering in his temples. He didn't know Trey Cottle from any other stranger who walked the street. But instinct told him that Cottle was a greasy weasel that they weren't to trust.

"We don't need you here," Lucien said. "We don't want you here. I don't know how word is getting about. I don't know who your sources are or who's been feeding you this ridiculous information. And even if you did have an info source, I'm certain you're not going to spill the beans on his or her identity."

"Au contraire," Cottle said. "I'd be happy to give you that information."

Evee's and Gavril's heads jerked back in surprise.

"Then who's contacted you and given you all this information about the Triad, about the Originals?" Lucien asked.

A long moment of silence passed between them.

"Just as I suspected," Evee said with a smirk. "You're not going to tell us shit. You're nothing but a lump of fat, sweaty clay that needs to be removed from here pronto."

Trey tapped a finger against his chin. "Now, owing to your inhospitableness, and your determination to go through this fiasco alone, I won't give you the whole picture. Just another piece of the puzzle. Let you figure it out for yourself. The source you are so anxious to know about is someone you know. Someone close to you." Cottle let out a nasally snort, his eyes darkening. "Chew on that for a while and see where it gets you."

Lucien fought hard to keep his hands balled into fists

at his sides. What he wanted to do was pummel Sweat Head and give Hook Nose a nose job.

With an odd bow, Cottle signaled for Black to follow him, and they quickly disappeared into the shadows from which they had come.

"What was that all about?" Gilly asked. "How did they know to come here? How do they know we're in trouble?"

"I'm not sure," Evee said. "Shandor met up with me earlier, here near the docks, whining about the same thing. Wanting to help, wanting to help. Same song and dance Cottle just gave us. Shandor wouldn't tell me shit about who'd told him."

"We'll figure it out," Lucien said, his mind already whirring with ideas. He turned to Gavril. "Once Gilly has her Chenilles back in the cemetery, meet us at Evee's café. We've got a lot to talk about. We've got to figure out who the snitch is. Chances are they snitched because they had something to do with the chaos we're experiencing."

"And the missing Originals?" Evee asked. "They have to be our priority."

"Oh, they are," Lucien assured her. "And we *will* find a way to get the missing Originals back here as quickly as possible. Come hell or high water, we'll make it happen."

Chapter 24

Somehow Gilly had managed to take the Chenilles to be fed and returned to the cemetery without any Cartesian incidents, which made Lucien and Gavril a bit nervous.

"We can always be grateful for small things," Evee said.

"Yes," Lucien said. "But things have been ramping up too quickly for the Cartesians to let that opportunity slide by."

They had all gathered at Evee's café—Evee, Lucien, Gavril, Gilly, Nikoli and Viv. As they relaxed in chairs, Evee had told everyone to make themselves at home with food and drink.

Nikoli and Gavril slammed down two ham sandwiches each, along with a Coke, while Viv and Gilly ate from a fresh fruit bowl they'd found in Evee's industrial-size fridge.

When everyone sat in the dining area again, Lucien said, "I have an idea. I don't know if it's going to work, but it might be worth a try."

"What is it?" Evee asked, edging her chair closer to his so as not to miss a word.

Lucien frowned as if considering his words carefully before he allowed them out of his mouth. "Instead of us running all over the city, we've got to remember that some of the Originals have moved outside the city proper to places like Chalmette. The last thing we want is for them to head off to other states."

"We already know that," Gilly said. "So what's your idea?"

"Are we okay, being here in your café?" Lucien asked Evee. "Are you expecting anyone to come in early to open and get things ready for your morning business?"

"Not for a few hours," she said. "I called Margaret, my manager, and told her I'd be running late today. She normally doesn't get here until six a.m."

Lucien checked his watch. "That gives us three hours. We'll keep the lights off in here just in case someone walks by and assumes you've opened early."

"And we're doing this why?" Evee asked.

"Here is safe from the Cartesians and the Originals. Here is where we might have a chance for you to channel Chank, the Nosferatu you lost when Pierre had to take him out."

"I see where you're going with this," Evee said. "Since I knew Chank well, and we know for sure he's dead, I can get a clearer picture of him in my mind's eye, address him directly and hopefully get some answers about the missing Originals. Maybe he can see something from the other side that we can't here."

"Exactly," Lucien said.

"Many of my Nosferatu are missing, but I might have a better chance of reaching Chank because I know he's dead and I knew him like a mother knows a child. I just might be able to connect."

"Great," Gilly said. "What do we have to do?"

Evee started pulling chairs and tables to the corners of the room. When the others caught on to what she was doing, they quickly lent a hand.

When the center of the dining area was vacant, Evee said, "Everybody sit on the floor, please, in a circle."

Lucien, Nikoli, Gilly, Gavril, and Viv complied without hesitation. Everyone sat cross-legged.

With everyone seated, Evee said, "Now put your hand on the knee of the person sitting beside you. For example, since Lucien is sitting to my right, I'll put my right hand on his left knee. Gilly's sitting on my left, so I'll put my left hand on her right knee. Like this…" Evee demonstrated what she'd tried to explain.

Everybody did as they were told. Not one funny quirk from anyone about how weird this seemed, which was usually a relief valve for someone feeling awkward in the moment. Instead, everyone kept their eyes on Evee, their expressions absolutely serious.

Evee should have been the one cracking jokes because she felt nervous as hell. The last time she'd tried to channel hadn't worked out so well. But now she hoped Chank, whom she knew from cauliflower ear to cauliflower ear, might just be able to come through.

"Everyone please close your eyes and concentrate," Evee instructed.

They all closed their eyes tightly.

Evee began to rock her body slightly from side to side. "Chank, oh Nosferatu of mine, I call upon you to come to me. Without harm or foul, use my body so that we might learn from you. So that we might see through your eyes, hear with your ears, and find the Originals who've left this place. Be our guide, not our distraction, and keep all who'd mean us harm to remain beyond the veil. It is only you I invite to use my body. Heed my words."

She continued to call for him, focusing on his face, his body in her mind's eye. She felt the grip on both of her knees tighten.

"Tell me, Chank, what you see, what you know from the other side. Certainly you see more than we see here."

"...big head."

Evee heard the voice, but as always it seemed to be coming from some distance away and belonging to someone else. In this case that someone else sounded no older than seven or eight years old.

Evee felt herself falling deeper into a trance.

"Big head...big house," the childlike voice said. "Not house, but like house. High, almost to the sky."

"Are the missing Originals there?" Evee heard Gilly ask.

"Yeah, but they can't leave. If they leave, they get dead."

Gavril asked, "Where is this big building? Is it close or is it far?"

"Far away. Yep, far away."

"Do you know the name of the building?" Lucien asked.

"Big building. Big head. Big body. They try to leave. But if they leave they get dead."

"We've heard that some Originals have left the city," Gavril said. "Are there more who've left here?"

"Yep, left city. Call back. All back or they dead. They don't stay still in big house, in big building. They fight the big man but him is stronger. Him is their boss. Him won't let them go. Him wants them to die."

Evee felt a cold sensation run down her throat, like cold milk sliding down her gullet. She opened her eyes, knowing the connection was gone.

"Well?" Evee asked.

"He showed up through you all right, but I couldn't understand a goddamn thing he said," Gavril said.

"He didn't give us direct answers. Not like we would have liked them to be. But maybe he's given us enough to give us clues."

"What did he say?" Evee asked.

"Something about a big head and a big house," Nikoli said. "From what he said, it sounded like they were trapped in this house because he said a big man was their leader, and he didn't want them to leave. He wanted them to die."

"It was like trying to communicate with a child," Viv said. "It was hard to understand him. To make sense out of anything he said." She repeated nearly verbatim all that had come through Evee from Chank.

Evee dropped her head in her hands. "What the hell? I can't make any more sense out of that than any of you. A big house and big head… I have no damn clue as to what that means." She grew so frustrated she pounded a fist on the floor. "Damn it. Even when our spells work, they don't. Chank didn't give us any information that we can work with here."

"Wait a sec," Lucien said. "He did give us one clue. He said there was one big man, and that man was their leader and refused to let them go."

"So there is one person responsible for all this…" Evee said thoughtfully. "I wonder if he's human, a sorcerer or netherworld."

"I should have asked," Gilly said. "My bad."

"We can always try channeling him again later," Evee said.

"Why not now?" Lucien asked.

"Because it takes a lot of energy for them to come

through that veil and speak through me. We have to give them time to build up energy so we can call them back."

"How much time?" Gavril asked.

"At least four to five hours."

"Damn."

"Yeah."

"But I'll tell you this much," Evee said. "Whatever time it takes and whoever this 'him' is, he may not be as big as Chank claims he is. But I swear on every living soul I know I will punch that son of a bitch in the face so hard he'll be sniffing his ass for the rest of his life."

Chapter 25

After everyone, including Lucien, left the café, Evee wasn't quite sure what to do with herself. She could have spent some time readying the café for its morning business, but Margaret would be in soon enough to take care of that for her. Besides, she didn't want to be in the café, not right now anyway. She had to check one more time.

Evee went back to the cathedral to make certain her Nosferatu were still tucked away safely in the catacombs.

When she finally arrived at St. John's and sneaked into the crypts, she saw all was well. Most of her Nosferatu were sleeping, some on top of crypts, others inside grave shelves, along with the bones of some former priests, bishops or deacons.

After seeing her brood was collected and sound, Evee felt better and headed back to the café to complete her duties.

Once there she made certain the appropriate amount of cash was in the register to provide change for early morning customers. Then she went into the kitchen area of the café to make sure they had all the ingredients needed for the day's morning and noon rush.

As Evee ticked off eggs, bacon, rice, sausage, tasso and biscuit mix from her mental list, Lucien kept weaving in and out of her thoughts. She'd never seen him that way before. Quiet, seemingly actionless. Like a man unsure of what to feel. Not that she blamed him. Had she been faced with the same situations they'd gone through in one day, she'd probably have crawled into a hole and walled off the rest of the world.

Still, she had been surprised when Lucien, who appeared so absolutely empty, had simply walked away when they were done with the channeling session. Pride had kept her from calling out to him.

As Evee worked to finish off her to-do list at the café, she recalled how Ronan had died. The scene kept playing over and over in her head. The long, crooked claws of the Cartesian jammed into Ronan's head. How he hadn't so much as whimpered when the Cartesian took him.

Ronan had saved her life, and now she had no way of repaying him for his kindness, his heroism, his sacrifice. Evee knew she'd carry the nightmare of Ronan's death until her own came to claim her. She'd also remember the last words she'd said to Lucien. How they couldn't be together anymore. Although she'd said it for his own safety and the safety of the other Benders and the Triad, her heart nearly collapsed in on itself. She never wanted to be without Lucien, but Ronan's death had caused her to think way past what she wanted.

There was no denying that karma meant to kick her ass, using everyone she cared about and loved. It was then she'd come to the heartbreaking conclusion that her sexual liaisons with Lucien had to stop. If adding one horror to another was how the universe planned on breaking her down, it had succeeded.

It was nearly 6:00 a.m. when Evee finished her chores in the café. Before heading home, she called Margaret, the café's hostess and general manager, to let her know she wouldn't be getting back to the café until much later. She told Margaret that all the supplies for today's meals had been accounted for, which meant Margaret wouldn't be starting her day at ground zero.

Once Margaret agreed to hold down the fort until Evee returned, she locked up the café and headed home.

By the time Evee made it home, she was so exhausted that she all she wanted to do was collapse in her bed. Which she did, telling herself she'd shower whenever she woke.

No sooner had her head hit the pillow than she felt sleep capture her. It refused to remain a constant, however.

She kept seeing visions of Ronan being slaughtered by the Cartesian, the sadness that radiated from Lucien as he witnessed his cousin's death, the heartache of loss swelling up from Nikoli and Gavril. With so many horrid memories rolling across her mind, piercing into her dreams, she found herself jolting awake every thirty minutes or so.

Evee finally gave up on any form of deep sleep around noon. She got out of bed, feeling more fatigued than she had when she'd gotten into bed.

After showering and taking care of her other bathroom duties, Evee went down to the kitchen for something to eat. Evidently, Viv and Gilly had already left, either to check on their businesses or brood, because they were nowhere to be found in the house.

Oddly enough, Hoot wasn't home, either. He always

did a flyby when Evee was preparing something to eat. She assumed he was out on one of his recon missions.

After making herself a grilled cheese sandwich, she ate it while standing near the stove. The house was quiet. Too quiet. The silence made her mind go abuzz with all that had happened over the last twenty-four hours.

The last thing Evee needed was to sulk around the house, reliving the nightmares that had stolen her sleep.

Having washed her grilled cheese sandwich down with a bottle of water, Eve left the house and went to a trolley stop about a block away.

The trolley jerked and shimmied as it stopped to pick up passengers or let some off along its ancient tracks. When it finally reached Canal, Evee signaled for a stop.

Exiting the trolley, she walked the seven or eight blocks to St. John's Cathedral. She wanted to check in on her Nosferatu once more before heading to the café and relieving Margaret.

She and Pierre had discussed how antsy the Nosferatu had been when they were off-loaded from the ferry. Fortunately, they'd been able to keep them under control. Antsy was never good when it came to a Nosferatu. One could never tell what it'd do next.

Inside the cathedral, Evee made her way to the side door that led to the catacombs. The door to the catacombs always stayed locked, which kept parishioners from snooping inside. Fortunately, the one small spell she used to open the lock on that door never seemed to fail.

Evee felt she might be getting a little OCD over her Originals. She'd checked on them only a few hours ago, and the majority of them had been asleep, which was usual for them after a feeding. They didn't start waking and grumbling until nightfall.

But worry was worry, and it would only be appeased when she laid eyes on her brood.

When Evee finally reached the catacombs, the first thing she noticed was the absolute darkness in the cavernous space. She froze when she walked into the dank, cool space below the church. The electric dome that had once lit up the catacombs like it held a thousand flashlights no longer existed.

The darkness was so complete she could barely see her hand in front of her face. Fortunately, she remembered that at the entrance to the catacombs, on a small table to the left of the door, stood two MagLite lights. These were used by the groundskeeper and by priests laying one of their own to rest.

Evee walked back a few steps, collected a MagLite from the table, then made her way back into the underground cemetery.

Her hands shook as she turned on the flashlight. And for good reason. Except for the decaying crypts and the wrapped corpses lying on burial shelves, the catacombs were empty.

She walked deeper into the belly of the catacombs, all the while calling out for Pierre and her other Originais. Her come-hither call was a high-pitched whistle that ended in a screech, much like the sounds Hoot made when he sensed danger. Her calls echoed back in the cavernous space until they overlapped.

No one appeared. No response to her calls. Not even from Pierre.

When Evee called out again and received no reply, her hands shook so badly that the light bounced around the catacombs in nonsensical patterns, turning it into a macabre funhouse.

Still seeing nothing of her Originais, Evee ran out

of the catacombs, out of the church and down Chartres Street. She felt tears burn her eyes and slide down her cheeks as she ran faster, as fast as her feet would allow. She had to reach her sisters to let them know.

Just as she turned a corner, heading for Snaps and Gilly, she ran into someone... She was so blind with worry she pushed away from him and was about to take off again when he grabbed her arm.

She looked down at the hand grasping her arm, then up at the face it belonged to. Lucien.

"What's wrong?" he asked, evidently seeing her tears, her wild eyes.

Evee didn't give a second thought about throwing her arms around him and sobbing.

Lucien held her tight. "Tell me," he said. "What is it? What has you so upset?"

"They're all gone," Evee wailed.

"Who's gone?"

"All of my Nosferatu! I just left the catacombs. It's empty. I don't know what happened. I went a few hours ago to check on them, and all was fine. Most of them asleep."

"There's no one down there?" Lucien asked. "Not even Pierre?"

She shook her head frantically. "No one. Not one Nosferatu. Nothing."

Without saying a word, Lucien grabbed Evee's hand and led her back toward the catacombs.

When they made their way inside, the only thing illuminated was the MagLite light that Evee had dropped when she ran from the catacombs. It lay on the ground, still burning brightly.

Lucien picked up the flashlight and walked through the catacombs, shaking his head. "I can't believe the electric dome is completely out. Do you have any idea where the Nosferatu might have gone?"

"N-no," Evee whimpered. "I haven't a clue. I called and called for them, but not one responded."

"Aside from the special call you give when you summon them, do you have any other way of contacting them?"

Evee sniffled, thinking hard, but her brain felt like it had clicked a pause button. She couldn't think of anything besides the fact that her entire brood was missing.

Suddenly, a thought hit Evee. "If any are dead, I might be able to channel one or more, like I did Chank earlier. See if they know anything."

"You feel comfortable channeling with only me here with you?" Lucien asked.

Evee sniffled again. "Of course. Channeling is no big secret society game. It's more like I open myself up to them so they can talk through me."

"Then let's try it," Lucien said.

"It's not as easy as that," Evee said. "I have to have a picture of the deceased in my mind's eye."

"Start somewhere, like maybe Pierre. He was responsible for watching over the Nosferatu when you weren't around, right?"

"Yes."

"Then logically, if Pierre was in charge of that group and now all of them are gone, chances are someone or something took him out."

"I can start there, but if he isn't dead, I don't know that I'll be able to find out anything. I can't attempt to summon every Nosferatu that's died. It would take forever."

"Understandable. But let's try Pierre. What can it hurt? If you can't summon him that way, it probably means he's still alive, which is a good thing."

Lucien held the flashlight so its beam pointed at Evee's feet. "It's at least worth a try."

Evee nodded, then quickly lowered herself to the concrete floor. She sat cross-legged and placed her palms up on her knees and closed her eyes. She tried visualizing Pierre, in human form and in his natural state.

Once her mind's eye was filled with the image of Pierre, Evee began to call for him.

"Pierre, oh leader of mine, I call upon you to come to me. Without harm or foul, use my body so that we might learn from you. So that we might see through your eyes, hear with your ears, and find the Originals who've left this place."

Suddenly, Evee felt a shiver run through her, always an indication that somebody or something wanted to come through and reside within her, if only for a moment.

She let her mind go blank, then felt her mouth drop open.

Evee heard a male voice from somewhere that seemed far way.

"They are all lost and near death," the voice said. "You stupid, archaic bitch. You and your spells are worthless. Completely asinine. Soon there will be no Originals for you to watch over. Very soon!"

Evee didn't recognize the voice and couldn't tell where it was coming from. It confused her, made her body shiver. She opened her eyes and looked over at Lucien. The expression on his face was nothing short of shock.

"I heard a voice," Evee said, "but it didn't sound like it was coming through me."

"Oh, it came through you all right, but I don't think it was Pierre."

"Who, then?"

"Possibly a Cartesian. Called you a stupid archaic bitch, and said your Nosferatu would soon all be dead."

Evee unfurled her legs, then pulled her knees up to her chest. She put her forehead against her knees and began sobbing uncontrollably.

Lucien leaned over and gathered Evee up into his arms. She clung tightly to his neck, still sobbing.

Lucien rocked her gently in his arms. "Shh. I'm here. We'll find them. I promise to stay at your side. Now that all of your Nosfertu are missing, we have to prepare for a great war. We'll find them and bring them home."

"But don't you see?" Evee said between sobs. "This is my fault. It's my fault they're missing."

Lucien took hold of Evee's chin and turned her so she faced him. His emerald eyes were fierce, piercing.

"For the last time, none of this is your fault, Evette François. The fault lies in the leader of the Cartesians. It has an agenda and will do whatever it has to do to accomplish it."

She looked down for a moment, slightly embarrassed.

Lucien lifted her chin once more, made sure Evee was looking directly into his eyes.

"And one other thing," Lucien said, his eyes softening. "In case you haven't noticed… I'm falling in love with you, Evette François, whether you like it or not. Despite the missing Nosferatu, Cartesian deaths and the curse that haunts you, I will always be by your side."

He pressed her head to his chest and whispered, "Evee."

Evee felt herself go limp in his arms and with her face pressed against his shoulder, she whispered with great trepidation, "And I love you, Lucien Hyland. Come hell or be damned, I do." She hoped her whisper had been too low for him to hear, but judging by how tightly he held her, how he kissed her forehead, her lips, he'd heard.

And in that moment, Evee knew in her heart of hearts

that with Lucien by her side, they'd win this war, despite the odds.

Evee had no idea about the how, when and where of it all. She simply knew they'd win. Lucien gave her strength.

She was a Triad, not a wimp. She had generations of powerful witches flowing through her blood. It was time to buck up and take control over what was hers. No more Miss Wimpy, which meant no more tears. The Triad was at war, and she concentrated on drawing the strength from her ancestors and from Lucien. The Benders were already warriors of great magnitude, not afraid to stare death in the eye. Ronan had proved that.

Now, Lucien deserved a partner just as strong, just as fierce and determined as he was. They'd set the Triad's world back on its axis and annihilate the enemy. Not only the Cartesians, but their goddamn leader.

Cut the head off the dog and the rest of the animal dies. Evee planted that goal deep in her heart, held tightly to Lucien. She and this man would find and destroy the enemy who'd taken so much from them. And with its death, she'd take Lucien as her own. Curse or no curse. There was no more to take from her, except Lucien, and she would fight at his side and protect him with her life.

She meant to spend the rest of her life with this man. If the curse stood true, Evee would lose all her powers.

So be it.

Better to lose every power she'd ever known than lose the one man who treasured her and made her feel whole.

* * * * *

Want to give in to temptation with steamy tales of irresistible desire?

Check out **Harlequin® Presents®, Harlequin® Desire** and **Harlequin® Kimani™ Romance** books!

New books available every month!

CONNECT WITH US AT:

Harlequin.com/Community

 Facebook.com/HarlequinBooks

 Twitter.com/HarlequinBooks

 Instagram.com/HarlequinBooks

 Pinterest.com/HarlequinBooks

ReaderService.com

ROMANCE WHEN YOU NEED IT

PGENRE2017

Looking for more satisfying love stories
with community and family at their core?

Check out **Harlequin**® **Special Edition**
and **Harlequin**® **Western Romance** books!

New books available every month!

Looking for inspiration in tales
of hope, faith and heartfelt romance?

Check out **Love Inspired**® and
Love Inspired® **Suspense** books!

New books available every month!

CONNECT WITH US AT:

Harlequin.com/Community

Facebook.com/HarlequinBooks

Twitter.com/HarlequinBooks

Instagram.com/HarlequinBooks

Pinterest.com/HarlequinBooks

ReaderService.com

Love Inspired®

LOVE
Harlequin
romance?

Join our Harlequin community to share your thoughts and connect with other romance readers!

Be the first to find out about promotions, news, and exclusive content!

Sign up for the Harlequin e-newsletter and download a free book from any series at

www.TryHarlequin.com

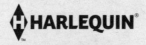

Reward the book lover in you!

Earn points from all your Harlequin book purchases from wherever you shop.

Turn your points into **FREE BOOKS** of your choice
OR
EXCLUSIVE GIFTS from your favorite authors or series.

Join for FREE today at
www.HarlequinMyRewards.com.

Harlequin My Rewards is a free program (no fees) without any commitments or obligations.

MYR17